1

Gideon's eyes shot open. The numbness was fading, but he immediately sensed that something was different this time. Something was off. Something was wrong.

His mind felt crisp and recovered from the light jump from Borroke, as it had the past four jumps, but his body was unusually numb and tingly. His fingers and toes felt disconnected. His feet weren't touching anything. His limbs were frozen—no, suspended in some way, restrained yet floating. He could hear nothing except his heart speeding up, yet even that seemed muffled. He squinted, his pupils frantically darting as he realized he could not move his head. He couldn't even move his mouth to scream.

All around him, he could see a blurry haze of white and grey. He was submerged in something, stuck like an insect in sap. It felt like jelly or some kind of goo, cold and firm, tight against his skin. He could see small bubbles all around, like those sporadically trapped in a vat of Jell-O. Maybe that was how he could still breathe. He wasn't suffocating, but that didn't ease his growing claustrophobia. Each breath felt normal, not at all labored. Where was he? Was he the only one? Did the others not survive the jump?

No matter how hard he strained, he could not move more than a small wiggle. The gelatinous surroundings had him completely immobilized. By the glow of light breaking through, he couldn't tell how deeply he was stuck or how thick the goop was. Why did his skin feel prickly everywhere? He wondered what kinds of chemicals were in the goo, if it was man-made or natural, and if he was going to survive its effects on his flesh. Even if he could somehow perform his cryptic blood-letting ritual and cut his shoulder, he would still feel fear rooting in his sanity.

Gideon had finally grown used to the process of light jump recovery. After visiting four planets through this incredible mode of transportation, the steps had become familiar: Hold tight to his companions, trust that Traveler, his guide, was not going to get them all killed as he raised his hand and harnessed the power of light, and then, whiteness.

Gideon had been thrilled to finally see Traveler's home, Whewliss, the most advanced world in the universe. Gideon was ready for his mission: Explore this ominous "fourth phase." He had thought he was ready. But now, this.

Wherever he had landed was a catastrophic leap in the wrong direction. His life didn't flash before his eyes, but the last few weeks did. Every experience leading up to the goo suddenly felt dark and deceiving. Had one of Traveler's little slip-ups gone too far? Doubt plagued Gideon's mind like flies on death. This couldn't be Whewliss. In the eternal vastness of space, and the endless possibilities on countless worlds that he could only begin to comprehend, there was no telling where he was or if he would ever escape the foreign confines. Gideon hoped he wasn't permanently stuck, or worse, that this was what death felt like.

He couldn't see any shapes in the smoky gelatin. Not even his own hands. No, wait. He tried to focus without opening his eyes too wide, lest the goo seep in through his lashes. He saw a faint bodily form not too far away. It wasn't hard to discern between the options and conclude it to be Timrekka. Gideon was able to make out the stubby body and spiky hair of the mad scientist. Even with Timrekka's denser, stronger cells, he appeared to be having the same luck when it came to moving. They were both stuck. Gideon tried harder to look around, but with his head held in place, his range of sight was limited, and his peripherals didn't offer much more. He assumed Traveler, Dumakleiza, and Cooby were somewhere nearby, perhaps behind him. He tried to call out, but he couldn't make any noise beyond a muffled mumble. Wherever they were, whatever they were in, they were powerless, left to the mercy of fate.

Gideon saw a bright glow coming from somewhere far beneath. The glow became a white light rising toward them. It rose fast, like a flat floor of blinding light. It elevated in seconds, surrounding and passing up overhead with a quick whirring sound. Gideon felt a wave of relief as he realized they were being scanned. They weren't stuck in some natural pool of, well, whatever they were in. Someone was watching them.

After the scan passed through them, the glowing beams of light shifted. Gideon's visual perspective changed with it at a slow but constant rate. He couldn't feel anything, but it was easy to tell they were descending, like toothpaste being squeezed through a tube. They were heading down toward something or someone, and whatever or whoever it was, it had absolute control over them.

As Gideon craned to look down to see how far they were going, the goo around him suddenly became as water, and he dropped. He yelled a muted cry, half out of fear and half out of excitement, in the downward rush of surrounding slush. He could breathe, but his arms and legs were still pinned by his sides as he fell. The goo glowed brighter and brighter until finally, *thump!*

Gideon blinked and gasped as he found himself standing. It happened too quickly for him to understand how, but he was free. He looked around, opening and closing his hands, trying to regain feeling. Every inch of his body was throbbing with titillating tingles. It was energizing, and he was still sopping with gooey residue. It had a minty odor and pine-like flavor. He stood in a white room, surrounded by a vibrating silence. He couldn't see much due to piercing white lights aimed at him from every direction. It felt like he was being interrogated. Observation suggested it was a decontamination chamber of sorts.

Thump! Gideon looked over to see Timrekka with the same bewildered expression on his wet face. Timrekka reached up, stared at his dripping hands, and then went to adjust his goggles, but they were not on his face.

"Where are we?" He looked around, trying to pick up on any visible clues. "I'm assuming, due to the clear nature of whatever that schmaltzy goop was, that it catches light jumpers inside of it as a screening process before entry is permitted; you probably also saw the scan light. I'm guessing it was a security measure, and once they recognized that we had no weapons or any threatening items, they filtered us down, but I wonder what would have happened if we *had* had weapons. Oops!" He covered his mouth. "Hopefully they didn't hear me say that; you don't think they did, do you?"

"I don't." Gideon couldn't help but chuckle as he realized they were both naked, completely covered in excess slime. He hadn't noticed when they were in the goop, but now that they could move, he saw every bit of Timrekka's nude body, along with his own. "I don't know. But wherever we are, I hope they enjoy helicopters." He chuckled and swiveled his hips.

Timrekka hadn't noticed. "Oh my." He covered himself as best he could. "Where are our clothes?"

They both looked up to see where they'd dropped from. A few feet above their heads, in the middle of a pearly white ceiling, was an opening about ten feet in diameter where the smoky, bubbly goo funneled down. There was no lid or door—just an uncovered, slimy circle that led up into the vat they'd been stuck in. They couldn't see very far into it, but they could see three silhouettes dipping down through the hole. Their feet were lowered and placed on the ground by the enveloping goop. Each extension detached and sprung back up with elastic retention, as if the slime had intelligent fingers.

Thump! Thump! Thump! Traveler, Dumakleiza, and Cooby landed. Dumakleiza's right eye was wide open. Her left purple dragon eye, sensitive to light due to its nocturnal ability, was squeezed shut. As soon as she could move, she reached for her knives. She gasped as she felt only the warmth of her own body. She was nude and unarmed. One of her hands immediately grabbed across her breasts while her other covered her groin. Her wide, right eye pleaded with her companions. They all looked as bewildered as her, except for Traveler.

Cooby was silent, still in unsure shock of what he'd just experienced. The nervous tanion scurried over to Dumakleiza, his six fur-covered limbs beating across the floor before he leapt up onto her back, sopping wet and all. He wrapped around her and nervously cooed as his beady eyes looked around. Dumakleiza took slight comfort in his armored back protecting her from a rear assault.

All of them stood naked, wet, confused, and unsure, waiting to see what was going to happen in the blinding white room. Only Traveler brushed some of the goo off his arms and hands as if it were an everyday occurrence. He smiled at the welcoming familiarity. After a relieving sigh, he glanced at his companions and smiled at their expected shock.

Gideon was about to ramble some questions to Traveler when a calming female voice spoke out from all around them. "Welcome to Interstellar Port, the welcoming center in the city of EBOO on planet Whewliss." The voice echoed around them. "What are your names? What are your home worlds? And what is your purpose on Whewliss?"

Traveler spoke for his stunned companions. "Recruiter Four Zero." He pointed at his recruits one-by-one as if displaying them. "Gideon of planet Earth, Dumakleiza of planet Cul, Timrekka of planet Thamiosh, and Cooby, pet animal of planet Cul. They are assembled recruits for the fourth phase expedition."

There was a heavy silence. Gideon, Dumakleiza, and Timrekka looked at each other as they waited. The voice returned with masked excitement.

"Please repeat that."

Traveler smiled as he nodded at the voice's disbelief. "You heard exactly what I said, Lady Melodeen." His smile grew as he proudly said the words he'd waited decades to report. "I have successfully recruited the first team for the fourth phase expedition."

There was a blatant smile in Lady Melodeen's tone as she responded louder than intended, "That is fantastic, recruiter Four Zero." There were some shifting sounds over the speakers. "Dress them, and I'll alert the council."

The lights immediately dimmed to a more accommodating level of brightness. The five of them blinked and rubbed their eyes to help adjust. Once visibility improved, they saw that the walls were smooth, without any corners. There was a single glimmering wall straight ahead of them, transparent as a window, but it bowed and flexed like a living thing. Behind it they saw people in clothing of vibrant colors. The Whewlights were watching them, studying them, and tapping away at projected screens on the large window.

Gideon's eager eyes glanced around. "I half expected there to be guns aimed at us."

"No need," Traveler said. "If they turn those lights up, we're instantly vaporized into nothing. Atmospheric fractal gases ensure strict security protocols."

"Fascinating." Timrekka stared at the lights. "What is fractal gas?"

"Microscopic reflective coated gas particles that direct any lit body trying to enter Whewliss's atmosphere directly to EBOO," Traveler said.

"Planetary defense against unwanted entry, that's brilliant."

Dumakleiza cowered down a little. "Light as a weapon. An entire world of science diviners." Her nervous energy transferred directly into Cooby, who clutched her more closely. "Grim, please do not abandon me."

Gideon smiled, captivated by the dimming lights. "Huh. I'm guessing most of your world runs on light technology."

"Yes, it does," Traveler said with hands proudly placed on his naked hips.

Five people appeared before them out of nowhere: A man, a teenage boy, and three women. A woman in a fashionable red jumpsuit walked directly up to Dumakleiza. She was a kind-looking brunette with eyes that smiled without her mouth having to. Her hair was as uniquely styled as her clothes. A variety of braids wrapped around her head like beautifully interwoven snakes. Even her walk had an elegance that almost appeared as floating. Not a single part of her was out of place. She gave a light bow and greeted Dumakleiza warmly.

"Hello, Dumakleiza, my name is Brasina. I'll be your personal host and assistant during your stay on Whewliss."

Dumakleiza hesitantly bowed, more out of reaction than respect. "Brasina of Whewliss. Where are my garments?" she whispered with veiled shame.

Brasina nodded to the expected question. "Step right over this way." She motioned to a spot on the floor. Dumakleiza squinted defensively but took small steps, making sure to keep herself covered. Once she was where Brasina had directed her to, a light appeared beneath her feet, glowing in a perfect circle. Dumakleiza squeezed her dragon eye shut as her right looked down in panic.

"What is happening? Am I in danger?"

Brasina gave a friendly smile and shook her head. "No, we are creating your gelatin suit. Please extend your hands out at shoulder height."

Dumakleiza's heart was racing. "I wish to trust you." She reached her hands out, exposing herself as she gulped down a mix of fear and vulnerability. She wouldn't feel such shameful fear if she at least had swords.

Brasina maintained her professionalism. "You're doing great, Dumakleiza." She motioned at the floor with her open right hand, palm up, and gently waved upward with her fingertips. As soon as she did, the outline of the glowing circle began to rise, slowly encasing Dumakleiza's legs with what looked like formed smoke. It was clearly still only light, but it concealed her like a tube. Everyone in the room stared at the rising curtain of light as it rose all the way up to Dumakleiza's throat. Only her hands, neck, and head were visible beyond the bright glow. Brasina turned her open hand sideways and then slowly moved it back and forth like a fishtail. The light surrounding Dumakleiza closed in on her as if it was going to shrink-wrap her body. It passed through her and disappeared.

Dumakleiza blinked a few times and then looked down to see that the gelatin coating her body was dry, and she was dressed in clothing similar to Brasina's. She stared at her hands and then slowly lowered her arms. A white one-piece garment covered her from her feet up to the base of her throat. Only her hands, neck, and head were uncovered. Dumakleiza had not felt any of the molecular alteration. She was speechless, unable to take her eyes off the outfit.

"H—h—how is this possible? Where is the drowning snot?"

Brasina looked Dumakleiza's body up and down to ensure that the gelatin had been properly and evenly applied. "The goo is a symbiotic, hyper-intelligent substance that we control until fusing light-shock transforms its properties into flexible, protective wear. It's what the suit is made from. The light shot that recruiter Four Zero gave you relays information about your body, health, and needs on a cellular level. You will be monitored and managed by the suit, so that you function optimally. The light shot has bonded to your cells, creating a network of optional and ever-expanding, personally customizable settings that you can adjust. During your stay on Whewliss, your light cells are activated, and you will be provided the best care by the suit, along with a guide—that's me—who will help you customize everything to your preference. The suit will monitor and regulate body temperature and assist your skin in selecting and absorbing chemicals and elements uniquely beneficial to you and

your health. Additionally it'll infuse you with your desired levels of nu-
tritional caffeine and will alarm you of any health concerns and/or needs
that may arise." Brasina stood up and smiled at Dumakleiza, who barely
understood a sentence of what was said. "How do you like it?"

Dumakleiza gazed at it as she calmed down and realized how comfortable she was. "I, uh—" She cracked a small smile. "I feel as though I
still wear nothing."

Brasina nodded. "Yes, it fits lightly." She chuckled. "A common play
on words here on Whewliss." She grinned at Dumakleiza. "Do you wish
for a different color?"

Dumakleiza's smile grew a little as she thought about actually getting
to choose her outfit. "Is there one the color of my eye?" she asked as she
pointed to her dragon eye.

Brasina's eyes sparkled as her face lit up with authentic surprise. "Oh,
how beautiful! I've never seen a dragon eye in person before. I've only
read about them." She squeezed her fists and nodded. "Fold your arms
across your chest and say 'purple.'"

Dumakleiza uneasily crossed her arms as instructed. She waited a
moment and then looked down. "Purple?" The instant she spoke the simple command, her suit became a vibrant purple. She let out a shrill giggle,
completely blown away. "How did it—?" She shook her head, dismissing
what she didn't understand. "It is beautiful." She smiled and looked at
Gideon. "Sir Gideon, do you approve of my garment color?"

Gideon nodded without hesitation. After remembering that his
shoulder was healed, his charisma had retreated. He wanted to give Dumakleiza's gelatin suit a more meaningful compliment, but he felt clammed
up. Dumakleiza looked back down at her outfit and continued admiring
it as one of the other women approached Cooby. The woman squatted
down and made some clicking sounds to get his attention. She had a calming face with an even more docile expression.

Cooby scooted backward, staring from Duma to the unfamiliar
woman. Sensory overload had him reacting a little slower to everything.

"Dumakleiza, is Cooby your pet?" the woman asked.

"Yes, he is my tanion," Dumakleiza accidentally said more protectively
than intended.

The woman smiled. "My name is Gruvelin, and I'll assist with his care on Whewliss. I'll ensure that he's well-fed, groomed, and has a pleasant stay. Does he like to play?"

"Oh, yes." Dumakleiza couldn't help reveling in Whewliss's hospitality. "I greatly appreciate that. I apologize for his apprehension. He only trusts Sir Gideon and myself."

Gruvelin nodded understandingly. "Trust must be earned." She withdrew a circular silver sticker from her pocket and stuck it to her hand. She reached out, so Cooby could smell it. "This is a mammalian pheromone patch that releases hormonal scents to help animals relax." Sure enough, as Cooby smelled it, he breathed a little easier and crawled up to her.

Gideon was slightly unnerved as a man approached him. The man, whose nationality looked similar to Earth's Hawaiian, stood a few inches taller than Gideon with a black, slicked back pompadour. His face was glowing and smooth, and his suit was black with silver collars. He had a slight sway to his step and was all smiles looking at Gideon. Flirtatious eyes led his suave demeanor. Gideon cleared his throat as he extended his hand to shake. The man stared at it curiously, unsure of what to do. He glanced up at Traveler for help.

Traveler smiled. "Gideon, you'll come to find that on Whewliss, the Earthly custom of shaking hands isn't reciprocated due to safety risks."

Gideon smirked. "Safety risks? You shook my hand when we first met."

"Yes," Traveler responded, "on Earth, where my implants were deactivated. But here on Whewliss, where they are activated, it's potentially dangerous to shake hands, as it could trigger unwanted reactions."

Gideon shrugged the answer away. "Okay." The honest response irritated him.

The suave gentleman smiled. "Hello, Gideon, my name is Kristuf. I'll be your personal host and assistant here on Whewliss. We're going to have a lot of fun." Even his voice had a twinkle in it.

Gideon feigned a smile. "Okay." He looked at Traveler with bothered eyes. "Would you, uh—" He nodded toward his shoulder.

Traveler took a hesitant breath and nodded toward Kristuf. "Do you have the index laser?" Kristuf nodded without breaking his smile. Traveler pointed at Gideon's shoulder. "He requires a scar from the top of his shoulder to the bottom in order to function at the best of his ability."

Kristuf's smile wavered. "I can assist." He touched Gideon's shoulder with his left index finger and carefully formed the rest of his hand into a fist with specific fingers overlapped. The tip of his index started glowing. Gideon winced as he felt a burning sensation. He grit his teeth and stared at his shoulder as Kristuf slid his finger down to the bottom of it. Kristuf retracted his hand and smiled at Gideon, hoping his assistance was satisfactory.

Gideon caught his breath. "That was intense." He looked at his shoulder to see an already healed scar. He exhaled and slumped a little, closing his eyes. "Thank you."

Kristuf looked to Traveler. Traveler shrugged. They watched as Gideon opened his eyes and immediately perked up.

"All right, is it my turn to make a jelly jumpsuit?" He smiled at Kristuf, who motioned for him take a few steps to his right. As Gideon moved into position, he glanced back up at the gooey portal overhead. "So, how's that stuff work? Like a futuristic TSA screening process?"

Kristuf started directing the tube of light up Gideon's body. "Yes. It's unlike anything on other worlds, isn't it?" he charismatically asked as if it were his first time hearing about it. "What's riveting is what happens if we catch an interstellar terrorist in it."

Gideon's eyes lit up with morbid curiosity. "What happens?"

"Well," Kristuf said, wagging his hand to finalize the goo's solidification, "if a threat is detected, we send an energy shock through the goo that instantly vaporizes the body under intense heat and pressure. It boils the flesh and tissue down until only its carbon element is left. After which the pressure intensifies, compressing it down to a gem made from dead terrorist—and done." Kristuf spiritedly opened his hands as he delivered the answer. "Terrorist gems."

"Seriously?" Gideon asked with wide eyes, not focused on the white jumpsuit wrapped around his body. "That's nuts." He chuckled. "Back on Earth, we just started offering carbon gems as a postmortem option, but I never imagined it'd be a security measure."

"Oh, yeah," Kristuff said with energetic arm movements. "We've only been using it for about fifty years or so, but it's proving to be quite effective. Though we've only had two terrorists, so I haven't gotten to see it happen myself. I probably shouldn't wish for one, but I secretly want to witness it." He leaned in and shushed Gideon. "Don't tell anyone."

Gideon chuckled. "I'm right there with you. That'd be insane to see. I'm more or less impressed with how openly you can just talk about it. On Earth we can't even say bomb in an airport, or we'll get arrested."

"Psh." Kristuf waved his hand. "We did away with human security measures a long time ago, so there's no risk for personal endangerment. You can say bomb, terrorist, kaboom, or anything you want. The goo is the only thing taking risk."

"That's so badass." Gideon thought about it. "Bin Laden!" Nothing happened. "Awesome."

The teenager who had appeared walked up to Timrekka. The young boy was wearing a bright blue one piece, and it looked like the right side of his mouth was smiling while the left was relaxed. His short blonde hair was buzzed, and he looked eager to meet the gorilla of a human. He stopped right in front of Timrekka and bowed his head.

"Hello, Timrekka, my name is Alik. I will be your personal host and assistant on Whewliss."

Timrekka grinned as he looked at the young man. "Nice to meet you, Alik. I look forward to your assistance and everything there is to learn. How old are you?"

"I'm fifty-two," Alik said plainly. "And if you'd step over this way, we can get you dressed."

"Fifty-two?" Timrekka was astounded. "You're of similar age to me, but you look like a child." He covered his mouth. "Oh, I'm sorry if that came out rude or ignorantly offensive."

Alik chuckled, "Nah, you're good. To me it's strange to think that *your* body has aged at the rate it has, so I understand your confusion."

"Wow." Timrekka smiled. "That's interesting. Would you mind if I took samples of your DNA and studied the intricacies to better understand the difference?"

Both sides of Alik's mouth curved up. "I take it you're the fourth phase scientist?"

Timrekka nodded. "Yes, and I can't wait to see more of Whewliss."

"All right." Alik snickered. "I'm excited to show you around."

While the recruits were tended to, the last woman approached Traveler. She looked to be middle-aged and had keen wisdom beaming from her eyes. Her sandy blonde hair was simply kempt. It didn't have the illustrious presentation of the other women's, but it was brushed and tucked behind her ears. Her suit was a subtle peach tone, and she wore a concerned smirk.

"Hello, Four Zero." She stopped a few feet shy of Traveler and looked him up and down. "Congratulations on your successful recruitment." She was impressed to the point of screaming, though her calm tone would never give it away.

Traveler gave a subtle bow. "Thank you, Lady Melodeen." He smiled, struggling to conceal his desire to jump up and down. "After many good recruits have fallen and every recruiter has failed, I am proud to present them to you."

"Their delivery is a monumental achievement. Your recruit from Thamiosh looks promising. Though I must be honest with you, I'm hesitant about the other two."

"Why is that?"

"A Culite? They have barely even begun their second phase. She will not likely survive."

Traveler nodded. "Understandable doubt. Though she has survived perilous circumstances already."

Lady Melodeen raised her eyebrows and shrugged. "Perhaps." She looked at Gideon. "And—an Earthling? They are so prideful and self-entitled and blinded by violent ambition. I fear a repeat of the past."

Traveler shook his head. "He is actually the most open-minded recruit I've ever met. I believe him to be the best candidate of the three." He looked back at her. "Besides they're the only three to make it this far."

"I hope you are right. *Your* judgement will be judged by their success or failure. I will not divulge their origins before you have the chance to tell the council yourself."

"Thank you."

"And actually—" Lady Melodeen dramatically paused, keeping eye contact with Traveler. "—they are not the first."

"What?" Traveler's eyebrows dropped. "When?"

"Yesterday, believe it or not."

"Yesterday?" Traveler asked in disbelief. "Who?"

"Recruiter Six One. She arrived yesterday morning with three recruits." Lady Melodeen looked around at Gideon, Dumakleiza, and Timrekka. "After so many years of a zero-success rate, our first two successful recruitments happen within two days. Remarkable. Just remarkable."

Traveler stared despondently at her as his heart sank. "Remarkable."

2

"So," Traveler sighed as his proud posture wilted. "What happens now?" Lady Melodeen smiled back at him with a calming nod. "Six One's recruits took last night to relax and enjoy Whewliss's hospitality, as they are unfamiliar with full-time productivity. They are scheduled to meet with the Lord and Council this afternoon." She looked around at Traveler's group. "Your recruits are offered the same welcome and will be meeting the Lord and Council tomorrow. Or, of course, you are all invited to partake in the introductory briefing today if you don't mind the rush."

Traveler's sense of urgency was more than apparent. He turned and looked at the three of them, obviously awaiting their answers. He hoped they wouldn't want to wait. He didn't want to play catch up behind another group.

Gideon looked back and forth between Traveler and Lady Melodeen. "Context clues suggest there's a second team that made it?" A smile exploded onto his face.

Traveler nodded, far less enthused. "Yes."

"That's awesome," Gideon yelled, shaking a fist. "A bigger crew for the expedition." He shook his head, realizing Lady Melodeen was waiting for an answer. "I'm ready. Let's go do this thing already. Like, now." He nodded with a fist to Traveler's shoulder.

Timrekka was beyond stoked. "Yes, I agree, as I know I, for one, require no more rest or downtime, and I want to keep moving."

Dumakleiza looked around, a little confused. "I, uh —" As her words fumbled in her mouth, Gideon looked at her. His eyes gave her all the reassurance she needed. She turned to Lady Melodeen. "I am in agreement. Let us continue this quest."

Gideon smiled. "See? We're all good after that light nap." He winked.

Brasina and Kristuf chuckled behind them as they continued looking the three up and down.

"He's got the light puns," Kristuf said, proud of his assigned person. "He'll fit in perfectly."

"Of course he will," Traveler growled under his breath.

Lady Melodeen gave a small smile and nodded. "So be it." She looked at the assistants. "Aid them with whatever is needed and then escort them to Prism Hall at thirteen ninety." She gave a final nod to the new arrivals. "I look forward to learning more about all of you." With that she vanished.

They stood there for a moment, adjusting to the fact that people appearing and vanishing was likely a norm on Whewliss. Dumakleiza, especially, was focusing on breathing. She knew it wasn't magic, but her upbringing kept surfacing and suggesting it was. She'd been breast-fed tales and nightmares of dark conjurers doing exactly what she was witnessing. Her fears were difficult to distinguish from this new reality. Timrekka was radiant with fascinated curiosity. He couldn't wait to get his twitching hands on all of Whewliss and experiment. Gideon was wide-eyed and smiling. He looked to Traveler.

"Spaceman, your world is incredible." Gideon patted Traveler on the back. "What's full-time productivity?"

Traveler turned and looked at him with a tensely cockeyed jaw. He steamed an exhale and looked to the assistants. "Anything they need." He turned and walked away.

Dumakleiza's eyes widened. "Where are you going?" She wasn't ready to be abandoned by their only familiarity on Whewliss.

"I'm getting a drink." A moment later, Traveler vanished.

"So emotional, that one." Gideon clicked his tongue. "So." He turned to Kristuf and the other assistants. "*You* get my million questions, ya lucky ducks. What's full-time productivity?"

Kristuf nodded before his eyes lit up. "Here on Whewliss, we are capable of staying awake all thirty hours a day. In EBOO each worker strives to remain productive for twenty-nine of them. We have one hour a day for breaks, and within that hour, we light jump around the planet."

Timrekka's pupils darted about the floor as he calculated. "Thirty-hour days, only resting for one, and one relatively instantaneous jump daily provides enough REM sleep to support full cognitive and physical function. Oh, the accomplishments that can be made without taking a third of one's life for sleep."

"Correct," Alik chimed in. "This guy gets it."

"So." Gideon ran his fingers along the arms of his new suit. "How does that work?"

Kristuf smiled. "There are light pads on most street corners across Whewliss, even more so in EBOO, for the benefit of our work. They are similar in appearance to the pad you stepped on for your suit." He pointed at the circles of light on the floor. "Whenever people feel their energy waning, they simply step onto a light pad. Their light cells are instantly activated, and they are whipped around Whewliss at the unhindered speed of light. They reappear at the same pad, refreshed, fully rested, and healed internally and externally. They then resume."

"That's crazy." Gideon chuckled. "So, at any given time, there are—" He looked up, imagining the sky through the white room's ceiling as he tried to calculate impossible math.

Kristuf understood. "I'm not sure, but my best guess would be, hmm, out of our population of nearly four billion, there are probably two to three hundred million people whipping within Whewliss's atmosphere at any given time."

"What?" Gideon and Timrekka exclaimed simultaneously.

"In fact," Brasina added, "we have found that, in addition to the other steps Whewliss has taken to keep our planet clean, the bodies of light constantly orbiting our world assist in the cleansing and purification of our air. We inadvertently decontaminate the ozone, removing pollutants a marginal amount with every jump."

"Really?" Gideon asked in astonishment. "Two hundred million maids cleaning up the planet's breathable air twenty-four seven, or thirty-seven—or whatever. You know what I mean."

"Exactly."

"Pardon my interruption," Dumakleiza said as she tried to process what they were talking about. "And I apologize if my question is naïve or ignorant in nature, but are you claiming that people do not sleep on this world of Whewliss?"

"Correct," Brasina said cheerfully. "Well, I mean, they do sometimes but only when they can't get to a light pad, or they can't afford it."

"Afford it?"

"Yes." Brasina nodded. "In EBOO, all light pads are free, as they assist in ensuring we are most productive in our work. Everyone here is performing governmental research, so they are complimentary. However, on the rest of Whewliss, they cost small fees for each use, just as any planet charges for means of travel or sleeping apparatuses."

"Mattresses?" Gideon clarified.

"Yes," Brasina said. "I've heard that is what is used on Earth. Mattresses." She mulled the word over. "Everyday familiarity to you. Relics to us."

Timrekka was beside himself. "I hadn't imagined that sleep would be obsolete, but now it just makes sense, and I could get so much more done."

"Yeah." Alik smiled. "You're going to get the understanding of this quickly."

"In fact," Brasina added, "outside of EBOO, there are museums showcasing obsolete relics that may be everyday familiarities back on your planets."

"Such as?" Gideon was beyond curious.

"Well." Brasina motioned to Dumakleiza. "We have exhibits ranging from Whewliss's medieval age, containing barbaric weaponry, like swords and early aerial assault tools, to—" She nodded to Kristuf, who looked eager to take over.

He smiled and motioned to Gideon as he spoke. "—to mattresses and other sleeping apparatuses we used to use. There are exhibits on primitive oddities, such as bulky modes of transportation, infirmaries, medicine, cr—"

"Hospitals?" Gideon asked with sincere bafflement. "Hospitals are obsolete?"

"Of course." Kristuf shrugged as if the answer was obvious.

"Then how—"

"Light heals everything on a cellular level, so there's no longer any need for hospitals, medicines, doctors, surgeries, or as we refer to it, consensual butchery." Kristuf dropped his professionalism long enough for a personal comment. "I can't believe you let other Earthlings cut into your body. Have you ever had a, uh, what's the word?"

"Surgery?"

"Yes." Kristuf cringed. "Why would you allow someone to mutilate you in the name of medicine?" He all but laughed to avoid vomiting.

Gideon smiled, realizing he could mess with them a little. "I've had a few surgeries." They gasped as Gideon started having fun. "I was tossed from a horse once, and when I landed, I tried to catch myself, but the impact was so rough that I dislocated my elbow."

"What?" Kristuf was disgustedly fascinated.

"Wasn't the worst part." Gideon turned his elbow, so they could look at it as he spoke. "I also tore and dislocated my tricep. It popped from my elbow and then rolled up into my shoulder. The doctors had to cut me open and dig around in my shoulder to find it." All the assistants held their hands to their mouths as they shook their heads with wide eyes. "Yeah," Gideon chuckled. "Once they fished the bastard out, they had to pull it down to my elbow and reattach it with metal screws."

"No!" Kristuf and Alik exclaimed in horror.

"Oh, yeah." Gideon nodded, enjoying torturing them. He thought for a moment. "So, what about broken bones and such? I get that you don't have doctors, but who sets those prior to jumps?"

"Oh, he's a smart one," Kristuf said, still trying to recover. "Almost as widespread as our light pads, there are gel pods. They are twice the size of the average human, filled with more of that." He pointed up at the goo portal in the ceiling. "If there's any anatomical alignment issues, people will climb in, submerge themselves, the pod will scan them for abnormalities, and then the gel will set the injury prior to jump with focalized pressure shocks. It's more efficient and less brutal than risking your flesh to human error."

"Huh," Gideon said, putting his hands on his hips. "So, I guess that's that. Hospitals are things of the past to you." He was riveted. "That's just nuts." The assistants waited while he chuckled. "So, are recruiters the only ones educated to set fractures, dislocations, and other random injuries by hand?"

"What?" Kristuf lowered his eyebrows.

Brasina stepped closer, looking at Gideon. "Recruiters are forbidden from practicing barbaric medicine—especially on the less developed."

Alik nodded. "It's very clearly stated in LOLA."

Dumakleiza was confused. "But the Diviner set Sir Gideon's leg and Timrekka's toe."

Gideon immediately tightened his lips as he realized they'd touched on something they shouldn't have. They could feel the assistants' energies negatively shift. They all looked at each other as Brasina shook her head.

"If Four Zero broke LOLA, I'm required to report it."

As she reached up to activate something in her ear, Gideon ushered her to stop.

"Hold on. Hold on. Hold on." He gave a lighthearted chuckled, hoping to disarm her. "If he hadn't, there's a good chance we wouldn't have made it. For the sake of the fourth phase mission, and for the sake of the bigger picture as a whole, please don't tattle. He did the right thing by helping us. Probably saved my life."

Brasina waited and then sighed as she brought her hand down. "I'm not happy about keeping secrets from my superiors, but I suppose what they don't know won't hurt them."

Gideon smiled, relieved. "We have that same saying on Earth."

Kristuf perked up. "Really? What a coincidence."

"Yeah." Gideon looked at Dumakleiza, who was embarrassed for divulging. He gave her a reassuring look before turning back to Kristuf. "We also say it's sometimes better to ask for forgiveness than for permission. Four Zero, as you call him, is an exceptional recruiter, and he did what was necessary for the survival of his team. You should be very proud of him. He's actually quite the badass sometimes."

Alik nudged Brasina, who still seemed uncomfortable with withholding criminal activity. "Ah, come on. It's exciting." He shivered with a childlike grin. "I've always dreamed of being a recruiter. I can only imagine the dangers they have to deal with on all those barbaric worlds."

"There ya go." Gideon smiled. "They're kinda your rock stars, aren't they?"

"Our what?"

"Celebrities, so to speak."

Kristuf nodded with an obvious smirk of admiration. "Oh, they are highly revered. What they do requires immeasurable courage."

Brasina finally exhaled and smiled, allowing herself to relax. "Okay. Well, I suppose we should start getting you all ready to meet the Council and Lord." Her perkiness returned. "Is there anything any of you need that we can provide for you? Food? Drink? Entertainment? We have three hours until you are expected at Prism Hall."

Dumakleiza nodded. "Yes." She'd been anxiously waiting. "My holy treasure. Where is it?"

Brasina smiled. "Your personal effects have been scanned, cleared, and stored. I will show you to them."

Dumakleiza smiled, knowing she hadn't lost her treasure again. "Thank you, Brasina of Whewliss."

Brasina nodded. "Of course. And then we can go get Cooby groomed if you'd like."

"Groomed?"

Gruvelin, who'd been busy loving on Cooby, finally chimed in. "We will bathe him in our finest salt baths. Then we'll primp and groom his fur, polish the plates on his back, trim his nails, clean his mouth, and feed him of course."

Dumakleiza's eyes lit up. "Yes. Of course. Never before has my little tanion been treated as royalty."

Brasina was enjoying Dumakleiza's rising excitement. "And you haven't shopped until you shop at Kaleidoscope Mall."

Duma squinted. "What is 'shopping?'"

Brasina's expression went flat. "You can't be serious. Oh, wait, perhaps you know it as going to market."

Dumakleiza shook her head. "I do not understand this term either."

"She lived alone," Gideon said to help. "Isolated on an island. She's never been shopping."

Brasina squealed. "For all the light shines on, you are going to love it!"

Gideon looked at Kristuf with eager eyes. "What kind of entertainment do you have?"

Kristuf thought for a moment. "Hmm, where to start? We have a virtual reality room where we've done our best to construct and mimic every world known. They're not perfect duplications, of course, but they are impressive. At least that's what the recruiters who have actually been to other worlds say. So, I can show you some digitally replicated planets if you'd like."

"Holy spirit, are you kidding me?" Gideon's jaw hung open. "Yes, yes, a thousand times yes." He laughed. "Yes, take me there yesterday. Let's go."

"Perfect." Kristuf's giggle matched Gideon's. "Let's see. I'll introduce you to some Brionites, Pa Int Blaalings, Teezles, and that might be all the time we have for today. Or!" He smiled. "Let's save that for another time. You come across as a man who might appreciate our anti-gravity room."

Gideon's jaw hung open a little. "Uh, yes. That. Let's do that. I love Whewliss. Is it possible to be in love with a planet?"

"Actually," Kristuf chuckled, "you'll see soon enough, but yes, that's a real thing. We're not supposed to judge people's customs from other worlds, but—" He straightened himself up and brushed his clothing, though it wasn't marred. "Love is love is love."

Alik laughed at their interaction and then turned to Timrekka. "Let me see if I can guess. You'd like to learn about Whewlight tech?"

Timrekka nodded vigorously. "Yes, I would absolutely be interested in that."

"All right," Alik said as he waved him forward. "Sounds like we all know what we're going to do."

With that, the assistants grabbed the hands of their respective visitors, and they all vanished.

3

That evening, Traveler leaned against a building's entryway, impatiently waiting for his team. They still had time, but his festering frustration put a damper on their arrival. He was clad in a white one-piece suit, perfectly clean and organized. Finally, after being on so many primitive planets, he was back in a state-of-the-art outfit. He tapped his feet and looked around at the familiar view of EBOO. Multi-shaped structures reflected the evening's colors with massive, mirrored walls. The cornucopia of vibrant yellows, oranges, reds, purples, and pinks dazzled across the city skyline. It was a spectacle to see Whewliss's sun dive toward the horizon, as EBOO was designed to glorify light in all its majesty.

It was comforting to see the city of a million lights instead of the decrepit, smoggy towns and citadels of Earth or Thamiosh. Cul and Borroke had provided necessary experiences, but the lack of hygiene had been nightmarish. Traveler tried to focus on the positives as he inhaled the cycled air, tasting the rejuvenating scents that came from multitudes of gardens and trees all around him. EBOO was famous across Whewliss for having innovative nurseries, gardens, and bountiful trees, budding with eclectic fruits and vibrant colors. He held the breath within his lungs and then exhaled. It didn't help. He couldn't shake the disappointment.

"Sup, Spaceman?" Gideon's voice turned Traveler's attention around to see Kristuf burning another new scar into his shoulder. Traveler feigned a small smile and looked between the arriving group.

"You do realize we use light transport for nearly everything, right? Are you going to have your assistant accompany you everywhere just to give you a new scar every few minutes?"

"Oh, good." Gideon chuckled. "I was worried you might have cheered up." He looked to Kristuf. "Any chance I could get that implant, so you don't have to do it every time light heals me?"

"Eh." Kristuf tossed his head side to side as he mulled the question over. "I have a strict permit for this one. I mean, it can be intensified to burn a hole through steel, though I've never actually done that. Most people that have this are police or governmental workers. It's a very difficult permit to get, and I've never heard of an alien getting one. But, I mean, the Lord will probably be more lenient with fourth phase recruits."

Traveler scoffed. "Gideon will probably manage to talk Lord Coyzle into permitting him the implant between his legs."

Gideon squinted with a curved mouth. "You are in rare form. This'll be fun."

Timrekka looked around at the entrance to Prism Hall. "Incredible." The massive dome towered overhead. He couldn't tell how many stories Prism Hall was, but he marveled at the green marble and reflective mirror swirling together to form a unique pattern on the outer wall.

Brasina glanced around at them with her signature smile. "Shall we?" She looked to Traveler. "Four Zero, lead the way."

Traveler nodded and walked toward the front doors as he forced some energy. "Here we go. Follow me."

They walked up some polished wood stairs and stepped through the front doorway, which appeared as a wall of dim green light. As they moved through, the green flashed brighter for each person. Dumakleiza's eyes widened.

"What is happening?"

Brasina smiled. "Many of our buildings have light doors. They serve a variety of purposes. We each get scanned when we walk through. It identifies us and assigns our suits a color in cases of specific formalities." She paused once everyone was inside and looked at the recruits. She gasped, along with the other assistants. "Oh, that's so exciting."

Gideon, Dumakleiza, and Timrekka looked down to see that their outfits had turned a speckled grey, white, and black. They studied them, wondering why the stippled pattern was their assigned color. In the center of their chests, there was a black circle.

Timrekka touched his suit, still amazed at its capabilities. "Interesting. Black and grey spatter. I wonder why it assigned us that."

Alik vibrated as he pointed at the black circle in the middle of their suits. "We've been waiting to see that design for a long time. It's for fourth phase recruits only."

Kristuf lit up like the city around them. "It's happening. It's finally happening, and we are a part of it."

"It's already happened," Traveler sourly added. "There's already a fourth phase team in there. Let's go before we're left behind." He walked away.

They followed Traveler through another light door into a massive auditorium. They stared around in awe at the tall ceiling, glowing down upon four commemorative statues. The lofty sculptures stood against the outer walls, towering high above. Each statue was carved out of perfectly smooth and polished marble, memorializing heroes of Whewliss's past. The enormous room was a perfectly circular dome with glowing walls, but no light bulbs to be seen. Timrekka studied it, wondering how they kept it lit. Here and there, vivacious colors accented the glowing pearl walls. Every inch of the large room was decorated and carefully designed. Even the floor swirled, as if it was a living thing. Colors and patterns slowly moved and flowed like water on the smooth surface. Gideon could only assume that even the floor provided some unusual benefit to their light cells. The entire room was a technological piece of art.

In its center was a smooth white table, shaped like a ring. It stretched twenty feet in diameter with sleek chairs all around. Sitting at the table on one side were three people in matching recruit suits. Joining them were three green assistants and one woman in a uniform matching Traveler's. Inside sat two women and three men facing the recruits.

Gideon smiled at the hall's pristine presentation. "This looks like a monstrous Catholic cathedral on steroids."

Dumakleiza was overwhelmed by the gaudy spectacle. It outdid any dream she'd ever had. Every vivid childhood fantasy and imaginative vision of her ideal heaven was dwarfed by what, to the people of Whew-liss, was simply an important room for their governmental officials. She was a little lightheaded as she processed the sensory overload.

Traveler led them up three steps to the risen center stage. As they followed, they noticed the floor responding to their footsteps. Small ripples of color spread beneath them. Gideon's mouth hung, watching it happen over and over. It was as if they were walking through a rainbow puddle after a light rain.

"Gideon," Kristuf quietly ushered him to pay attention as they reached the table. Gideon looked up to see everyone waiting on him. He gave a small wave and then sat down in a chair Kristuf had pulled out. Strange sensations instantly shivered through him as the chair massaged his back, butt, and legs. Unlike massage chairs he'd experienced back on Earth, this one sent subtle electric currents through his body. He could feel waves of energy, random focalized zaps seemingly massaging inner organs, muscles, and even his *bones* felt pampered. His eyes fluttered as he looked around to see Dumakleiza and Timrekka experiencing the same confused pleasure.

"Peoples of other worlds." Lady Melodeen's voice caught their attention. "I would like to formally welcome you to the city of EBOO. More importantly, I would like to welcome you to planet Whewliss. Your arrivals here mark a new epoch for humanity as a universal species, and your mission will mark you as heroes, never to be forgotten."

She, along with the four others in the inner ring of the table, spoke in unison. "Welcome." The unexpected blend of voices made all six recruits look at each other with nervous excitement.

She continued, "I have previously met you upon your arrivals, following the security gelatin, but allow me to formally introduce myself. I am Lady Melodeen, council member and governor of EBOO." She motioned with her right hand to the woman seated next to her. "This is Lady Skorric, council member and keeper of the IPOK, our Interplanetary Pool of Knowledge." Lady Skorric was a grinning, tight-cheeked woman with light skin. She was smaller in frame than any of the other council members, but her aura exuded nothing but confidence. Lady Melodeen pointed to a brawny, bald black man with a contagious smile under his bushy mustache. "This is Master Keevind, council member and captain of the EPF, EBOO's police force." Master Keevind gave a gravitating belly chuckle and nod. Lady Melodeen motioned to the next man in the inner circle. "This is Master N'kowsky, council member, governor of the City of Light, and Whewliss's LOLA ambassador." Master N'kowsky was a dashing man of tall stature. His charcoal black hair was perfectly combed back, and his smile stole a beat from all six recruits' hearts.

Gideon watched Dumakleiza blush at Master N'kowsky's piercing eyes, and he couldn't blame her. He quickly composed himself and tried to focus on Lady Melodeen introducing the last council member.

"This is Master Brawd, council member, general of Whewliss's military, and head of the fourth phase expedition." Master Brawd was a massive man with reddish-brown skin. He had shoulders as wide as Timrekka's, a jaw thicker than his cranium, fists as hefty as oak, and he appeared completely incapable of smiling.

Gideon noticed an iridescent emblem on each council member's chest, so shimmery and silver that they nearly looked like light themselves. It was the shape of a hand with fingers spread and what looked like light beams extending from each finger and thumb. Five beams for five members.

Lady Melodeen postured herself properly. "Lastly, and most importantly, allow me to introduce you to Lord Coyzle." She motioned behind herself, toward the center of the table's inner circle. "He is our planetary commander, leader of all Whewliss."

In a flash, four men appeared out of nowhere. They stood in the middle of the table in a square, facing out toward the recruits. It only took a couple seconds to realize that all four were identical. They were exact digital copies of one another. Well-trimmed beards wreathed rosy smiles on full-figured faces. Warm green eyes took time to look at each recruit. The men's suits were unlike any of the council members', or anyone else they'd seen on Whewliss so far. The unfamiliar material they were composed of was reflective and incandescently clear. It was like staring into the reflective surface of water at sunset, but it wasn't blinding. Rather, it was soothing on the eyes. Mesmerized, the recruits stared in silence as the four men moved in perfect synchronicity.

"Greetings, alien recruits," the four identicals spoke as one voice. "I cannot begin to tell you how exciting and groundbreaking your arrival is. On behalf of myself, EBOO's council, and of Whewliss, congratulations on completing and surviving your individual tests. I look forward to hearing about each of your stories, as they could possibly earn a pivotal place in our history."

Lord Coyzle smiled a jolly smile at their baffled expressions. "I know there is much on Whewliss that will be immediate cultural, planetary, and developmental shock. Please feel free to ask any questions and use your personal assistants for guidance in exploring our world. It's what they've been assigned to you for." The four identicals looked to the two recruiters and bowed. "Recruiters, you have my utmost respect. You two are the first of the twelve that were sent into the vast and ever-expanding universe to return successful in your missions. I can only begin to imagine what you've witnessed, experienced, lost—" He gave a moment of solemn silence. "—and ultimately, accomplished. I hope that the light will guide the recruits into the fourth phase and return them with glorious discovery. You have placed your lives and our fates into their hands. That trust is one that we must, in turn, place ours. Thank you for your risk. Thank you for your sacrifice. Thank you for your bravery. Thank you for delivering six souls to venture to the fourth phase, not just for us, not just for them, but for the future of every human of every world." Lord Coyzle confidently postured himself to sum up the end of his welcome speech. "Recruits, as you will often hear here on Whewliss, may the light guide and protect you." With that, all four of Lord Coyzle's identicals turned. "Lady Melodeen."

"Thank you, Lord Coyzle." She bowed to him and then returned her eyes to the recruiters. "Recruiter Six One, you were the first to arrive. Therefore, you will introduce your recruits first. Who are they? What LOLA planets are they from? And what tests did they pass?"

Traveler quietly scoffed in irritation. Each time it was voiced that he hadn't returned first, it felt like a personal slap in the face. Gideon gave an encouraging nod, but Traveler kept his disappointed eyes on the other recruiter. The dismissal allowed Gideon a moment to realize what Lady

Melodeen had said. Neither he, Dumakleiza, nor Timrekka were from planets that had discovered light travel, let alone heard of LOLA. He sat back in his chair, preparing for an eventful introduction.

All eyes turned to Six One. She was a thin blonde. Her hair was tightly pulled back into a collage of braids, and her eyebrows were so naturally curved that they looked like checkmarks. She had a proud smirk on her face, holding eye contact with Traveler before looking away.

"Thank you, Lady Melodeen. It is truly an honor to be the first to deliver a suitable crew for the fourth phase." She motioned to her left with an open hand. "In order of discovery, allow me to begin with my recruit of science, Izzy Bonifaas of the planet Jurael." There were immediately some murmurs among the council members, approving the planet. Traveler and his recruits studied Izzy. He was a round-headed man with buzzed hair, a stoic face, and an eager twinkle in his eyes. His radiantly dark skin looked to Gideon like a blend of African and Asian. Izzy's bushy right eyebrow looked twitchy enough to jump right off his face, and his fingers had been nervously tapping the table since first sitting down.

The council spoke simultaneously, "Welcome, Izzy of Jurael."

Izzy nodded toward them with a probing expression. "Grateful. May the light guide and protect you."

Six One looked proudly from Izzy to the council. "As you know, Jurael has transformed into a much more peaceful world since its introduction to LOLA. They have grown united in their efforts to advance as a planet and focus on the future. Only nine provinces remain stubborn, refusing to surrender to LOLA, and I assure you, I did not find Izzy within their rebellion." She bowed at Izzy as she spoke of him. "He is a renowned doctor within the province of Schmitusch and is a brilliant physicist with military background. In fact, he was a member of the team that discovered the properties of light on Jurael." There were some impressed "oohs" and "ahhs" at his résumé.

Master N'kowsky smiled at him, nodding receptively. "That's remarkable. You have carried your society into a new age." His eyes were even more flattering than his words.

"Grateful," Izzy said. He held his head high at the praise. "Just trying to catch up to Whewliss."

Master Keevind gave another belly laugh with a light slap on the table. "Isn't light travel amazing?" His contagious energy brought everyone other than Master Brawd a smile.

Lady Skorric maintained skepticism as she turned to Six One. "What was his test?"

Six One cleared her throat and met Lady Skorric's demanding eyes, trying not to weaken at their expectation. "I—I brought him to planet One Three Seven, a habitable world currently without human life."

"I'm familiar with it," Lady Skorric replied.

Six One swallowed and continued, "I instructed him to document an uncharted continent. He did so with incredibly intricate detail. He discovered a new gaseous element and survived four days without sleep as he explored, unafraid of the weather."

Lady Skorric squinted. "What was the weather?"

"Uh." Six One blinked rapidly. "The days reached one-hundred-and-thirty-degrees, and the nights dropped to below zero."

Master N'kowsky nodded. "Impressive."

Lady Skorric's expression didn't falter. "Tell us about your next recruit."

Gideon gave Izzy an encouraging thumbs-up from across the table. Izzy optimistically shrugged back with a puffed-out bottom lip. It made Gideon chuckle under his breath. Unlike Traveler, he didn't see Six One's recruits as threats or competition. He saw them as more, exciting people from unheard of worlds who could fortify the team and explore together. Dumakleiza and Timrekka felt the same way, but they were apprehensive, worried about what two teams might mean.

Six One's confidence stumbled a little as she threw her words together. "Next I found my recruit of faith, Tsuna Negwing." All eyes turned to Tsuna, a man sitting next to Izzy, with only one eye visible. His slick black hair neatly swooped down in front of the other, hanging around his head like stalactite spikes trying to stab into his cheeks and neck. An odd expression of melancholy painted him difficult to read.

Six One continued composing herself. "Tsuna is from the planet Gawthraw, which as you are more than aware, feels profoundly honored to be the newest addition to the worlds compliant with LOLA."

The council simultaneously addressed Tsuna, "Welcome, Tsuna of Gawthraw."

Tsuna slowly moved his hand through the air as though he was caressing something precious. "May the light, beautiful and often temporary, guide and protect you." He didn't look at them as his voice trailed off, his eyes fixated on his fluttering fingertips.

Dumakleiza studied him, confused and unsure of what type of spiritual figure he could be with such mannerisms. His strangeness perplexed her in a way that tore her between uneasy and curious. Her plan was to keep her distance and study him. She was also beginning to wonder if she was expected to address the council the same way these recruits had so far. Traveler hadn't given them instructions.

Everyone remained awkward and silent after Tsuna's greeting. Even Lord Coyzle's four identicals stared down at nothing, waiting for anyone to move the introductions forward. Lady Skorric and Master Brawd had unwavering eyes locked on Tsuna, unsure what to make of him. They didn't share any concern, but they weren't willing to tolerate anything or anyone who wouldn't benefit the mission.

Master N'kowsky maintained his charming expression as he patiently waited. Lady Melodeen was a little taken back, put off by Tsuna. She cleared her throat, though she didn't physically need to.

Six One spoke up, hoping to wow the council and regain their interest.

"I took Tsuna to planet Earth. Now, I need not remind the council of the absurdity of that world. Technologies within a century or two of discovering light travel, and yet they still bicker amongst themselves like children. They still fight for dominance over their first phase when they've breached their third. Lunacy. It's comical, really." She shook her head in disappointment, not catching Gideon's smirk to Traveler. She ran long fingernails along the side of her head. "But no matter how much of Earth's spiritual hypocrisies, division, and slaughter in the name of numerous gods, Tsuna maintained his holy resolve. Not once did he falter, and he survived their barbaric animosities, proving himself a truly ideal spiritual recruit for the fourth phase."

Master Keevind didn't miss a beat with his belly laugh. "That's great." He looked around at the other council members and the recruits with his permanent smile.

Master Brawd's stern expression hadn't budged in the slightest since the meeting began, and his response to Tsuna was no exception. Ladies Melodeen and Skorric looked at each other, unsure of how to reply.

Finally, Master N'kowsky filled the silence. "Well, welcome, Tsuna. We're all impressed and grateful you survived your test. We look forward to seeing you further contribute to this project."

Tsuna briefly glanced up at him before returning his eyes to his still fluttering hand. "The holy celestials bless us." His words slid out like molasses.

Six One didn't wait for anyone else to speak. "And lastly I found my recruit of adventure, Jasss of the planet Ojīptian." There were some immediate council murmurs about the risky chance taken by recruiting an Ojīptian. They showed specific concern toward the color of Jasss's skin. Traveler's recruits and the council turned to assess Jasss. She was a bright, green-eyed woman with a light and fair complexion. Her waving hair was naturally full of volume, and her large breasts were making it difficult for some of the men to focus on her face. A quirky expression teased feistiness, but she had an underlying aura of fear. The puzzle pieces didn't fit.

Six One continued. "As the only planet operating under LOLA that still practices slavery, Ojīptian was not an obvious choice for finding a recruit, but I'd heard of a woman who'd escaped captivity and spent her days sabotaging slave encampments," she said with her first genuine smile. "I was curious, so I sought out Jasss. She was difficult to find, but once I did, I knew I had to test her." She looked at Jasss as she went on. "She spent a week with the Honixlets on their barbaric planet. It was a strange and dangerous quest, spending nights camping in their daunting wildernesses, avoiding bandits, all in order to hunt down a gaggle of tar sharks that had made their way into the honey pits. They'd been killing Honixlets' herds of kilobessies." She nodded, proud of the memory. "When she was presented with the test, I didn't read any rising levels of blood pressure or detect any odor of fear. Jasss just leapt at the opportunity. Not only did she survive, she dove straight into a honeycomb pool after one of the sharks, and then, show them, Jasss." She motioned impatiently. "Show them."

Jasss smiled as she held up a thin necklace dangling on her chest. The leather was a dried blend of black and yellow. Swinging at the front of it were three shark teeth, each about an inch and a half long. She stared at them fondly, barely even noticing Master N'kowsky's impressed voice as her mind drifted to distant nostalgia.

"...kill the tar shark?" Master N'kowsky sounded amazed, drawing Jasss's attention back. She dropped the necklace, feeling the razor teeth clank against her skin. Master N'kowsky recognized her mind's distraction, so he repeated himself. "What did you use to kill the tar shark?"

Jasss squinted as she tried to recollect what happened beneath the golden surface. "I don't remember. My hands, I think." She bunched her lips. "Plucked its eye out and fisted its eye socket elbow deep." She chuckled.

Master Keevind couldn't help his signature laugh.

Lady Melodeen shifted uncomfortably. She'd psyched herself up, planning to expect the unexpected with recruits from different worlds, but they were still making her feel unsafe on her own planet."

The council addressed Jasss simultaneously, "Welcome, Jasss of Ojīptian."

Jasss's smile lit up as she looked around at the council. "Thank you. May the light guide and protect you all." Her professionalism returned as though she hadn't just grown giddy at tearing out an animal's brains.

"All right." Lady Melodeen maintained speed. "Six One, you have successfully brought an eclectic three. Moving forward, we will see how capable they truly are."

"Thank you, Lady Melodeen." Six One's shoulders slumped as she finally allowed herself to relax. She'd delivered three recruits. She'd done her job. She was done. She smiled and breathed freely. It didn't matter that Master Brawd hadn't engaged her or any of her recruits. She was just happy that her presentation was over.

Traveler silently assessed Six One's recruits more harshly, judging them behind his narrow eyes. Izzy struck him as an easily distracted arsonist, obsessed with creating weapons and explosives. Tsuna was obviously a self-righteous, harebrained, emotionally erratic, high-risk gamble. And Jasss seemed like she'd gone somewhat mad after liberating herself from enslavement. Traveler had visited two of the three planets they were from, and he didn't feel confident in their ability to unite and operate as a team. He scoffed to himself, excited to see them fail as their testing and training continued.

Lady Melodeen turned to him. "Four Zero, you may now introduce your recruits. Who are they? What LOLA planets are they from? And what tests did they pass?"

4

The council stared at Traveler, anxiously waiting to meet his recruits and hear their stories. Master Brawd stared past everyone, glaring through the walls of Prism Hall. He cared nothing for the formal introductions, and he remained impatient for this trivial portion of his day to end. Lady Skorric focused on studying the subtleties of Traveler's nuances and expressions. Something wasn't right. Masters N'kowsky and Keevind waited with polite smiles, neither urging Traveler to hurry. Lady Melodeen was growing impatient, as she was the meeting's hostess.

Lord Coyzle wanted desperately to hear stories. Having never traveled from Whewliss himself, he thrived on harrowing adventures of others on distant worlds. He absolutely loved the tales of heroism and thrills. His duties were to his people on Whewliss, but his dream was to spend more time getting his hands dirty and exploring the corners of the universe. Only after his curiosity about their stories was satisfied would he be able to focus on the fourth phase and all that came with it.

Six One smirked, waiting with her three recruits, eager to see how Traveler had fallen short as she was familiar with him doing. By his slow response, she knew there was something he was reluctant to share. Her recruits, on the other hand, were eager to learn about them. They were more familiar with Whewliss and its customs, but the spectacle of aliens from other worlds never ceased to intrigue and dazzle.

Traveler finally looked up, his head oscillating to look at each of the council members. He turned to Lord Coyzle. "My Lord." He bowed his head and then lifted it. Lord Coyzle smiled and nodded in response, anxious to continue.

Lady Melodeen repeated herself with a respectful but firmer tone, "Four Zero. Your recruits, their names, their planets, and their tests. If you're ready to join us."

Six One smirked to herself.

Traveler smiled in a moment of impulsive clarity. "Yes, Lady Melodeen." He suddenly felt a liberating indifference toward reprimand or punishment. His expression grew more assertive. "Council members." He forgot the speech he'd recited repeatedly in his head, choosing rather to improvise. "In order of discovery, allow me to first introduce my recruit of adventure, Gideon Green of the planet Earth." He delivered the word "Earth" with poise, knowing full-well what was coming.

"Earth?" Six One spat out without realizing it. "For all that light shines on, why?"

The council members shifted in their seats as concerned comments susurrated.

Lady Skorric leaned toward Traveler, disturbed. "Four Zero, you selected a recruit from a world that does not abide by LOLA? From a world that has not even discovered the powers of light?"

Traveler held his head high as he calmly responded, "Is that a crime?"

Lady Skorric studied his blatancy as Lady Melodeen answered him for her, "No, Four Zero, it is not a crime. It is not illegal. Yet. You may be within your rights, but you have been advised repeatedly by each member of this council. It has been strongly, even adamantly advised that you *not* recruit on such young worlds." She breathed in frustrated control. "It is not condescending elitism that drives our disappointment in your reckless and careless actions; it is the guarantee that your blind risk will not only cost mass quantities of EBOO's funding, time, and resources, but also result in the deaths of your three recruits. They have minimal exposure to worlds beyond their own, and even less experience to help guide them into the unknown of the fourth phase. It is an illogical waste of Whewlight effort."

"Additionally," Lady Skorric said, "you know that successfully delivering to us a recruited three speaks for your reputation and the future of your career. Your name accompanies their success or failure regarding the fourth phase. Do you truly have faith in someone from Earthto venture into a place that *we* do not dare?" She shook her head. "You have committed no crimes, broken no laws, but I do not approve of the brazen disrespect you've shown this council by ignoring our guidance. If you waste our time, I'll personally see that you are permanently banned from EBOO."

The quiet tension that followed had the recruits stunned in fear of the council's wrath. Dumakleiza, Timrekka, and Six One's recruits looked at each other nervously. Gideon, on the other hand, was fixated on Traveler, curious how he was going to respond—especially knowing that no matter how much they disapproved of Earth, they would be just as upset about Thamiosh, and especially Cul.

Traveler looked to the other council members, waiting to hear what the rest of them had to say before he made a case for himself.

Master Keevind shook his head and shrugged. "This is not my area of expertise." Even with his flippant disapproval, his smile remained. "I can guarantee the recruits' safety within EBOO. But once they leave here..."

Master N'kowsky reluctantly showed his disapproval, as well. "I mean no disrespect, Four Zero." He looked at Traveler with warmth. "I simply don't see an outcome where the Earthling's inexperience doesn't leave him vulnerable." He gave a small shrug, trying to dig out some positivity. "Maybe you'll surprise us. Maybe." He flashed his charming smile. "I do enjoy surprises."

Master Brawd said nothing.

Traveler humbly nodded at what they had to say. "Council members, I respect all of your concerns. It is not out of disrespect that I sought out younger worlds but out of necessity and of my own experience." The council members stared at him, scrutinizing every word coming from his mouth. "I spent many, many years recruiting only on LOLA-abiding worlds, as I was instructed. I strictly followed every word and rule, afraid to stray. I discovered promising recruit after promising recruit. But no matter how much potential *I* saw in them, their tests either proved them unworthy or claimed their lives." Traveler tensed as honest remembrance poured out. "And that's when I had an epiphany." He looked directly at Lady Skorric. "There's a raw survival instinct in younger worlds, a natural ability to survive what we have grown to fear. Why is it that a barbarian will charge another on the battlefield with a bludgeoning weapon while we stand safely at a distance with laser implants?"

Lady Skorric rolled her eyes. "Because we've adapted, learned, and bettered ourselves with technological advancements after centuries of hard wo—"

"Courage!" Traveler passionately corrected. "True appreciation for the *fragility* between life and death. They possess a ferocity and absolute, daring, relentless valor that we have long forgotten."

"That is completely incorrect," Lady Skorric growled. "We, as a people, are—"

"Why are we recruiting on worlds other than Whewliss?" Traveler shouted the wakeup call. "Because we are too cowardly to risk our own lives. We are seeking out worlds less advanced *because* they have more courage, *because* we are afraid of the fourth phase." He exhaled through his nostrils as his pulse quickened.

"Yes," Lady Skorric barked back, "we seek one, maybe two steps back, to worlds that at least know light travel is possible. We don't recruit on worlds so primeval that they still wage war like Neanderthals in order to establish dominance over their first phase."

"We?" Traveler scoffed. "You have not once left the comfort and safety of Whewliss. Please remind me what 'we' you are referring to."

Master N'kowsky tried to dissolve the rising tension. "Let us not start—"

"I *mean*," Lady Skorric sneered, "Six One followed a simple command and recruited on LOLA-abiding worlds. And she managed to find three recruits who survived their tests, and they sit before us now. Is that because she's a better recruiter, a better leader, or simply knows how not to kill her recruits?"

Six One silently gloated with a pretentious grin.

The other council members and Lord Coyzle awkwardly lowered their heads, unsure how to quell the situation.

Traveler leaned forward, glaring at Lady Skorric through burning eyes. "As our keeper of the IPOK, your job is to study, maintain, and update our library of knowledge. You learn about ourtravels from the safety of EBOO. *Do not* lecture me on the recruits I've grown to care about and lost, that I've invested time, hope, and memories into and then witnessed die in an attempt to deliver them to you. How dare you. I risk my life every time I leave Whewliss. I am usually in matching danger to my recruits. No matter how different our points of view, no matter what we disagree on, you have no right to be so disrespectful as to mock the deaths you've only read about, but I have held in my hands in their last moments." He fought against burning tears. "They may merely be stories to you, numbers, statistics, but to me, they are memories, pains, and faces I carry—knowing that it was to impress me and serve you that they died."

Goose bumps flew down Gideon's arms. Traveler had always been collected and reserved. Gideon wanted to jump up and applaud, but he refrained.

Lady Skorric took a deep breath and held her fiery tongue as she realized she'd gone too far. "I apologize for that comment, Four Zero. I simply meant to say—"

"And of course Six One's recruits survived." Traveler sharply motioned toward her. "Two out of her three recruits didn't even have tests."

Six One scowled. "Excuse me? I did an excellent job testi—"

"Having one recruit go camping? He survived camping?" Traveler turned to Izzy. "No offense, Izzy, it is not you nor any of you recruits that I'm upset with. But spending a few days outside is nothing compared to the danger and risk that you have blindly volunteered them to venture into. Spending time on Earth and 'surviving' religious oppression by the multitude of disagreeing cultures is not preparation for what is to come. Are you serious?" He looked to Six One. "Do you truly have confidence in Tsuna to survive the fourth phase because he didn't let mockery break him down? No offense to Tsuna, but we teach that tolerance to children."

Six One didn't have a good retort. She scoured her mind, desperate to find an argument that wouldn't make her look foolish.

Traveler turned, looking at Gideon, Dumakleiza, and Timrekka. "I have lost thirteen recruits." The weight of his own words hurt. They made Six One cringe. "I did not lose them due to negligence nor my own incapability. I've made my long list of mistakes along the way, just as all of us recruiters have, but I did not cause the deaths. I lost them because I take the fourth phase seriously. It is dangerous enough to terrify us incapable of exploring it ourselves, and I want the recruits I send into that darkness, that unknown, to be as prepared as they can be. How can I establish that confidence within them? By giving them tests as dangerous as the fourth phase. I didn't train my recruits with pillows for an enemy with swords." He stopped talking before repeating himself, looking around to see if the council had more to argue.

No one said anything. A couple of them averted their eyes, unwilling or unable to match his passion. Traveler nodded and spoke toward everyone. "Now, shall I continue introducing my team, or shall I return them to their worlds because they're not up-to-date on Whewliss's dinner etiquette?"

Gideon smiled as he recognized Traveler's line. It was the same argument he'd made to convince him to recruit Dumakleiza back on Cul. He couldn't help feeling some pride at Traveler reusing it to argue against his superiors.

Lord Coyzle finally spoke. "Four Zero." Traveler looked up to see rosy cheeks perked up with an impressed expression. Lord Coyzle's jolliness masked an observant wisdom that only surfaced when it needed to. He motioned toward Traveler. "Your speech brags an exciting story of life-threatening tests. That's a lot to boast. I pray you can deliver, and don't disappoint after, uh, all that." He smiled. "Please continue."

At his instruction, the council held their tongues. It didn't matter what their reservations were. Their Lord had spoken.

Traveler nodded and spoke directly to him, ignoring the council. "As I was saying, I found Gideon on Earth. He was a thrill-seeking wanderer. However, upon first impression, it wasn't hard to discern that though he had no home, he belonged anywhere and everywhere. It's difficult to explain until you have a conversation with him, but even after all of the planets I've visited, I've never felt gravity like that of his charismatic personality." He smiled as he reminisced with himself. "His magnetic aura aside, during that first moment meeting him, he dove off a mountain in a wingsuit that he'd never had any training using." A couple of the council members murmured to each other. Gideon smiled at Traveler bragging about him. It was fun harking back. Traveler maintained his focus on Lord Coyzle. "I've tested him continuously since then. First I brought him to the Roaring Valley on the only habitable world in the Leshreaf galaxy."

"What?" Six One couldn't help her outburst. "You actually *went to* the Roaring Valley?"

Traveler nodded, taking some pride in her disbelief. "Yes, and when I asked Gideon if he wanted to jump, he leapt before I even finished the question."

Master N'kowsky gasped. "No Whewlight has ever actually been to that world, let alone jumped. I don't believe anyone else has done more than stare at it through telescopes." He shook his head and gawped at Gideon. "You jumped? You jumped off the six-mile-high cliff at the Roaring Valley?"

Gideon nodded, excited to reveal more to the story. "So did Traveler, er, recruiter Four Zero." The instant his words left his mouth, Traveler shot him wide eyes that silently screamed for him to shut up.

"What?" Six One and Master N'kowsky blurted out together.

"You bet." Gideon nodded with wild energy. "He jumped with me, and we landed together." It felt good to brag about Traveler to the judgmental council. Traveler deserved it. "He may be recruiting us for the sake of our super badass courage, but he himself is brimming with it. He's got the stuff."

"Four Zero," Lord Coyzle gasped in captivated veneration, "did you really risk your own life — both of your lives — for a test?"

Traveler slowly nodded as his eyes trailed up to Lord Coyzle's. "When Master Brawd reviews my optical recordings, he will confirm it."

"Wow." Lord Coyzle smiled. "Then what happened?"

"Well." Traveler's eyes widened as he recalled everything. "Let me think. I abandoned Gideon on the planet Cul to see if he was capable of surviving unexpected dangers under the impression of me being shadowed. When I found him, Gideon had speed dueled on a faihrgrrey and was knighted as a vaquilemun. He later stormed into a blinding mist and confronted the legendary ghost king, Yagūl." Traveler motioned toward Dumakleiza. "I believe she killed four or five men before Gideon recognized the potential in her, talked her out of killing both of us, and convinced her and myself that she was a perfect recruit of faith. Then he started a revolution on the planet Thamiosh, uniting two violent rival gangs, ultimately sparking the liberation of Thamiosh's oppressed people against the tyrant, Highness Trollop. That allowed me to recruit Timrekka as our resident scientist." Traveler took a couple breaths. "Gideon was crowned an Eyrayor on Borroke after surviving a gladiatorial match against an entire village of Vulgairs. He's been sentenced to execution twice, threatened with death by nature and man numerously just in the time that I've known him, and has always managed to turn his enemies into friends. And, as he said, he's helped me overcome many of my own fears. I can confidently say that he's taught me as much as I've taught him. In my life, I have traveled the stars, visited many habitable planets, met more multitudes of humanity within the pantheon of life than I ever fathomed to be possible, and searched for the smartest, bravest, most driven individuals to exist in all of creation. And now, after decades of recruiting, I can say with absolute certainty that Gideon is the one and only human I believe capable of venturing into the fourth phase completely alone and surviving. That is who he is, thatis the courage the Earthling effortlessly breathes every day; thoseare just some of his *many* tests so far, and thatis the first recruit I'm delivering to you."

As everyone sat in silence, processing Traveler's ardent narrative, Dumakleiza beamed. Her full smile glowed as she reveled in the tales of Gideon's unequaled heroics. She gazed at Gideon, who was grinning at Traveler's bragging. It wasn't often that Gideon thought it best to bite his tongue, but he decided that he should wait to see what the council members said before he spoke.

Timrekka's eyes were aimed down. His whole head was bowed, preparing for more screaming from the council. He was bad at confrontation, and the palpable tension between Traveler and the council had him wanting to hide.

Lord Coyzle tentatively grinned. "I was planning on returning to the City of Light after this meeting." He looked from Traveler to Gideon, assessing him with his own judgments, curiosities, and excitement. "However, now I believe I will join Master Brawd in reviewing your optical footage." His comment didn't get a flinch out of Master Brawd, who was still staring forward, impatiently waiting for the meeting to be over. Lord Coyzle's voice grew hushed. "Did I hear you say that she —" He motioned openhandedly toward Dumakleiza. "— is from the medieval planet of Cul, and that he —" He motioned toward Timrekka. "— is from Thamiosh?"

Traveler nodded without a shred of shame. "Yes, my lord." He could see Lady Skorric losing her mind in an attempt to bite her tongue. She wanted to make a hurricane of objections and rules needing enforced, but Traveler only cared about Lord Coyzle's approval.

Lord Coyzle's identicals chuckled a scoff. "Your common sense is missing, Four Zero. You're mad, and you gamble with more recklessness than all eleven of the other recruiters combined." Six One smiled at Lord Coyzle's lecturing. Lord Coyzle slowly nodded, contemplating as he mulled over the unsoundness of Traveler's medley. His expression grew to a smile. "Only time will tell if it's a madness worth having or if it will be your downfall, but maybe, just maybe, it's what we all need to aspire toward."

The comment surprised everyone, except Gideon. He'd heard its promise in Lord Coyzle's tone. The council looked at one another, unsure of what to make of it. Six One glared at Traveler through a façade of smiling congratulations. Even Traveler was confused by Lord Coyzle's reaction, expecting further reprimand.

Lord Coyzle smiled, recognizing Traveler's side blinded surprise. "Don't leave us—in the dark." He grinned. "Tell us about them."

"Ooh! Ooh!" Gideon nudged Traveler's shoulder while raising his hand. "Tag me in."

Traveler sharply turned and glared at Gideon for his interruption. "Not now, Gideon. Be quiet."

Gideon nudged him again. "Let me introduce them. Give you a break after all that fun."

Traveler's eyebrows lowered, embarrassed. "That's not how this meeting is conducted."

Lord Coyzle raised his hand, claiming everyone's attention. "This meeting has been beyond unorthodox since you began your introductions, Four Zero." He shrugged, enjoying the break from tradition. "And if Gideon is the recruit you say he is, I'd be very interested in him introducing the rest of your team." His rosy cheeks smiled without his mouth having to.

"Yes, my lord." Traveler was honestly relieved to hand over the reins.

Gideon smiled and turned to the council. He put his hands together as if praying and then bowed his head. "Council." He looked up. "Lord Coyzle." He was addressing the heads of the most advanced and most powerful world known, and he was reveling in every second of the new adrenaline rush.

The council greeted him in unison, "Gideon of the planet Earth."

Gideon put on his most professional expression, trying to focus his excitement. "I take more pride and pleasure in speaking to you than you know. This planet is awesome. Everything you guys have accomplished is incredible—absolutely incredible, and I can't wait to find out what this dang fourth phase is." Three out of the five council members stared at him in stillness, waiting for him to get on with it. Only Masters Keevind and N'kowsky chuckled at Gideon's infectious energy.

Gideon continued. "Anyways, let me introduce you to these two little rascals. First we have the lovely pirate princess, Dumakleiza Yagūl, last of the Yagūlamites. She's beautiful, she's fierce, she's passionate, and she's devoted to her god, Grimleck. She's one of a kind. Now, I know what you're thinking, she's from Cul. It's a scary, primitive world that makes even Earth seem advanced. But she's lived her entire life bathed in violence, preparing for the unexpected, single-handedly fighting off scores of men at a time, and always living her life in crazy awesome honor of Grimleck. She handled Thamiosh like a boss, and here on Whewliss, the technological advancements and cool, 'magical'thingamajigs haven't fazed her."

He smiled at Dumakleiza smiling back at him.

"Trave—Four Zero explained that people from lesser-developed planets typically lose their minds being exposed to other worlds, but not Duma. No, sir. She's a badass heroine-and-a-half. I may not know what the fourth phase is, but I would put my life in Duma's hands through it. She's already saved it more than once." He turned his smile toward the council and Lord Coyzle. "You're all very lucky to have her."

Lord Coyzle stared at Dumakleiza, teeming with wonder. "Welcome."

Master Keevind leaned toward her, trying to be polite and speak at a pace she could understand. "Hel-lo, Du-ma-klei-za." He nodded to help ease the understanding. "Wel-come to Whew —"

"I do not speak with such labored difficulty," Dumakleiza plainly stated. "I may not understand Whewliss, but people are similar on every world. So is rudeness. I request that you do not patronize me due to the world from which I hail."

Master Keevind brought his head back, blushing. "My apologies."

Lady Melodeen overcame her own prejudices for a moment and bowed. "You are a true beauty, Dumakleiza. I apologize for our predetermined judgments of those from younger worlds. Rudeness is not our intention. We council members simply do not venture beyond Whewliss. Our responsibilities are here, and sometimes that narrows our vision on all that exists beyond. Reading about it and living it are two different colors that often bleed together in our minds. Only Master N'kowsky ever visits other worlds, and even then, only worlds technologically advanced enough to have elastic light." She sat back, feeling lectured by her own words. She sighed. "Only our observers and recruiters have ventured to younger worlds and civilizations." She looked to Traveler. "I suppose the correct thing to do would be to trust our own selections and judgments. We must trust that we appointed the right recruiters. As a council, we must trust in our recruiters' judgments and decisions, for they are extensions of our own guidance." She and Traveler exchanged appreciative expressions before she turned to Gideon. "Gideon of Earth, please continue."

Gideon grinned, enjoying the meeting's evolution. "Yes, ma'am." He'd been so engrossed in their back and forth that he'd forgotten to collect his thoughts. "Uh." He looked around. "Oh, right, ahem—well, next is the one and only Timrekka." Gideon giggled as he thought of how he would have described Timrekka to his Earthling friends. He would have hammed it up without needing to embellish anything. "Timrekka is a crazy, mad scientist from Thamiosh." He smiled at Timrekka, sheepishly grinning back. "Where to start with that man. He's brilliant, more inventive than any physicist, surgeon, or crackhead I've ever heard of, sometimes transcending what should be humanly possible with his whackadoo creations and —" Gideon debated whether or not to deliver the finale. "In fact, Timrekka —" He smiled as Traveler reluctantly shrugged, knowing exactly what Gideon wanted to reveal. "Timrekka was shadowed."

Confused silence seized the room.

Six One stared at Gideon, sure that he didn't understand what he was saying. He must be confused. Even Master Brawd looked at Gideon, waiting for him to correct himself.

"What?" Lord Coyzle's identicals blurted out. He leaned in a little. "Repeat that last part."

"Yes," Lady Skorric added. "Did you say he was shadowed? Are you aware of what that means?" She didn't intend to come off as condescending, but Gideon's storytelling had taken a dangerously ignorant turn.

Master Keevind's perma-smile dwindled as he stared at Gideon, randomly flickering his eyes toward Traveler and Timrekka. "We must have heard you incorrectly."

Gideon waited, savoring their confusion and undivided attention. "I said shadowed, right?" Lady Skorric immediately nodded, curious how he'd correct himself. Gideon brought his head back with a peculiar smirk. "And shadowing is where someone is accidentally intercepted during a light jump by an unforeseen body of mass in space, right? The leading cause of Whewlight deaths?"

Master N'kowsky slowly nodded, unsure of Gideon's assured tone. "Yes. So there must be some confusion in what you think happened. It's a serious risk we face every time we jump. No one has ever survived."

"It's not a joking matter," Lady Melodeen added.

Gideon solemnly nodded. "I agree." He reached over and placed his hand on Timrekka's shoulder. "And I was not confused nor mistaken in my choice of words. Timrekka was shadowed between Thamiosh and Borroke."

"Impossible," Master N'kowsky said before Gideon finished.

Six One looked to the council members and Lord Coyzle with nervous eyes. She wanted to see if they believed Gideon's story. There's no way they would be gullible enough to place faith in such a ludicrous, insensitive claim.

Lord Coyzle turned toward Traveler, his eyes lingering on Gideon.

He was looking for the slightest shred of falsehood, a sign of deception. There was none.

"Four Zero, you know the sincerity of Gideon's claim. Can you testify to this?"

Traveler shrugged, relinquishing control over what would come next. "As you said, Lord Coyzle, you will see the truth of everything that happened if you review my optical footage with Master Brawd. Scroll back through our jump history."

All eyes turned to Timrekka, who hid his face downward. The weight of it made him dizzy. He wanted to crawl under the table where no one could stare at him.

Lady Skorric squinted. "Timrekka of Thamiosh, if what is being claimed has any truth to it, how did you survive what no one else has?"

Timrekka fretfully cleared his throat and glanced up at her. "One of my inventions."

As everyone stared, slack jawed, Gideon smiled and leaned back. "Oh, this is going to be fun. So, what happens next?"

The room remained quiet while the council and Lord Coyzle digested everything. Some of it sounded ridiculous, some of it made up, and most of it impossible. They weren't sure what to make of it all. If Timrekka had truly survived being shadowed, if that was even possible, then they had a miracle on their hands. Even whispering a doubt might break the possibility of it being true.

Finally, Master N'kowsky regained his poise. His dazzling smile returned, along with the twinkle in his eyes. "Four Zero, Gideon, Dumakleiza, Timrekka." He delicately turned. "Six One, Izzy, Tsuna, Jasss, today is a historic day filled with excitement, achievement, wonder—*and* doubt, hesitance, and disbelief. Maybe even fear. The full spectrum of emotion is swirling around us right now. After waiting so many years for this moment to be a reality, it begins feeling like fiction, like a dream that will never actually come true." He smiled professionally. "You have had to accept much that you did not understand, and you have done so with grace. We, in turn, will do our part to accept that which even we do not yet understand. Together we will pioneer a new age for all of humanity." His cheek dimples deepened as his smile grew. "You are all miracles in my eyes. I have visited more worlds than any Whew-light—possibly than any other living soul, so please understand the magnitude of me saying that you are the most promising group of eclectic humans I've ever seen." He ended each sentence with the finesse. "I have waited a long time for your arrival, and without even meeting you, I've had such inspiring visions of the future we will create together." He bowed to his superior. "Lord Coyzle."

Lord Coyzle nodded back. "Thank you for wording what we cannot, Master N'kowsky." He looked to the recruits. "I don't know what we'd do without him. He's our poet. A graceful tool in helping new worlds feel comfortable entering into LOLA." Lord Coyzle took a deep breath and focused. "Like he said, we will do our part in accepting the truths you claim." He smiled. "At this time, your assistants will take you to enjoy some of EBOO's fineries for two hours. At the end of those two hours, they will assist you in beginning your first resting light jump. That way you can begin living a lifestyle of full-time productivity. During the time you are gone, Master Brawd and I will review the recruiters' optical foot-age and further debrief them. When all is said and done, if everything that was said during this meeting is confirmed, we will reconvene at Dark to Light Hall."

He, along with all five council members, turned to face Six One's re-cruits. As one they tilted forward and bowed. They then turned to Traveler's recruits and did the same thing. Lord Coyzle smiled.

"Thank you for everything you have already done and for everything we move toward. As always, may the light guide and protect you all."

Traveler hoped it would. He swallowed hard and bowed.

5

They exited the massive dome and began down a glassy sidewalk that glistened with smoky luminescence. On either side, lush gardens decorated every open space. Vibrant colors burst like small explosions from the cornucopia of flowers, fruits, and effervescent plants. Random clusters of trees sprouted overhead like cartoon springs. They reminded Gideon of palm trees with additional leaf spines spiraling down their trunks.

The recruits took in the view of EBOO's mirror-coated buildings reflecting the sunset. For a moment, the paradisiacal view, saturated in colors that defied reality, silenced even Gideon as they stopped to savor it.

"Wow." Gideon's eyes widened at the majesty. "Bob Ross would roll over in his grave if he knew this was here."

Kristuf racked his mind for Earthling references. "Who would what?"

"My favorite artist, slash lullaby voice." Gideon smiled. "So, where are you taking us?"

"That depends on you recruits," Kristuf said with an eager grin. "Our prompt is to entertain you until Lord Coyzle is ready for you and to assist with you getting to know each other."

Dumakleiza's spine was tense. On one hand, she was glad there were another three recruits to accompany them, but on the other, she didn't trust them, and historically she killed those she didn't trust. She didn't have any weapons on her, and she assumed she wouldn't need them, but just having a knife or two accessible would make her feel more at ease.

Timrekka was still. He was a sponge with unfamiliar people, and with so many new faces, he was silently listening, absorbing everything he could. Both he and Dumakleiza trusted Gideon to be their voice.

Gideon looked at Six One's recruits. "Well, hmm." He tilted his head back and forth as he thought. "If that's what we're supposed to do, then how about we go to that hologram, virtual reality room you were telling me about? You said it has pretty good renditions of every world you know, right?"

Kristuf nodded.

Gideon smiled again. "Perfect. Then we can hang out and chitchat while taking virtual tours of each other's worlds, right?"

Kristuf nodded as he realized what Gideon was wanting. "Oh, that's a good idea." He turned to the others. "As long as that's what everyone wants to do."

Dumakleiza nodded toward the other recruits. "I would feel more trusting if I were shown their origins."

Timrekka nodded, keeping his hands clasped together, shifting his weight back and forth.

Izzy smiled. "That sounds like a great bonding opportunity. I've never seen a virtual reality room. It would certainly acquaint me with Four Zero's recruits."

Jasss puffed her bottom lip out and nodded.

Tsuna lackadaisically sighed. "Submerging our souls in electronic ghosts of distant worlds. Sounds like a dream built on desperation." His assistant tried to hide some annoyed impatience.

Gideon chuckled. "Sounds like we're all down. Can we? Can we? Please?" he playfully begged.

Kristuf resumed walking down the glossy sidewalk with the other assistants. "Follow us."

Gideon looked at him curiously. "We're not jumping there? Going for a *light* jog instead?"

Alik chuckled from behind him. "We do walk places. We're not that jaded by technology. Do we come off that lazy?"

"No." Gideon smirked playfully. "Just giving you crap."

Kristuf squinted. "Give us crap? Please tell me that's a saying from Earth and not a literal intention."

"It is not," Dumakleiza chirped in. "I do not believe Sir Gideon is the type of man who would bestow fecal gifts to new acquaintances."

Jasss walked a little faster so she could hear them better. "Oh, I want to watch if you're giving him fecal matter."

Gideon laughed. "Holy spirit, you guys are killing me. Yeah, yeah, it's just a saying."

Everyone but Tsuna either smiled or laughed.

The assistants led them into a two story, cube-shaped building. Once they passed through the doorway scanner, they stopped in the entry room.

Brasina fervently took lead. "Before we enter, you get your next implant."

"Optical?" Gideon guessed with shaking fists.

"That is correct."

The assistants smiled as they faced their assigned recruit and extended open hands, palms up. Placed upon their palms were small platters with thin layers of fluid. Centered in them were two contacts.

Izzy's assistant spoke for the rest of them. "Place these in your eyes. They are biodegradable micro-tech. Once removed from the solution, they dissolve and activate upon moisture, so insert them immediately."

The recruits tentatively reached for the contacts, carefully picking them up with trembling fingertips. They each struggled to insert them into their eyes. There was blinking, tearing up, stretched faces of concentration, and cross-eyed aiming.

Dumakleiza stared at hers fearfully. The idea of sticking somethinginto her eyes sounded barbaric. She couldn't believeadvanced people thought it was a good idea. The only experience she had with contacts was watching Gideon with the chameleon eyes, and that did not give her confidence.

Brasina leaned in and whispered, "It's completely safe. I promise." Her words gave Dumakleiza just enough of a push to reach for the small, transparent discs.

As the recruits finally got their contacts situated, their assistants double-checked to make sure they were put in properly.

"Your eyes will absorb the micro-tech carried within the thin film," Brasina said. "And then you will be able to see much more of Whewliss. They will never need to be replaced—above the ripples."

"I don't see anything different," Gideon said.

"You shouldn't yet," Kristuf slyly commented. "Follow us this way."

The assistants led them through a hallway to a door. Within the doorway, nothing was visible since the lights were off. It was the first time any of the recruits had seen any darkness on Whewliss. Once they passed through an entryway, lights came on from all around them. The floor, walls, and ceiling were each individual, massive panels of light. The room was made of a milky white glass covering a wire grid. There was no spectacle, just what looked to Gideon like a chicken wire cage wrapped in light bulbs.

"Well." Kristuf looked around at the walls. "How does it look?"

Gideon searched the room, trying to see if there was something he was missing. "I still don't see anything."

"Okay, good. You're not crazy." Kristuf and the other assistants chuckled at the initiation joke.

Brasina raised both hands above her head and then brought them down toward her sides in an arching motion. As she did, the lights dimmed. Her movements were as poised and disciplined as a dance. By the time her hands reached her sides, everyone in the room was swallowed in pitch black. Gideon moved his hand in front of his face, seeing nothing at all.

Then, out of nowhere, stars appeared all around, above, and below them. Gideon felt like he was back on a middle school field trip to a planetarium. Every direction was comprised of distant constellations, galaxies, nebulas, planets, and countless celestial bodies moving in real time. They couldn't see any of the floor, walls, or ceiling. It was as if they were floating in space, regardless of still feeling the floor.

Brasina looked at the recruits. "Without your contacts, you wouldn't be able to see any of this."

Most of the recruits gawked in amazement of the digitized universe, but Dumakleiza's breathing quickened. She was trying to maintain her cool acceptance of everything beyond her understanding, but being suspended in a perfect rendition of space had her feeling light-headed and powerless. She'd never seen anything like it. She understood the basic concept of what they were experiencing, but it was far more over-whelming than she had prepared herself for. She couldn't see what she was standing on, she couldn't get a grasp on where the room had gone, and she couldn't help wondering if she was actually lost in space. It was too much. Her knees buckled and she fell over, failing to catch herself on the floor she couldn't see.

"Oh, shit." Gideon dropped down and scooped up Dumakleiza under her arms. He carefully lifted her back to her feet. Dumakleiza widened her eyes, trying to force feeling into her extremities.

Brasina looked at them as she maintained her hands' positions. "Are you all right?"

Dumakleiza fuzzily nodded. "Yes. I apologize." She shook her head and feigned a smile. "I will be fine."

Brasina gave an understanding expression. "Your suit will recognize your shortness of breath. It'll infuse you with a higher dose of oxygen and assist in spiking your adrenaline." As soon as she finished explaining, Dumakleiza felt it. She took a few deep breaths and nodded to Gideon.

"I am okay. Thank you, Sir Gideon." She smiled at his concern. She hated having someone help her, but she couldn't deny that it felt good to have Gideon concerned about her well-being.

Tsuna scoffed, "She collapsed during a digital rendering. Whatever the fourth phase is, it is not for her." He giggled to himself as he continued looking at the spectacle around them.

Timrekka turned and glared. "Do not call her weak."

Tsuna scoffed again, keeping his eyes elsewhere. "We will see, grand-father dwarf."

Izzy backhanded Tsuna in the chest. "Go back to humping dirt, prin-cess eyeliner." He looked to Dumakleiza and Timrekka. "Sorry about him. He's bad at relationships with things that aren't insentient spheres."

The murky comment made Tsuna shake his head and look away. "I pray for her sake that the Earthling is ready to catch her repetitively. We've barely even begun."

Gideon held Dumakleiza's shoulders and looked deep into her eyes to make sure she was all right. "Don't listen to him. You've got this." He winked and kept his arm around her to keep her up.

Dumakleiza glared at Tsuna as she whispered to Gideon. "When we are done here, I need to be with Cooby."

Brasina resumed once everyone was ready to continue, "Another function of your contacts is translating written language. Similar to the translators implanted into your inner ears, the contacts will translate most foreign languages that you see into readable text you can understand." She waved her right hand toward the ceiling. "For example."

Something else came into view in the digitized universe. Over each celestial body, names appeared. They read in clear translation to each recruits' native language. Gideon's mouth hung open as he stared at the fully immersive map all around them. Everywhere he looked, stars, planets, nebulas, galaxies, and even shooting stars, asteroid belts, moons, and everything visible was titled with small, glowing letters.

"Well, that's just one of the coolest things ever," Gideon said as his eyes reflected the high-definition wonder.

"It never ceases to amaze," Kristuf said, enjoying their first-time excitement. "Brasina, where should we start?"

"Hmm." Brasina thought over the appropriate answer. "We should probably go in order of recruitment. Izzy, remind me, what world are you from?"

Izzy's assistant answered immediately, "Jurael. That way." The assistant pointed off into virtual reality space.

"Ah, yes." Brasina shifted her hands in the air, outstretching her arms and bringing them together in front of herself. Suddenly they launched forward, streaks of light passing them as they flew through space. The virtual architects had even added a vibrating *whoosh* sound to amplify the sensation of light travel. All the recruits swayed a little at the unexpected visual. They chuckled as they regained their bearings, knowing that they hadn't actually moved at all. Brasina laughed with them as she continued moving her hands like a ribbon dancer. Wisps of light passed so fast that they couldn't discern stars from galaxies, planets from supergiants. Colors blurred together in beautiful harmonies of the full spectrum, leaving curious trails of everything they passed. Gideon had no idea how Brasina was keeping track of where they were, but she looked perfectly in control and confident in her steering through countless lightyears and trillions of miles.

Then, as suddenly as she'd propelled them forward, she spread her arms and they stopped. Everything came to a standstill. Everyone stumbled forward as their minds again fell victim to illusory inertia. They looked around at their new surroundings. In front of them, they saw a galaxy with a large yellow sun in the center of six orbiting planets.

Jasss stepped forward and reached for one of them as it slowly orbited in front of her hip. Her fingers went through it as if it wasn't there. She smiled. "Fist me, that's beautiful." She turned her head toward Brasina while keeping her eyes on the planet floating away from her. "Do these have names, as well?"

"Oh. Yes." Brasina shook her head. "Sorry. Here they are." She flicked a finger, and then the names of everything appeared in floating white text.

Jasss leaned in close to the planet next to her hand. "Centringole."

"*That's* Centringole?" Izzy stepped up next to her. "Huh." He nodded. "It certainly is. Which means —" He turned, tapping his finger on his lips as he studied the other floating planets. "—thatis Jurael. Yes, it is!" He walked a few steps over to the familiar orb. He cupped his hands near it, wishing he could touch it.

Gideon curiously studied the green and blue planet. It reminded him of Earth from afar. There were green bodies of land, blue bodies of water, and swirling white clouds. Aside from the differently shaped continents, it looked like what he was familiar with on maps and globes. He'd only visited other worlds directly. He'd never stared at them from outer space.

"So, do all habitable worlds look the same?"

"Relatively," Brasina said. "Oceans and lands are pretty consistent. The greenery varies depending on the topographical makeup of each world. Some are made of more forests, jungles, deserts, tundras, frozen wastelands, varied by smog, density of cities, etcetera. But oceans are a giveaway. It's actually a large part of how we find inhabited worlds. Though, many habitable worlds, early in their development, look quite different." She paused and took a moment to appreciate the wonder on the recruits' faces. "Would you be interested in visiting Jurael's surface?"

Izzy turned to her. "We can actually go there in here? I thought this was as close as we could get."

"Oh, of course we can." Brasina grinned. "You really think that all-we're capable of on Whewliss—in EBOO nonetheless—is looking from afar? No. No. No." She smiled and walked up to Jurael as it floated next to Izzy. She extended one finger toward it. "We are capable of much-more." She tapped the digital rendering.

Whoosh! In an instant, they launched forward as if they were in a shuttle flying down to Jurael's surface. The virtual visual around them zoomed down, leaving space behind. Some of them screamed, as it felt like they were going to crash into Jurael's surface. They passed through the planet's outer atmosphere and continued downward through clouds, illuminating themselves in white wisps. Then, as fast as they'd shot toward the planet, they stopped, finding themselves standing on Jurael's surface.

They looked around, catching their breath. It felt like they were truly there. The virtual reality was so vivid that they momentarily forgot they were really standing in an empty room. There was no buffering, no vague clarity of limited pixel quality. It was real. Vast deserts of hazel sand stretched as far as they could see. Only on the distant horizon could they faintly make out treeless mountains.

"Wow," Izzy exclaimed. "This is impressive. This is the city I'm from."

Gideon looked around, trying to see anything that resembled civilization or structures. "This is a city?"

"Yes. On Schmitusch—this province—it's too hot for living conditions, so we re-built our cities in valleys and then buried them in sand. Keeps us cool and safe from Thormaggen's rays."

"Thormaggen?"

"Our sun."

"Oh, okay." Gideon continued studying the desert landscape. "Mole people. That's cool. So, where's a door? Or whatever you use to get down into the city?"

"Uh." Izzy looked around to see how accurate the rendering of his home world was. "That really isimpressive. The Whewlights got it right." He pointed off toward what simply looked like a barren stretch of desert.

Brasina followed his indication, steering them forward. The ground passed beneath their feet without them walking. They hovered, coasting over sand, detailed plant life, scurrying desert animals, and even a light breeze sending tumbleweed by. Brasina brought her arms out and stopped them once she saw what Izzy's finger was aimed at. Centered between them on the ground was a metal cylinder built into the sand.

Izzy nodded with an amazed smile. "That's one of I believe thirty-five entrances to Trihead, the city beneath." He glanced toward the assistants. "Do you have renderings of Trihead that I can tour us all through?"

Brasina shook her head. "No, unfortunately our observers and re-cruiters haven't gathered enough data on your sub-cities for us to accurately generate them."

"Aw," Gideon sighed in disappointment. "I was really excited to see what an underground city would look like. You'll have to take me there someday."

"Okay." Izzy smiled, happy to share his home world. "We literally have everything we need down there."

"What about agriculture?"

"That, too. Solar mimicking bulbs make it possible to farm under-ground. It's something I've helped develop ever since discovering the power of light. It's not as efficient as Thormaggen, sure, but we can sur-vive underground for months at a time without needing to surface for maintenance and whatnot."

"This is the coolest show-and-tell ever." Gideon smiled. "What was it like to discover light travel for your world?"

Izzy's eyebrows danced. "Well." He smirked. "Recruiter Six One didn't tell my story quite right. I am a physicist, but I wasn't when I dis-covered light travel. I was an undercover arms dealer that specialized in explosives."

Timrekka leaned in at what sounded like inventing. "How does one get that confused with physicists?"

Izzy shrugged. "I don't know. I think she's ashamed of that part of my past, so she left it out. I was a member of a police unit trying to infiltrate a terrorist organization called the Vem. They had taken credit for three terror attacks that left a total of thirty-eight dead from detonations. Our goal was to infiltrate and cut the head off the flang, so to speak. My squad and I were experimenting with hydroelectric laser-bang tech, trying to fashion a new dirty bomb that would ultimately lead to arrests." Everyone stopped looking at Jurael to listen more intently to Izzy. "We were far away from Trihead, in a more desolate valley where the Vem had taken refuge." His right thumb rapidly tapped against his thigh as he spoke. "One energy particle laser-bang blast later and *boom*!" Izzy threw his hands to the left. "Out of nowhere, I found myself twenty-nine miles away from where I had been. It was disorienting and *so* surreal."

"What a discovery." Timrekka eagerly scooted closer. "Were you aware of what you'd stumbled across, as in did you know that light had transported you? I can only imagine how lost you must have felt."

Izzy scoffed. "Oh, we had no idea. We were all so amazed at what we thought was a triggered wormhole that we lost focus on our tasks—the Vem included. Undercover cops and terrorists alike leapt the twenty-nine miles over and over and over. It was like a never-ending theme park ride."

"Huh," Gideon said with crossed arms, amused. "So, what happened? With the Vem? And when did you know you'd discovered light travel?"

"Well," Izzy chuckled and pinched the bridge of his nose as he laughed harder at the memory. "In our distraction, we provided enough of a window for more police to amass and successfully surround the encampment. They arrested all the Vem, so that was a win. And then our resources went into studying the phenomenon of 'the wormhole.'"

Izzy's assistant nudged him. "There's more to Jurael's history than that. Don't leave out the most interesting details."

"Oh." Gideon smiled. "Spill the beans."

Izzy stared quizzically at Gideon's comment and then went on. "Well, once it was confirmed that we were dealing with light travel and not a wormhole, my government used the incarcerated Vem as test subjects. They shot them into space with no idea of where they were aiming. It was said that it was to see if they would discover life beyond our world, but we knew the truth." Izzy shook his head, ashamed of his government's actions. "They just wanted to see the looks on the Vem's faces before they blindly sent them into oblivion."

"Wow," Gideon said. "That's a hell of a bedtime story."

Jasss laughed. "I love that Jurael turned its 'bad guys' into shooting stars."

"They burned their world," Tsuna said, upset. "So it spat them off itself."

Timrekka lowered his head a little. "I'm not sure if they deserved that or not, as it's certainly a moral dilemma, but if it saved innocent lives from their terrorism——"

"Yeah," Izzy said, clapping his hands together. "Well, that's Jurael for you. Shortly after that, we were visited by Master N'kowsky and introduced to LOLA." He sighed, eager to step out of the spotlight. "Shall we move on to someone else's world?"

Brasina nodded and whipped her hands around, choreographing their departure. Within seconds, they were flying back up into the sky, passing through clouds. Everyone fought for balance as they reentered the void of space, surrounded by millions of distant stars. Brasina looked around to the recruits floating in the vaccuum.

"I vote we go back and forth between groups. Gideon, you were first for Four Zero, correct?"

"Yup. Yup. Yup," Gideon answered, eager to see how good of a job they'd done mimicking Earth. He couldn't even begin to imagine how they created such intricate details.

Brasina looked around. "Hmm, Earth."

Gideon blatantly coughed, "Milky Way." He patted his chest. "Excuse me."

Kristuf chuckled, "You are fantastic."

Brasina smiled and nodded. "Right." She maneuvered her hands and launched them to the right. Once again stars streaked by in rapidly vanishing blurs. They flew through space, barely noticing subtle right and left shifts that Brasina made. "And here we are." She brought her arms out, and they came to a sudden stop.

As everyone stared at the cosmic blackness around them, they searched for Gideon's home galaxy. They weren't sure if they were missing it, but they didn't see anything resembling one anywhere. It didn't look like any solar system any of them had ever seen. It seemed darker, bereft of any celestial bodies aside from one single sun floating directionless behind them. Even the assistants, with all they had studied, felt unfamiliar with where Brasina had taken them. They'd never seen space so empty. Wherever they were, it had a haunting aura to it. Discomfort was immediately palpable within the group. The virtual reality of the room was forgotten, as they all felt a swallowing claustrophobia ebbing in. They were lost somewhere they didn't want to be, somewhere they didn't belong.

Alik turned to Brasina. "This isn't where Earth is located." He looked around. "I don't think anything is over here. Where are we?"

Brasina squinted in the darkness. "I'm not sure. I must have gotten lost." She flicked her finger, searching for any floating names, hoping something familiar would pop up and give her a sense of direction. Everyone helped search their surroundings for any sign of documentation or familiarity. They were sure that at least one of them would know where they were. The blackness only seemed to be getting darker.

Dumakleiza cocked her head to the side as her dragon eye faintly noticed something no one else could see. "H. P. What is H.P.?"

"What's what?" Brasina tried to follow Dumakleiza's gaze, barely visible in the blackness. She slowly steered them forward, zooming in on whatever Dumakleiza was talking about. After flying blindly, it became visible to the rest of them. The initials "H.P." were floating in white text above a smoky sphere in the distance. There were no visible oceans, no land, nothing except for dark, swirling clouds. The recruits dismissed it as an uninhabitable world, a random planet floating in the vast void of the cosmos, but the assistants leaned in closer.

Alik was the closest. "What is this world? I've never heard of it. What do the initials stand for?"

"I'm not sure," said Jasss's assistant. "Have any of you heard of it? It appears to be habitable."

Gideon grew interested. "Habitable, as in a young world that can support life? Or do you mean that there are already people on it?"

Brasina shrugged. "I don't know." She looked to the other assistants, still hoping maybe one of them had read something about it. "I have never heard of any habitable world named H.P."

Timrekka took a single step backward. "It feels like we shouldn't be here." He immediately felt silly for acting fearful in a digital rendering of something countless lightyears away.

"I agree with grandfather dwarf," Tsuna muttered, unsettled by their location.

"Well." Gideon smiled, unbothered by the mysterious world. "Let's find you two a sitter while we —" He looked to Brasina. "—zoom in and find out who lives there."

"Yes," Brasina mumbled out, unsure why she felt uneasy. She shook her head and cleared her throat before reaching forward to touch H.P. Whatever it was, they were going to zoom down to its surface and figure it out. Everyone tensed in anticipation. Brasina's finger slowly extended and then she touched it.

Nothing happened.

Brasina jerked her head back, confused, and tried again. Still nothing. "It's —" She narrowed her eyes. "—restricted? What does...hmm." She leaned in to read the fine print. After double-checking what she thought she'd misunderstood, she looked to the other assistants. "Have you ever been denied access to a planet?" They all shook their heads. Brasina turned back, leaning in as close as she could to the digital rendering of H.P. "It says it's habitable. There's no indication as to whether or not it's habited, but why wouldn't we be able to explore it? I've never seen 're-stricted.'"

Alik shrugged, perplexed. "There must be something Lord Coyzle doesn't want anyone to see."

"Him and who else?" Brasina puzzled. "Who all knows about this? Is it dangerous? Who lives there?"

"Or what lives there?" Gideon said dramatically. "Dun, dun, dun." He cracked an unseen smile and grabbed his chin with his thumb and index finger. It still felt weird to feel it shaved. "It couldn't possibly stand for Hewlett-Packard? A digital rendering of a computer planet. Oh! Or does it mean Harry Potter? A wizarding world?"

The assistants looked at him with no idea what he was referring to. "Harry Potter?" Kristuf asked.

"Never mind." Gideon waved the question away. "So, we've stumbled upon something we're not allowed to see? It feels like we're teenagers who found our parents' secret porn folder and don't know how to open it." He chuckled.

Brasina exhaled sharply as she stepped back, keeping her eyes on the foreign world. "I have no idea." She shook her head, realizing she needed to focus on the recruits and not her personal curiosity. "We will inquire about it later." She forced her perky personality to the forefront of her mind. "For now let's redirect and find Earth."

Gideon sighed heavily. "Ugh, this whole moment has been like licking the tip and then walking away. Such a tease."

Dumakleiza stuck her head into his line of sight. "I am beside myself with excitement, Sir Gideon. I wish to see the world you hail from." She gently grabbed his hand, hoping to see matched appreciation in his eyes.

Gideon feigned a starry-eyed smile and nodded. "I'm excited to show you around."

With that, Brasina maneuvered her arms and launched them through streaming stars and galaxies.

6

After visiting all six of their home planets, the recruits had been taken to do their first resting light jump. Their assistants helped them with EBOO's light pads and sent them into orbit around Whewliss. As with their previous jumps between worlds, the time they spent lit around the planet felt like a blink, their reappearances instantaneous. They landed on the exact light pads they'd jumped from, fully rested, alert, and greeted by their assistants.

Afterward Kristuf had cut Gideon's shoulder before they'd been taken to eat at one of EBOO's finest restaurants. They devoured a smorgasbord of flavorful dishes accumulated from different worlds. There was a dish comprised of tentacles that reminded Gideon of octopus, except the ends looked like human fingers with long nails. The earthy flavor was rich enough to distract them from the unnerving appearance. They were given a dish of thin pasta, but it was on fire when it had been served. Some of the drinks had fish swimming around in the liquid that the recruits had been instructed to swallow whole.

They shared stories and laughs while the assistants explained more facets of Whewliss. Finally, after resting and getting their fill, they headed to Dark to Light Hall to reconvene with Lord Coyzle and the council.

Dark to Light Hall wasn't as large or majestic as Prism Hall, nor as well-guarded with a scanning doorway, but what it lacked in height, it made up for in length. It actually looked like a massive hallway. The structure was long and wide, looking like a walled-in airplane runway. The outside was coated in shimmering, reflective paint. In the darkness

of night, the only reflections were of the stars above them and the surrounding lights of EBOO. The abundance of mirrors and extravagant
decorations took some getting used to for the aliens from other worlds.
In the day, it was easy to at least make out the shapes of the structures,
but at night, each building made EBOO go on for eternity. Gideon assumed that was one of the goals of the architects: to create a stunning
spectacle, doubling the size of everything visible, as one mirror reflected
another and another. It was dizzying but too captivating and mesmerizing
to look away.

Inside Dark to Light's entryway, couches lined the walls of a smaller
room, and dim lights created a calm ambiance. The only brightness was
a light pad in the center of the floor, similar to those they'd used for their
resting light jumps.

Everyone relaxed on the couches while they waited. Just like the
chairs at Prism Hall, the couches adjusted to each person's gelatin suit,
tending to individual musculature, gently kneading and massaging sensed
tensions with stimulating electric pulses. While the assistants were jaded
to the sensations, they did enjoy watching the exhilarated expressions on
the recruits' faces. Only Tsuna had insisted upon staying outside so he
could sit in one of the gardens. He'd explained that he needed to connect
to Whewliss and identify with her soul. His assistant courteously stayed
out with him against his will.

Dumakleiza stared at the floor, still in shock from the digital rendering
of Cul. "My island appeared so small and unimportant from afar." Her
disappointment was near mourning.

As Gideon touched her shoulder to comfort her, Timrekka beamed
at him. "I still haven't recovered from how unique and creative your an-
cestors' burial methods were in those pyramid structures."

Gideon nodded while looking at the intricate murals painted on the
walls. "Conspiracy theorists think aliens taught the ancient Egyptians
how to build them." The murals were difficult to see in the dimness. They
looked like black and white swirls trailing off into elaborate designs. Gideon grinned. "After all of this, maybe they're right." The mural reminded
him of the red and yellow roads in *The Wizard of Oz*. He squinted, trying
to see more.

Kristuf recognized his difficulty. "A convenience you now possess with your biodegraded contacts: Look up and wink your right eye to dilate and let more light in, or look down and wink your right eye to prevent light from coming in, darkening your view."

"What?" Gideon aimed only his eyes toward the ceiling. He winked, and the room became a little brighter. "Well, that's cool." Once he was satisfied with the brightness level, he looked around, smiling at the clarity of the painted walls. "Nifty indeed."

Dumakleiza quietly tried the same trick. She wanted to master it before joining in the conversation. Even though she didn't fear conflict, embarrassment at disability or misunderstanding was a bitter taste she wanted to avoid having to choke down. She cracked a smile as she saw the room's brightness change with each of her winks. It was a magic that she had control over.

Jasss grunted in frustration. "I can't wink." Everyone looked over to see her looking up and blinking. She flexed her jaw and tried again. No matter how hard she tried, she couldn't single out one eye. The others couldn't help but chuckle at her simple handicap. After a few more attempts, she joined in the laughter. "Fist it, I'll just deal with this romantic darkness all by myself."

Dumakleiza took the laughter as an opportunity to ask something. "Tell me." She leaned toward Jasss. "Why does Tsuna of Gawthraw distance himself from us with veiled hostility?"

"Oh." Jasss rolled her eyes, one of them fluttering in distaste for Tsuna. The room grew brighter for her. "Oh! Ha!" She smiled victoriously. "I can blink if I'm trying not to vomit." She chuckled and looked back to Dumakleiza. "Tsuna worships planets." She scoffed. "He believes Gawthraw is the highest deity there is and that the rest of our worlds are lesser gods. If I were to guess, I would bet that he's outside right now, whispering to Whewliss, kissing, maybe even humping the dirt just to get an intimate understanding. Ugh." She shivered. "He's a creepy, creepy creep."

"How curious," Dumakleiza said, scooting forward with piqued interest. "How does one worship a planet?"

Jasss scoffed again as she leaned back, sprawling her arms across the back of the couch. "You would have to go ask the psycho outside."

"Well," Gideon chimed in, "he seems to be a lot of things, but he certainly is devout."

Dumakleiza shot him a distasteful look, unappreciative of him defending Tsuna. "Well, I — " She looked back to Jasss. "I've never thought of gods being worlds. It is truly strange."

While Dumakleiza and Jasss continued talking, Gideon looked to the assistants. "So, is there any clue or hint you guys can give us about the fourth phase?"

Kristuf and Alik looked to Brasina, knowing she was the most fluent with explanations. All three of them smiled in silent understanding, as if they'd been expecting the question. They seemed almost reverent, heightened by the fourth phase's mentioning.

"Everything we do in EBOO is top-secret," Brasina said. "The rest of Whewliss knows we exist. They're aware that we deal with other worlds outside of those that abide by LOLA, but they do not know anything else about them. There is civilian travel between LOLA-abiding planets for business or vacation. However, Whewlights don't know the details, the people, or anything beyond those worlds. We operate in governmental-decreed confidentiality. However — " She paused and looked from the other assistants back to Gideon. "The fourth phase is classified above top-secret. Only Lord Coyzle, the council, and the recruiters know exactly what it — well, they know more than anyone else. I don't think anyone actually knows what it is."

Gideon raised an eyebrow and tittered in amused frustration. "After all this, it'd better not be nothing."

"It is certainly not nothing," Lord Coyzle said, surprising them.

Everyone turned to see that he, both recruiters, Master Brawd, and Lady Skorric had appeared on the white circle in the floor. Only then did Gideon connect the skylight in the ceiling being a doorway, not a window. The assistants stood to their feet and bowed. The recruits realized they should follow, so they stood to their feet and bowed, as well. Tsuna's assistant escorted the unenthusiastic alien inside to join the others.

Lord Coyzle smiled at Gideon. "So you're trying to get started without us? Tsk. Tsk." He shook his head.

"Just excited to get a move on," Gideon said with a grin. "So, how'd show-and-tell go?"

Lord Coyzle looked to Traveler and Six One with an impressed look before turning back. "I'm still trying to process everything." He shivered a smile. "I'm jealous of the adventures you've gotten to experience. If my duty wasn't here, I'd want to go see other worlds myself." He slowly nodded as he looked around at each of them. "And to answer your question, Master Brawd and myself are in agreement." He waited a little longer, enjoying the leveraged tension he had them caught in. With another smile, he nodded. "We approve of you all."

Traveler and Six One's smiles shone brighter than the lights in EBOO at the commendation. They put their differences aside for a moment to congratulate each other as the recruits clapped for them.

Master Brawd even acknowledged the recruits' existence. "Welcome." It sounded forced, instructed, but they were willing to accept any comment from his stern presence.

Lord Coyzle's energy felt like that of a magician, excited to perform. "Have your assistants told you why we're gathered here?" The recruits shook their heads as a couple of them looked around the entryway for hints. "Well." Lord Coyzle smiled, knowing he got to explain first. "Lady Skorric is going to take us on a tour—a history lesson rather—from the discovery of light travel all the way until the discovery of the fourth phase."

"Finally," Gideon blurted out with fists thrown above his head.

"That is, of course, if you'd all be interested in that," Lord Coyzle said with a rosy-cheeked wink.

"Yes!" Gideon couldn't help shouting. "Let's do this."

Timrekka was trying not to run around the room in anticipation. His enhanced strength filled him with more energy than he was familiar with. He peered through his goggles and turned to Lord Coyzle.

"Where are the other council members?"

"Oh." Lord Coyzle realized he'd forgotten to explain. "Lady Melodeen returned to her post at the gelatin. She enjoys spending her days reading while overseeing arrivals. I'm pretty sure she's read every book we have on Whewliss—twice. She's probably working on the third time around."

He took a deep breath and looked at their hungry eyes, all impatient to get a move on. "Master Keevind had to return to work at EBOO's police headquarters, and Master N'kowsky departed for another world. He frequents every planet operating under LOLA to ensure that they're abiding by its laws."

Izzy nodded. "We're always excited to see him on Jurael when he visits."

Lord Coyzle rolled his eyes in playful contempt. "Oh, yes, we know. He is a universal celebrity. That's what we get for sending a striking, charming, walking smile like him through space." He chuckled. "I'm just kidding. He's loved everywhere he goes. He's perfect, and that's why we hate him."

Lady Skorric's smile was courteous but impatient. "Shall we?" She motioned to a doorway. As she reclaimed their attention, she turned and led the way. Gideon, Dumakleiza, and Timrekka were beside themselves, barely able to contain their excitement. Six One's recruits were less enthused since they already knew much of Whewliss's history. Everyone followed behind Lord Coyzle and Master Brawd as they kept on Lady Skorric's heels.

Through the doorway was the first true great hall they'd seen. From where they stood in, it visually stretched away like an eternal tunnel. They couldn't see its end. On one side, the walls were painted in vivid murals from top to bottom. Every inch was exhaustive art, meticulously painted throughout the entire hall, not a single spot left without. The details were difficult to see from the doorway, but it looked to illustrate outer space, worlds, people, battles, fire, structures, large murals of iconic individuals, and a wide array of further storytelling. They didn't look cartoony or abstract. Realism had clearly been strived for by the artist or artists. Everything the recruits' wide eyes soaked up was methodically crafted art, and it reminded Gideon of the Sistine Chapel. Strangely, the right side of the hall was white, blank, and void of any art or decoration. It was the first part of Whewliss that they'd seen without any clear purpose.

Lady Skorric proudly stared down the hall at what was familiar and personal history. Each painting struck a passionately emotional chord within her. She'd studied every inch, every stroke of paint, every captured moment. To her it wasn't art. It was pain. It was hope. It was one of the truest mementos of what they'd endured as a people. It was a national monument, a treasure, a holy relic, priceless and sacred. She turned to check if the recruits shared her awe at the decorated walls.

"Welcome to Dark to Light Hall. These paintings tell the story of light that predates even Whewliss's knowledge of it. We display these walls to honor the history of the very light that has become the foundation of our modern society."

"I've heard stories of this hall," Izzy said, starstruck by the art itself. "I've read much of Whewliss's history, but I am humbled to hear the details firsthand."

Lady Skorric nodded with a smile. "There is much the history books leave out, and for good reason." She turned and motioned to the beginning of the wall next to the doorframe. A large black mural depicted space with one planet in its midst. "The power of light's original discovery took place more than nine-hundred Whewliss years ago. We don't know exactly how long ago it was, but that's the best we can guesstimate." Her usually strict tone melted away almost instantaneously, as her passion for history flowed through the voice of a natural born storyteller. "The story of light's history begins on another world—an old world, where the first society we know of to ever exist set events in motion that would forever change the future of us all." She reached toward the painting of the planet but stopped a few inches shy, her fingers contorting uncomfortably before she retracted them. "This is the planet Daemoana, the only world we know that is older and more advanced than Whewliss. To our knowledge, it is the oldest habitable world in existence."

Izzy leaned in and whispered to Jasss, "I'm barely fathoming that we are actually hearing this from a Whewlight council member. This is a dream come true." His fists quivered with giddiness.

Lady Skorric slowly walked forward as she stared at the wall's continuing story. "Somewhere around nine-hundred of our years ago, a Daemoanik man by the name Stagvayne first stumbled upon light travel. We don't know how. He unintentionally combined the exact right chemicals to adapt his cells to those of light's, and boom, light travel was discovered."

"That's crazy," Gideon said as his eyes traced every outline of the painting they were walking past.

Lady Skorric nodded. "Once they began experimenting with light travel and discovered that other habited worlds existed, the Daemoaniks united as a planet and militarized their newfound technology." Pictures of normal people portrayed the Daemoaniks experimenting with light and venturing out to other worlds. Long hair poured out of their heads like fountains. Gideon thought the rough expressions and braided hairstyles resembled Vikings.

Lady Skorric went on. "They sent observers to visit other worlds, much like we do today, except their purpose was different. At first their intent was no more than visiting and learning about aliens. But back on Daemoana, they were compiling information about each individual world's defenses, natural resources, technological and military advances, and the potential usefulness of the indigenous aliens that lived on each world."

"Eek," Gideon murmured. "I can see where this is going."

"The Daemoaniks quickly learned there was no world that exceeded their own technology or that was even aware of light travel. They walked among us, blending in, making no impact. For years their spies existed on Whewliss and other worlds alike, studying us in broad daylight, living among us for an unknown number of years, and reporting back to Daemoana."

"Cooby would have smelled them out if they ever came to Yagūl's isle," Dumakleiza confidently stated. "I would not be so easily duped."

The paintings were becoming eerie, haunting even, in their presentation of foreign men and women with hungry eyes standing unnoticed in oblivious crowds.

"Back on Daemoana, the measures to guarantee success were ghastly, horrifying by any standard. All their resources went into designing technologies to advance their weaponry in order to subjugate all and slaughter as many necessary along the way. Subsequently, they began working on themselves, experimenting on their own flesh, often mutilating themselves and each other to create super soldiers. Soon they shelved their weaponry and focused all of their efforts into their bodies."

The correlating paintings on the wall made the recruits' stomachs churn as Lady Skorric's words painted even more vivid mental images.

"We do not know how many drones of them died in their quest to turn themselves into—what they became. We only know *some* of the experimenting they did. At first their endeavors were arguably fascinating advancements in human capability. They began testing light's ability to heal them instantaneously, designing grueling exercise programs that brought them to the brink of death, probably oftentimes actually to death. Then they would overload their bodies with nutrients until they were about to burst. At which point, they would light jump and heal, ultimately expediting the process of building stronger muscle tissues and bones."

"Super bodybuilders." Gideon listened intently while leaning in closer to look at the depictions.

"As soon as they would land, the program would restart. They would repeat this process tirelessly, jumping multiple times every day, devoting years to hardening their bodies internally and externally. Their flesh became well beyond that of any human in existence. Their skin was coated in unknown chemicals that hardened their tissues and compressed their DNA into denser callous every time they landed. It only toughened their outer tissues a fraction of a percent each time, but after tens of thousands of treatments, it added up. Additionally, they designed combative training programs that killed who knows how many more of their own in an effort to maximize their lethality. Bones were intentionally broken, shattered. Knuckles, wrists, elbows, knees, shins, and every body part intended to inflict damage was beaten until bruised and broken. Then they would jump and heal them until over time, bones were reshaped and sharpened to be made more proficient at cutting, bashing, breaking, killing. Eventually it became legally commanded that each Daemoanik undergo extensive surgeries to have the majority of their nerves seared until their bodies barely retained any ability to feel pain orpleasure. Many sharpened their teeth, some removed them altogether. Eyes were enhanced to hunt like nocturnal creatures, bones coated in protective armor modeled after insect exoskeletons, skin flayed to graft and attach protrusions for bludgeoning or stabbing with extensions of their own bodies, their own flesh and blood—all made possible by the ability to send dying and mutilated bodies through light

jumps and miraculously heal their diabolical experimentations. Their physical capacities developed beyond the point of fathomable possibility. And,
as I'm sure you can imagine, the majority of them went mad from the never-
ending agony, leaving their mangled psyches with an insatiable lust for
violence—for bloodshed, to destroy and conquer everything and everyone.
Many just went mad."

She shook her head in disgust at the facts she knew all too well.

"It wasn't uncommon for them to be drowned in water or blood, suf-
focated, strangled, or beaten to death, and then resuscitated in an effort
to coarsen their minds."

Timrekka couldn't look at some of the paintings illustrating Lady
Skorric's words. Even he, as a supposedly *mad* scientist, couldn't stomach
some of the brutally explicit images. Paintings of the Daemoaniks en-
during hell to transform themselves into nightmares were instantly
scarred to his memory.

Lady Skorric sighed as she slowly continued down the hall. "After
countless Daemoaniks died, what they were left with was an army of
monsters, an entire planet's population of enhanced abominations prepared to act out unspeakable evil—and eyes set upon the rest of humanity
across the stars."

Dumakleiza growled, "What happened?"

Lady Skorric stared intensely into Dumakleiza's dragon eye, wondering if she could handle the answers she sought.

"They invaded."

The gravity of her statement left the great hall haunted. "Millions
of Daemoaniks landed on eleven worlds. Whewliss was one of them.
They tore through our defenses, obliterating our unprepared militaries
with enhanced physicality, the likes of which we'd never even imagined
possible. At first each world didn't fight back. We were in a state of
shock—of terror. We'd never seen anything like them—so grotesque,
monstrous, barely any humanity left in them, let alone visible on their
bodies." She shook her head at the memory. "They were our introduction to the existence of aliens. We had no idea at that point that there
was life on other worlds."

Lady Skorric ran her fingers through her hair, trying to shake her frustration. "We didn't know what to do. Our weapons barely affected them at all, and theirs were nothing short of devastating. Their first wave was a statement, and that statement was death. The number of lives we lost during that time has never been fully calculated, but by many guesses, it was between one and two billion Whewlights, driving us nearly to extinction. Across the universe, I don't even want to know how many they slaughtered."

"Shit," Gideon said. "Did you resist?"

"No," Lady Skorric said in shame. "Their arrival introduced us to light travel, and they were at least a century ahead of us developmentally. Maybe more. We were a reclusive, peaceful people. They were alpha predators, and they overtook us like a hurricane." She sighed, staring at an artist's representation of their defeat on the wall. "We were conquered. In every sense of the word, we were conquered. Every planet they set their sights on was conquered. There's a famous Daemoanik quote from that time. 'We prepared for a battle that was never waged.' They overthrew us so easily, slaughtered us so effortlessly, that they were disappointed by how painless it was." She shook her head. "We lived in subjugated fear of their tyrannical butchery. For years, their way of life became our prison, *our* way of life."

Dumakleiza's blood boiled with rage for a time long past. "What did they do to you?" She longed to avenge the Whewlights, to leap into battle with Cooby on her back and kill the Daemoaniks.

"Those who survived were enslaved, as those who are conquered typically are. We worked for them, building their cities on our worlds. Some of us were transported to Daemoana to work there or to be sold for breeding purposes. Countless of us were—eaten. Any resistance was met with immediate death. They had enough of us as slaves that they could kill as many as they wanted and still have countless leftover."

Jasss's sass dimmed as she stared despondently through the floor. The story struck a chord as she thought back over her own enslavement.

"How did it end?" Gideon asked, his eyes empathizing for their suffering. A small fraction of his mind hoped the Daemoaniks still existed so he could see one, maybe talk to one, but the larger portion of his common sense knew he shouldpray that they'd been eradicated.

"Well." Lady Skorric took a couple steps forward, motioning to some vivid illustrations. "We had to develop superior technology if we were going to survive, but it had to be done in secret. Anything we built, designed, or invented that was found by our overseers would render our heads physically pulled off our bodies, their favorite method for public execution." She shook her head as her eyes burned red. "They would literally dislodge our spines from within our torsos and rip them out with their bare hands, like pulling the meat from a crab shell." The recruits silently absorbed the historical horror. "But regardless of the looming threat, a few brave Whewlight souls risked everything by jumping between worlds to incite a revolution from the shadows. These men and women were the predecessors to our observers."

Lady Skorric led them past a painting of people hiding in darkness, out of sight from Daemoaniks, who were depicted as haunting monstrosities.

"One thing that was learned to be ubiquitous of every world and culture the Daemoaniks had conquered was their method. They relied on their desire to physically experience killing, to literally feel death in their hands. There were no weapons of mass destruction used, no chemical warfare. Handheld, aerial weaponry was the most advanced form they used, as they preferred melee tools for physically experiencing the slaughter. They wanted to *feel* the life leave our bodies. That was what they found the most satisfying. And *that* would be the seed of their downfall."

Timrekka grimaced at the thought. He wasn't sure how to voice his maelstrom of newly acquired fears, so he kept quiet, brooding within his fragile mind. His thumbs twiddled together, trying to find any outlet aside from crying or crumpling.

"So," Gideon nodded as he read ahead. "You took advantage of their bloodthirst and designed chemical weapons to kill them in mass quantity."

Lady Skorric nodded. "That became the goal, yes." She continued forward. "We had to evolve our weaponry beyond what it was. We were still using physical projectiles similar to the bullets most of your planets are familiar with." The comment made Dumakleiza ponder as Lady Skorric went on. "They couldn't pierce the hardened skin of the Daemoaniks, so we studied light further and realized that we could manipulate it to create implantable lasers powered by our sun and the electricity generated within our own bodies. Once we managed to mass produce that technology, we distributed it in secret, and thus began the — "

"Universal Liberation War?" Gideon blurted out his guess.

Lady Skorric paused, staring at Gideon through narrow eyes. She turned to Traveler, looking at him for a moment, and then back to Gideon. "I see Four Zero has given you this history lesson before."

"No," Gideon said. "He's just mentioned the ULW before, so I put two and two together."

Jasss cocked her head to the side. "Four?"

Gideon chuckled. "No. Never mind." He motioned for Lady Skorric to continue. "I'm sorry for interrupting. Please go on."

She resumed, "Their invasion was the beginning of the ULW. Our resistance finally gave them the fight they'd prepared for. As a universally united resistance, our orchestrated surprise attack was a massive success. It was executed simultaneously on each world, so they wouldn't have a chance to call for aid. Our lasers managed to pierce through their skin, effectively killing the invincible creatures they'd become. The war lasted an additional year before their loss was great enough for their survivors to retreat back to Daemoana."

"Hell yeah." Gideon nodded with a big smile on his face. "That's so badass." He looked around, noticing that the Whewlights in Dark to Light Hall didn't share his triumphant zeal. He slowly brought his head back. "Something tells me that that didn't equal happily ever after."

Lady Skorric shook her head. "No. The terror we had experienced up to that point became a fairytale compared to what came next." Everyone went silent. Lady Skorric's voice lowered as if she was afraid of what she was about to say. "The leader of Daemoana, King Slaughtvike, realized he was fighting a losing war. United, we had become too powerful and resilient to defeat. So, in an act of desperation, he turned to the one man that the Daemoaniks, as an entire people, feared."

Dumakleiza stood still, as if there were suddenly ghosts in the hall. "There exists a man who *they* feared?"

"Only one." Lady Skorric held up a finger to drive her point deeper. "He was one of their own, a Daemoanik. But he had no part in their invasion. He played no role in their universal conquest."

Gideon's eyes beamed with curiosity. "What is his name?"

"*Was* his name, and no one knows." Lady Skorric's breathing became audibly shallow. "Not much is known about him. We call him Shadowmaker." She whispered the name, visibly afraid of the mere sound. "All we've been told is that he was an assassin long before they discovered light travel. He had already killed for a living before lust for violence overcame the rest of his people. He was already the Damoanik's most effective killer without everything that light could provide. And while we're pretty sure he took advantage of light, enhancing his body's strength and whatnot, he took no part in invading other worlds. That much we know. While the rest of the Daemoaniks mutilated in transformation, he studied. He studied war, breaking it down to a microscopic science. We assume he spent time traveling to as many worlds as he could just to study their warfare, martial arts, weaponry, and technologies, all so he could amalgamate as many cultures' tactics together as he could. He was a ghost, an apparition in the void, always watching and learning, a student of death itself—perfecting himself—becoming a legend, a myth. While the rest of his world set their eyes on us, he hoarded knowledge, studied and predicted patterns, setting elaborate traps across entire worlds, hunting his targets with stealth and precision, designing weapons so advanced that we may still not have matched them today." Lady Skorric looked at the recruits' uncomfortable faces. "Much of what we know is speculative guesses we've accumulated over many years. We can't confirm what he was or how he became that way. All we know for sure is the destruction he wrought—however impossible it will sound to you."

Paintings on the wall vaguely depicted a silhouetted figure surrounded by Daemoanik soldiers. The artists had no idea how to render him, so he was a shapeless horror.

Dumakleiza's spine tensed as if Shadowmaker was in the room with them. "What was it that he was capable of, Lady Skorric of Whewliss?"

Lady Skorric stared through the paint as she recalled the story she thought she'd been prepared to tell. "King Slaughtvike hired Shadowmaker to assassinate the leaders of the resistance on every planet." She paused and looked at Lord Coyzle, whose head was slightly hung at her words. She inhaled. "Lord Coyzle, I believe you should tell what happened next."

Lord Coyzle took a deep breath and held it before looking at her with compromised eyes. "Yes, uh." He blinked a few times and then looked at the painting. "My father was one of the men Lady Skorric spoke of. He heroically helped incite the revolution. He spearheaded the Whewlight portion of the resistance, and, uh—Shadowmaker killed him."

Dumakleiza stood taller. "Your father was a man of great honor."

Timrekka slumped as if the news was new.

Lord Coyzle composed himself. "But it wasn't that he killed him. It was *how* he did it that made him so dangerous." He stared at the wall as if braindead before continuing. "My father was killed by a coin that shot straight down through his body headfirst." Two more composing breaths. "When we dug the coin out of the dirt, we saw strange markings on it." Lord Coyzle shook his head as everyone looked at a painted rendition of the coin on the wall. It was a black silhouette in front of a red backdrop. Lord Coyzle glared at it as he went on. "The angle of the kill, the trajectory, everything—it was as if it had been shot straight down from the sky, perfectly timed, aimed, and executed with such precision——it's mind-boggling, an impossible shot. From *galaxies* away."

"Wait." Gideon tilted his head, making sure he was understanding what Lord Coyzle was saying. "What do you mean by that?"

Lord Coyzle nodded again as he reminded himself of the truth of it. "At first, we assumed it was a fluke, an unfortunate, unpredictable tragedy. Inexplicable but certainly not an assassination. How could it have been? The idea was ludicrous. But we soon learned that resistance leaders on the other planets had been executed the exact same way by coins with the same marking."

Gideon squinted. "But you use light travel. There's no such thing as spaceships, at least none that travel between worlds. How did—" He was confused. "Where did the coins come from?"

"Exactly." Lord Coyzle nodded. "It took us a while to figure it out. But when we did—" He shook his head, still in disbelief. "—we realized that someone had shot them *from* Daemoana." He turned and stared at everyone so they could feel his sincerity. "Shadowmaker sent an inanimate object through space, something our technology *still* isn't capable of. He strategically planned the time and place to send eleven of them to assassinate eleven different targets, all lightyears away. He coordinated and perfectly planned exactly how to assassinate my father from the safety of Daemoana—with a coin." Lord Coyzle took a deep breath as everyone else digested the impossibility. "We've done the math. The instant my father died was the equivalent of two of our days after Shadowmaker originally sent the coin. When my father's last breath left his body, Shadowmaker had probably already forgotten about sending it at all."

Gideon glanced down at Lord Coyzle's clenched fists. "But how could he—that's, uh——no, that's impossible, right? The calculations necessary to—"

Traveler looked at him and spoke for the first time since they'd entered Dark to Light Hall. "Has anything you've seen since you left Earth supported your definition of possible?"

"Well, no. But that's—" Gideon felt dizzy trying to mull it over. "This is something different entirely."

Traveler's eyes lowered, humbled by familiar terror. "The greatest long-distance killers on other worlds—and I mean the absolute *best*—are typically capable of execution from less than a mile away, and that's with their most advanced aerial assault weapons. They have to calculate distance, gravity, wind, temperature, humidity, and even the rotation of the world they're on in order to accurately hit their target." Traveler took a deep breath. "But that's the average record for distance. Not only on individual worlds, but across the stars. Managing to calculate the exponentially compounding mathematics of the exponentially compounding factors as distances increase becomes humanly impossible. Even the most highly advanced warships, planes, missiles, and even our light cannons are incapable of pinpointing that accuracy across our own world—let alone our galaxy. And certainly not between galaxies." Traveler looked up at Gideon. "Shadowmaker was able to execute multiple targets on separate worlds, calculating details so intricate and miniscule we don't even know how to begin understanding it. The tactical mastery of his mind was the most powerful weapon we know of to ever exist. The only things more mysterious are black holes." Traveler cleared his throat as his body went cold. He saw the recruits' legs threatening to give way. "Welcome to the knowledge of what kind of people exist in the universe."

None of the other recruits said anything. They stared at the paintings in stunned silence.

Lord Coyzle took a deep breath and continued, "After that the Daemoaniks invaded again. Without our leadership to unite us, the Daemoaniks came a second time, and the ULW continued. Bloodier, with hungrier, more determined monsters. And death. So much death."

Timrekka spoke up, hoping to douse his fear. "Are you sure that Shadowmaker exists? What if it was just the technology of the Daemoaniks that killed your leaders? What proof was there that it was one man? Couldn't the Daemoaniks have sent the coins? Are you sure it was some-*one* else?"

Lord Coyzle looked at him sternly. "The Daemoaniks were advanced barbarians. They didn't possess the intelligence to orchestrate such precise assassinations from worlds away. They thrived on hand-to-hand violence and tearing people apart with claws." He shook his head. "No, Timrekka. I hate telling you as much as you hate hearing it, but Shadowmaker was real. If you are religious and believe in any form of the devil, the bogeyman, the dark one, true evil, Shadowmaker is not that. He is the one the devil fears."

Timrekka lowered his gaze, unwilling to contest Shadowmaker's existence any further. He didn't even want to say the name again.

Dumakleiza blinked a few times, trying to process all of it. "How did you defeat the Maker of Shadows?"

Lord Coyzle shook his head, trying not to relive it. "Lady Skorric, would you mind taking over?"

She nodded. "Of course, my lord." She turned to Dumakleiza. "We did not defeat him. We couldn't. No one could. He was an enemy so far beyond us that even with our combined efforts, we were nothing to him but gathered sheep for the slaughter."

"Then how—"

"Lord Coyzle, Master Brawd, and Master N'kowsky were there for the ULW. They were young soldiers fighting toward the end of the resistance. Master Brawd is the only person we know of from any world who's ever seen Shadowmaker and lived."

"What?" Gideon's question burst out of him as he spun toward Master Brawd. "What did he look like?"

Master Brawd's eyes stayed glued to the painting of the coin as he finally spoke. "It was night." His voice was deep and quick, as he gave only the facts. "Thirty-three of us resistance members had just cleared a building of Daemoaniks when everything went dark. The lights shut down unaccountably. I heard screaming. Some was from my group. Some was from me. The lights came back on. I was on the ground. I do not remember falling. Didn't feel it. I looked around to see everyone dead with holes in their bodies, holes I didn't hear happen, and I didn't see what made them. I had two holes in my torso. Both hit vital organs. As I lay dying, I saw him walking through us. The last thing I remember was his belt. It had the same coins. Some were missing." Master Brawd's voice was flat, as if the memory had no effect on him. "I woke up later after being resuscitated by light. Shadowmaker was gone." Master Brawd slowly turned and stared at the recruits. "We had more advanced weapons than the Daemoaniks. We had better armor. He killed us instantly. Silently. Killed everyone. Only I survived, and I almost didn't. We never saw him coming. No one saw him leave. We never saw how he did it. Beneath a cloak, he didn't look mutilated like the other Daemoaniks. But somehow he was less human than they were."

The recruits stared at Master Brawd without saying a word. They were already intimidated enough by him. Hearing about his firsthand encounter with the horror that all Whewlights feared rendered them speechless.

"Not long after," Lady Skorric took over and resumed walking forward, "in a fatefully cataclysmic turn of events, a miracle occurred. One of the rarest events ever witnessed in the cosmos took place. Daemoana collided with the nearest planet in its solar system."

"What?" Gideon uttered, unsure if he'd heard her correctly. "Like, full on crashed into another, like—" He clapped his fists together, pantomiming an explosion.

"Yes," Lady Skorric said, wrapping up the story suddenly. "It's known to happen, but it's so rare that it's only occurred three times that we know of, including Daemoana."

"Holy shit." Gideon looked at the other five recruits to see if they were as wowed as he was. They were. "How does that even happen?"

"We don't know," Lady Skorric responded. "Somehow they collided, and the extinction-level-event killed everything on Daemoana. The humanity, the animal life, probably even the plant life. The collision threw Daemoana off its axis, its orbit, presumably rendering it uninhabitable. We've never visited it to find out. It now floats within the same galaxy, as mutated as its inhabitants, two planets bulbously smashed together, circling their sun in a newly formed orbit."

The painting of the planetary collision was crafted with vibrant colors, explicitly showing the two worlds smashing together. It was illustrated with such effervescence that they could tell it had been made as a celebratory piece——an icon.

Dumakleiza was the only one to hastily move past it, as she didn't fully comprehend what they were talking about. "What became of the devils still on your worlds?"

"They were divided, left without a home world to return to or get reinforcements from. Slowly, we hunted and killed the remaining Daemoaniks. It took years to find them all, as some went into hiding on our planets without anywhere else to go. But now they are believed to be nearly extinct."

Before any of the recruits could react, Lord Coyzle returned to his chipper, jolly self and took over. "After the war was over, all planets involved met and agreed upon peaceful terms for universal harmony. Thusly birthing LOLA. From there, the history you're all already familiar with took place. We sent observers out to ensure we would never again be blindsided by a violent world bent upon universal domination. And during that time, we stumbled upon the fourth phase of human exploration."

Gideon shook his fists. "Yes!"

They all looked to the painting to see what the depiction of the mysterious fourth phase was. The recruits stared in confusion as they saw

Lord Coyzle motioning to the back wall at the end of the hallway. It was black. There were no pictures, no illustrations. The end of the hall was nothing but a flat black wall.

Gideon looked back and forth between the wall, Lord Coyzle, and Traveler. "The fourth phase is a black wall?"

Lord Coyzle took a breath as he looked up, trying to find his words. "For lack of a better description, yes. It's where you're going tomorrow."

7

"So, is the blank white wall of Dark to Light Hall being left for what is discovered in the fourth phase?" Gideon asked as they exited Dark to Light Hall.

"Yes," Lady Skorric said. "Half of the hall is in memory of the pain we suffered to survive and overcome extinction. We're hoping that the other side will celebrate our restoration and achievements after."

"That's really cool. Solid symbolism."

Lord Coyzle looked at their faces, enjoying seeing them still digesting everything. "You will leave for your introduction to the fourth phase in a few hours. Until then, you wi—"

"With all due respect, Lord Coyzle," Gideon excitedly yammered out, "let's not waste time. I think I speak for all six recruits when I say we're ready to just get a move on and go now."

Lord Coyzle chuckled, his rosy cheeks rising. "Four Zero, you found some ambitious aliens. That gives me hope."

Traveler gave a grateful nod and then looked at Gideon, embarrassed by his outburst. "Gideon, look up. What do you see?"

Gideon earnestly stared up into the night sky, feeling philosophical. "I see stars. I see an eternal depth holding secrets yet to be discovered. I see—"

"Darkness," Traveler plainly stated. "You see darkness. It's dark. It's night. The location of the fourth phase requires a light jump, which requires?"

"Light." Gideon cracked a one-sided smile at Traveler's irritation.

"There's my intelligent recruit," Traveler said before glancing at Lord Coyzle apologetically. He turned to Gideon. "So, as you Earthlings would say, hold your elephants."

Gideon cocked his head to the side. "What? Oh." He nodded with an understanding chuckle. "Horses. Hold your horses."

"Yes. Whatever. Either is too heavy to be realistic." Traveler shook his head, annoyed. "Be patient. We will leave soon."

"Yes, sir," Gideon said with a smile as he saluted him.

"I have a question," Jasss blurted at Lord Coyzle.

"For me?" he asked.

"Yes." She studied him the same way a fox would a rabbit. "Why don't you have more security with you while you're around us aliens? Seems risky that you'd just freely walk among us without bodyguards."

Jasss's comment made Master Brawd turn to her.

Six One shot her a damning look, hoping she'd get the hint and close her lips.

Lord Coyzle's smile disappeared and then came back, "Well, I could have explained, though I'd hoped I wouldn't need to. While on Whewliss, you're expected to behave properly. We are a diplomatic and nonviolent people. We will treat you with peaceful respect, and we expect you to return that civility."

"Of course," Jasss said, changing her tone to a sweeter softness. "I'm just curious what you would do if one of us suddenly became hostile." She shrugged, unsure of why her curiosity wasn't shared.

"Well, if you must know," Lord Coyzle said in a lower tone, "defensive countermeasures are programmed into my suit. It's a state-of-the-art reflection suit. It took a few decades to fully conceive and create. Mine is the only one in existence, and it was designed specifically to protect me from *any* attack, including an assassination like the one Shadowmaker used to execute my father. So, believe me, there is nothing you could do to assault me." He stared sternly at her.

"Oh," Jasss said, disappointed with the anticlimactic answer.

"And," Master Brawd added, "he could command your suit to incinerate you." His direct threat was heard loud and clear. "You or anyone else could be instantly vaporized at the lord's whim. Only your head and hands would remain."

"Oh, that's much better," Jasss said with excitable eyes.

"And if none of that was effective enough," Lord Coyzle added, "I have Master Brawd to defend me. Personally, I'd prefer being vaporized than being on the wrong side of him."

Timrekka lowered his eyebrows at Jasss, worried about her sanity. He turned to Lord Coyzle. "Our suits sound like an effective defense mechanism, and I'm curious how they work and what kind of materials are used in the gelatin to make it so hyper-intelligent and programmable."

Lord Coyzle chuckled, easing some of the growing tension. "That is not why we're here, nor would I feel comfortable divulging those details."

Gideon raised his hand. "As long as Four Zero here doesn't get mad at me for asking more questions, I have another."

Traveler bit his tongue, allowing Lord Coyzle to handle Gideon however he saw fit.

Lord Coyzle turned to him. "Ask it."

Gideon smiled. "What do you do with criminals who don't get executed or vaporized, or killed in the gelatin, or anything like that? Do you still use prisons? How do you incarcerate people who can play musical planets? A light prison or something?"

Lord Coyzle nodded. "The answer to that actually ties in well to the differences of our nights and days. Without light, most of our world would cease to function, as it has grown reliant upon it." He turned and led them down a sidewalk. "As Four Zero mentioned, we are less capable in darkness without the power of our sun. However, the answer to your question assists in keeping Whewliss's cities running at night."

"Okay, I'm really intrigued," Gideon said as he imagined alien criminals in black and white striped suits running on giant hamster wheels to power EBOO.

Lord Coyzle reached up and gently pressed on his right ear's tragus. "Master Keevind." After what sounded like silence to everyone else, Lord Coyzle spoke again. "It went very well—yes, they—yes, they think

Shadowmaker sounds terrifying—what are you laughing about?" Lord Coyzle chuckled and shook his head. "Are you available to meet us at the Winkloh Star?" He rolled his eyes at the recruits' amusement. "Yes, that works perfectly. See you then." He retracted his finger. "All right, come with me."

Gideon, Dumakleiza, and Timrekka looked to Traveler curiously after hearing Lord Coyzle say "Winkloh Star." Traveler sternly stared back, demanding silence. It had something to do with him breaking more of LOLA.

Kristuf burned a fresh scar into Gideon's shoulder after they landed. Lady Skorric had to return to her duties, so she reluctantly left Lord Coyzle and Master Brawd alone to introduce the Winkloh Star. Once Gideon's ritual was complete, Lord Coyzle introduced them to their new location.

"This is what we call a light prison. Close guess on the name, Gideon."

In front of them was a large, cubed structure made entirely of what looked like cement. Each square wall looked to measure about thirty feet across. There were no windows or decorations, only a single door that led in and out. The large grey building was the first blank structure they'd seen, as everything else in EBOO was so magnanimous.

Master Keevind appeared next to Lord Coyzle. He smiled his regular smile and looked at the recruits. "Hey there!"

His contagious energy immediately brought grins to everyone except Master Brawd and Tsuna. Master Keevind was no longer wearing his council attire. Instead, he donned a new suit with rich blacks, purples, and blues, which they all assumed must be his EPF chief uniform. He turned and headed toward the door. "Well, let's go inside, shall we?"

His energetic tone made them wonder what was in the building since they were expecting to see an actual prison. "Oh." He stopped and turned to them. "Before we go in, adjust the aperture of your eyes to their darkest settings." At his instruction, the recruits curiously mimicked their assistants looking downward and winking their right eyes. After they finished, they looked up with readiness. Master Keevind's toothy smile was a little harder to make out with their dimmed sight, but it was still there. "All right, let's go inside."

He walked up to the door and put his hand on a scanner.

"Oh, cool," Gideon commented. "It's neat seeing that you guys still use *some* similar tech as we do. We have fingerprint and hand scanners back on Earth."

"It's not scanning my prints," Master Keevind corrected. "It's reading my DNA. Our scanners require specific DNA and a pulse. If someone tried to fake my fingerprints, they wouldn't gain access to anything secured. If they cut off my hand, they'd have the DNA but not the pulse."

"Okay, I stand corrected. Once again, y'all are just cooler than every side of the pillow."

"Additionally," Master Keevind added, "I have to scan my eyes. If heightened stress or threatened responses are detected, access is denied. I can't be held against my will and forced to grant access to an antagonist. What's inside is too sensitive to even consider my own life."

"That's intense." Gideon shook his head. "I love Whewliss."

Master Keevind nodded and belly laughed as he leaned up close to the door. After the additional retinal scan, the door opened. *Click.* Inside, the recruits could see nothing but pitch blackness. Knowing that the building was some form of prison and then not being able to see inside was disconcerting. Nonetheless, they walked in. Once everyone was inside, Master Keevind closed and locked the door behind them, removing even the light from outside. No one could see anything.

Only Dumakleiza was aware of more than blackness. She couldn't see much of anything either, but her dragon eye managed to make out some of the details of the room. As it turned out, there really weren't any. They were standing in a tiny hallway, barely big enough to fit all sixteen of them standing shoulder to shoulder. On the opposite end was another door that looked similar. The hallway was a safety measure to ensure that no light got in or out. She wasn't sure why. Everything they were learning was beyond her.

Master Keevind went through the same process on the second door, scanning his hand and his eyes. *Click.* The moment the second door cracked open, light spilled into the small hallway. It was so bright that they could immediately tell it would have blinded them had their eyes not been dilated to the darkest setting.

Master Keevind ushered everyone into the bright room and then closed the door, once again locking it. With the entryway closed behind them, their eyes fixated on a massive glass ball of blinding light. Gideon, Dumakleiza, and Timrekka recognized the design from Thamiosh, but this Winkloh Star was pristine. It was about twice the size, and there were no visible seams. The Winkloh Star Traveler built on Thamiosh had been stunning, but to see one presented the way it was intended to was breathtaking, poetic even. Organized wires and cords ran out the bottom of it, feeding the power it provided to numerous outlets.

Lord Coyzle and Master Brawd stared at the Winkloh Star as if it was a normal piece of machinery. Master Keevind smiled at it, basking in its light like a lizard. After allowing everyone to come to their own conclusions, he turned to explain.

"The Winkloh Star was invented by a Whewlight named Ievan Van Winkloh as a means to two ends. It is constructed of two-sided mirrors, the reflective side facing inward. It's one of our more impressive feats, in my opinion. Whenever one is constructed, I like to stand inside before it's closed off. The visual from being surrounding by a sphere of inward facing mirrors is—well, dizzying to say the least." Gideon, Dumakleiza, and Timrekka were trying to read ahead. They had some surfacing questions as Master Keevind went on. "Much like older technologies that operated on airflow or water flow, the Winkloh Star operates on the continuous flow of light."

"The continuousflow of light?" Timrekka asked, confused by the lack of scientific credibility.

"Yes, continuous," Master Keevind confidently responded. "The light is trapped within the mirrors, unable to escape the glass, so long as the rest of the prison is kept dark."

"But," Timrekka argued, unable to let it go, "light only continuously flows as long as the light *source* continues emitting light, and how can an empty mirror sphere generate light when there's no other source in this prison? I don't understand the mechanics of this."

Master Keevind looked to Traveler with a mischievous expression. "Would you like to explain?"

Traveler looked back and forth between them and then nodded. "I can." He organized his thoughts and then turned to Timrekka. "How do we travel?"

"At an amplified speed of light."

"No," Traveler corrected. "We don't travel atthe *speed* of light. We would cause a gamma explosion that would destroy us and everything miles around us. We travel *as* light." Timrekka nodded while simultaneously shaking his head, knowing that he should have gotten the question right. Traveler asked a second one. "When do we land?"

"Uh." Timrekka tried to redeem himself. "When we, *as* light, come in contact with a solid surface or anything that light shines on."

"Correct." Traveler nodded. "So, if I were to shoot you into the Winkloh Star, into a sphere of inward facing mirrors, when would you land?"

Timrekka mulled it over. "I wouldn't. I would continue bouncing around inside the walls forever until the glass was eventually broken by another source—possibly even ultimately swirling around within the sphere due to the circular nature of the glass until I was spinning, still at the same speed of light that I had originally been shot in at." The answer logically poured out of him without him even realizing what it suggested.

Traveler nodded more slowly. "And, as Gideon says, what happens when you now put two and two together?"

It didn't take long for all the recruits to figure out what it meant.

Timrekka's eyes widened as a flood of thoughts and questions entered his head. "There are *people* in there?"

Gideon's mouth dropped. "*That's* where you send criminals?" He couldn't tell if he was amazed, dumbfounded, or appalled. All the Whewlights nodded. It was old news to them, an everyday way of life. Gideon looked down, trying to wrap his mind around it. He looked back up at the Winkloh Star in a new light. "Who is in there?" He all but whispered the question.

Master Keevind took the lead again. "Well." He stared intently into the Winkloh Star, clearly seeing something with his optical implant that none of the recruits could. "It looks like we have fourteen criminals in

this one. Eleven of the incarcerated are Daemoaniks. They've been distributed between Winkloh Stars across Whewliss."

"What?" Gideon gawked as he stepped closer to the Winkloh Star.
Part of his mind wondered if he were to get closer and peer in with more
focus if he'd be able to see them. He knew he wouldn't, but he couldn't
help trying.

Master Keevind puffed out his bottom lip. "They can hold up to somewhere between fifty to sixty people before the energy becomes too great
to contain. It all depends on the mass of each criminal. We safely allow
no more than forty criminals per Winkloh Star." He thought for a moment. "It's actually a testament to how safe EBOO is that in over a
century, we've only accumulated three Whewlights in ours."

"Are they—can they feel anything? Are they aware?" Gideon shook
his head, immediately knowing the answer. "I know the answer. Duh.
They can't. But can they?"

"No," Traveler answered. "As you know, when you are light, your
body experiences such shock that you are in a constant comatose state
of perfect health. They can't feel anything. They're not aware of anything.
They're healthier than they've ever been. Preserved. If they were released,
they would have no knowledge that any time had passed."

"Dear God. So, in theory, they will be in there, spinning forever unless
the glass breaks." Gideon exhaled. "I imagine that's a controversial means
of punishment."

"Yes," Master Keevind answered. "There have been protests but very
few. Most everyone on Whewliss is in support of Winkloh Stars due to
the fact that the only convicts sentenced to them would otherwise be sentenced to death. Plus, no one's actively trying to save the Daemoaniks."
He allowed the information to sink in. "Additionally, instead of their lives
simply being thrown away, they are instead kept alive and put to use for
the benefit of the rest of the population. They power our cities through
a continuous flow of light. The Winkloh Star requires no maintenance
aside from dusting the outer glass from time to time, and it provides more
electricity than any other power source aside from our sun."

Dumakleiza stared at the Winkloh Star sorrowfully. "But should they
eternally not be allowed to die, how will their souls venture on?" As she

thought more about it, the idea weighed heavily on her heart. "If they live within the star of Winkloh for all time, how can they enter heaven or be condemned to hell?" Her eyes welled up at the gravity of their loss. "These souls are stuck in purgatory. This is hell."

Tsuna slowly nodded. "Their bodies should be allowed to be eaten by the dirt. Whewliss hungers for their judgment."

Lord Coyzle wasn't in the mood for a religious debate. "Nothing lasts forever. No matter how far we advance, we will all one day come to an end. No matter how long Winkloh Stars last, one day Whewliss will be consumed by our sun. All worlds are condemned to the same inevitable fate. Then every soul in every Winkloh Star will be freed to whatever the afterlife holds. Until then, I have no sympathy for them." He didn't want to ruin the mood with his hatred, but he couldn't help his honesty.

Timrekka had been brainstorming during the conversation. He finally gathered the courage to ask Traveler.

"Highness Trollop, Captain Diggid, did you—"

"What's H.P.?" Gideon quickly asked to bury Timrekka's question. He already figured out what Traveler had done on Thamiosh, but it wasn't something that should be discussed in front of his superiors. The high ranking Whewlights all turned to Gideon, caught off guard.

Lord Coyzle's smile dwindled. "What did you say?" He'd heard Gideon just fine, but he was hoping that maybe he hadn't.

"What is H.P.?" Gideon repeated himself. "It's a planet we stumbled upon in the virtual reality room that we couldn't explore."

Kristuf, Brasina, and Alik looked at each other, their suits reading rising stress levels. They were worried enough about asking Lord Coyzle about H.P. themselves, let alone one of the alien recruits probing about something restricted.

Lord Coyzle quickly composed himself. "H.P. is, uh, a habitable world that we are unable to visit. It is capable of sustaining life. However, we have no idea whether there is actually human life on it. The entire world is covered in thick, gaseous clouds that prevent us from landing there, or more importantly, escaping if we did find a way."

"Is that why access wasn't granted to viewing it more closely?" Gideon bravely asked.

Lord Coyzle refrained from glaring. "There are things you are not qualified to know, Earthling." He stared into Gideon's eyes, challenging him to inquire any further. After no response, he nodded and then looked around at the recruits. "It's not important, and it does not affect you." He smiled. "Focus on the fact that you will soon be leaving for your introduction to the fourth phase. You won't have free time once you arrive there. Take the next few hours to enjoy the last down time you will have for a while."

He returned to his warm aura. "Now, I must return to the City of Light." He sighed, clearly disappointed at not being able to continue with them. "Master Keevind will be going back to work now. So, Master Brawd will be in charge. Otherwise, your recruiters can join you, though they aren't required to. Their jobs are henceforward completed."

Gideon, Dumakleiza, and Timrekka looked at Traveler, wondering if he was going to go. Knowing that he could leave them in the hands of Master Brawd and not go any further scared them a little. It felt like a potential void in their bonded team. They might never see him again.

Similarly, Six One's recruits looked to her, hoping she wouldn't abandon them now that her job was complete. Only Tsuna appeared indifferent.

Lord Coyzle's smile turned to an ambiguous squint. "I hope you're ready."

8

The fourth phase was imminent. Dumakleiza needed to see Cooby. A few hours was too long to spend apart, and she was eager to see what pampering he'd received. She also needed to spend time with Grimleck before they ventured off. The fact that Lord Coyzle had defined it as a black wall had Dumakleiza feeling uneasy.

Alik took Timrekka to one of EBOO's labs to show him what they were working on. He promised to let him dabble and tinker alongside their scientists to a limited extent. Timrekka's eyes lit up when he learned he could actually experiment with Whewlight technology and base elements. He hadn't gotten to build or invent anything since they'd left Thamiosh, and his creative side was itching.

Lord Coyzle and Master Brawd vanished shortly after. Six One, her recruits, and their assistants went their separate ways. Master Keevind kindly wished everyone a pleasant farewell and then returned to his civic duties. The last left was Gideon, Traveler, and Kristuf.

Kristuf looked to Gideon. "How about you, handsome? What would you like to do with our last few hours together?"

"Hmm." Gideon thought. "I'm not sure." He looked to Traveler, who was standing a ways away, staring up at the night sky. Gideon smiled. "I think I'll see if I can annoy Four Zero here for a while longer, being that this may be the last time we see each other."

Kristuf nodded, disappointed. "Okay. Should you need me, have him contact me and I'll return."

"Thank you," Gideon said with a pat to Kristuf's shoulder. "Will you be there to see us off?"

"Oh, pfff, of course," Kristuf remarked with a chuckle. "I wouldn't miss that historic moment for the world—any world."

"Perfect. I'll see you then."

Kristuf returned Gideon's friendly smile. "May the light guide and protect you." He turned and walked away before Gideon could respond.

Gideon took a moment to appreciate the quiet. They'd been inundated by so much newness and culture shock since they'd arrived that even though their bodies were perfectly healed, it felt good to have some unwinding time. Gideon looked around at the glimmering lights of EBOO's reflective buildings. With no one else around, he recognized crickets, or a similar insect, in the night. It was comforting to hear familiar songs so far from home. Their simple melody reminded him of late-night campfires under the stars. He'd spent countless nights doing just that on travels across the Earth. He brought a deep breath of cool air into his lungs, savoring it before letting it out. It was therapeutic and needed. With the awe-inspiring technology saturating the Whewlight way of life, it was grounding to appreciate the nature that still existed on even the most advanced world.

Gideon looked at Traveler, who was staring up as if lost. His expression suggested a despair or hesitance. It didn't look like he was even aware that Gideon was still there. Traveler was consumed by his own thoughts that Gideon could only begin to guess. His eyes reflected the night sky in their glassy shimmer as if the stars themselves existed within him.

Gideon took a couple slow steps forward as he, too, looked up at the heavens. "Mind if I join you?"

Traveler didn't look away from the sky. "Please do," he said calmly, though his expression remained an ocean of mystery.

Gideon tried to follow Traveler's exact gaze, wondering if there was something specific he was looking at in the vastness of the night sky. "I suppose congratulations are in order."

Traveler looked at him blankly. "For what?"

"For completing your mission. Your job's done. Congratulations, man."

"Ah," Traveler said with a dismissive nod. "Yes. That. Thank you, Gideon. It's been a long time coming."

"So, what do you say?" Gideon playfully asked. "Time to retire? Pretend old age matters to you guys. Settle down and live for a couple hundred years in Whewliss's version of Florida, wherever that is." He chuckled, assuming Traveler wouldn't get the joke.

Traveler scoffed. "That was certainly the goal for many years. Successfully deliver three qualified recruits was supposed to feel conclusive. It was supposed to be one of the greatest accomplishments of the human race."

Gideon puffed out his bottom lip and nodded. "Well, I mean, don't detract from it. It is impressive. There are only two of you in history to ever get the job done. You're definitely my favorite of the two, though. I'm kinda biased, but yeah." He smiled. "I'd say that's worth more than a simple atta boy."

"No, I know." Traveler returned to gazing up at the stars. "Don't play the ignorant fool with me, Gideon. You know what I'm struggling with."

"Oh, I know." Gideon smiled. "I get it." He stepped closer. "Will the fearful Four Zero reign supreme or will the adventurous Traveler surprise us even more than he did with that Winkloh Star stunt?"

Traveler couldn't help a proud smile. "That's a secret you're taking to your grave, which may be sooner than you think."

Gideon laughed. "I can't believe you seriously did that. *You.* You snuck into Supreme—by means of light whipping, I'm guessing, which means you probably had to endure a couple more rounds of Timrekka's supersoldier serum upon landing there and back. You hunted Trollop and Diggid down, somehow forced light shots down their giant throats, jumped them back to Grezzik's house, stuffed them into his basement, and shot them into the star." He scoffed with slow applause.

Traveler gave a sly nod, impressed by his own feat. "It was surprisingly easy with a few tranquilizer darts, compliments of Timrekka."

"Timrekka was in on it?"

"Oh, no. He had no idea. He just gave them to me when I asked for them. Let me tell you, Thamioshlings are heavyalready, let alone when they're deadweight." They both laughed. "And Trollop was actually heavier than Diggid."

"Ha! I wish I could have seen that. I'm a little upset you didn't invite me." Gideon shook his head. "If I had a hat, I'd tip it to you, sir. You powered Darchangel territory — er, sorry. I mean, as Grezzik would have said, *terri'try* — using the unconscious bodies of the tyrants you liberated them from. That's gangster poetry. And you kept it under wraps, you dog."

Traveler nodded. "Indeed. And now they will bounce around in that prison for as long as the Darchangels unknowingly let them." He chuckled. "They sure would be in for a surprise if the glass broke."

"Yeah, something tells me the Darchangels wouldn't let them make it very far."

"Indeed."

They stood for a moment without speaking, crickets chirping around them as they stared up at the stars.

Gideon realized a sudden curiosity. "So, your optical implants recorded everything you've done? Everything we've done?"

"Surprise," Traveler said with a lackluster hand raise. "Like I've told you many times, we're all constantly being tested."

"Right." Gideon moved directly past Traveler's point. "But my concern is with you breaking LOLA. How are you not in super big trouble with Lord Coyzle and Master Brawd after them reviewing it?"

Traveler huffed. "Those two don't care about the means we used to get here. Lord Coyzle wishes he could visit other worlds, so he sees every broken law as intrigue. Master Brawd couldn't care less. He wants to skip the formalities and get on with the fourth phase expedition. It's the other council members I didn't want knowing. They wouldn't have moved on from arguments about protocol. They'd likely demand that I start over and follow the rules with new, legally recruited aliens."

"Ah." Gideon nodded. "Fair enough. So, any BTS on what was said behind the curtain?"

"BTS?"

"Oh, come on. You guys love acronyms here in *EBOO*. It means behind the scenes."

"Oh." Traveler stared intently at some specific stars. "All you missed was seeing Master Brawd be Master Brawd. Nothing impresses him. Ever since the ULW, he's just been Master Brawd. He has severe PTSD. An acronym I believe our worlds share." They both chuckled. "And Lord Coyzle, on the other hand, thought every moment was the most exciting thing he'd ever seen. He agrees that you've helped me find more courage than most Whewlights."

Gideon waved the subtle compliment away. "Oh, please. Based off your tomfooleries on Thamiosh, it sounds like you've had a pair for quite a while already."

"No. That was a desperate means to an end. We had to move, and I was impatient. It's like making a decision when you really have to urinate. You simply take action without overthinking." Traveler glanced at Gideon staring up with him. "Thank you for being who you are."

Gideon slowly nodded, taking time to acknowledge Traveler's sincerity. "You're welcome, Spaceman." He smiled. "I'm happy to be your gubernaculum. You can just call me goober."

"What?" Traveler spat out his question with a concerned chuckle. "What on Whewliss is a gubernaculum?"

Gideon laughed. "Like 'what on Earth.' I get it. A gubernaculum is — I don't remember exactly, but it's some part of the balls that helps them drop during puberty. Or something like that. Basically, I help your balls drop." He rolled his fingers through the air. "Over and over and o——"

Traveler burst into some much-needed laughter as they said it at the same time, "Holy spirit." They laughed harder.

Traveler shook his head as his smile finally felt real. "Goober it is. That is a well-earned nickname."

Gideon tried it on for size. "Goober and the Spaceman. It sounds like a B-rated, buddy cop movie from the eighties."

Traveler raised a finger. "Fun little fact about puberty: We wait until children have gonethrough puberty before beginning them on full-time productivity. Up until then, they are only permitted light jumps for health purposes. It ensures that they're fully developed before we slow their aging process down."

Gideon laughed. "You don't want a bunch of wobbly thirty-year-old toddlers running around?"

"The early stages of light travel were very exciting, but in our obsession, there were some creepy moments." Traveler shook away the memories of underdeveloped adults. "Until puberty, they sleep the natural way, the way you're familiar with."

"It's comforting to know that it's not a completely outdated idea."

"Indeed. They sleep in centrifuge pods just like anywhere else."

Gideon laughed with closed eyes as he shook his head. "We sleep on mattresses. Most worlds sleep on some form of mattresses. You were so close with that one."

"Indeed," Traveler said, annoyed by the obvious mistake.

Gideon looked down from the sky to address Traveler more sincerely. "So, tell me, is this where Goober and the Spaceman's adventure ends?"

Traveler sighed, trying not to rush his response. "I used to stare at the stars and dream that one day I'd venture farther into them, but I was afraid of danger." He scoffed. "I'm feeling confident with my courage. My only remaining fear is that I'll slow you three down once we get there—if my fear defeats my courage down the—" Traveler bit his tongue and sighed.

Gideon could taste the vulnerability. He mulled it over. "You know, Miss Frizzle, before you invited me on your Magic School Bus, I was very good at saying goodbye. For a long time—well, at least a long time for Earthlings, I spent every day on the move, and it was easy. I could meet a stranger, experience the timelessness of a single moment with them, the dazzling unexpectedness of a first impression, and then part ways with a high five. Heart strings were never plucked too hard. You know what I mean?" He stared upward, appreciating the serene starscape. "I could survive my entire life on a strict diet of sonder and namasté cocktails." His eyes lit up. "Fun fact. Did you know that one of the most accepted translations of namasté includes 'I honor the place in you in which the entire universe dwells'?"

Traveler shook his head. "No. I assume that has taken on more meaning now."

"Oh, absolutely. I can't wait to go back to Earth someday and say it again. No one else will appreciate it. So much for philosophical yoga classes." Gideon's smile went down a little as he returned to the conversation. "Some aspects of life are easier being alone. Avoiding developing relationships, for example. Long lasting relationships of any kind take work. Duh. Everyone knows that. And I'm not knocking it or insulting the importance of helping others. In fact, I love it, aiding strangers. It's my favorite thing. But cultivating and tending a relationship is a different kind of work. It's not just the magical first impression. There's something so pure to me about touching someone's life, or them touching yours, and then disappearing. It makes you a vision in their mind, an angel of sorts. I prefer letting people dwell only on that moment and not sharing my demons with them." He chuckled. "I'd be lying if I didn't say Dumakleiza is becoming more difficult now that we're way past first impressions."

Traveler smiled slyly. "She wants more after your night in the tent, doesn't she?"

"Yes." Gideon nodded in exhaustion. "Not unusual after people spend a night together, but I normally never stay long enough to get this far. We don't necessarily have anything lasting. We really aren't anything more than fellow recruits, confused, exposed, dazzled, and amazed by everything we're being introduced to, but we're in a situation where it's bound to become more than that. The four of us are facing destiny, tethered together as we head into something none of us understand. Not even you. The chances of romance blossoming from that dependence is kinda expected I guess." He sighed as he tried to find the right words. "It's nothing I expect anyone else to understand since the American dream is to find a woman, marry her, make crib midgets, buy a house, and then chill 'til death comes for a friendly visit in your sleep." He shivered. "That just sounds like a boring nightmare made of cookie-cutter greyness. My life would only be worth perpetuating the species, and it's gotta be worth more than that. It just has to be." He scoffed to himself. "Could you imagine me as a dad?"

"Ha. No. Is that why you always say, 'may death not find you sleeping' instead of goodbye?"

"I just think life has more potential than expected routine and preparation for death in the comfort of a hospital bed. At least give me a centrifuge pod or whatever you said." He chuckled in frustration. "I want to explore. I want to make mistakes. I want to meet new people every day. I want to try everything I can. I want to try everything I *can't*." He shook his head. "I feel like so many people long for near-death experiences but avoid near-life experiences. I want to do what no one else ever has. What's more exciting than that? I—I don't want to look back on my life and see a pattern day after day. I guess you could say after losing the last girl I cared about and beginning down this fly-by-the-seat-of-my-pantslifestyle, I'm just afraid of what a relationship might do to me. I'm afraid of an anchor." He laughed at himself. "Is that normal? To be afraid of people after the first impression? When they see you for who you really are?"

Traveler turned to him. "I think it's very normal." He looked at the ground as he approached one of the rare moments where Gideon stopped hiding behind charisma and sarcasm. "It actually makes me feel like I can relate to you. And let me tell you, that's rare." He chuckled. "Earth is one of my favorite planets to visit precisely because our cultures are similar. The United States, in particular, and EBOO both seek out foreign aid in dire circumstances. At least historically."

Gideon cocked his head to the side. "What do you mean?"

"Simple," Traveler stated. "Underdeveloped worlds segregate more adamantly. If a region, country, or any group of people need help, they'll stubbornly refuse from their neighbor, and especially their enemy. The more a world advances, *usually* they open to foreign aid because they understand its necessity. It's a step toward planetary unity. The discovery of alien existence is typically the final nail in the corpse, as you'd say."

Gideon chuckled away a correction. "You've got my curiosity, Spaceman."

"Well, Goober, nearly everyone in your culture lives behind a pointed finger, policing others, telling them how to live, how to exist by a variety of personal and bias standards. But your government is trillions of dollars in debt to other countries, and your citizens don't agree on anything."

"I like to think of it as an ever-evolving need for each other, whether it be money, military, technology, food, and what have you."

"I appreciate your open mindset on a planetary scale." Traveler nodded. "But *universally*, here in EBOO, we sought you out to solve our problem that we're unwilling to solve ourselves." He looked from Gideon, up to the stars. "I don't know. I suppose I find comfort in the imperfections that are the same on our worlds, regardless of developmental differences."

Gideon nodded as he, too, stared upward, making shapes out of the foreign constellations. "That's fair. Each world has to figure it out their own way, in their own time."

Traveler tightened the left side of his mouth. "It took us getting invaded to realize we weren't the center of the universe and that we needed to change. Earth will figure it out. Because, like you say on Earth, there are more ways than one to skin a baby."

Gideon slowly turned to face traveler, horrified. "*Cat.* There are more ways than one to skin a *cat.*" He shook his head, laughing with worried eyes as Traveler closed his at the mistake. Gideon chuckled. "Dear God, you're not allowed to use Earth sayings anymore."

Traveler snickered. "Skinning a cat doesn't make much more sense to me, but I suppose it's better than skinning a baby."

Gideon laughed harder. "Yes," he said with an unshakable smile. "Yes, it does. Come on, man." His eyes sternly lingered on Traveler before looking back up at the sky. "I sure hope we can get our shit figured out before Earth gets invaded."

"Well, if we have anything to say about it here on Whewliss, there won't be any more invasions happening on any world. We monitor every planet with light technology, and LOLA restricts anything resembling anything even close to invasion preparation. Master N'kowsky keeps close watch over every world capable of light travel."

Gideon nodded. "He's a smart move on Whewliss's part. Your world really is an incredible place. You guys seem to have universal peace and safety wrapped up with a bow on top."

"Indeed. I believe we do." Traveler sighed. "It's been work, but you're safe here." He looked at Gideon with an eyebrow raised. "So, if I don't want death catching me sleeping—"

Gideon smiled. "Then you'd better get your mopey ass excited to go explore the fourth phase with us."

Traveler nodded and looked down, staring at the ground. "You're sure you're not too afraid of developing our friendship? We're way past first impressions."

"If you can find the courage to overcome your fear of unknown, how am I going to justify being afraid of getting to know an old man like you?"

Traveler smiled at him. "You know what's scary? You're probably the best friend I have."

Gideon slowly nodded. "Right back at you. Definitely didn't think you'd be the one to stick around when I met you all spic-and-span atop Auyantepui Mountain."

"Indeed. What about Dumakleiza? Are you going to be all right spending more time with her?"

Gideon grumbled. "You just had to ruin the moment, didn't you?" He groaned. "Ah, I don't know. It stresses me out. Now I'm all anxious and nervous again. I don't know." He looked at Traveler, hoping for some real advice. "It's stupid to be afraid of feelings for someone, right? I'm just being a child, aren't I?"

"I'm not a good candidate for a relationship counselor." Traveler smiled. "I've never had a girlfriend."

"Really?" Gideon was shocked. "Never? That's ridiculous. I'm going to have to play matchmaker for you." He made a sound composed of a chuckle, a groan, and a scoff. "I mean, we shared a bed with a Vulgair woman. Does she really want something to come of that kind of romantic origin?"

Traveler shrugged. "Firstly, I'm not an expert on women. I'm an expert on light sciences and space travel. Secondly, I also shared a bed with Vulgair women, and Ihad a greattime." He grinned at the memory, which seemed crazier in retrospect. "Thirdly, is any man reallyan expert on women?" They both shook their heads. "Fourthly, keep in mind, she is from a completely different world, culture, and advancement than either of us. Night and day. Her views on relationships, love, sex, *marriage*— they're all very different than either of ours. She might have just engaged in the threesome to try to impress you. I don't know. And fifthly, neither of us have all the answers, but there's one thing we both know."

"What's that?"

"She is protective of you, and she indubitably has feelings for you."

Gideon nodded. "I know." He closed his eyes and exhaled, relinquishing control of destiny. "Hey, what ifthe fourth phase is an adventure into the labyrinth that is the female psyche? Because that would be dangerous."

Traveler fervently shook his head, "You and I would not survive." As they both laughed, Traveler looked at him with genuine curiosity. He was always confused and mesmerized by the mystery of Gideon's inner workings. "Since you brought up our first impression, how is it you managed to weave such magical poetry about romance and love when we first met, but now you're scared of the first woman interested in you since? Well, aside from the Neanderthal."

Gideon sheepishly shrugged. "Because I suck. I don't know. It scares me. *She* scares me." He sighed and looked deeper into the night sky, hoping to find the perfect words somewhere in the cosmos. "Dumakleiza never scared me when she was pointing an arrow at my face, but the helplessness I feel when she looks at me with that beautiful dragon eye of hers—that scares the crap out of me."

Traveler smiled at him. "From what I've been told and read, that's got love written all over it, my dear friend. Sounds like *you* need a gubernaculum."

"Way too soon for the L word," Gideon chuckled. "Your inexperience is showing." He took a deep breath and smirked. "Do you have anything to drink?" Traveler nodded with a sudden burst of enthusiasm.

Gideon smiled. "Perfect. What do you say we go toast to all the upcoming adventures that scare us?"

"That sounds like the perfect way to prepare for the fourth phase." Traveler hadn't thought of tossing drinks back into the night, but now that Gideon had suggested it, there was nothing else he wanted to do. "Come with me." He turned and eagerly walked away with Gideon close behind him.

Gideon laughed to himself. "I can't wait to see what kind of what-if questions you start proposing when you're drunk. Well, honestly, I just can't wait to see what you're like with a little liquid courage."

Traveler shook his head. "I'm already regretting this. And we're not going to drink toomuch. I feel like if I get drunk around you, we'll both somehow end up on another world, married, running against each other for president of some strange country with tattoos of each other's faces *on* our faces."

Gideon gasped. "Can we do that?"

9

Once Whewliss's sun rose, a small crowd gathered to see the recruits off. The bright morning weather was perfect for an outdoor celebration. There was no wind or cloud cover. It was as if Whewliss itself was ready to see them depart for the fourth phase. Lord Coyzle, three council members, the assistants, and a handful of EBOO officials stood around what looked to Gideon like a helipad on the roof of one of the city's taller buildings. It had the same hand symbol as the council members' suits shining up from it, clearly ceremonious for interplanetary departures. Everyone was eagerly expressing congratulations, excitement, and wishing success and good fortune to the departing.

Traveler looked around at the crowd of less than thirty and then leaned in close enough for his three recruits to hear. "This is everyone in the universe who knows about the fourth phase."

Dumakleiza brought her head back. "You toy with our minds. There are no others? Not even on other worlds?"

Traveler shook his head. "No. This is it. Only N'kowsky and Melodeen aren't here. I'm surprised she's not present to witness this. That's unusual. She must be welcoming someone from the gelatin or be lost in a book." He refocused on Dumakleiza. "But yes, the fourth phase is not public knowledge. One day it might be, but that depends on you."

"What an honor," Dumakleiza said. "Privy to a secret of the stars." She held her head a little higher.

Traveler nodded. "One more will greet us upon our arrival at the Wall."

Gideon, Dumakleiza, and Timrekka were dying to know what the Wall was but knew they'd be there shortly. It was almost time to find out what all the veiled secrecy was all about. It was almost time to see the fourth phase.

Cooby was on Dumakleiza's back, cooing and pawing at her. His fur was combed and shampooed to a bright sheen, bringing the richness of its colors to surface. His armored back had been buffered and waxed. All the accumulated residue, gunk, and mossy buildup had been scrubbed away. His claws were trimmed, teeth cleaned, and wing skin washed. He looked like a brand-new animal, and he could feel the warmth of everyone's attention. The tanion visibly bathed in their adoration. His reactive instincts were still twitchy, being met with happiness and kindness versus aggression and violence.

After a young woman asked Timrekka to pose for a selfie from a camera he couldn't see, he turned to Gideon and whispered, "Gideon, Alik and I made these. You should try one." He held out a spray bottle filled with murky liquid. It was opaque with little black beads rattling around inside.

"What is it?" Gideon squinted at him.

"It activates all your vocal chords, triggering vibrational patterns beyond what you can control on your own, allowing you a much higher vocal range and possibly even allowing you to speak in multiple voices, or I mean, tones and volumes at once."

"Possibly?" Gideon smiled. "It's always comforting to know that you're not cheating on me, Timmy, old boy. I get to be the first to try this, don't I?"

Timrekka nodded at the obvious. "There's also a chance it could damage the vocal cords and eat away the tissue until you're mute, so no one's been willing to try so far, but I figured you'd be unafraid."

Gideon feigned some fluttering eyelashes. "You know me so well." He took the spray bottle from Timrekka's gorilla hand and sprayed it into the back of his mouth without a shred of hesitation. It tasted like mango, which was a pleasant surprise. His throat started scratching. It was as if he had a hair lodged in his esophagus. He coughed a few times and waited.

Lord Coyzle gathered everyone's attention. "The time has come." They all turned. "It feels unreal to actually be announcing this. It's something that's gone from a dream to an impossibility. I honestly feel like I'm dreaming, but we live in a time where sleep is obsolete, so I know I'm not." He chuckled, unable to contain himself. "Ever since our ground-breaking discovery on the Wall, we have searched the universe for souls brave enough to venture where we dare not. Our fear is the platform for their courage. Their courage is the catalyst for our future. And our future will discover answers to mysteries that could very well change the destiny of mankind across the stars."

Everyone cheered. It was still strange to Gideon to hear cheering without any applause. He shrugged and clapped regardless of being the only one. As he cheered, it sounded like three different voices came out of him: one shrill, one normal, and one deep. No one else noticed amid the other shouting. Only Timrekka caught it and smiled at his invention's success. They smiled at each other and then turned their attention back to Lord Coyzle as he ushered the crowd to quiet down.

"We are literally worlds apart. Our cultures, epochs, technologies, physiologies, beliefs, and ways of life differ in nearly every way. But we are all explorers, learners, students, and travelers possessing human fundamentals. We each have aspirations, hopes, dreams, goals, and determined minds set on improvement. And what better way to advance ourselves than to explore together? United we stand, facing the darkness of fear. We venture into what scares us all: the unknown." His smile disappeared as he looked around at the gathered faces. "And it doesn't matter what deities we believe in or don't believe in. Regardless of faith, science, known, unknown, I pray to whatever higher powers may or may not exist. I pray that we are taking the right course of action and that whatever lies beyond will pioneer us into a future beyond our comprehension."

More cheering erupted, echoing out from the rooftop, invigorated, and inspired.

"Now," he continued, "with the level of discretion we wish to maintain with the fourth phase's mere existence, I will not keep you any longer." He took a deep breath, reluctant to part ways. It pained him to see them venture off into the unknown while he remained behind in the known. "Six One." He turned to see her standing with Izzy, Tsuna, and Jasss. "Does your journey end here, or are you braving the fourth phase with your three incredible recruits?"

Six One smiled back at him with charm and shine. "My journey ends here." Her recruits immediately looked at her with veiled disappointment. She smiled back at them with nebulous encouragement. "I send them forth with absolute confidence in their ability to succeed. However, the fourth phase is not a journey I'm brave enough to explore." Her smile grew, obviously a presentation for the crowd. "Perhaps when they returnI will then be willing to follow the path they will have blazed for us."

Lord Coyzle nodded. "I sympathize with your hesitation. It is, after all, why we originally recruited them." His understanding released her from a large portion of her lingering guilt. She just wasn't going to look them in the eyes for a few minutes. Lord Coyzle turned to Traveler. "Four Zero, does your journey end here, or are you braving the fourth phase with yourthree remarkable recruits?"

Traveler looked at Gideon, Dumakleiza, and Timrekka, considering the gravity of the choice. "As Gideon would say—" He turned and looked confidently at Lord Coyzle. "—why not?"

A light gasp hissed through the air. The crowd stared at Traveler in shock. They knew the offer would be presented, but they expected him to politely decline. After all, it's what every other Whewlight would have done: smile as they courteously avoided what terrified them. But not Traveler. Six One stared at him with peeled eyes, genuinely worried for him. All her competitive arrogance melted away as she heard him commit to doom. He may as well have proclaimed that he was going to commit suicide, and while smiling, no less.

Traveler basked in their disbelief, a foreign feeling of empowerment budding from within it. He had so much he wanted to say, to explain, but allowing their dumbfounded minds to feel the freefall of surprise was more rewarding than he had anticipated.

Lord Coyzle struggled to find a response. "You actually—" He resituated himself. "When did you decide this?"

Traveler smiled, his posture straightening. "I've wanted to find this specific courage longer than I've wanted to succeed as a recruiter." He motioned to Gideon. "And my gubernaculum helped me develop myself and grow into the person who can actually brave the unknown."

Everyone was speechless. There was no cheering, no murmuring. Nothing. They were unsure if they'd heard him correctly.

"Oh!" Gideon threw a finger in the air. His harmonious triple-voice echoed, distracting everyone's befuddlement. Gideon unslung his backpack and fished around inside. After a moment, he withdrew a worn, rolled up paper bound by a cracked rubber band. Gideon smiled and slid the rubber band off it as he walked toward Lord Coyzle. "I like giving parting gifts to people who've affected my life."

His voice was down to two pitches vibrating together, but he was too focused on his task to care how he sounded. "I know you wish you could come, or at least leave Whewliss sometimes." He unrolled the paper scroll, exposing an old map of Earth. Lord Coyzle looked at it as Gideon stepped up to him. Gideon smiled fondly at the nostalgic keepsake. "And I know this isn't as exciting as all of the cool worlds you guys know about, but up until meeting Four Zero, this was my greatest exploring aspiration."

Lord Coyzle studied the atlas held out in Gideon's hands. It was a scribbly mess with red dots marking many of the countries, states, provinces, and arrows aimed over a few of the oceans and seas. Lord Coyzle smirked as he tried to figure out what all the markings meant.

"What is it?"

"It's my diary," Gideon said with a doting smile. "The only memoir I've kept of my own personal explorations and adventures when I thought Earth was all that there was. I mean I've always wondered if there was life on other planets, but you know what I mean." He handed it to Lord Coyzle as the throat spray dissolved back to one voice. "I don't know, maybe it could be a way for you to vicariously feel the same rush of leaving your home and journeying into the great beyond."

Lord Coyzle smiled as he felt what it represented. "Thank you." His rosy cheeks swelled. He stared at it for a moment longer and then rolled it up to keep it safe. As he slid the rubber band back over the map, he looked at Gideon. "Regardless of what you discover in the fourth phase, this will be an artifact for future generations to see. The fact that all of you came from younger worlds and are joining this voyage is astounding. This map is a great reminder of your courage and faith." He smiled. "And yes, I hope to one day join you on one of your adventures. Perhaps if we ever elect a new lord, it will allow me the opportunity." He sighed, knowing it was unlikely. He stepped back and addressed everyone together. "Without further ado, Master Brawd, is everything prepared for your departure and arrival?"

Master Brawd gave a barely visible nod. "Yes, my lord."

"I have a question." Timrekka threw his hand in the air. "Do we need other outfits, or will the gelatin suits be okay on this wall place?"

Lord Coyzle smiled. "We have Whewlight technology at our outposts on the Wall. Those suits will be sufficient—for now."

"Okay." Timrekka brought his hand down, refraining from asking his plethora of other questions.

Izzy smiled. "I'm growing partial to mine. It would make working in a lab a lot easier without all that cloth getting in the way."

Timrekka matched his grin. "That's very true; I hadn't thought of how helpful that would be."

Lord Coyzle gave one last look around. "Recruits, I look forward to seeing you when you return. I cannot express in words how excited I am to hear what you discover. And I cannot even begin to fathom what future you will pioneer us toward." He respectfully took a moment to look each of them in the eye. "On behalf of every Whewlight and every human to ever venture into the unknown—"

All the gathered Whewlights spoke as one, "May the light guide and protect you."

The recruits responded in turn, "May the light guide and protect you."

Gideon smiled at the crowd gathered around them. "Whewlights, may death not find you sleeping."

He got a few questioning looks as the Whewlights tried to figure it out. It was an odd saying, but some of them smiled as it resonated, providing an odd sense of promise.

As the crowd looked at the six aliens with their earnest hopes and dreams resting on their shoulders, Master Brawd spoke, "Recruits." He stood in the middle of them and offered his hand to Traveler, who immediately took hold. Master Brawd wasted no time as he looked up into the bright midday sky and reached upward, closing his fingers around the unseen. It was weird to the recruits to see a recruiter falling back and following someone else. Traveler being outranked was strange.

One by one, the recruits took each other's hands, nervous excitement rising within them. It was time. Gideon's heart raced as he looked from Traveler's nervous face up to the bright sky. Whatever was out there, wherever they were going, it was time. Gideon couldn't help but laugh to release some energy. He was bursting, overflowing. Every second they waited for Master Brawd to find the right forecast felt like an hour.

The gathered crowd waited in silence. The jump wouldn't be anything new, but what it represented was unprecedented. All eyes were on Master Brawd's closed fist.

Master Brawd gave one last look to Lord Coyzle. "My lord."

Lord Coyzle smiled back to his war buddy. "May the light guide and protect you, old friend."

With that, Master Brawd opened his hand, and they vanished.

10

As the light faded from Gideon's eyes, he begged his body to hurry up and recover. He was intoxicated by anticipation. He desperately wanted to know where they'd landed as soon as he started coming to.

Come on. Come on. Come on!

Finally, the bright haze faded, leaving him in darkness that took a moment to adjust to. Wherever they were, it was the dead of night. As soon as he could see clearly, the first thing he noticed was all his traveling companions standing next to him. A skimming headcount confirmed that everyone had made it. Good. Onto wherever they were. Gideon turned to look around. He paused. His mind struggled with what he saw.

The first thing he noticed was that they were standing on pitch black soil, but the more he stared at it, the less like dirt it appeared. He squatted down on his haunches like a child. The fine, dark dirt under his feet looked more like little beads. At first, he thought it was his mind playing tricks on his eyes adjusting in the limited visibility. As he saw more clearly, his piqued curiosity was raised by the confirmation: The beads were beads. He ran his fingers through the ground. It felt soft to the touch, and the beads were natural, not manmade. There was an earthiness to them, and yet it still appeared unnatural. Stranger still was the smell. It emanated a musky scent that was strangely reminiscent of cooking spices. Gideon couldn't put his finger on which one it reminded him of most, but he was brought back to his childhood, smelling his mother cooking for him in their humble, one-bedroom apartment. It was so novel and unique yet familiar that the dirt-like black beads were instantly painted to his olfactory memory.

All right, enough with the ground, he thought. He looked up, jumbled as he processed what he saw next. The other recruits' curious murmurs and sounds bypassed his ears as he stared, unsure, at the eccentric foliage around them. Standing about two heads high was a forest of trees, but nothing like any he'd ever seen, even on other worlds. He wasn't sure if he could even classify them as trees. They were so warped and twisted in shape and design that they appeared cartoonish, with vibrantly colored leaves and fruit that looked like black coconuts bunched in blackberry bulges. They were so mesmerizing and silly that it was a struggle to look beyond them.

Gideon's eyes trailed up and looked skyward. What he saw next left him speechless. For a brief second, he thought the night sky was filled with northern lights. The colors were too close to the ground, and fainter. He squinted and shook his head, trying to slow his mind to make sense of it. Spanning across the entire night sky, looking to be twenty-or-so feet above the ground, was a light blue shimmer. The blackness of the sky and the clarity of the distant stars were perfectly visible—but in the distance, in every direction, the sky had a baby blue tint. It almost felt like they were underneath a giant glass ceiling. Gideon knew they weren't, but he didn't understand what it actually was. It didn't appear solid. It had more of an opaque haze.

Gideon took a moment to focus on the stars, and it made him stutter a breath. Their crystal clarity bested any night view he'd seen before. It felt like there was nothing between them, as if he could literally reach out and touch the stars with his own hands. The magnificence of space felt mere inches away, and it floored him. He'd never been much for astronomy, but for a moment, it was all that mattered.

Gideon waved his fingertips to Traveler, blindly reaching for him as he pointed up. "What is that, uh, blue?"

Traveler gave a small smile as he, too, looked up at the shimmering. "That is the edge of the Wall's atmosphere. It's only eighteen feet high."

Gideon mouthed some silent guesses, doubting what the answer meant. "So, that would mean that nineteen feet from the ground is—"

"Space?" Timrekka finished his guess for him.

"Yes." Traveler threw open hands in the air, excited to share what he'd been legally withholding. "Oh." He stepped forward and touched his left index finger to the top of Gideon's shoulder. "While we were on Whewliss, I got the implant so I could do this for you." Bright light appeared between his finger and Gideon's shoulder as he burned a line from Gideon's clavicle down to his bicep. Gideon winced a little but kept his eyes on the blueness of the distant sky. He was almost too distracted to care about his cathartic scar.

Dumakleiza stared up at what Traveler called the edge of the atmosphere. She had a limited understanding of what those words meant, but with what little she knew about air and space, it left her feeling claustrophobic. It suddenly felt like she couldn't breathe, as if the sky was shrinking down toward them, and soon there wouldn't be enough air to fill her lungs. She closed her eyes, trying to control herself. Cooby recognized her nervousness, so he held onto her tighter, cooing comforts as his own fear matched hers. It didn't take long for their melding energy to transform Duma's fears into protective aggression. Her eyes shot open, immediately scanning their surroundings for something to kill. She had no idea if there was a threat in the night, but if there was, she was going to be ready for it. Even with her dragon eye, she saw nothing but darkness and strange trees. She saw no lifeforms beyond their party.

"Grim," she whispered under her quick breathing, "keep me alert."

Izzy stood next to Timrekka, hoping to find a like-minded curiosity within the fellow scientist. "What kind of planet has an atmosphere only three heads high? Or in your case—" He looked at Timrekka and grinned. "—maybe four."

Timrekka giggled. "I have no idea, but I wonder if that means we're on a larger world like mine or if this is smaller. I can probably find out if I hit something because if it's like Thamiosh, I'll hurt my hand, but if it's smaller, then I'll break stuff."

Izzy nodded, anxious to witness it. "Or you could technically be able to leap out of the atmosphere at that height. Although—" He slumped. "—you'd probably start floating away into space."

Timrekka trembled. "I'm glad you mentioned that because I almost jumped just to find out."

Jasss hesitantly stared around, looking for any exits if they became necessary. Her eyes remained narrow since first opening. The silence of the dark forest had her teeth grinding. There were no crickets. There was no sound at all, and the dead silence had her ready to run. Silence was the home of hunters.

Tsuna squatted down, running his fingers through the black soil. His condescending attitude was missing. Instead, he had a softness about him as he buried his hands in the ground and whispered like he would in a lover's ear. A couple of the others glanced at him but quickly looked away as he made them uncomfortable.

Master Brawd looked around, making sure no one was shadowed. Once he finished the headcount, he turned his eyes back to the sky. He wanted to stare at Whewliss in the distant forecast one more time before devoting his full attention to the fourth phase. He couldn't help feeling delight rising from within.

Traveler retracted his finger once he was satisfied with Gideon's cauterized scar. "That should be sufficient." He smiled at his work. "I think I have a good handle on this implant. Going to be helpful, I think. At least with you."

Gideon's eyes hadn't left the sky, and he barely realized he'd reached over with his right hand to feel the scar. He sighed with subconscious relief.

"Thank you." He brought his head down and looked back and forth between Traveler and Master Brawd. "Is this the fourth phase?"

"No," Master Brawd answered. "This is where we found the fourth phase."

There was something immediately different about Master Brawd's tone and energy, and everyone noticed. He wasn't tense or withdrawn. His sternness hadn't budged, but there was an enthusiasm, an underlying energy. Wherever they were, it was where his mind had been, and now that they were there, he was reunited with his thoughts. He didn't care about the politics on Whewliss. All that mattered was the fourth phase. He looked to the recruits.

"Our outpost is a short walk from this clearing. To understand the fourth phase, you must first understand the Wall." He turned and started walking.

Traveler followed close behind, keen on hearing the description he'd heard many times before. The recruits followed. The mysteriousness of the bizarre forest had them spooked, and even Traveler allowed himself to feel a little fear of what he knew he didn't need to. The blackness held much he still didn't understand.

Master Brawd wasted no time. "Well, as we began exploring the universe, theories about what we would find were prime discussion among our council, philosophers, and scientists. Were there worlds more advanced than ours or Daemoana? Was there nonhuman intelligent life as the dominant species on other worlds? Would we find the origin of all life itself? What would we discover?"

The recruits listened with entranced attention. Only Dumakleiza and Jasss kept their eyes focused on the darkness as they walked. Dumakleiza was rattled. Something felt dangerously out of place. Wherever they were, it left an ache of helplessness in her stomach.

"After many years," Master Brawd continued, "we detected a life-supporting atmosphere here, but it wasn't a planet." Everyone was unsure of what he meant. "We assumed our equipment was faulty, but after many tests, we read life-supporting conditions spanning across an impossibly large portion of space, much larger than any world we'd ever seen. We had no idea what we were reading in our space forecast, but after we gathered up the courage, a few Whewlights made the jump. They landed here."

"The Wall," Gideon guessed.

"Yes. Now here's where it gets interesting." Master Brawd's tone went up a few octaves. "This isn't a planet."

Timrekka adjusted his goggles as he dug for a hidden meaning. "What?"

"It's flat." Master Brawd's response left all six recruits with squinted eyes filled with questions. Master Brawd gave them some time to consider the idea.

"We have spent many decades exploring the Wall. We have light jumped, light whipped, and travelled trillions of miles in every direction, charting every single inch of the Wall. We always have hundreds of expeditions out, documenting and mapping everything here. The information gathered alone has required us to advance our technologies just to hold the exponentially growing amount of data." He took a deep breath before telling one of his favorite facts. "Every one-thousand-miles, we've planted tracking beacons into the ground, so we can measure whatever *here* is. The massive grid is currently made up of multiples of billions of beacons, all creating a three dimensionally digitized map we can measure, observe, and study. But no matter how many we plant, the grid has only given us one single piece of information about the Wall."

"What?" Timrekka spat out, so desperate to know that he was sweating.

Master Brawd stared through the trees in front of him as he walked. "It's perfectly flat." It wasn't new information to him, but it still blew his mind. "Across trillions of miles, the beacons haven't measured a single iota of a fraction of a percent of curvature in any direction. For as far as we've measured and as far as we can hypothesize, there is no end to this. There is no sphere. We have no evidence that suggests anything other than an eternal surface. There are no edges, no hills, mountains, cliffs, no change in shape. Just...the Wall. The edge of space."

"What?" Timrekka's mind raced. "That's impossible; there has to be shape, at least a hill here or there, and certainly an end to this body of mass, it can't just go on eternally because that concept is, well, it's just impossible." He couldn't tell if deep down he wanted to believe Master Brawd or not.

Master Brawd stopped. He turned and stared down at Timrekka, his dark eyes intimidating the stout scientist. He looked around at each recruit, daring them to challenge his knowledge. He cracked a small smile on one side of his mouth that came off as more of a sneer. "Climb up and see for yourselves." He motioned to the trees.

"Yup!" Gideon leapt. Before the other recruits could consider the idea, he was already shimmying up some warped branches. It didn't take long to climb. As soon as he popped his head over the tree line and looked, his jaw dropped. What he saw didn't register. "Y—y—you guys *have* to see this!"

It didn't take any more coaxing. The other recruits ran over to different trees and climbed up as fast as their hands and feet would carry them. Timrekka accidentally ripped one of the branches off a tree with his zeal. He was definitely stronger than anyone else on the Wall, but that's not what he cared about. Once everyone got good footholds and grips on their trees, they, too, peered out over the tree line. They held on tighter as the sight made them all light-headed.

Stretching out farther than anything they'd ever seen, the forest spanned eternally in every direction. It was lit only by the crystal clarity of the stars, showing a sparkling ocean of treetops. The recruits were all so naturally accustomed to seeing the curvature of their own planets that they were struggling to understand it. Normally, on any world, the view of the horizon would curve downward in the distance, and if they were high enough, they could even see the shape of the planet. However, on the Wall, the endlessness appeared as if it was warping upward. It was like they were in a valley looking up a distant grade in every direction, even though everything they could see was perfectly flat.

They stared blankly, trying to comprehend it, but it just wasn't happening. Even the blueness of the atmosphere was playing tricks on their minds. Since there was no curvature to it either, it went on unendingly parallel to the treetops. There was no top or bottom to the view as they turned, looking every which way. There were no clouds, so everything was visible as far as their vision was capable.

Hearing Master Brawd explain everything was one thing, but seeing it with their own eyes overwhelmed them to the point of orgasmic nausea; it was simultaneously the most beautiful view they'd ever seen and the most intimidating reality. None of them moved. None of them spoke. They barely breathed.

Gideon couldn't lift his jaw. "Flat Earthers would shit out of their dicks if they saw this."

The only variance in the eternity of trees was what looked like a small village a little more than a mile away. They assumed it was the Whewlight outpost they were walking toward.

Cooby didn't care. Once he climbed a tree, he happily screamed and leapt to another one, enjoying the feeling of air catching beneath his wing flaps again. Branches and leaves shook as he pounced from one tree to another, screeching and yelling with glee.

It took a few minutes for the recruits to make their way back down. Master Brawd didn't rush them. He understood all too well what they were feeling: the helplessness, the powerless insignificance, the fear, the wonder, the unknown, the millions of questions, and the utter inability to even think. It was too much, and he was willing to give them as much time as they needed. Shattered perspectives required time to pick up the pieces.

Everyone stood in overawed silence. They stared through the trees, through the ground, aimlessly into space.

Dumakleiza, being the most unfamiliar with space, spoke first. "This is the end of all that exists? Because of science?"

Master Brawd gave a slight nod. "It's been debated and argued that it could be more of a ceiling looming *over* us or the floor of space spanning *beneath* us——some end or another. No one knows. There is no way to know. We simply call it the Wall because it is the least threatening of the three. It permits us to keep our sanity." He looked up at the clear stars above them. "No one likes to think the Wall is a ceiling that could fall down on us or a floor that we could fall to. Everyone has their own what-if theory about what the Wall could be."

Traveler leaned toward Gideon and whispered, "That's the origin of my favorite game."

Gideon slowly nodded, barely able to focus on anything. "Makes sense."

Timrekka shook his head and raised his hand. "I have so many questions, like if all of that is true, how are we standing here so simply? Shouldn't the gravity be so high that we instantly die and compress as thin as paper, and shouldn't everything be being pulled into the Wall in massive cataclysmic devastation? How does it have such survivable gravity, and if it's eternally spanning in every direction, how do you light jump from here? If there are no stars close enough to power a jump, such as a galaxy's local sun, which would be in closer proximity to habitable planets, are we stuck here permanently, and will we ever be able to leave? And have you studied what the ground is comprised of because it's clearly not dirt, but I don't know what else to call it, and once again, this *isn't* the fourth phase?"

Jasss and Izzy chuckled at how fast Timrekka spoke and how much he was able to cover in a single breath. Dumakleiza looked around apprehensively as Gideon nodded along with all Timrekka's questions.

Tsuna scoffed. "The Wall speaks to me. I know not why everyone else fears it so. It is a misunderstood soul that doesn't deserve to be treated as such an outsider, an oddity." He scowled at Timrekka. "The dwarf insults her."

Jasss laughed at him. "Shut up, planet humper."

Master Brawd calmly and collectedly addressed Timrekka's concerns. "First, you're being caught up to speed on the second-greatest phenomenon we've ever discovered. We don't have all the answers, but we are constantly searching for them." He looked around at their curious faces before turning back to Timrekka. "The gravity is something we've puzzled over since the Wall's original discovery nearly eighty Whewliss years ago. We don't understand it, and we share your hypothesis about the magnitude of power it *should* have but doesn't. We've measured the gravity, and it's seventy-nine-percent as strong as the gravity on Whewliss, which makes it even more confusing." He stared at Timrekka, who clearly wanted to argue even though he knew there wasn't reason to. The Whewlights were just as curious about his questions as he was.

Master Brawd continued, "Even more baffling is that the entire universe is moving away from the Wall, as if it somehow originated here. Or the Wall somehow birthed everything. We don't know. Just more theories. But it's literally operating in the exact opposite fashion than a celestial body should. Instead of dragging all toward itself with gravity that should rival thousands of black holes, it's pushing everything away. We have continuously compounding questions about that and no answers."

Everyone stared at him, flabbergasted and unable to think of anything to respond with. They were completely staggered. Master Brawd thought back over Timrekka's other questions. "Your curiosity about light jumping is a good question."

"Are we stuck here?" Timrekka nervously repeated himself as the fear resurfaced.

"No." Master Brawd looked up and pointed out at the vast ocean of stars. "The first Whewlights who landed on the Wall hopelessly thought they were. There is no star near enough the Wall, so it's never dayhere. It's always night as we perceive it. Anyway, we believed the lost observers, dead on another world, floating somewhere in space, or shadowed in transit. They didn't return to Whewliss for over two years. They experimented tirelessly and developed our light tech, creating more advanced methods of grabbing onto light. They tried everything they could to further manipulate its elasticity. They ended up utilizing the weak light from every distant star in sight, creating an elastic tension from thousands of different stars at one single time." The concept tickled Timrekka's mind. "At first, they struggled to aim with that many power sources at once, but after a while of perfecting it over the course of their years stuck here, they made their first successful jump back home." He smiled at the proud memory. "We worked as a people, experimenting on and perfecting their newfound method before visiting the Wall and attempting it for ourselves. Now it's the second most popular jumping method we use between celestial bodies. It's known as chariot jumping."

"Oh, cool." Gideon smiled. "Because of all the horses pulling the one chariot. I get it."

Master Brawd looked at him, confused. "What?" Everyone else also looked at Gideon, unsure of what he was talking about.

Gideon chuckled and puffed out his bottom lip. "Uh, never mind." He glared at Traveler. "Hey, you told me last night on Whewliss that we couldn't come here early because it was night and we needed light to jump. You liar, liar, pants on fire."

Timrekka scratched his head, suddenly pondering the same thing. "I don't know why I didn't think of that."

Traveler smirked, "Yeah, I just wanted you to shut up."

Gideon squinted with an annoyed smirk. "I don't know if I'll ever be able to trust you again."

Master Brawd readily addressed Timrekka's next concern. "The ground here has been named black bead. It's not creative, but it is what it is." He looked at the recruits. "Grab a handful of it," he ushered them eagerly. His sternness hadn't transformed into friendliness by any means, but the difference in his social interaction with them was night and day. The recruits squatted down and picked up handfuls of black bead. It spilled through their fingers as they held it up to study.

"As you can see," Master Brawd explained, "it's very light and only one millimeter in diameter."

"That's a precise measurement," Izzy commented. "It doesn't vary?"

"No, every single bead is the same," Master Brawd said, fully aware of how ridiculous the fact sounded. "And what we still have trouble accepting is that we can't break it down."

"What do you mean?" Gideon asked as he stared at the little pile of black bead in his hand.

"Simply that," Master Brawd responded. "We can't break it down to study its smaller makeup. We can't break the black bead apart. Nothing in our vast array of tools can split it. Nothing chemical, nothing blunt, nothing nuclear, not even our expansive light technology. It's a blow to the pride for Whewlights. None of our tools can study black bead in any smaller form than it's already in."

"Huh?" Timrekka said, suddenly hungering for the chance to try his hand at the challenge.

"It gets stranger," Master Brawd said. "When we've tried to dig into the ground, we get exactly eighteen inches."

"What happens at eighteen inches?" Timrekka and Izzy asked at the same time.

"Nothing," said Master Brawd. "Our tools stop. Nothing of ours can get any farther. We are unable to dig any deeper than eighteen inches anywhere across the Wall. Personally, I wouldn't be surprised if an entire planet collided into the Wall and didn't go any deeper than eighteen inches. A world-shattering impact would only destroy the world. The Wall would remain unscathed, as if it never happened."

"Hm." Timrekka thought about it, trying to take in all the information.

Master Brawd nodded. "It's maddening." After a long pause, he turned and resumed walking. Everyone picked up their feet and followed. Master Brawd continued. "There is much more to this place, but those are the introductory basics. The Wall is a humbling reminder of how small and powerless we ultimately are in the universe. It doesn't matter how advanced we are as a planet or a species. Nature is always in final control. All we're allowed are brief delusions of having it ourselves." They kept walking. "Oh." He paused and turned to look at them with heavy demand in his tone. "And *do not* climb above the atmosphere. You *will* float away into space, and there's very little we can do to help you. We have lost good people to curiosity."

Timrekka looked at Izzy. "Good thing I didn't jump."

Gideon peered ahead at where they were walking. It looked the exact same as everywhere else around them. There were more vibrantly colored trees with black fruit, and below their branches was eternal darkness. He had no idea how Master Brawd even knew his way around when the Wall was the same everywhere. Maybe the constellations, like explorers of old. He shook his head, trying not to succumb to the overwhelming magnitude of it all.

"Where are we going now?"

"To where your adventure begins."

11

They walked through the last grove of trees standing between them and the Whewlight outpost. The recruits were surprised by the lack of spectacle before them. After being on Whewliss, they were expecting to see futuristic technologies and structures that challenged their comprehension of what kinds of engineering was possible. Instead, what they saw beneath the vibrant stars was an outpost comprised of what looked like elaborate shacks nestled in the endless forest.

Bright lights shone through windows, bringing the first manmade light to the Wall. The buildings felt out of place, standing out amid the perfectly flat and uniformed Wall. The eight shacks, each standing up to a few feet below the atmospheric line, were built in a circle, all facing the center yard between them. They were identical in design and structure. They were spacious and flat on top. If they were any higher, they would risk venturing beyond the atmosphere and out into the dangers of space.

Even in the limited lighting, it was easy to recognize the wood that the buildings were built from. Every part of the walls, the framing, the roof, everything had been made of the trees on the Wall. It appeared that the outside had been sanded down to make each massive shack look more presentable, though there really wasn't much of a reason for them to be. All eight of the buildings were like a neighborhood cul-de-sac, each about forty feet apart, and in the middle of them appeared to be a barren stretch of the Wall with no trees. The darkness made it difficult to see any more details.

"This is the Wall Post," Master Brawd said with an ambiguous energy. His announcement of the name made Gideon bite his tongue to avoid making a Facebook joke. Master Brawd continued. "Whewliss is considering building cities here one day and solving overpopulation with the Wall instead of empty habitable planets. But for now, the Wall Post is the only civilization on any part of the Wall—that we know of."

The recruits looked at the eight buildings, feeling less wowed than they were hoping to be. They weren't dumpy, but they were profoundly simple in comparison to Prism or any other building in EBOO.

Gideon smiled. He thought they looked campy, like a getaway in the mountains or a summer camp. His imagination begged for a bonfire in the middle of the eight buildings where everyone would gather and socialize, maybe eat some hot dogs and s'mores, ending each night tossing back beers and telling ghost stories. In the back of his mind, he was hoping they were going to end each day that way, spending the night chatting and laughing about their adventures. He immediately laughed at himself for thinking that there was a difference between night and day on the Wall, where there was no local sun providing light. It was always night.

"Mackel!" an excited voice shouted from inside one of the buildings.

Master Brawd smiled and walked toward the shack. Everyone else stayed behind, waiting to find out who the stranger was.

A woman came running toward them from behind one of the buildings, arms flung out. She had vibrant tattoos all over, shimmering and glowing, flickering like subterraneous ocean life. She barreled into Master Brawd, wrapping her arms around him and squeezing him as hard as she could. In the dimness of the Wall, the recruits couldn't get a good read on the woman, but watching her and Master Brawd embrace, they made a few assumptions.

Gideon leaned in next to Traveler. "Mackel?"

Traveler nodded. "Master MackelBrawd."

"Oh my," Gideon said with a playful smile.

Master Brawd released the woman and turned to the recruits. "This is my wife, Candelle. She's the Wall's lead observer, and she's in charge of the mapping."

Candelle turned and looked at the newcomers with a smile visible in the darkness. "Aliens!" she shouted with outstretched arms.

The recruits all said hello, a couple of them waving.

Master Brawd motioned to them. "Candelle, these are the—"

"Fourth phase recruits," Candelle exclaimed. "There are seven." She did nothing to conceal her disbelief. "I've waited a lifetime for three, and now I get *seven*?" She smiled and ran forward, crashing a hug into Timrekka. Her arms latched as far around him as they could, squeezing harder than Timrekka was expecting. "Welcome!" She quickly worked through all recruits, hugging each of them. When she got to Traveler, she paused. "Wait." She looked closer to make sure her eyes weren't deceiving her. "Aren't you, uh, Four Zero?" She gawked. "Why are *you* here?"

Traveler smiled confidently. "I'm going."

Candelle brought her head back. She stared at him to see if he was joking. After some unwavering eye contact, Candelle's eyebrows rose.

"One of *ours* is going? Well—" She looked to Master Brawd. "—sounds like I have a lot of catching up to do."

Master Brawd nodded as he walked up to her. "Let's go inside." He turned and started toward one of the shacks with Candelle's hand in his.

As the other recruits followed behind them, Gideon hung back and whispered in Traveler's ear, "I didn't figure Brawd for a family man."

Traveler quietly scoffed and whispered back, "Master Brawd has four wives and two husbands."

Gideon paused, his eyes widening as he slowly panned over to face Traveler. "He wha—that *dog*." He whispered a snarl with sassy eyebrows. "Is that common among Whewlights?"

"Yes. Monogamy is still the prominent relationship dynamic on Whewliss, but I'd venture to guess that one in seven relationships is comprised of varied polygamy."

Gideon nodded. "Back to your requirement for minds to operate like parachutes, that's pretty open of you guys."

"Indeed. It's becoming more commonplace. But if you bring it up at all around Candelle, just make sure you address her as Master Brawd's favorite. It's imperative to acknowledge her position, or you'll have to deal with Master Brawd."

"Oh, is she his number one?"

"Yes."

"Oh, man, that's fun. There's still so much about you peoplethat I have yet to learn."

✳

Inside, the recruits looked around. There wasn't much to see. Desks made of the Wall's trees lined one side of the room with hand-sized electronics strewn about. On the opposite side of the room, three beds were built into the wall. The fact that there were relics like mattresses, pillows, and blankets brought up some curiosities. In the middle of the shack stood a wooden table, also made from the Wall's trees, with four chairs around it. Stacked board games and other items that the recruits assumed were Whewlight card games were scattered about. They had been used recently, as much had spilled onto the floor. Gideon was anxious to know what kinds of entertainment they amused themselves with. He hoped that maybe he'd get the chance to join them for a round or two. They continued looking around, but the room was otherwise empty.

Candelle stepped into the middle of the room and fumbled with a green and black oval game piece. As she turned to see their reactions to her home, they finally got a good look at her. Her suit was made of the same gelatin material, but it didn't cover her shoulders or arms. It started halfway up her chest, exposing half of her breasts and wrapping around her mid-upper back. It was black with images of yellow explosions that resembled fireworks. She had intricate tattoos covering every visible part of her. An artistic balance of what looked like tribal patterns and unfamiliar birds were crafted together over her skin. The recruits were mesmerized by the way her tattoos reacted to the lights in the ceiling. As Candelle moved, her tattoos glowed. The closer to any light source, the brighter they shimmered, like butterfly wings struck by lightning. Every tribal portion of her tattoos was black, but they shimmered electric greens and yellows. It was hard to look away from her body.

Gideon was surprised and impressed that Master Mackel Brawd had such an alternative-styled wife when he gave off such a strong conservative impression.

Candelle put the game piece down and looked at the recruits' reactions to her home away from home. "So, this is it. Home, savory home."

"Alone?" Izzy asked.

"Oh. No." Candelle waved her hand. "There are six of us on the Wall right now. The others are off mapping. We really don't see each other very often." She leaned forward and spoke with some feisty undertones. "But when we do, we have fun." She pointed to the messy table. "Add some strong malt to sazeal juice and you're going to have an unforgettably good night beneath the stars…that you're probably actually going to forget." She chuckled with a flare in her eyes.

Cooby sniffed the air. Once he realized he was in a safe environment, he climbed down Dumakleiza and started exploring the large one-room shack. He crawled around the floor, skulking like a fuzzy spider as his nose processed the new smells.

"What is sazeal?" Gideon asked.

Master Brawd pointed out of a window. "The trees. The fruit is the only food native to the Wall, and it's fully comprehensive."

"What do you mean?" Gideon wanted to try one.

"Sazeal has a full spectrum of vitamins, carbohydrates, proteins, and a lot more. I'm not very knowledgeable on the details, but apparently they're all you need. Unlike planetary fruit, it doesn't cause digestive issues if consumed in high quantities, and if eaten without any other food, it sustains life without any negative side effects, at least none we've noticed. Their existence makes me wonder about intelligent design."

"That's crazy," Gideon remarked. "How do they taste? What about water?"

"Uh." Candelle tilted her head side to side. "They're sweet but not overly. They're kind of sour. And rich. Bitter at times. Sometimes they taste kind of meaty." She chuckled. "It's hard to explain unless you've eaten one. Just another unexplainable part of the Wall. It's strange not having variety, but they can be prepared in a variety of ways to keep me sane for a while. And their juice keeps us well hydrated, but I definitely need to visit a habitable now and then just to submerge my head in water and drink my weight's worth."

"Okay, I have a question," Gideon said. "How are there trees here if you can't dig any deeper than eighteen inches? How are their roots able to take hold and create tall trees? Do *they* have the ability to go deeper?"

"Yes," Candelle said plainly. "The black bead allows the roots deeper into the soil. We've tried manipulating prosthetic replication, leveraging it, but nothing we do can duplicate it. We can't dig deeper, we can't dig with the roots, nothing we've tried can mimic it, and once we uproot a tree, the black bead seals up where the roots were, and the ground is immediately impenetrable." She shrugged, uncaring about the debilitating truth. "There's no doubt in my mind. The Wall is infinitely beyond our understanding and even further from our control. It has its way of life, and there's nothing we can do to have any effect on it. We're just guests here. We can't even get any other kind of plant seed to take in the black bead."

"So," Izzy brainstormed, "if there are such limited resources on the Wall, why not program an unmanned vessel to carry supplies from Whewliss to here? I know it's an outdated technology but—"

"We have." Master Brawd's answer turned some quizzical looks his way. "After a short while here, we decided to resort back to the spaceships we had originally designed to explore the third phase. We rebuilt three of them. The Roshik, the Whewlaw, and the Dianaise. We stocked them full of supplies. They are juggernauts of cargo ships we designed to carry mass amounts of provisions. They're filled with raw building materials, equipment, tools, defensive weaponry, and enough supplies to create a small settlement as technologically advanced as Whewliss was thirty-six-years ago."

Gideon smirked. "You're planning on designing an outpost here based off an older Whewlight era?"

Traveler answered for Master Brawd. "Gideon, why would a spaceship bring technologies from thirty-six-years ago through space, all the way to the Wall?"

Gideon closed his eyes with a mortified smile. "Because it was *sent* thirty-six-years ago."

"Correct," Traveler said proudly. A few of the recruits' eyes widened at the answer. Traveler went on. "The ships are estimated to arrive in another twenty years. Their mission isn't our primary objective, but when the day comes that they actually get here, it'll be a luxury to have all that they provide available on the Wall."

"Wow." Izzy shook his head and looked at Timrekka, only to see the same flabbergasted appreciation for the vastness of the universe. "That's fun to think about."

"The supplies won't be *too* primitive," Master Brawd said. "They mostly have raw materials like steel, other wood types, and—"

"Boring!" Candelle yelled out. "They do that all the time, don't they?" She pointed at Master Brawd and Traveler, directing her question to the recruits. "Just yapping on and on about stuff and how it works. Such. A. Waste. Of. Time." She gave a playful wink to Master Brawd, who glared in response. "They love bragging about how much they know to aliens from younger worlds." She scoffed. "Who cares about stuff that will be fifty-years-old when it gets here? Let's talk about the future." She shone an animated smile at the recruits. "Do you want to go see the fourth phase?"

"Yes!" Gideon answered, almost running for the door.

"Yes. Let's go see this thing," Jasss said impatiently.

Timrekka's and Izzy's minds were already spinning, making scientific conjectures and theses about what could possibly be. Based on everything they'd just learned about the Wall, all sorts of new ideas were springing up in their minds. There had to be some clues or subtle scientific facts that could give them insight into what the fourth phase was.

Tsuna leaned against the doorway with reluctant participation. He'd just wanted to be outside ever since they'd stepped foot into the shack. The Wall Posts were a disgrace to the purity of the Wall.

Dumakleiza nodded. "I would like the mystery torn asunder, that I may finally see the phase of four." She clicked her tongue, motioning for Cooby to return to her so they could be ready.

"That's what I want to hear," Candelle said. "Mackel can bore you with stories of archaic spaceships another time." She walked over to a small desk and opened a small wooden case. "Come grab a headlight and let's go."

Everyone grabbed a headlight, strapped the small elastic bands around their foreheads, and followed Candelle outside into the darkness of the Wall. The elastic seemed a little outdated for Whewlight technology, but the lights that fitted into them were glowing marbles. Gideon wasn't sure how they worked or what powered them, but they were impressively bright.

The recruits couldn't help aiming the small, quarter-sized lights at Candelle as they walked. It was mesmerizing to watch the way her tattoos reacted with dancing sparkles. The lights were powerful enough to illuminate the blackness of the woods around them, and it gave the Wall an eerier look. The strange trees and their vibrant leaves gave neon flashes whenever shined upon, casting deep shadows, like black souls stretching out behind them. They were all but expecting to see the reflective eyes of an alien predator lurking in the darkness. There were no crickets, no late-night chirping birds, no rustling in the distance, no breeze, nothing. They were bathed in silence. The only sounds were their feet lightly crunching the endless black bead and their anxious breathing.

The recruits were so desperate to finally see what the fourth phase was that not even Gideon was talking. They kept their lights and eyes ahead of them, trying to see what they were walking toward, trying to predict, to anticipate. Nothing looked any different than anywhere else on the Wall. Every step they took, there were just more trees, more fruit, more black bead, more stars shining down upon them.

"Fun fact," Candelle said as she led them through the Wall's forest. "Since the Wall is endless, it's theoretically visible from any part of any planet in the universe." She glanced back to see expected confused expressions. "Due to every world being spherical, it's always possible to look in the direction of the Wall. There's always an angle. It's obviously too far away to actually see, but you're able to look in the right direction, regardless. Cool, huh?"

Gideon smiled, starry-eyed. "That's really cool, actually."

"No," Tsuna said. "You fail to consider canyons, tall treed woods, mountainous valleys, city buildings blocking views." He shook his head. "Not a fact at all."

"Oh, good." Candelle grabbed Tsuna and shoved her face into his personal space. "They have someone like *you* around. That'll make the trip super fun!" She released his bewildered expression and continued forth.

Gideon walked up closer to her. "That's kind of blowing my mind— along with everything else here."

Candelle nodded. "And depending on the current rotation of the planet, you could stare up into the sky and technically be facing nothing but the Wall."

Gideon's eyebrows rose. "That's kind of terrifying, actually." He mulled it over. "And since we've been raised thinking spherically, the whole concept of staring at something eternally flat is nearly impossible to fathom."

"Exactly. Without experiencing it, our minds have trouble comprehending or even imagining what it's like. It's simply not in our conceptual vernacular." Candelle smiled. "Sometimes I climb up on top of one of the Wall Posts and lie on my back. I like turning my head side to side and staring at the never-ending Wall one way and then the other. It kind of makes me dizzy the more I lay there and think about it. It's like a drug, mind-expanding and brilliant."

"I want to try that." Gideon stared up at the stars, imagining lying on the ground back on Earth and stargazing. He felt lightheaded as he tried to wrap his mind around the concept of the Wall. He'd had more than an hour to accept it as fact, but it still didn't feel real. He salivated at the thought of all the late-night philosophical conversations that could be had about it, all the what-ifs. "You guys have had decades to wonder about this." Gideon shook his head while his eyes searched the heavens above. "I can only imagine all of the theories you've got." He directed a playful look toward Traveler. "I wanna know all of your what-if talks you've had about the Wall."

Candelle nodded as they continued walking. "There have been quite a few books written about it, some about the facts we know, some theoretical, others fictitious."

"What about movies?"

Candelle scrunched her nose for a second and then nodded. "Right, you're from Earth, aren't you?" Gideon nodded. "Relatable," Candelle said. "Whewliss has similar entertainment in our virtual reality rooms. Basically a massive, three-dimensionally immersive experience, where you're submersed in the story all around you. You'll never care about movies again after you've been to one of them. And yes, there have been plenty made about the Wall. The public knows about the Wall but not about the rest."

"Oh, that's so cool." Gideon's walking almost turned into skipping. "I can picture it now." He held his hands out in front of himself, deepening his tone as he did his best to mimic the movie man voice. "This summer, the Wall is the edge of space—the edge of *the universe*. But —" He paused dramatically, enjoying himself. "—what is on the other side? Dun, dun, dun!" He chuckled to himself. A few laughs came from the other recruits, but Traveler, Master Brawd, and Candelle all stopped in their tracks. They turned and looked at Gideon with unsettled expressions. They looked scared, unnerved. Candelle's free-spirited energy melted away in an instant.

The recruits stopped to look at their strange behavior, waiting to see what was wrong. Gideon brought his head back, confused by their response to him playing around. Then it clicked. His eyes slowly widened, and his heart began to race.

"How far are we?" His words shot out, no longer playful.

Candelle pointed in the direction they'd been walking. "We're nearly there."

Gideon turned and ran. No fear, no hesitation, just burning curiosity flooding his veins near the point of bursting. He didn't feel his hurtling feet barely making contact with the black bead as he ran pell-mell through the sazeal forest. He didn't hear the cries from Traveler, Master Brawd, and Dumakleiza to stop, slow down, and be careful. He barely heard Candelle yell not to fall down something. All he was focused on was keeping his light aimed ahead. He could feel how close he was to finally seeing what the fourth phase was. After being tortured by answerless mystery, he was going to see what had the most advanced humans in the universe terrified. He was about to understand why they had spent the better part of a century recruiting aliens to do what they dare not. No more waiting. No being cautious. It was time for Gideon to be Gideon and break free from everyone else, go off on his own adventure, and discover for himself.

He reveled in the adrenaline spike of running toward the unknown all alone. It was spiritually liberating. He passed through trees, hurdled over a couple felled tree trunks, and darted under branches, his light flashing all over the Wall.

Then, as Gideon burst through a tight grouping of trees, his eyes shot open at what looked like a massive crater stretching a few hundred feet in diameter. He threw his body down and backward in a desperate attempt to stop before running straight over into free fall. He crashed into the black bead and slid, his hands wildly clawing at the ground to slow his momentum as his feet slid off the edge of the cliff. The ground disappeared out of nowhere. He barely managed to stop in time to have both elbows and arms frantically gripping the ledge as the rest of his body dangled over nothingness. In a moment of panic, Gideon managed to look down to see what was beneath him. There was an almost nonexistent flash of white light in his peripherals that faded away and disappeared. All he saw beneath him was darkness.

It looked to be a bottomless pit, vast, black, at least three-hundred-feet across. At first glance, it seemed to be a perfect circle. At least that's the best he could make out with the limited light shining across the black abyss from his forehead light. He groaned and strained as he pulled with all his strength, dragging his body back up. There it was again, another flash of white light spreading as he moved. It dissipated into nothing. It looked like an electric pulse or something. He wasn't focused on it. He squinted, confused, and then continued pulling himself up. His forehead beaded with sweat. His heart was beating out of his chest and his muscles burned, but after a few struggling pulls, he rolled up over the edge. He quickly scooted away from the cliff, his breath pouring from his lips. There was a near-death smile plastered to his face.

"Sir Gideon!" Dumakleiza yelled out as Gideon saw their array of lights approaching in the darkness.

"Gideon!" Traveler screamed, not seeing him anywhere.

"I'm over here!" Gideon yelled with a joyful tone. "Watch your step. There's a hole!"

The group quickly caught up, their lights beaming straight at him. They stopped once they realized he was okay, a couple of them catching their breath in relief. Dumakleiza dropped down and punched Gideon square in the jaw, knocking him back down to the black bead.

"How dare you worry me with such reckless abandon! I could not aid you if fearlessness claimed your life!" She roared as she threw her arms around him, holding him against her chest. Gideon's eyes were wide open in surprise and pain as he smiled. He gave a quick, reassuring hug back.

"I'm sorry." He shook his head and moved his jaw around, wincing at the sting. Before he could recover, two strong hands sternly grabbed around his shoulders and yanked him into the air. Master Brawd glared at him with furious authority.

"Get ahold of yourself." His gritty tone growled the instruction into Gideon's face without a fiber of pity. He squeezed tighter, making Gideon whimper at the cut on his shoulder. "You want to be reckless? Fine. You're off team. If you want to learn how to explore the fourth phase *with* your team's best interest in mind, you're on team. It's that simple. If you endanger a single person from here on out, I will personally send you back to Earth and leave you there." He pulled Gideon closer, so his words could literally hit him in the face. "You are not special to me. You are not irreplaceable. You're not here for your personality, and who you are inside will not guarantee your involvement. You are qualified. That's it. I will scrap this entire project if I deem the team unworthy, and we will start at the beginning, recruiting replacements. Do you understand?" He glared so deep into Gideon's eyes that Gideon was momentarily shaken from his usual response to threats.

Traveler froze at the idea of losing his favorite recruit. Gideon's wildness was constant, but in every previous situation, he'd managed to chinwag his way out of it. He knew it wouldn't be that easy with Master Brawd. He knew for an absolute fact that Master Brawd had meant what he'd said about banishing Gideon from the mission at the slightest slipup. Traveler prayed Gideon would muster a respectful response.

Gideon sighed. He also knew he was in too deep with everyone involved to simply talk his way out of their bad graces. It would have to be earned. He also knew that once they began the fourth phase, they would have to operate as a unit, something else he didn't prefer. He'd much rather go on his own and feel free to adventure, but that wasn't an option. He slowly nodded in Master Brawd's vice grip.

"Yes, sir. I apologize," he said as calmly as he could. Master Brawd's glare didn't falter. He stared at Gideon, forcing his lecture to further absorb. Gideon understood. He'd apologized, but that wasn't enough. However, there were questions that needed answering. He impatiently waited for Master Brawd to place him back down on his feet. "What is that?" He looked at the massive chasm.

Everyone shone their forehead lights at the crater. They paused, staring at the enormous void in the otherwise unvarying flatness of the edge of space. The descending walls looked like calcified black bead, multi-colored chemical deposits creating a more stone-like surface on the way down. The nine of them leaned forward, trying to see how far down the hole went, but the bottom wasn't visible. Their lighted vision disappeared farther and farther down, shining on nothing as the void swallowed into blackness.

Candelle squatted down and grabbed a handful of black bead. She held it for a moment, some loose grains spilling between her fingers. She waited until everyone curiously looked at her. She tossed the handful out over the chasm.

As the hundreds of beads rained down, bright white appeared out of nowhere. Ripples of light spread, like pebbles thrown into a pond. It was as if there was a flat, unseen surface spreading over the entire crater. Hundreds of small currents continued spreading and fading as the white circles thinned farther and farther out. The recruits' eyes peeled open as they stared at what looked like a magical forcefield blanketing the pit. Then, as soon as the ripples had appeared, they dissipated into nothing, leaving the recruits in darkness once more.

Gideon leaned forward, shining his light down the hole as he tried to see the surface Candelle disrupted. There was nothing. Once again, it looked like nothing more than a giant, bottomless chasm.

Dumakleiza's eyes were wide open. "Is this devilry more of your science?"

Gideon glanced at her and shrugged, honestly unsure.

"Oh, lover," Tsuna said to the hole as he squatted down, his eyes feasting on the anomaly, "you are a beauty to behold."

"Is it some kind of portal?" Izzy asked. He knew portals were conjectural, but what he'd just witnessed flirted with the impossible.

Timrekka was silent as his magnified eyes darted around, searching the hole for any clues or scientific giveaways. Jasss, too, was quiet, fear gripping her throat as she struggled to swallow her nerves.

Gideon brainstormed as he stared into the abyss. He'd almost fallen down it, and he knew his body had disrupted the ripples. After a millisecond of considering the consequences, he walked forward and knelt by the cliff's edge, reaching his hand below the nonexistent surface.

He didn't feel anything, but his eyes lit up in wonder. Sure enough, bright light mimicked ripples in broken water, spreading around his wrist. The other recruits gasped, unnerved by the unknown, wondering if Gideon's arm would burn off or if something would emerge to drag him down.

Nothing happened.

Gideon stared at his hand with uncertainty. He hadn't felt anything happen. There was no physical surface he'd breached. He didn't even feel any shift in energy, no electric shock, not the faintest sensation. It was like his eyes were playing tricks on him. He waved his hand around, watching more light ripples spread like water.

Candelle stared into the darkness with quickened breaths. "Welcome to the fourth phase."

12

"This is the fourth phase?" Tsuna asked with a disappointed slump. "A big hole in the ground?"

"Yes," Master Brawd stated with outright reverence as he peered deep into the blackness below. The hefty Whewlight felt just as insignificant and exposed as the rest of them as he gaped.

Tsuna shook his head. "What a boring end to an already dull journey."

The other recruits ignored him as they stared down the pit. Its murkiness was consuming, as if something somewhere deep down within it was staring back up at them. Everyone stood in silence. After all the buildup, all of the clandestine mysticism, after all of the waiting and the unknown, finding themselves face-to-face with a giant black hole in the edge of the universe had them feeling tiny, powerless, and vulnerable. Gravity was feeling less relative and more theoretical as their grip on reality sputtered.

Timrekka was the first to shake free of his stupor. "What was the light?" He blinked, shaking his head. He had to keep recalibrating his mind. "I don't see any water."

Traveler responded since Master Brawd and Candelle weren't paying attention, distracted by the ominous pit drawing their souls downward. "I'm afraid—" He paused. "—that this is where we run out of answers."

"You mean—"

"—that we don'tknow what the light is. We only know some of what happens when we pass beneath it."

Gideon glanced back at the hole. "I slipped and almost fell down it. The light ripples were maybe up to my chest, and nothing happened to me." He was suddenly curious if he was going to experience some side effects. Maybe he'd acquired superpowers.

"Oh, good," Traveler said in relief. "At least your head didn't — Tsuna, don't!"

Everyone turned to see Tsuna on his belly at the edge, dipping his head beneath the ripples. White circles of light spread from his face as he breached the unseen surface. He stared deeper into the darkness beneath, cocking his head. He thought he heard something: a voice. It sent chills down his spine. He couldn't understand what it —

"Tsuna!" Master Brawd barked. "Stand up!"

Tsuna rolled his eyes at all the hollering. He didn't feel anything different after submerging his head, at least nothing physical. But did he hear something? He wasn't sure. Nothing bad had happened, though. He retracted himself, sneering at Master Brawd.

"What?" he yelled, irritated that his intimate moment had been interrupted. Then, as he stood up to spit foul distaste, he stopped, squinted, and looked around, confused.

"Tsuna, what's wrong with you now?" Izzy asked.

"What?" Tsuna's helpless tone worried the other recruits. He looked fine. Nothing appeared out of place or affected by the white ripples, but he was acting like he didn't know what was going on.

Master Brawd shook his head. "Religious imbecile. Our implants don't work inside the hole. In fact, they're permanently disabled once they enter." He nodded to Candelle and then turned back to the recruits. "Tsuna's translator is done. He can't understand what anyone is saying."

Candelle walked over to Tsuna. It wasn't the first time she'd seen the fear—the sudden fear of everything after experiencing the ripples. She pointed into his ear and shook her head. There was no point in trying to explain anything verbally.

Tsuna blinked a few times, trying to figure out what had happened. He suddenly felt very alone on the Wall. Candelle gave a comforting smile and then led the priest back to the Wall Post so she could replace his translator.

As soon as they walked away, the other recruits had a plethora of new questions. Master Brawd and Traveler had been anticipating them. Five pairs of impatient eyes begged them for answers, and they could only provide so many.

Master Brawd stepped past them and peered down into the darkness. "When we first stumbled upon the hole, one of our observers climbed down beneath the ripples. Fully submerged. His finger light implant immediately turned off and wouldn't turn back on. He climbed out to see what had malfunctioned to perform repairs, only to discover that every single one of his implants had stopped working. They weren't broken, they weren't fried, there was nothing physically wrong with them. They simply wouldn't work. Nothing electrically powered works beneath the ripples."

Izzy and Timrekka immediately stepped closer to the edge to take a better look. Their fears were momentarily cast aside, replaced with intrigue. They silently asked the same questions, hoping to arrive at a theory before the other.

Timrekka adjusted his goggles. "Is there some kind of electromagnetic pu—"

"No," Master Brawd interrupted him, knowing where his question was heading. "There's nothing. There's no readable energy of any kind. There's literally nothing quantifiable in any form aside from visual light. There's no climate change, no variation in temperature, there's nothing measurable to explain why none of our technology functions below the surface—nothing that we can detect, and believe me, we've exhausted our resources in an effort to understand it."

Timrekka toyed with curiosity. "Since I don't have any of your implants in my hand, is it okay for me to stick it in? I want to experience it for myself, unless of course you think something bad will happen to me." He cringed at self-made fears. "I just want to understand it."

Izzy nodded, wanting to get his hands dirty, too. "Yes, should we? Or is it ill-advised?"

Master Brawd motioned toward the abyss. "Right now the only parts of you that would be adversely affected would be your ears and eyes. Your translators and contacts would be permanently deactivated. Your suits are fine, your light cells are fine, and the rest of you, as far as we know, won't experience anything bad——or good. You should feel nothing."

Timrekka and Izzy knelt at the edge. They looked at each other, challenging the other to back away from nerves, but they were both too curious. They reached their hands down into the barren dark. White ripples spread as their fingers entered, flowing away like beautiful water. Neither of them felt anything anomalous. Their minds were abuzz with unsatisfied expectation. Seeing the light flow away from them demanded that they feel something, but they didn't.

Gideon blew an embarrassed raspberry through tight lips, ashamed he hadn't leapt to join the scientists. He stepped over and dropped down next to Timrekka, instantly plunging his whole arm through the nonexistent surface. Just like water, the ripples expanded in thicker waves due to how quickly he'd reached through. They even responded to each other, one set of ripples bouncing off another.

Dumakleiza and Jasss tentatively approached the edge, hesitant to join the boys in their hasty interaction with the unknown. Slowly, unsurely, defensively, they squatted down next to Gideon and Izzy. They stayed on their feet rather than their knees, as their instincts warned them to be prepared to run, something none of the men seemed to care about. They kept pace with each other, starting with one finger. They dipped their indexes into the surface and watched as small ripples spread.

Jasss was instantly on edge, worried about the consequences of meddling with powers beyond understanding. Dumakleiza, on the other hand, stared in wide-eyed wonder. Her dragon eye reflected like purple fire, relishing in the dark, peering into the blackness, hoping maybe she'd have an advantage and see something no one else could. Cooby watched over her shoulder, holding tightly. His animalistic instincts warned of danger he didn't understand.

Timrekka's eyes widened as he jumped to his feet in a fluster of concern. "Wait, how are we supposed to go into this if we all speak different languages and our translators will be useless?" He looked around at the other recruits, hoping not to lose communication with them. "And do you have any idea what the internal makeup of this hole is, like how deep it goes, or have you dropped a light down it to see if it is bottomless?"

As if he'd anticipated all of the questions, Master Brawd reached up and pulled the small light ball out of his headband. It glowed brightly in all directions once removed, like a marble of pure light. Master Brawd stepped over to the edge and waited for the recruits to step up on either side of him.

Gideon was practically leaning over the ledge, flirting with the fall. His toes extended beyond the cliff's lip, tempting fate or a surprise breeze to push him over. The other four were cautiously about a foot away, leaning over just enough to see. Traveler slowly stepped up behind them, more interested in reading their responses than seeing the demonstration again.

Master Brawd spoke slow and calm. "This is all we know about the internal structure of the fourth phase." He squeezed the small battery-powered sphere of light. As if he flipped a switch, it glowed brighter. Master Brawd continued squeezing, upping the wattage output. The recruits all squinted, Dumakleiza covering her throbbing dragon eye. Master Brawd kept squeezing it until the light was nearly blinding. Once it was as bright as he could get it, he dropped the ball into the hole.

The recruits blinked furiously as they looked over the edge. It took a moment to dilate back to the darkness, but their eyes finally managed to fixate on it. They watched as the wall of the hole was illuminated lower and lower. Ten seconds went by. Fifteen. Twenty. It continued falling, beginning to dull the farther down it went.

Then, barely observable at the depth, they saw it bounce and jog left. Their eyes tried to follow as the light faded into some kind of tunneling curve deep within the bowels of the abyss.

Gideon kept his eyes peeled in case he managed to see anything else. "Where did it go?"

"We don't know," Master Brawd said with frustrated honesty. "That's why you're here." He stared out over the crater. "And while we have no ability to dig through the black bead, periodically we'll find that the hole widens. We've never witnessed it, but since we first discovered the hole, it—it almost appears as if something has dug it wider. But once again, it could just be randomly crumbling as any rock does. But it's bizarre since we can't dig it ourselves. Begs the question how the hole came to be in the first place."

Gideon squinted at him with adventurous hunger. "What do you think's down there?"

"Maybe nothing," Master Brawd said. "Perhaps it's just a dead end, a deep tunnel in the impenetrable edge of space. The only one we've found over trillions of square miles."

"Right." Gideon shrugged. "Or?"

"Or——" Master Brawd hesitated. "——perhaps it leads somewhere. Maybe the afterlife exists beyond the Wall—another plane of existence altogether. Our astrophysicists have hypothesized numerous dimensions we wouldn't be able to understand, even if we explored down the hole, impossibly advanced beyond our three-dimensional existence, and that's why nothing electrically powered functions below the ripples. Perhaps heaven, maybe hell, another universe altogether, and those ripples are the portal. There could be life forms down there, living within the Wall. Maybe Homo sapiens, maybe somethingelse, maybe nothing. There have been countless theories and guesses, and we're tired of wondering. We're tired of being scared of what *could be* out there. We want to know what *is*." Master Brawd looked to Gideon. "First impression, what would you guess is down there?"

Gideon's eyes widened. "Uh." He glanced from Master Brawd to Traveler, then to Dumakleiza and Timrekka. "Maybe Jesus, Buddha, and Grimleck in lab coats playing with beakers and microscopes." He scoffed and thought about a real guess. "I don't know." He peered back down over the edge. "But whatever's down there, beyond the edge of space, if there's anything at all, is either something we were never meant to see or our ultimate destiny that our very souls are fated to discover."

Traveler silently smiled with pride at Gideon's answer. He'd been keeping to himself so that Master Brawd could lead the way, but he was itching to get involved. It was relieving to have Gideon redeem himself a little by showing that he was more than just an adrenaline junky. There was depth to Gideon that he didn't always let others see. Traveler wanted to sit on the edge of the hole with him, their feet dangling in as if they were relaxing at a pond's edge, and just talk. It was a strange feeling to simply want a heart-to-heart with his best friend. He still wasn't accustomed to the idea of having friends, let alone a best one.

While Master Brawd nodded, agreeing with Gideon's answer, Timrekka inched a little closer. He needed more answers as his questions compounded upon themselves, but he was nervous about overstepping his bounds with interruptions.

"Uh, have you tried lowering whatever form of recording devices Whewlights have on a rope or anything, or do they not work either?"

Master Brawd finally brought his eyes away from the hole. "Electrically powered items don't work. Battery powered items sort of do. Anything with its own independent power source functions in the hole the same way it does outside of it, except the battery life is much shorter. The hole drains battery faster than we've ever seen."

Timrekka's eyes lit up at the answer. "So, we *can* lower a recording device down the —"

"We have." Master Brawd cut him off. "They manage to function for a short time with their own power source, but they come back having only recorded static. There is some unexplainable interference right below the —"

"—ripples." Timrekka finished the statement with a hauntingly curious tone. As he mulled it all over, he slowly nodded. "I see why you're afraid of it, why no one's gone down. It's a huge black pit in the edge of space, which is already impossible to explain or understand, with an invisible surface that defies the thin veil between science and magic, and either nature or a deity has created a gate that you must pass through in order to explore it, and no manmade technology works down it, and you don't know what's down there, possibly nothing, possibly another side, possibly something spiritual, possibly something we're not even guessing." He sighed. "I admit I am feeling quite small. I admit that I, too, am scared of going down there."

"How long will that ball you dropped glow down there before it stops working?" Gideon asked.

Master Brawd shrugged. "From what we've measured, our best guess is minutes. Outside of the hole, those lights last decades."

"Wow." Gideon nodded. "Yeah, that's a little shorter." He chuckled. "So, how are we supposed to see when we go down there?" He looked to Master Brawd. "What if it's a long journey? Like, say, for the sake of argument, a year. How are we supposed to see? I'm assuming it's pitch black down there."

Master Brawd shrugged. "We don't know."

Timrekka wasted no time. "I'll start looking for the missing pieces to that puzzle."

Izzy nodded. "I'll help." He smiled, keen on buddying up.

"Oh, this will be fun!" Timrekka exclaimed, suddenly realizing how happy he was not being the only mad scientist.

Dumakleiza timidly leaned over next to Traveler. "What am *I* to do? I feel as though I misjudged my purpose coming here."

Traveler looked at her for a moment, unsure of why her question had struck him the way it had. He felt strangely protective, especially since she was the least technologically developed. The realization hit him like a cold wind. It was the first time he'd felt they were equal in their raw vulnerability and lack of understanding. Thousands of years of human development separated them, and yet, there on the Wall, staring down the fourth phase, they were the same. He gave a warm, understanding smile.

"I know you're afraid. We all are. It's why we're here, and especially why *you* are here." He thought for a moment. "Your purpose here isn't to build anything or lead the charge. The entire reason you and Tsuna were recruited is because you are the souls of this journey—though, in my estimation, you're the only soul worth anything. You're the heart. All we ask of you is that you pray." Dumakleiza's chest deflated at the comforting instruction. Traveler maintained his smile. "I'm not a spiritual man. Well, I'm open, but I'm unsure. But whether or not you're right about *who*God is, you are at least absolutely certain that there is a god. That's a hope that we will likely need in the darkness. When our fear takes hold, and I guarantee it will, especially mine, we're going to need you as a pillar of faith to guide our souls through what we don't understand." He stared off. "It's been said that the more technology advances, religion becomes an insurance policy."

"What does this mean?"

"Means that the more we can prove, the less we believe." Traveler looked to Dumakleiza. "I find comfort in knowing you're not religious but faithful."

Dumakleiza smiled as she recognized Traveler beginning to care for her. "I will pray without ceasing, Diviner." She tried to conceal her cracking vulnerability. "Grimleck has been my light in the dark. I am happy to know I am no longer the only one his winged warriors protects."

Traveler blinked a few times, the gravity of what was to come finally hitting him. "Thank you, Duma" He shook his head. "Sorry. Dumakleiza."

"No," Dumakleiza replied with a warmer tone. "Our journey has brought us far. I wish for you to call me Duma." They smiled at each other.

"So," Gideon's loud voice disrupted their moment as he looked at Master Brawd. "You never told us how we're supposed to communicate with each other down there once our translators go out. Won't we just be seven aliens from separate worlds making weird whistles and clicks?"

"Yes," Master Brawd answered. "That is one of the primary preparations that needs to be practiced. Once you were approved as recruits, Whewlight translation books were printed in each of your native tongues. They're back at the Wall Post. You will each need to study them thoroughly and master them before you go down since you likely won't be able to read them in the darkness."

Gideon's eyebrows rose. "You want us to master an entire language before we go down there?"

"Much of it, yes. It may take months or years, but you've been introduced to light. You have time. You don't have to be fluent, but the closer to fluent you are, the better chance you'll have in communicating efficiently. Once you return from your venture, new translators will be implanted, and life will resume as it does now."

"Wow." Gideon shook his head. "That's quite the task. Okay, so we need to go back to the Wall Post, study and master Whewlight translation, try and figure out a permanent, portable light source, pack a few hundred sack lunches, grab some climbing gear, and then we're ready to go?"

"Minus a few more preparatory tasks, yes."

Dumakleiza's eyes widened as she thought about learning a second language for the first time. Back on Cul, she'd never needed to. The only communicating she'd done with people from other parts of her world was shooting flaming arrows at them. She gulped down some nerves and looked at Traveler.

"And what is Sir Gideon's purpose in the phase of four?"

Traveler chuckled. "To stay crazy."

13

Everyone sat together inside one of the Wall Posts. They'd been given their personalized Whewlight translation books and were leafing through the pages to get a feel for the task.

It was rare for Gideon to be able to focus on something as simple as reading for more than five minutes, but the prospect of learning an alien language was actually pretty cool the more he thought about it. He was completely immersed. Every word he read in English was followed by a translation broken down into English sounds. The fact that alien worlds existed and that he could visit them had sunken in. He'd accepted it, and it was part of his reality, but for some reason, learning one of their native tongues stirred the mystery and wonder of it all over again.

Dumakleiza was doing her best to make sense of the book. Even the quality of its structure impressed her. She wasn't familiar with books back on Cul. They had some scrolls, but nothing of the extensive magnitude held within the thin pages in her hands. She kept finding herself blinking, forcing her mind to focus on what seemed impossible. She heard Cooby screaming outside as he ran off his energy, leaping into the sazeal trees and coasting through the air. The louder and happier his cries, the more Dumakleiza wanted to put the book down and go explore with him. She was a little worried that he may try to leap up and inadvertently find himself suffocating outside of the atmosphere. He probably couldn't with how high it was from the treetops. It should be out of reach, but the anxiety remained. It took everything in her to sit and focus. She refused to head down the pit and be the least able to communicate. She already felt like the group's outsider, and that would only exclude her further. She was going to master the book and be the most fluent in this Whewlight language.

Timrekka and Izzy were sitting in a corner. They'd flipped through their books and then shelved them for later study. They were whispering ideas about the fourth phase's expedition, both eager to experiment and invent something helpful. Their previously silent conversation was gradually growing louder as they thought of something. Izzy got up and ran around, scrambling for a piece of scrap paper as Timrekka looked for a writing utensil.

Master Brawd, Traveler, and Candelle walked inside, appearing somewhat spooked. The recruits looked up to see them talking quietly amongst themselves.

Gideon studied Traveler specifically. He had gotten to know the Spaceman well enough to recognize his expressions. Traveler only got that lost look when there was something he didn't understand on a bigger scale. Gideon set his book down and stood. He waited until the hush-hush conversation was done and then made his way over. He heard the words "Tsuna" and "child's voice" repeated as he approached. As soon as they noticed him, they stopped talking. Master Brawd looked to Gideon and then at everyone else awkwardly staring.

"How are your translation books?"

"Good," Gideon dismissed. "How's Tsuna?"

"He's repaired," Master Brawd answered. "His translator has been replaced." Whatever they weren't telling the recruits, they weren't even making much of an effort to hide it.

Master Brawd, Traveler, and Candelle awkwardly stood there for a moment and then dispersed, heading off to do remedial tasks while the recruits studied. Gideon squinted. He enjoyed playing detective. He stepped through outside and looked around.

It was surreal to step back into a night setting. He didn't know exactly how long they'd been inside reading, but it felt like it had been a few hours. He was internally programmed to expect a difference in lighting, seeing at least pretenses for a rising sun. But not on the Wall, not where it was always night. He assumed it would get old, that he'd eventually long for the day, but for the time being, he enjoyed it. It felt like a true escape, which was all he ever really desired. He looked around, appreciating the darkness of the sazeal trees, lit only by the windows and looming ocean of stars. He immediately wondered a plethora of Wall-specific questions that didn't really matter but would be fun to figure out. How far could he run there before he tired? What direction would a compass aim? Other than peeing on a random tree, where did the Whewlights go to the bathroom? He chuckled to himself, knowing that some of the other recruits might be too ashamed to ask outright. He'd already used a couple sazeal trees.

A loud scream from an exuberant Cooby caught his attention as the large fur ball leapt between trees somewhere nearby. His jolly squall echoed across the Wall as branches and leaves rustled. Gideon smiled. He couldn't see the tanion, but he could imagine the mad expression of happiness on its fuzzy face.

Gideon took a few steps away from the building as he heard some quiet mumbling. He strained his eyes, trying to see in the blackness. It dawned on him that he could change the brightness through his contacts. The convenience was still unversed. After a little adjusting, he saw Tsuna sitting in the black bead a ways away from the Wall Post. Gideon smiled and took a jaunty walk over to him.

"Tsuna? Can you understand me?"

Tsuna jerked his head up and glared at Gideon somewhat fearfully. "Yes." His chest deflated at the familiar face. "I have a new translator." His rattled eyes aimlessly wandered away.

Gideon nodded and sat down against a tree a few feet away from him. "That was pretty crazy what happened at the hole. How are you feeling?"

Tsuna's eyes refocused on the ground. He dug his fingers into the black bead and grabbed a handful, submerging it up to the wrist. The instant he had a grip of dirt, he seemed to calm a little.

"I don't—" Tsuna struggled to organize his thoughts. "I do not believe we are meant to go down into the Wall. She doesn't want us there."

Gideon was intrigued. "What happened? Did you see something?"

Tsuna shook his head. "I heard a voice."

"A voice?" Gideon leaned closer. "Like someone down at the bottom?"

Tsuna shook his head again. "It was all around me. Coming from all around me, like I was submerged under water, and the water was a voice, a whisper. It wasn't an echo. It was just...everywhere."

Gideon's mind buzzed. "What did it say?"

Tsuna blinked a few times, his eyes darting around. "It greeted me."

"Hmm." Gideon puffed out his bottom lip. "Simple enough. I wonder how it—wait." He looked at Tsuna. "Your translator was broken, and you understood what the voice said?"

Tsuna nodded. "It wasn't in my language. I didn't recognizethe words, but I understood it. I felt it."

Gideon sat still for a moment, trying to figure out what he meant. "Okay. Was it a scary voice or something?" He wanted to understand why it upset Tsuna.

Tsuna shook his head again, squeezing the black bead tighter. "It sounded young, prepubescent." He looked ashamedly at Gideon. "It knew something I didn't. I could feel it. I've never felt—that. Hearing someone I couldn't see as I stared into—" He looked around. "I feel like it's gone now, like it lives in there."

Gideon wasn't sure what to make of it. "I mean no disrespect by the following question, but I'm just unfamiliar with the details of your faith. Don't you normally converse with planets? Or their spirits or however it works?"

Tsuna stared him dead in the eyes. "This wasn't that," he said with absolute confidence. "This was something else." He looked down at the ground, staring through it. "Speaking to the essence of a world takes years of meditation, focus, surrender." He shook his head. "I heard this voice as clearly as I hear yours now." He relived it. "And it didn't come from any one direction. It came from every direction." He shivered and reaffirmed his decision. "I'm not going back down there where that—that thing lives."

Gideon immediately wanted to go dip his head into the hole and see if he could hear anything for himself. He knew Master Brawd would probably get upset for some odd reason and send him back to Earth. He sighed, constipated with curiosity.

"Did it sound threatening?"

Tsuna glared at him. "Listen, Earthling, I know you feel like you're a preordained hero destined to spearhead the fourth phase, surrounded by riches and adoration, and maybe that is written in the heavens for you, but *do not* belittle my fear. Something sinister awaits us, something we are ill-prepared for. I *felt* it." His tone only intrigued Gideon further, but Gideon respectfully listened to the tongue-lashing. "I've been to your world. How can you expect to unite us as a species across the stars when you can't even unite yourselves as a planet?" Tsuna shook his head, done with the conversation. "When you climb down there, you *will* die." Before Gideon could get a word in, Tsuna was already up on his feet, storming away into the sazeal forest.

Gideon nodded and then patted the ground reassuringly. "Hey, I'm sorry you two had a fight," he said to the black bead. "Every couple goes through hard times." He got up. "Personally, I think you need to see other people—maybe a recently single moon or a slutty planet, like Uranus." He chuckled to himself.

Traveler stepped outside, knowing Gideon was about to come find him. He only had to walk a few feet before they made eye contact. Traveler sighed and then walked over. Gideon smirked a sly grin back. He could see the apprehension on Traveler's face.

"How's it hanging, Spaceman?"

Traveler shook his head with a half-assed smile. "Just ask." He stopped a couple feet shy of Gideon to keep the conversation private.

Gideon nodded, happy to see that they were on the same page. "Well, if we're skipping the foreplay, why don't you just explain?"

Traveler looked off in the direction of the hole, gazing through the dark forest. "The observer that went down the pit, the first one down the hole—"

"Yeah?"

"He's the only other one who's ever had their head beneath the ripples."

Gideon slowly nodded as he began to understand. "And let me guess. He heard it, too."

"Indeed," Traveler said softly, as if he was trying to prevent the trees from listening. "We dismissed it as a fluke until we saw how badly it had damaged his sanity. Just another reason we haven't wanted to go down into the hole ourselves. If it's something we hear just beneath the surface, we're worried about what we'll find if we venture to the bottom and whatever lies beyond."

"You have no idea what it is?"

"We know it sounds like a child's voice and that it's everywhere. That's all the observer said. It was documented history, but it's never been paid much mind. However, now that Tsuna reported the exact same experience, there's no ignoring it. Another horror we have to consider and prepare for before we descend."

Gideon scrunched his face. "I always love these talks because you usually teach me something crazy. It's strange having you in the same boat as me. Not sure if I like it." He thought for a moment. "No, I take that back. I like it. It's exciting." He chuckled and looked at Traveler. "So?"

"So what?" Traveler responded, his mind lost in distant thought.

"*So* this is the perfect platform for your favorite game. Don't tell me you don't have one selected what-if question that you favor above the rest."

Traveler exhaled through his nose and tightened his lips. "Right now the only what-if question I can't shake is: What if it's just death? What if I've brought you here for nothing more than a false quest that leads to our immediate demise?"

"Well." Gideon thought for a moment. "According to my favorite movie genre, horror, that would mean that we'd be stuck together for eternity, haunting this place, and you'd neverbe rid of me." He winked.

Traveler chuckled. "A fate worse than death." He laughed a little louder, enjoying releasing the pent-up tension. Everyone else on the Wall shared his fear of the unknown down the hole, so having Gideon's sarcasm was a welcomed relief. "I don't understand how your mind works, but in this *one* instance, it's appreciated."

"I'd be happy to give you a tour sometime."

"I would sooner take one of your wing suits down the fourth phase." They both laughed. Traveler slumped, relieved at the laughter purging the cloud clogging his mind. "I actually have a question I've wanted to know about your superstitions surrounding that."

"Surrounding what?"

"Haunting where you die. You Earthlings obsess over that concept. But if that's true, wouldn't there be dinosaur ghosts literally everywhere?"

Gideon smiled. "I always love talking about dinosaurs with you." Normally he would have explored the concept further, but there were more pressing theories. "So, what do you think the voice in the hole is? A spirit? A demon? God? The voice of the Wall? An actual child stuck down the hole? Should I call Lassie?"

"I don't know. I don't even know what to guess," Traveler said. "I haven't heard it."

"Well, let's go check it out," Gideon said with sudden excitement.

"Absolutely not."

"Why not? We're going to eventually anyway. Why not better acquaint ourselves with it first?" He stared impatiently at Traveler as he mulled it over. "And don't hit me with the 'but our translators' crap." He chuckled. "Bring your little implanter doohickey and just give us new ones after we stick our heads down." He waited as Traveler continued his contemplation. Precious time was being wasted. Gideon leaned forward and smiled. "Unless you're backsliding and going all scaredy cat on me again, *Whewlight*."

Traveler glared at him. "You're supposedto be memorizing your book."

Gideon threw his hands in the air. "Okay. Okay. Okay. I'll go study the book." He started walking toward the Wall Post. "Scared of a child's voice."

Traveler scoffed and shook his head. "Fine. You can study the book in the morning."

"In the morning?" Gideon asked, caught off guard by the comment.

"Yes, in the morning. At first light."

Gideon cracked a smile as he turned and followed Traveler walking toward the hole. "Was that a joke? Did you just make a joke?"

"Shut up. Come on."

"Goober and the Spaceman!" Gideon used his movie man voice again. "Turns out *Spaceman* is the comic relief. Who would've guessed?"

"You're the worst at shutting up." Traveler brushed some large sazeal leaves out of his face.

"Yeah, I failed Shut Up Class three years straight. Got held back. Now I'm just a loud man child that you get to babysit forever."

"Holy spirit, Gideon, *shut up*." Traveler shook his head as they walked on.

Once they reached the crater, they squatted down near the edge. Pitch blackness stared up at them as only the glowing stars battled its consuming gravity. Being surrounded by a dark forest and an even darker pit drew them deeper. From above, the atmosphere's subtle blue tint lightened the mood a little, making them glow as they peered down.

Gideon tossed a small handful of black bead into the giant chasm just to watch the ripples. As they spread, his eyes lit up. It was hypnotic, and he couldn't get enough. He had to know more. After the ripples faded, he looked at Traveler with a hunger for exploration.

"Well, shall we?"

Traveler smiled, unable to deny that he was looking forward to dipping his toe in adventure. "I recruited you to lead, remember?"

Gideon got down to his hands and knees and peered into the blackness, his face mere inches from where he thought the ripples to be. He took a deep breath to psyche himself up and then tilted forward. He blew out his lungful, so he could see the subtle ripples before his face broke the surface.

Traveler tensed as he watched Gideon's head dip below. White ripples spread around it and then faded away. Neither of them made a sound. Gideon tried not to breathe so if even a fly farted, he'd be able to hear it. Traveler's eyes were glued to Gideon's expression, waiting for the faintest shift.

After nothing happening, Traveler's impatience got the best of him. He had to join. He couldn't just be a bystander anymore. After years of fearing the fourth phase, it had boiled down to him squatted down next to one other person. He got to his hands and knees, taking his time, cherishing a moment he knew he'd remember. He took a deep breath, as if he was about to dunk himself in water, and then dipped his head down. There was no pain, no abnormal sensation, nothing noticeable. They both waited and listened, neither breaking the silence.

Out of nowhere, they both felt it: a child's voice, innocuous but resolute, and it was all around them. It was loud, consuming, and yet didn't cause a single ripple to spread. Gideon squinted. Traveler froze. It wasn't a vibration, but it made their skin tingle as it faded away. They instantly knew exactly what Tsuna had meant when he'd said that he couldn't understand its words but that he'd feltwhat it was trying to convey. It sounded like it somehow knew them. It was violating, leaving them vulnerable and exposed.

Traveler's throat tightened. He felt the voice penetrate his mind, like it was staring straight through him. Gideon could feel his heart speeding up, but he wasn't focused on it. He couldn't see anything down the black hole, but it felt like something was watching him. For the first time in a long time, Gideon Green felt fear.

After the voice faded away in a haunting echo, they stayed perfectly still, marinating in the silence that followed. It felt unreal, as though they'd imagined the entire thing. One look at the other's face and they knew they'd both heard it. Something had spoken to them.

Without thinking of possible repercussions, Gideon took a deep breath and broke the silence.

"Hello?" he yelled back into the abyss, his voice echoing down.

Traveler froze with eyes peeled open. He was terrified. What if something answered Gideon's call? What if he'd awakened something? What if it started climbing up the walls of the pit? They'd never see it until it was too late. What if it was already coming? He wasn't sure if he should wait to hear if something responded or if he should get up and run back to the Wall Post as fast as he could. It had four walls and a door. He'd be safe in there, right? It suddenly felt as though no matter where he took refuge, whatever had spoken to them would be able to find him, that whatever it was had his scent, and that there was nothing he could do to hide.

Something answered back.

Something in the deep blackness bellowed up. The voice returned, and Gideon and Traveler both felt it in their bones. It was deeper than before, not a child anymore. It shook their bodies, causing them both to lurch backward. They jerked their heads from the ripples with wild expressions and looked at each other.

"We—" Gideon gasped. He shook his head as his ears rang. "We have to tell them."

14

Dumakleiza and Jasss were the only recruits still studying their books. Jasss had already worked her way through a third of hers. She wasn't focused on memorization so much as seeing if the Whewlights had included any curse words. Dumakleiza was still struggling, but her determination pushed her through page after page. She was going to be fluent. There would be minimal accent, and she'd be able to spout them off without having to search her memory for them. She wanted Traveler to be impressed when she mastered his native tongue.

Timrekka and Izzy had a rough sketch of their concept. They beamed as they double-checked it and scribbled adjustments. They looked up to see Master Brawd holding some game pieces, looking at them as he rolled his fingers around their edges. The dreaded part of his job had arrived: the slow, monotonous waiting around while the recruits studied. The old war hero was bored.

"Excuse me, Master Brawd," Izzy said as he approached. "I think we have a solution for the darkness problem down the hole."

Master Brawd looked up, trying not to roll his eyes at their enthusiasm. "Nothing you can invent will function down there, and fire will eventually burn out, no matter how much fuel we bring."

"It's not something we invented. It's something you invented," Izzy blurted out, unable to contain himself.

"What?" Master Brawd stepped forward. "That *I* invented?"

"That you Whewlights invented," Izzy clarified before smiling at Timrekka, who was practically shaking the paper.

Master Brawd marched two steps up to Timrekka. "What are you talking about?" He snatched the paper from his hands and looked at it. He immediately recognized a rough outline of a Winkloh Star, but the dimensions were all wrong, and there were detailed scribblings in a foreign language. "A Winkloh Star? That would never work down the hole."

Izzy bounced a little, happy to hear Master Brawd respond the way they'd expected. He looked at Timrekka and nodded for him to explain.

Timrekka smiled, allowing Master Brawd's doubt to linger a moment longer. "We knew you'd say that, and you're right, a Winkloh Star would never function down the hole with its sheer mass, and the fragile state of the glass would inevitably shatter at some point; however, if we make a Winkloh Star out of thick, clear rubber, then coat its inner lining with reflective paint and shoot in a small biological lifeform that could fit inside its dimensions as light, then, according to our calculations, it would theoretically hold light in the darkness down the pit in a portable and relatively indestructible package that we could simply strap to one of our backs. No electricity, no battery, just light." Timrekka took a deep breath, replenishing himself after spurting everything out. He hoped he'd explained it thoroughly enough.

Master Brawd's eyes darted around the page, seeing it in a new light. He glared as his mind reactively troubleshot the idea. He took the paper and turned to walk away. They could hear him mumbling ideas under his breath. He opened the Wall Post door with his eyes glued to the drawing.

Timrekka and Izzy glanced at each other, confused by the lack of response.

"Where are you going?" Izzy asked, worried that maybe they'd messed up.

"Sending a message back to EBOO," Master Brawd replied as he walked out. "We need supplies." With that, he closed the door behind him.

"Good job," Izzy said, eagerly shaking Timrekka's arm.

"Timrekka." Dumakleiza's concerned tone interrupted as she marched over. They looked at her with big grins, triumphant, ready for their deserved praise.

"Dumakleiza, did you hear? We have a solution for the darkness in the pit, so we're that much closer to being ready to go," Timrekka exclaimed, raising his fists alongside his spiky white hair.

"I heard," Dumakleiza answered, but she did not sound pleased. "I heard *everything*." Her eyes narrowed. "You are plotting to put Cooby in this smaller star of Winkloh, are you not?" Her steadfast eyes made Timrekka's waver.

"I, uh—"

"Yes," Izzy shrugged, not realizing how delicate the subject matter was. "He's a little large, but he's close to the appropriate size for a smaller Winkloh Star, and he would be perfectly preserved until we released him later." He smiled, satisfied with his answer. "And we wouldn't have to worry about his well-being down there."

"Izzy," Timrekka sharply whispered.

Dumakleiza lurched forward, grabbing Izzy by the throat. "You will find your head inside your star of Winkloh before I *ever* allow my Coobs to be confined in a prison of light." She released him and glared at Timrekka with ravenous disappointment. Her ferocity was all he needed to feel her threat loud and clear. He lowered his head, mortified. Izzy threw his hands up in shocked surrender. Dumakleiza pointed at both of them and then walked away to resume reading. Timrekka and Izzy looked at each other, embarrassed.

Jasss smiled at the tense moment from the opposite corner of the room. "You all right, Izzy?" Her question was less concern and more amusement. He looked up at her through his eyebrows and gave a humiliated nod. Jasss chuckled and turned her eyes to Dumakleiza. "Don't worry, princess. He's harmless."

Dumakleiza scowled back, still offended. "I assume their male genitals are small enough to fit inside their star of Winkloh," she snarled. Neither Izzy nor Timrekka said anything to defend themselves.

Jasss's expression turned sour as she nodded. "I'll cut'm off for you and we can find out."

Izzy jerked his head back.

"I'm just kidding." Jasss winked and then looked at Dumakleiza mouthing, "I'll do it."

Dumakleiza was completely lost and rather put off by Jasss. One way or another, she felt unsafe around the other recruits. She longed for her bow and arrows back on Cul.

The door flung open. Gideon and Traveler burst in, covered in sweat. They looked around wildly, gathering everyone's attention.

Dumakleiza's anger shifted to concern as she saw Gideon's face. "Sir Gideon, what is wrong?"

Traveler scoped the room. "Where are Master Brawd and Candelle?"

Izzy pointed at the front door. "Contacting Whewliss. Is everything okay?"

After rounding up Master Brawd, Candelle, and Tsuna, everyone gathered inside. Any argument they had for being busy was overruled when Traveler had told them that they'd discovered something at the hole. Gideon even chased Cooby down to make sure that literally everyone was accounted for. The worn-out tanion was happily cooing in Dumakleiza's arms. Books were down and attentions were undivided. Master Brawd stared at them impatiently.

Candelle bunched her lips. "What's wrong, Four Zero? You're so sweaty."

Gideon scratched his ear, still tender from the freshly implanted translator. "We stuck our heads beneath the ripples to see if we could hear the voice." The comment immediately made Tsuna uncomfortable. He shifted in his seat.

Master Brawd leaned forward. "You tampered with the fourth phase without my authorization."

"No disrespect," Traveler said, "but trust me. It's important. Please listen, master."

Gideon looked at Master Brawd. "We heard it. It's exactly as Tsuna said."

The other recruits looked at each other, puzzled. They hadn't been told about a voice inside the pit.

Gideon continued, "You can't understand what it's saying, but there was no mistaking a greeting." Traveler nodded along as Gideon explained. "So I said hello back, and whatever it is, it responded."

Candelle didn't move, but her tattooed chest bowed with quickened breaths. "What did it say?"

Gideon and Traveler exchanged glances. Gideon gulped down a cocktail of nervous excitement before answering.

"Again, we couldn't understand it, per say, but Four Zero and I felt the same thing." He paused a moment longer. "It was afraid, defensive. Like, I'd say it sounded like a territorial animal."

Master Brawd waited. He wasn't sure how much belief to invest in their claim, but he couldn't dismiss it. "Did you *feel* any kind of warning? A threat?"

"Uh." Gideon looked at Traveler, knowing that Master Brawd would be more receptive if it came from him.

Traveler took a deep breath and then took over. "It only felt as threatening as it needed to be. It seems as apprehensive of us as we are of it, whatever it is. That's what we got from it. We both unmistakably agreed that we felt it was asking if we lived 'down there.'"

"Down there?" Master Brawd asked, confused. "It thinks we live inside the hole?"

"Yes and no," Traveler answered, knowing how crazy and confusing he sounded. "The tone, er, or the perspective was all wrong."

"How so?"

"It didn't feel like it was asking if we *also* lived down the pit, where it clearly lives from our perspective. It felt like it was outside of the hole asking down—as if *we* were at the bottom and *it* was leaning over."

Candelle squinted. "What does that mean? I don't know what that means."

Gideon was trembling with anticipation. "We think we do." He was smiling from ear to ear.

"Well?" Master Brawd barked.

"We think it means that whoever or whatever it is, it's also leaning in."

"What *do you mean*?" Master Brawd was getting irritated at the vagueness.

"I mean, we don't think it's a pit. We think it's a tunnel." Gideon waited for everyone to consider the possibility. "And something is talking to us from the other side but — " He paused. "We don't believe it's human."

The room was instantly tense. No one spoke or moved.

Tsuna's eyes bore holes through the floor. "I'm not going back in there."

Master Brawd leaned farther forward and stared into Traveler's eyes. "Do *you* truly believe that?"

Traveler nodded without hesitation. "I know it sounds absurd, but Gideon is telling the truth. There's no denying it. I heard it with my own ears." He tried to slow his pulse. "You should hear it for yourself." He glanced around at everyone looking to him for answers. "I believe the Wall is literally that, a wall, and that there is another side to it. The Wall is a line in the sand, but I'm not sure what it's separating us from." He looked at Gideon and then back to everyone else. "Based off what we felt the voice saying, that's our shared theory."

Master Brawd sat back. "You believe the Wall is an eternally spanning barrier between two universes, and some *creature* is trying to communicate with us from the other side——a creature that you don't understand but you feel?"

Traveler slowly nodded, unable to deny any of it. "I don't expect you to accept my testimony as evidence."

Candelle had been running through scenarios in her mind. She finally stood up, unable to contain herself. She paced around the room, her thumb and index fingers rubbing her chin. No one spoke. They all waited for someone else to ask the right questions. Finally, Candelle stopped and turned to Gideon and Traveler.

"Well, you two have already made contact. It knows we're here." She reconsidered her idea for a moment and then decided to go through with it. "Why don't we go back and see if we can find out more from this crea-ture or being or whatever it is?" She looked at Gideon and pointed at him. "Something tells me you wouldn't mind sticking your head back down beneath the ripples."

Gideon took a deep breath, his adrenaline spiking. "Like Traveler said, it's why I'm here."

15

Everyone gathered near the hole. They stayed about fifteen feet from its edge, where the illusion of safety still existed. The comfort of the sazeal tree line was much more reassuring than the openness near the drop. After hearing that there was some sort of being in the abyss, they'd lost interest in playing with the ripples. Flirting with magic had no allure when monsters lay beyond, perhaps climbing up to grab them.

Gideon nonchalantly walked up to the edge and squatted down. He was a little nervous, but he thrived on the infrequent treat of something making him hesitate. He took a few deep breaths and then got down to his belly. With his face hovering over the vast darkness of the hole once again, he waited, taking a moment to consider what might happen. He'd spoken with every kind of person he could back on Earth. He'd conversed with kings, monks, pirates, warlords, presidents, homeless, criminals, everyone of every color and every walk of life. But now, for the first time, he was talking with something—else. He glanced over his shoulder.

"You sure none of you want to come hear this? Master Brawd? Candelle? Anyone?"

After waiting in still silence, Candelle was the first to respond. "I will stay by your side, but I'm not sticking my face in there." She tentatively walked up and squatted next to him. She was merely preparing to grab him and yank him back if he slipped.

Gideon paused. "Hold on now. How on earth do you—okay, that was the wrong way to word that." He chuckled. "How the hell do you guys plan on going down this thing if none of you are willing to even dip your head in?" No one moved or responded. Gideon rolled his eyes. "All right, let's break this down. Jasss, you're supposed to be the other adventurer, so you'd better get your ass over here and join me."

Jasss grunted. "Yeah, yeah, yeah." She shook her head and cautiously stepped forward, hating that Gideon was right. It was either find her courage or turn back, and she hated the idea of being labeled a coward.

Gideon continued glaring at everyone else. "Dumakleiza, Tsuna, you two had better at least be praying over there." They didn't need to be told twice. Gideon's instruction made perfect sense to both of them. "And you two science junkies—" He pointed to Timrekka and Izzy. "—had better be doing something science-y right now."

"Oh, we have something in the works to help with the inability to see down there, so don't worry about us because we're doing our part," Timrekka said. He hoped it'd be enough to keep Gideon from dragging him over to the edge and forcing him to converse with whatever lived in the depths.

Dumakleiza fervently prayed under her breath. "Grim, I beg not to allow Sir Gideon to fall or be swallowed by the darkness. Please allow no foul spirit or monster to devour his soul." She held tight to Cooby's paw as he stayed wrapped around her back.

Tsuna squatted down and muttered his prayer with a handful of black bead squeezed in his fist. "Mighty Wall, I see you for the dark deity you truly are." His eyes narrowed at the others. "If you must kill them for their blatant insolence, spare me, for I wish to be nothing more than your slave."

Traveler and Master Brawd watched Jasss lay down on her stomach a good distance from Gideon. She didn't trust him near a fatal fall, or anyone else for that matter. She wasn't going to interact with the ripples until he did. Gideon was the craziest of them all in her eyes.

"Well, here goes nothing." Gideon smiled at everyone and then dunked his head. As the ripples faded away, Jasss tightened her lips and forced herself to follow in suit. White ripples spread around their heads and faded away.

Jasss immediately regretted her decision once she realized she was going to have to suffer a new translator. "Gideon…" she said, but it only sounded like nonsense to him. Jasss chuckled as she kept talking.

Gideon grinned and faced the black chasm below. "Hello, darkness, my old friend!" His voice echoed away, disappearing into the deep.

Jasss's eyes froze. The noise didn't bother her. She'd been plenty loud just moments before, but intentionally addressing whatever might live in the hole instantly focused her attention. All fun and games were gone.

Without any warning, the voice appeared. It swirled around them, consuming their faces with subtle vibrations. This time, whatever was addressing them was a quiet whisper, barely noticeable, but its presence was undeniable. Goosebumps flew down Gideon and Jasss's spines, making them arch their backs. The whispering grew louder, as if one voice had split into four and then suddenly ten. It susurrated until it sounded like a roaring wind of shrill voices eerily harmonizing, like they were in a storm of startled ghosts.

"Shit!" Gideon yelled, shaking his head as he yanked it out. He lurched to his feet and stumbled backward. Jasss did the same, her hands rushing to cover her ears.

"What was that?" she yelled, struggling to regain her footing. "What was that?"

"Wait!" Master Brawd quickly stepped forward. He pointed to Traveler. "Give them new translators *now*."

Traveler wasted no time following the instruction. He sped over and stuck the implanting device into Gideon's ear. *Click.* Gideon didn't even wince at the stinging pain in his inner ear. He just stared out into the distance as if he'd been lobotomized. Whatever he'd felt the voice say, it left him stunned, and that made Traveler uncomfortable. He made his way to Jasss and gave her the implant as well. *Click.* Again there was no reaction.

Master Brawd paused in case there was any subsiding discomfort. "Don't tell us what you heard. Not yet. I have to be sure." He motioned to Candelle. "You and Jasss go over there." He pointed away. "Whisper what you heard to Candelle. And Gideon, come tell me your account. I want to know what you two felt or heard *separately*."

Gideon's eyes stared through Master Brawd as he numbly approached. He leaned in next to his ear. It took him a moment to compose himself enough to whisper.

"It told me...not to bring any of my darkness into the hole." He brought his head back, his eyes darting around aimlessly. Master Brawd stared at him, studying his haunted expression. It was unsettling, and he didn't like it. From above the ripples, he hadn't heard anything other than the two recruits screaming. He crinkled one side of his mouth and looked over at Candelle. She had the same taken aback expression after debriefing Jasss.

They walked over to each other, leaving Gideon and Jasss alone in their sullen silence.

Traveler and the other recruits uneasily watched. Barely any interaction had taken place with the fourth phase, and their team was already shaken.

Candelle leaned in and whispered into Master Brawd's ear, "She said she felt it ask her if she was a night creature."

"What do you think it means?" he asked as he brought his head back.

"I have no idea," Candelle said, trying not to let her apprehension show.

Master Brawd slowly turned to face everyone. Gideon and Jasss were still standing where they'd left them. After taking some time to mull over what their accounts could mean, Master Brawd cleared his throat and walked back to the group. He narrowed his eyes as he jostled some ideas around. The severity of the voice's effect on the two adventurers was undeniable, and he wasn't sure what to do with the information.

He looked at the group. "There's no purpose in secrecy here." He took a second to appreciate the fear in their eyes. "Gideon felt that it said not to bring his darkness with him, and Jasss felt it asking if she is a night creature."

Before anyone could do or say anything, Tsuna shook his head. "I'm not going down there. It's cursed. Send me back to my world. Now. I'm over it. I'm done."

Everyone ignored him as they looked to Master Brawd to hear what instructions he had. They were hungry for leadership in the face of the unknown, but to their dismay, he looked just as lost as them. After some deliberation, he looked from the ground back up to their fretful faces.

"I must consult with Lord Coyzle about this. For now, let's go back

to the Wall Post. You all focus on resting and memorizing your books."
He looked at Timrekka and Izzy. "There will be Whewlights arriving
soon with handheld supplies for you to create your miniature Winkloh
Star. I want all your efforts and thoughts going into that. Don't dwell on
this. I will."

Candelle walked over toward Dumakleiza. "Dumakleiza, now would
be a great time to pray for our mission. I think I'll join you, if it wouldn't
bother you."

"Me, too," Jasss nervously added. "I don't want to be alone right
now." It was an abnormal truth for her.

Dumakleiza smiled amid everyone else's unease. "I would be honored
to assist you both in finding guidance."

"Me, too," Gideon shakily chimed in as he made his way back over
to them. "I could use some Jesus right now." He wasn't normally the
praying type, but his roots were screaming for him to pray to the God
he was raised on.

Timrekka raised his eyebrows at Izzy. "Let's go build something."

"Yup," Izzy quickly agreed, welcoming the distraction.

As everyone turned and followed Candelle back toward the Wall Post,
Traveler hung back a moment and stared down into the hole. It had
shaken Gideon, the one man he'd hoped wouldn't be affected by it at all.
Gideon was supposed to be their strength, the fearless hero to lead them
through the unknown. Traveler stared down into the darkness. It almost
felt wrong to look away, like it would expose the cracks in his resolve
and that the beast in the pit would shine through them. He shook his
head and blinked a few times before kicking some black bead into it. He
watched the white ripples fade and then turned to follow everyone else.

Master Brawd had made his way to the front of the group by the time
they approached the Wall Post clearing. He entered the openness and
then stopped once he saw the familiar structures. His energy immediately
shifted. His breathing pattern alone made everyone behind him take
pause. His posture looked like that of an interrupted predator. Nobody

said anything at first, as they wanted to see what had startled him. He was studying the buildings. Something was off. At first no one understood, but then they saw it. The front door to the Wall Post was open, and they remembered having closed it on their way out. Someone had been there, and whoever it was could still be inside. Master Brawd held his hand up, instructing everyone to wait.

Timrekka blinked as sweat beaded on his face. He reached up and adjusted his goggles as his throat tightened. He wished he had at least been armed with his regular utility belt. Then he'd have some lines of defense.

He whispered, "Could it be the Whewlights bringing supplies?"

"No." Master Brawd whispered back as he studied the Wall Posts for any sign of movement. "They shouldn't be here for a few more hours. It will take them longer to gather the correct supplies in small enough packages to be able to carry with a light jump."

"Could it—" Dumakleiza feared the words coming out of her own mouth. "Could it be the Maker of Shadows?"

Master Brawd slowly shook his head as he grew tenser at the stillness. "Even if he was alive, if he was here, we would already be dead."

"It's the Wall's demon," Tsuna gasped.

Jasss thwapped him in the stomach. "Shut up."

Gideon lifted his head, trying to see anything. "I'll go check, if that'd make everyone feel better." He smiled, eager to know who had opened the door. His nerves had finally worn off. Risking safety always perked him right up.

"No." Master Brawd was getting frustrated seeing no signs of life inside.

"Come on," Gideon whispered back. "This is kind of my job description, isn't it? Running blindly into danger to find answers for you guys? And besides, you've got your finger laser thingies, right? Cover me."

Master Brawd hated to admit that Gideon was right. It was exactly the job they'd hired him for. After failing to think of a better option, Master Brawd nodded and lifted his hand.

"I'll cover you." He pointed his right index finger at the open door, prepared to fire a beam of light through anything or anyone that moved.

Traveler patted Gideon's arm. "Master Brawd is one of our best shots."
Gideon smiled. "Think of it as training for me."

Master Brawd shook his head, annoyed with Gideon's reckless happiness. "Go."

Without needing further instruction, Gideon got to his feet and started across the clearing. The Wall Post with the open door was about two-hundred-feet-away. The distance closed fast, especially with Gideon's brisk pace. The darkness of the Wall turned him into a silhouette as soon as he walked away from the group, making them more nervous. They could barely see him as it was, and the farther away he got, the less sure they were about Master Brawd's marksmanship.

Gideon neared the Wall Post enough for its light to shine on him. He paused and looked around. He couldn't see or hear anyone. The lights were all on. There was no mess or disruption anywhere, and he couldn't hear anyone rummaging around inside. After seeing nothing, he turned and shrugged back in the general direction he thought the group to be. He couldn't see them anymore. He turned around and faced the open door.

"Hello! Is anybody there?"

"Hey!" an unthreatening voice yelled out from inside. "Gideon!" It sounded familiar, but everyone's nerves were too high to focus on who it was.

Master Brawd aimed his finger at the doorway, ready to fire at whoever walked out. He was perfectly still. He hadn't had to shoot anyone in a long time, but his military instincts returned with fiery readiness.

As they waited, somebody walked out of the Wall Post to greet Gideon.

16

Master Brawd lowered his aimed finger. "Master N'kowsky?" Everyone leaned forward, narrowing their eyes in the darkness. They saw him, too. The beautifully handsome man was instantly recognizable, his radiant skin practically glowing in the starlight.

Master N'kowsky smiled at Gideon and then turned, staring straight at the huddled group. He had no difficulty seeing them in the darkness. His sparkling eyes and chiseled jaw perfectly framed a growing smile as he waved.

"Greetings! I hope I didn't startle you all with my arrival," his caramel voice called out over the cool air.

"Why are you here?" Master Brawd bluntly asked with dissecting eyes. He sounded surprised by Master N'kowsky's arrival, almost put off by it.

They gathered inside the Wall Post, sitting on the chairs and beds. The recruits looked at Master N'kowsky as he leaned against a wall, habitually brushing his suit off. He was donning a purely white outfit, shimmering like a milky diamond. He turned to answer Master Brawd.

"I figured I'd surprise you," he said. He ran his right hand through the feathery hair hanging by his eyes. "I wanted to come see how preparations are going." He winked at Dumakleiza. "Lord Coyzle doesn't know I'm here. Kind of a surprise all around," he bragged and looked to Master Brawd. "How *are* things going here?"

"They are advancing," Master Brawd said, unable to shake his caution.

"Are they?" Master N'kowsky chuckled and looked around at the ragtag group. "Just by the looks on everyone's faces, it appears the fourth phase has already done what it does best." Even his derisive comment sounded like flowing lace.

Master Brawd stood taller. "Master N'kowsky, why have you come?"

Master N'kowsky smiled and nodded with closed eyes. He was too excited to keep his reason a secret any longer. With a beaming smile, he opened his eyes and threw his hands out.

"To tell you I've resigned!"

Candelle gasped and joined the conversation. "As Whewliss's LOLA ambassador?"

Master N'kowsky nodded. "Yes. It's been a long time coming." He slumped, happy to say it out loud.

The recruits studied the Whewlights' reactions. They were surprised that Master Brawd wasn't congratulating him. Resignation or retirement were both momentous occasions deserving of merriment. It was presumably true of any world or culture. Traveler appeared to be doing the same thing, waiting on Master Brawd for guidance.

Master Brawd tilted to one side as he stared at him. "What are you going to do now?" They'd both been on the council for so long that the idea of resignation had never even crossed his mind, let alone abruptly quitting. "And who's replacing you?" He leaned forward. "How did Lord Coyzle react?"

Master N'kowsky dismissed the questions with a wave. "Details, my friend, details. In time. More importantly, I wanted to celebrate with the fourth phase team on the Wall. I can't believe I can finally say that. That's been an even longer time coming." He chuckled with obvious admiration. "Let's drink some sazeal, heavy on the liquor." The suggestion finally got some smiles from a few of the recruits. "Oh, and I'll obviously no longer be going by MasterN'kowsky as I am stepping down from the council. You can call me Abdabriel N'kowsky now. Or just Abdabriel. I'd rather be known on a first-name basis with the fourth phase team." He flashed another dazzling smile at the recruits before looking to Master Brawd.

"But first I really do want to hear about the updates on the fourth phase. It's so exciting, isn't it?"

The recruits all gave the same unsure expression. They wanted to share his enthusiasm for their expedition, but after recent events, they were uncertain. Traveler recognized Master Brawd and Candelle's hesitance. He wasn't enjoying the awkward silence, so he answered for them.

"We're experimenting and establishing some plans, but there have been some setbacks and concerns that we're dealing with. It was to be expected."

"Oh, without any doubt. The fourth phase is a terrifying mystery." Abdabriel nodded, his piercing eyes sympathetically meeting Traveler's. "The voice, I'm assuming?"

"Yes," Traveler answered. "It's been confirmed. I've heard it with my own ears."

"Wow." Abdabriel shivered. "I don't possess the courage to overlook that—and to climb down anyway?" He raised his hands, freeing himself of the responsibility.

Master Brawd was growing impatient. "Why else are you here? Is there something you need to tell me?"

"Oh, not just you, old friend," Abdabriel said with a smile. "I came to tell all of you. But first, sazeal shots. Who wants one? This is a time for celebration! You — " He looked at Master Brawd. "—certainly need one. You're so tense. Not that that's ever a surprise from the one and only. Relax and share a drink with me while I share news. I promise it's worth your time."

Master Brawd didn't budge. "We have some important issues that need to be addressed immediately. If what you've traveled this distance to tell us is so important, share it. The time for celebration isn't now." Everyone leaned back a little as his comment made the room palpably tense.

Abdabriel waited a moment, accepting that he wasn't going to be able to convince Master Brawd to let his guard down. He resisted the urge to roll his eyes as he pushed away from the wall.

"Of course. I apologize for my insensitivity. The fourth phase is no joking matter." He paused and looked off as he smiled. Everything he had to say possessed such magnitude that he didn't know where to start.

"Back on Whewliss, when we were first introduced, I told you all that I saw so much potential in you and that together we would pioneer a new age for humanity as a whole." His eyes lit up. "I meant that. I meant that with every fiber of my being." His smile grew. "However, what I didn't tell you is that I wasn't talking about the fourth phase." No one knew how to react. Abdabriel grinned at the expected response. "I've come here to offer you—*all* of you, every single person in this room—an opportunity beyond your wildest dreams, more promising than the fourth phase." Even though he delivered the news with a quiet voice, his tone was vibrating with bridled excitement.

Master Brawd breathed slowly. "What are you talking about?"

After a dramatic pause, Abdabriel slowly exhaled. "I have set in motion a plan to unite the human race." His entire being pulsated as he spoke. "I have a dream where every human being across the stars will be aligned as one soul, one team, one harmonious species. I want to lead us into a new future, beyond any shore, beyond any one world, and unite us with a common goal: universal peace." His introduction faded into silence as everyone stared at him, confused and undecided. Master Brawd didn't say anything. He looked stuck in place, as though what Abdabriel had said went right over his head.

Gideon crossed his arms. "Okay, I'll bite. Seems like a rather hefty undertaking. How are you planning on going about that? Door-to-planetary-door flyers?"

"By speeding up the process to updated immediacy," Abdabriel said simply. "With every world I've visited, I've seen just how many are advancing to light travel. As anything else in life, they're beginning to increase exponentially. When I first began introducing LOLA to the worlds that had crossed that threshold, there were only a handful. Now the frequency at which I visit new worlds has increased to the point of unstable escalation. The inevitability of every world reaching that technology and having access to each other is closer than we think. It's only a matter of time until there are no worlds that can't, and when that happens, the universe is going to become a much smaller place." His smile slowly faded to a glare. "And when that happens, I promise you it will also become a much more dangerous place. LOLA will not be enough to keep the peace as leaders and governments of different worlds fight for dominion over one another. I've seen where the universe is heading, and it's going to be Daemoana all over again, but multiplied. It's in our genes. It's human nature."

Candelle studied Abdabriel's unwavering eyes. "What exactly are you planning?"

"A preemptive establishment of law and order," Abdabriel said without a shred of hesitation.

He suddenly had Master Brawd's full, undivided attention. "Master N'kowsky, you better not mean—"

"Abdabriel," Abdabriel said.

Master Brawd ignored the correction. "What have you done?"

Abdabriel chuckled at the reaction. "I have prepared, old friend. I've seen the warning signs for many, *many* years, and I've prepared." He looked at the unsteady eyes staring at him. "I knew my foresight would be met by fear and dismissal from Whewliss, not understanding. So, I've prepared in secret as a contingency plan to the imminent threat around us."

Master Brawd was visibly steaming. "Tell me what you've done."

Cooby held tighter to Dumakleiza as he sensed the unrest.

Abdabriel looked down for a moment and then back up at Master Brawd. "I have assembled enough logical, critical thinkers from many worlds that share my concern. Patriots to the human race itself. They've cast aside their allegiances to any leaders or worlds that blindly cling to human division and have sworn oaths of loyalty to my vision. These are people who don't want to see another ULW. Men and women who are afraid of the unseen threats hiding in the stars and are willing to do what's necessary to effectively prevent any threat from slaughtering *any* people. We are unwilling to wait until it's too late." He looked around at the faces silently waiting for more information. He smiled, knowing that they were growing more and more uneasy. "Together we are going to visit every world one-by-one and remove the blinders from their eyes. We're not going to wait around for them to discover that they're not alone in the universe any longer. We will tell them that they are not and that they are part of something much bigger. We will share the glorious news that there are countless planets among the heavens, a vast network that they are a part of. We will unite them as individual worlds, showing them that their differences are petty and detrimental to their survival. And once each world is brought to peace, we will provide them with technology to bring them up to date, so they can advance with us as one unified species." He smiled, unsure as to why no one else was. "Under one ruler, the entire universe will stop fighting itself, and humanity will be safe from its own implosive nature. There will be peace. There will be harmony. There will be no more wars, and the stars can rest easy without bloodshed for the first time in human history. *That* is the real fourth phase of human development. Not some hole in the ground at the edge of space." He finished with a flick of the tongue and a confident eyebrow raise. "What do you think?"

"What do I think?" Master Brawd snarled without wasting time. "What you're suggesting is breaking every facet of LOLA. It's treason. You're wanting to conquer other worlds under, I'm assuming, *your* rule."

Abdabriel nodded. "Yes, but you have to see my vision. It's not to enslave but to set free from—"

"From themselves, their wars, and their conflicts," Master Brawd spat out. "I heard. Your charm isn't disguising what that entails."

"Please," Abdabriel said with sincerity, "tell me what cost is too great for universal peace."

"Do notpatronize me," Master Brawd barked. "You want to remove each planet's right to govern itself. You're taking away their liberty, their freedom, and their unique story. Each world dictates its own fate. You're suggesting hostile takeovers veiled as peace-keeping missions. Do I really need to quote LOLA to you?"

Abdabriel chuckled and shook his head. "Any hostility from us will be warranted solely by those who resist my army of light while we unite the human race. I'm not intending violence, but I will dole out what is necessary to achieve peace."

"You're invading!" Master Brawd yelled out, trying to reach his friend. "There's no way to disguise what you're suggesting! You are plotting to lead alien invasions!"

The recruits were dead silent. They weren't sure what to do. If what Master N'kowsky was promising was going to come to any fruition, they realized that each of their worlds was set in his sights. Gideon knew that the leaders of Earth wouldn't surrender to foreign rule, especially after just learning of the existence of other worlds. They would defend their freedom and fight back, and when that happened, Abdabriel and his alien army would slaughter millions for the sake of billions. And that would just be Earth. Gideon's eyes fluttered. He saw that the other recruits were thinking similar thoughts. The maelstrom of emotions and responses flooding through their minds had them frozen in place as Master Brawd and Abdabriel argued.

"Merely perspective, old friend," Abdabriel said, maintaining his cool. "The only people who will see my arrival as invasion are those unwilling to join the future—a peacefulfuture where we stand as one. Those who recognize me as the savior of the human race won't even question why I'm there. They will lay down their arms and join me. Translators for all, light travel for all, one governing rule for all. No more division based on color, belief, gender, riches, development, and now even planet. How do you not see the benefit in that logic?"

"Logic?" Master Brawd roared. "You just called yourself the saviorof the human race." His eyes were on fire. "What happened to you, *old friend*? You've lost yourself."

Abdabriel slowly shook his head while maintaining eye contact. "Oh, no, I've found myself. I have discovered my true purpose, and no one is going to convince me otherwise. The future I see is too bright." He breathed coolly through his nose. "I have visited more worlds than all of you combined, and I have bared witness to the grotesque nature of man that currentlyunites us all. They fight each other for scraps, killing each other in drones, oceans of blood-spilling among the stars as countless wars for trivial pieces of dying worlds kill trillions every single day."

Master Brawd nodded. "As tragic as that is, each world still has the right to its own destiny. You have no right to tell them how to live on their own planet."

"Don't give me an empty speech of freedom. Too long have we turned a blind eye to their needless suffering." Abdabriel squinted. "Open your mind to the potential guidance wecan provide. I want to take you with me. You have so much wisdom and strength. You can help these worlds as much as I can. You can lead my armies, keeping the peace on every world. You'll stay the general you already are, but on a scale we've never aspired to," he said, his voice quickly returning to its delightful eminence. "That's why I'm here." He looked around at the recruits. "The nine of you would be perfect leaders. Brave. Eyes set on the future. Examples to the rest of humanity. Each of you would flourish as you govern your own planets." He smiled. "You would unite the very worlds you love, establish planet-wide peace, and have more fame and power in that position than you ever fathomed. We will be loved for the harmony and safety we provide."

Master Brawd stepped closer to Abdabriel, his large frame looming. "That's enough. I've heard enough. We all have." He turned and walked toward the door.

Abdabriel tilted his head to the side. "Where are you going?"

"I'm going to Whewliss. The council needs to know what you're plotting. We're going to get you the help you need before it's too late."

"You're wasting your time." Abdabriel shrugged. "This plan is inevitable, and it's a good thing."

Master Brawd grabbed the door handle and shook his head. "You know what they say: Light heals the body, not the mind."

"Funny," Abdabriel chuckled as Master Brawd opened the door, "that's exactly what Lord Coyzle said before—" He paused.

Master Brawd let go of the door handle and slowly turned around. "Before what?" His tone was more of a threat than words could be.

Abdabriel closed his eyes and quickly shook his head. "Nothing. Nothing. It's not important." He opened his eyes to see Master Brawd's index finger aggressively poised by his side, ready to hold him at laser point. "Old friend, that would be unwise."

Master Brawd didn't care about threats. "What did you do to our Lord?"

Abdabriel lowered his gaze, his voice turning hostile. "I came here to peacefully invite you to join me. I'd hoped you'd see the light." He sighed. "There doesn't need to be any antagonism. A simple 'no' would suffice."

Master Brawd lifted his hand and aimed his index finger directly between Abdabriel's eyes. "Tell me what happened. I won't ask again."

Fft. A sharp static sound drew everyone's attention to Master Brawd.

He was frozen in place with a painfully confused expression. His finger was still aimed up, and his eyes were twitching, but before anyone could say or do anything, he fell forward and crashed onto the floor with the rigidity of a wooden board.

"Mackel!" Candelle screamed as she leapt up to run to his side. *Fft.* Another vibrational static stunned Candelle and dropped her to the ground.

Abdabriel sighed and stepped forward as the recruits backed away. "I don't want any of this." He groaned at the inconvenience. "Don't worry, they're not dead." He glanced out the open door and nodded. "Mentrauffo just subdued them. They'll recover soon. But please." He turned to the recruits. "I want to take this time to talk to you without their interruption."

Three men walked through the doorway.

Abdabriel smiled at their entrance. "Recruits, these are three soldiers in the army of light. They are ready to unite humanity." He pointed to the two taller men. "This is Kengreed and Mentrauffo." He motioned to the third, shorter man. "And this is Greotz." They gave a polite nod and then stood in the doorway, ensuring that everyone stayed where they were. Abdabriel sighed. "I'd like to apologize for this impression. It was never supposed to go this way. I was truly hoping for this to be a celebratory visit. I wanted it to be a momentous time that would forever be recognized in our history books as the moment when we began the unity of the human race." He smiled bigger. "And I also want to apologize on behalf of my people, of the Whewlights. We are not good leaders." He scoffed. "It's no fault of any of yours, but ever since your arrival on the Wall, I'm assuming there's been poor leadership? That Master Brawd and Candelle have pointed you at the fourth phase and instructed you to just figure it out?"

Tsuna slowly nodded, hesitant to engage. "Other than giving us translation books, yes."

"Exactly," Abdabriel said, throwing his hands out. "I can tell just by looking at you all that you're not functioning as a team out here. You have poor leadership. Again, it's not your fault. Do any of you feel lost? Purposeless? Discouraged?"

The other recruits silently listened as Tsuna spoke up again. "Yes, I do. I feel like we're in over our heads. It's perilous. We shouldn't be here."

"Thank you." Abdabriel shook his head. "I've never understood my people's obsession over it." He turned and looked at the three men in the doorway. "For example. These three know nothing of the fourth phase. Kengreed, Mentrauffo, Greotz, you've just been introduced to the Wall. It's scary, right?" All three of them glanced at each other and then shrugged or nodded. "Well." Abdabriel played into it. "What if I told you that not far from here, there's a giant hole through the edge of space? It's pitch black, we have no idea how deep it is, where it leads to, or anything about it for that matter. None of our equipment works inside of it, and everyone who's ever even been in it claims to have heard a child's whisper calling out to them. Would you like to go down it?" The three men squinted and shook their heads without having to look at each other. Abdabriel nodded and turned back to the recruits. "Exactly. Instead of leaving well enough alone, my people have recruited some of the bravest souls in the universe and told them to explore a hole." He shook his head. "I apologize for what they've asked of you. They don't deserve your sacrifice when there's no promise of reward. There's not even any promise of survival." He clicked his tongue. "That's unacceptable. The fourth phase of human development exists, but it's not a death sentence as you've been led to believe. Let's go spelunking?" He shook his head. "No. That's nothing. The *real* fourth phase is universal peace. It's not darkness. It's light." He shrugged, hoping for more of them to engage in the conversation. "Why should we explore something we don't understand when we can't even get along on the worlds we *do*?" He took another step closer, begging them to see his vision. "I'm offering you leadership and actual guidance with a purpose. You will rise higher in ranks than you ever could anywhere else in the universe, and you'll be making it a safer place for the people you care about."

Gideon slowly nodded, finally wanting to speak up. "So, to make sure I understand the eggs you're willing to break to make your grand omelet, you're prepared to kill billions in order to save trillions?"

Abdabriel nodded. "A high body count of collateral damage that I wish to avoid, but if it unfortunately comes to that, it's no more than I expect would die in their own bickering wars. In fact, due to the fact that their attention will be focused on us, it could very well be less than would kill each other meaninglessly. This may come off as cold, but mathematically there is no downside."

Gideon winced. "And that doesn't kinda make you just wanna not do it?" He urged. "You know, your soul and all of that? Kind of feels like a damning move."

"Every great step in mankind's history has required sacrifice," Abdabriel answered. "Every *god* demands sacrifice. Whether you're looking at this religiously or logically, death is inevitable in the process. Many will die, yes, but exponentially more will be spared violent fates. I am establishing the widest network of peacekeeping soldiers that humanity has ever heard of."

Gideon grinned. "And that doesn't sound at all megalomaniacal to you? Like at all? Zero percent?"

Abdabriel chuckled. "I expected that you out of all the recruits would see the fruitful reward that a crazy idea can bring."

Gideon nodded. "Ah, well, you got me there." He shrugged. "Crazy is more life-sustaining than blood when it comes to the pursuit of destiny." He had to take a moment to be honest with himself. The man he'd been for years normally would have accepted the bizarre twist of circumstantial direction. If his life was on the line, he always found a way to survive, no matter the cost. He was always capable of riding the tide, and he couldn't deny that some of Abdabriel's logic was in fact logical. Naturally, his instinct was to abandon the other recruits and accept Abdabriel's invitation. He looked around at Traveler, Timrekka, and ultimately, Dumakleiza. His heart made up his mind as her dragon eye melted him, and he could feel the sinking inevitability of fate. He looked to Abdabriel. "Listen, man, normally I would let destiny seduce me, no matter the dance." He paused and sighed. "But if billions of souls are the carnage left in the wake of our passions, I couldn't live with it. For your sake, I'm really hoping you rethink this." He returned one of Abdabriel's signature winks.

"Ugh, you would be *perfect*," Abdabriel groaned. "Did you hear what just came out of your mouth? I'm incredibly good at reading people from other worlds and convincing them of the truth, but something tells me you may give me a run for my money. An Earthling saying, I recall." He pointed at Gideon. "I'm keeping a spot open for you in hopes that maybe one day you'll see the light." He sighed. "But no, it's too late to turn back now. I have secured a force of over fourteen-million-soldiers who've rallied to this cause, and more are seeing the light every day. The majority of those are actual soldiers from some of the most developed worlds and advanced armies that exist. We have been developing new technologies, new weapons, and new defensive countermeasures ever since I first conceived this vision. We will be unstoppable, and once we've swept through the cosmos, it'll be a better place for it—free of hatred, prejudices, and most importantly, war. Children will feel safe regardless of where they are. Do you realize how amazing that will be?" He looked around at the other recruits and then turned back to Gideon. "You've visited what, seven worlds, including the Wall, if I remember correctly?" Gideon nodded as Abdabriel nodded with him. "And how many of those planets had even a glimmer of worldwide peace in their future?"

"Only Whewliss," Gideon answered, knowing where Abdabriel was heading. "We should probably hold guns to the others' heads and force them to play nice. Don't you think?"

"And even on yourworld, Earth, there are wars being waged to this day. This very second there are multiple battles being fought over lands, religions, resources, etcetera. And millions are dying. And that's just ononeplanet. Don't you want to see an end to that?"

"Of course I want to see an end to war," Gideon scoffed. "But not by waging my own and forcing the losers under my thumb. That's hypocritical and ultimately makes you the bad guy. You really do see yourself as the good guy with this, don't you?" Abdabriel just looked at him, disappointed with the response. Gideon sighed. "There's no way to talk you out of this, is there?"

Abdabriel shook his head before posturing himself and looking at the other recruits. "That was an unsatisfactory conversation." He exhaled and cleared his throat. "I have so much respect for all of you. Truly. I admire your courage and faith, and I could use heroes like you on this journey. I have no intention of causing any unnecessary pain. I mean that. I will leave you all to your mission down the hole." He looked around one last time. "Are there any of you that would like to leave this place and join me?"

"Yes!" Tsuna blurted out as he stepped forward. "The Wall is a lone creature, wishing not to be troubled by our presence."

Abdabriel twitched at the babbling planet worshipper. "Welcome to our cause, Tsuna of Gawthraw." Tsuna was the least desired, but Abdabriel believed any fourth phase recruit would be beneficial.

"Tsuna?" Izzy couldn't help reaching out. "What are you doing?" He caught himself whispering the question, even though everyone could hear him.

Tsuna turned around and glared at Izzy as he brushed hair from in front of his eye. "He's right. We're unraveling without guidance. We're drooling over a hole." He spat on the manmade floor. "I'm ascending. As should all of you."

As they spoke, Gideon caught some subtle movement out of the corner of his eye. He saw Dumakleiza inching into a coiled position. It was barely noticeable, but he recognized her predatory form. She was planning something with Cooby on her back. There were no weapons, which meant she was going to try to take Abdabriel by hand. Gideon had no idea what her plan was or how she was expecting to survive his three guard dogs if she killed their master. It seemed like a bad idea—his favorite kind, but not at the expense of someone else's well-being. He tried to silently get her attention with stern eye contact and eyebrows, but her gaze was fixed on Abdabriel. Gideon knew he had to help somehow.

"You know, Abdabriel, we have a saying on Earth." He exhaled and took a step forward.

"What's that?"

"It is said that something as small as the flutter of a butterfly's wing can cause a typhoon halfway around the world." He spoke loudly enough to ensure that everyone's eyes were on him. He quickly shot a glance to Timrekka and ever so subtly nodded toward Dumakleiza before looking at the three men in the doorway. It was vague, swift, and he was worried it wasn't enough to deliver the message.

Abdabriel nodded. "Yes, I've heard many quotes like it on other worlds. It suggests that my actions are going to cause a much larger outcome than

I'm anticipating and that I'm not prepared for the consequences." He smiled and leaned in close to Gideon, his expression turning to a fire-breathing glare. "I admire the life lesson, Earthling, but I promise you: When I am done beating my wings, the typhoon will be a solar flare so bright that even God will shield his eyes."

Gideon smiled at Abdabriel. "Oh, I'm not talking about tsunamis worlds away. I'm talking about here. In this room." His smile grew. "Now!"

As soon as he yelled, he dropped and lurched backward, throwing himself at the three unsuspecting men's feet, hoping to hit them low. Luckily, at the same time, Timrekka yelled a panicked scream with wide eyes as he leapt toward them. He had no idea what he was going to do, but he had to try.

Abdabriel burst out laughing. "What are you — "

Oomph! He was caught off guard as the wild pirate princess hit him from the air, instantly twisting around his body and maneuvering her arms around his throat. Abdabriel frantically reached up to grab her as Cooby clawed at his face and chest.

Timrekka flew toward the bodyguards, but they raised fingers and fired. *Fft.Fft.Fft.* Three simultaneous shocks petrified the Thamioshling midair. The men scooted aside as Timrekka fell onto Gideon, who had failed at making much impact against their legs. Gideon yelped as Timrekka crushed him and rolled over, frozen in place.

Fft.Fft. Two quick shots rendered Dumakleiza and Cooby unconscious. They fell off Abdabriel and landed on the floor, twisted and statuesque. Abdabriel stepped back, brushing unseen hands from his face as he collected his bearings.

"Wow, I did *not* see that coming!" He laughed away his anger at how close she'd come to causing any real damage.

Traveler, Izzy, and Jasss watched in horror at what was happening before them. Everything had been undone. Five of their own were unconscious on the floor, Gideon was struggling to breathe, Tsuna had abandoned them, and their worlds were in Abdabriel's sights. They didn't move.

Abdabriel ran his hands over his head, brushing his jostled hair back into place. He felt the cuts and scrapes all over his face and neck. There was bruising from where Dumakleiza had almost choked the life out of him. He smiled and widened his eyes for a second.

"Well." He shook his head and looked around at everyone. "That was unexpected. I didn't think you had it in you." He directed his comments at Gideon. "It was a good attempt, but let's be honest, you're not a well-oiled bunch. The word 'team' doesn't even apply to you. As a ragtag group of misfits, disassembly is inevitable. Come find me when you've seen the light, and I will provide you with much-needed structure. With open arms, I might add." He winked at Gideon and then turned back to his men. "This right here is a prime example of how we handle those who stand against peace." His men and Tsuna smiled, excited for a demonstration of power. Abdabriel walked over to where Master Brawd was lying. He squatted down next to him and placed a hand on his seized shoulder. "Old friend, under these circumstances, I would not hesitate to make an example out of anyone else." He gave a sympathetic headshake. "No matter how much I know I should, I just can't kill you. You are still too dear to me, no matter how blind you've proven yourself today. But—" Abdabriel stood. "—a punishment must be administered." He turned to his men. "Take his wife."

"No!" Traveler yelled out. "Master N'kowsky, please!" He jumped to his feet but stayed his ground with hands raised.

"Abdabriel," he corrected. "I'm sorry, Four Zero. A bright future is upon us, and I must ensure that no one sees promise in resistance. But rest assured, I will not harm you or any of the recruits, so long as you stay where you are."

They watched in tears as one of his men grabbed Candelle's stunned ankles and dragged her body outside. Just the sound of her sliding across the floor had tears streaming down Traveler's face. The other two men had their fingers aimed out at the rest of them, ready to fire at Abdabriel's command. There was nothing any of them could do.

Abdabriel walked over to Dumakleiza's body and stared down at her, gazing upon her complexion. "Such a shame." He shook his head as he admired her rich skin, bright freckles, and dragon eye. "She's so beautiful, so full of passion and potential. She's come all this way, only to reveal herself as an animal."

Gideon struggled to sit up as he pleaded, "Don't hurt her! Please!"

Abdabriel slowly nodded. "She needs to be put down. She attacked me, an offense punishable by immediate execution."

Gideon forced his way to his knees, almost passing out from something internally broken. "Abdabriel, please. Kill me instead."

Abdabriel sighed. "I wish to be known as a merciful god. She is no more a threat to me than a child is to a chrome lion. She deserves death, but she is loved by you, Gideon Green of Earth. That means more than you know because I'm holding out for you. I will spare her in hopes that it will help you see the light. However —" He turned his gaze to Cooby's body. "—an example must be made."

"No!" Gideon begged. "Just no! You don't need to hurt anyone!"

"Pain instructs obedience, and through obedience, I shall establish peace across the universe." Abdabriel nodded to one of his remaining men. "Take the animal out and toss it into space, as well." He shook his head. "Such a waste."

"No!" Gideon's helplessness was driving him mad as tears welled. "I knew there was something wrong with you. You were too perfect, and now I see why. You're insane. You're a sociopath, not a leader."

Abdabriel walked to the table as his acolyte dragged Cooby outside. "These will help you recover once you wake up." He placed a capsule of pills on the table. "As I said, I am merciful, and I will honor my word. You may resume your exploration of the fourth phase. I won't get in your way. I am truly sorry for how this visit played out. It's not what I wanted. I truly hope you find something worthwhile inside the pit. It would be a shame if you made the wrong decision and wasted your lives when you could have lived as gods. If any of you see the light, I will be waiting." He gave them a mourning nod. "May the light guide and protect you all."

Fft.Fft. Abdabriel's last soldier subdued the remaining recruits. Only Traveler was left. As the man turned to fire at him, Traveler cried out.

"Master N'kowsky, why? After everything you and Lord Coyzle have built?"

Abdabriel held out a hand to his man and sighed tenderly at Traveler. "Four Zero, whatever your real name originally was, it's time to stop following blind leadership. You are the bravest recruiter that's ever been. Use that courage and find your wisdom. I want you by my side in this."

Traveler didn't know what to do. "Where are you going?"

"In order for peace to be achieved, I must first neutralize the greatest threat to its fulfillment: us." He sighed. "The next time you see Whewliss, it will be transformed. It will be the birthplace of universal peace."

Tears welled in Traveler's eyes as he realized what that meant. *Fft.* He fell over onto his side, and everything went black.

17

Dumakleiza woke with a start, immediately aching as she tried to move. Electric currents pulsed through her veins in random spurts. The sensation was foreign. Between Highness Trollop and Abdabriel, this was her second time feeling it. It took a moment for her eyes to adjust to Jasss kneeling over her, urgently shushing her. Even with Dumakleiza's instinctive defenses, she recognized the sincerity on Jasss's face. She refrained from groaning as Jasss put a finger to her lips. Dumakleiza squinted, trying to recall how she'd ended up asleep on the floor. The memory of attacking Abdabriel came rushing back.

"Where is —" Her yell was instantly silenced by Jasss's full hand smothering her mouth.

"Stay quiet," Jasss sharply whispered before looking around to see if anyone had heard her.

Dumakleiza nodded and waited till Jasss's hand was gone before whispering back, "Are you all right, Jasss of Ojīptian?"

Jasss raised an eyebrow and nodded. "Of course, I am. I was the only one smart enough to sneak out before they stunned you all. I've escaped from enough bad situations to recognize when one is spiraling. Lucky for you, I woke you up. You would probably be asleep for another few hours." She handed Dumakleiza one of the pills Abdabriel left them. She'd anticipated Dumakleiza's trepidation with trusting her, but there was no time. "Take it. It'll kill the jitters."

Dumakleiza slowly sat up, wincing as she looked around and swallowed the pill. It was flavorless, and as soon as it was down her throat, it was out of her mind. She was the last to have been roused. Everyone else was experiencing the same aching and groaning as they tried to recover from the electric coma. They were either on their knees or sitting, and based off Jasss's hand motions, Duma understood that she needed to stay low.

Everyone appeared gammy and incapacitated, but Gideon was the only one clutching an actual injury. Dumakleiza barely remembered seeing Timrekka fall deadweight onto him. She wanted to tend to his wounds once she could breathe and stand, but first she had to check on Cooby. After a quick scan of the room, her alarm sounded. She didn't see Cooby. She double-checked as she shakily got to her tingling feet. The ache in her muscles no longer mattered.

She grabbed Jasss and whispered, "Where is Cooby?"

Since everyone was awake, Jasss skipped the one-on-ones and addressed them all. "No sudden movements." She looked around with frantic eyes while staying crouched. She motioned for Dumakleiza to get lower. "Two of them are still outside."

Master Brawd finally convalesced well enough to recognize that Candelle wasn't in the room. "Where is Candelle?"

Jasss barked a whisper, demanding their attention. "I watched Abdabriel and two of his gofers light jump away. I'm assuming they went to Whewliss. The short man and Tsuna stayed behind to—" She swallowed hard. "They're going to throw Candelle and Cooby beyond the atmosphere."

She could feel Master Brawd and Dumakleiza's eyes bore holes through her with fire. Master Brawd forced himself to his feet, still trying to regain control of his nerves and muscles.

"Where?" He followed her finger to a window. Staying low, he hurried over and placed his back against the wall. The bottom of the window began at his standing chest height, which gave him just enough cover to look without being spotted. He turned to peer outside. They were barely visible in the darkness, but the short man and Tsuna were in the yard between the Wall Posts. Their silhouettes were working on something, but Master Brawd couldn't tell what it was. His fists clenched tight enough for his knuckles to turn white. He kept his eyes on the outside as he quietly spoke to everyone.

"Here's what's going to happen. We're going to—"

"Where's Dumakleiza?" Gideon asked.

Everyone turned their attention from Master Brawd to where Dumakleiza had been. She was gone. The door was wide, and no one had heard it open.

In the cover of darkness, Dumakleiza climbed the outside wall with burning determination. She didn't feel her fingers aching with residual shocks as she ascended a building that wasn't designed for climbing. She still didn't have a weapon, but it didn't matter. If she managed to save Cooby, the two men were going to die quickly. If she was too late and she had to watch Cooby die, the two men were going to die slowly. Nothing else mattered. She was torn between praying to Grimleck and telling him to look away from what she was about to do.

Sweat trailed down her face and neck as she silently reached the roof and crawled across until she was at the edge, peering over. She couldn't see much with her right eye, but her dragon eye saw with burning clarity. The short man and Tsuna were placing Cooby's unconscious body onto a square device. She could only assume it was designed to launch his body into the air. She had to be fast and she had to be precise. They were about eight paces from the building, and that was a long jump for her without Cooby's wings. As she brainstormed, she heard Tsuna chuckle.

"I want to do this one." He reached down, fumbling with the device. "I can't wait to rid the Wall of this thing's wretched shrieking. That purple-eyed bitch should thank me."

Dumakleiza's eyes shot open as she bared her teeth like fangs. There was no more time for stealth. She rolled back to the other edge of the roof and stood as high as she could without poking her head above the atmosphere. It only allowed her a hunched position, but it would have to do. She ran as fast as she could in the short distance and leapt.

A loud spring echoed out as Tsuna flicked a switch. He and the short man watched as Cooby was shot upward, flying into the sky. Then, just before he reached the edge of the atmosphere, an unexpected figure dove through the air and snatched him by one of his legs. Both men jumped back. They watched as the two silhouettes fell to the ground, crashing and tumbling out of sight.

"What was that?" The shorter man craned his neck, struggling to see in the darkness.

Tsuna immediately backed up. He couldn't see what it was either, but he didn't have the courage to find out. "Uh," was all he managed to sputter.

The shorter man remembered Abdabriel had given him implants. He lifted a hand and angled his fingers to create a light shining forth. There was nothing where the silhouettes had landed.

"Where did they —" Aggressive footsteps turned the man's attention to his right. He spun just in time to — *thunk*. Dumakleiza sped by, burying a chunk of sazeal bark deep into the side of his throat. The man gurgled, clutching wildly at his neck as blood spurted out of him. His legs immediately gave way, and before he even hit the ground, Dumakleiza had Tsuna. He screamed as she ripped his arm and swept his leg out from under him, violently spinning him through the air and body-slamming him facedown into the black bead.

"Dumakleiza!" Master Brawd's yell turned her focus as she wrenched Tsuna's arm to a breaking point. He wept at the pain. The recruits all stopped, pausing behind Master Brawd as they saw unsatisfied bloodlust in Dumakleiza's eyes. Master Brawd marched forward with the same look in his. He glanced at the dead man on the ground. Even in the darkness, he could see the pool of blood spreading around the lifeless body. It only fueled his indignation. He turned back to Dumakleiza. "Give him to me."

Dumakleiza's snarl was carved to her face. She wanted to snap Tsuna's arm out of its socket and watch the terror in his eyes as she continued dismantling him piece by piece. All she could manage was a slow head-shake. Tsuna needed to die, and nothing Master Brawd said was going to change her mind.

Master Brawd didn't bark at her as she'd expected. Instead, he squatted down next to them and looked at her with the same hatred in his eyes.

"I'm not pardoning him, Dumakleiza. I just need to know." He turned his gaze down to Tsuna's anguish-ridden face. "Where is Candelle?" At the name, Tsuna stopped crying. His trembling eyes widened at Master

Brawd. There was an eerie pleading in them, terrified, begging, voiceless. Master Brawd leaned in, resisting the urge to smash Tsuna's skull in two. "Where is she?" he growled.

Again, Tsuna didn't respond. His lips quivered as saliva dripped from them. It was barely noticeable, but his eyes flickered, looking up for a split second. Master Brawd paused. He kept his eyes on Tsuna. He didn't want to look up. He flexed his jaw, a cold sweat beading on his neck. He exhaled and looked upward.

"Oh, no," Timrekka quietly moaned.

Master Brawd's expression didn't change. He was locked in place as he stared at Candelle's silhouette gently floating away from them a few feet beyond the atmosphere. She was motionless, arms and legs spread out like a doll sinking underwater. Her outline glowed in the starlight as her weightless hair spread. Master Brawd's eyes twitched as his mind went blank. He shook in place, unable to think, unable to move. She was right there, just out of reach, and there was nothing he could do to bring her body back to hold one last time. He had to watch as she slowly floated away, forever to be lost in the endlessness. The haunting obscurity of her silhouette only broke his heart into more pieces. He longed to see her face, but all that was left was darkness. Only her glimmering tattoos seemed to be reaching back for him.

"Dumakleiza," he said, monotone and forthright. "Give him to me."

Tsuna immediately resumed whining. "No! Just let me go," he cried. "Oh, mighty Wall, help me! Help me!"

Dumakleiza let go of Tsuna as she saw Master Brawd's rage surpass her own. She crawled off, getting to her throbbing ankles. The landing had been rough, and now that Cooby was safe, her pain caught up.

Tsuna scrambled away once he was free, but Master Brawd's powerful grip pinned his throat in place. Master Brawd stood up, lifting Tsuna into the air, dangling him with haunting calm. Tsuna grabbed his burly wrist and pulled up for some starving breaths. Master Brawd looked from his panic-stricken face over to the device they'd used to launch Candelle. He stared at it, considering his options. No one else moved.

"No," Tsuna gurgled, turning white without circulation. "I'm sorry." He gagged. "I'm sorry. Just let me go." His words were barely discernable, but they got Master Brawd to look at him. After letting his callous linger, Master Brawd spoke low and controlled.

"I'm not going to." He stared through Tsuna. "You don't deserve to be up there with her."

"Thank you," Tsuna whimpered as Master Brawd returned his feet to the ground. "I'm so sorry. I just —" His words were choked out as Master Brawd squeezed his throat tighter and marched away.

The recruits watched as Master Brawd dragged Tsuna into the darkness of the sazeal trees. They didn't know what to do, if they should even be doing anything at all. Tsuna's gurgled screams echoed in the black forest, terrified, futile. No one moved. They listened as the cries grew quieter and quieter. They'd lost sight of Master Brawd, but they had a good idea where he was heading.

Dumakleiza ignored the screams. They were nothing new to her. She had no pity for whatever fate Master Brawd had in mind for Tsuna. All that mattered was reviving Cooby.

"Jasss, assist me with Cooby's resurrection." Her tone made Jasss jump and hurry over. They approached the unconscious tanion lying in the black bead. Dumakleiza shot Jasss a demanding glare.

"Okay. Okay." Jasss knelt down next to Cooby and placed her hands on his small chest cavity. She gulped, worried that if she failed to wake Cooby, Dumakleiza would find more bark. She started devising an escape plan should it come to that. After a brief collection of her thoughts, she pressed down over and over in quick succession. The response was instant. Cooby snarled and snapped awake, panicking and lurching to his feet.

"Coobs!" Dumakleiza yelled. The rattled tanion leapt into her arms, twitching as his furry body struggled to recover from electric shocks. They held each other, swaying back and forth as Cooby cried and cooed, clawing at Dumakleiza's suit. "Shhh," she comforted. "I have you, Coobs. Jasss of Ojīptian has brought you back from the lightning death."

Jasss slumped at avoiding Dumakleiza's rage. "He's okay?"

"Yes. Thank you." Dumakleiza looked at her, finally dropping her aggression. There was no need for it anymore.

❋

"Stop! Please!" Tsuna pleaded as Master Brawd dragged him farther away from the Wall Posts. "I'm sorry." There was no response as Master Brawd effortlessly hauled him through the darkness, scraping his body against trees and rough patches of black bead.

Tsuna screamed as he was hauled to the clearing surrounding the hole. He fought, clawing and kicking the large Whewlight but to no avail. It seemed that the more he struggled, the less Master Brawd cared. His vice grip around Tsuna's throat was unbreakable.

"Master Brawd, I'm sorry! It was necessary to gain their trust. I was going to gain insights into their plan and then report it back to you so we could stop them together. I swear that was my plan! I'm sorry!" he wailed. "Don't do this!"

Master Brawd walked him to the edge of the hole and held him out over it, staring lifelessly into his eyes. Tsuna mumbled through mucous-filled tears as his feet dangled over the void. Blood streamed down Master Brawd's arm from where Tsuna clawed him, but he didn't feel anything.

Tsuna closed his eyes and cried to the only thing he could. "Mighty Wall, please come to my aid! Spare me! Spare me!"

Master Brawd glanced into the abyss and then looked at Tsuna. "Allow me to unite you with your god." With that, he released Tsuna's throat. Tsuna screamed and scrambled, holding onto the thick arm as hard as he could. They made eye contact for a brief second before Tsuna's fingers failed and he fell. Bright white ripples spread as he disappeared into the blackness of the pit. He screamed, echoing farther and farther down. Master Brawd stood perfectly still until he heard the screaming stop.

18

Everyone sat in the Wall Post, trauma bleeding despondence. Master Brawd had his elbows on his knees as he stared through the floor in a disarray of anger and grief. He hadn't spoken since returning. Whatever dark world his mind had descended into, nobody was saving him from it.

Traveler knew that until Master Brawd returned to the land of the living, he was next in command. The remaining recruits would look to him for guidance. He had no idea what to do or say. He wanted guidance himself, but he bit his tongue and waited, allowing his own emotions to take their course.

Timrekka had Gideon propped up in a corner, trying to set his injuries. He'd blabbered a desperate apology, which Gideon had waved away with a pained smile.

Dumakleiza sat next to them, coddling Cooby as she studied Gideon. Her temper had transformed into relief and sympathy. Cooby had been saved, preventing her from feeling alone in the universe, but Gideon was hurt.

Izzy and Jasss were sitting together on the edge of a bed. They were all each other had from their team. Six One left them in Master Brawd's care and Tsuna betrayed them. They felt like outsiders in the universe's expanding enormity.

"Oh!" Timrekka jumped to his feet. "Idea!" Everyone watched him scuttle over to his utility belt he'd stashed against a wall. He rummaged around for a moment and then hurried back with some kind of rod. "Izzy, I could use your assistance."

"Okay." Izzy was grateful for the distraction.

Timrekka opened his hand to expose what looked like a sharp metal dowel about six inches long. The spherical tip was needle sharp, and the back end was made of glass with what looked like a syringe plunger.

Gideon raised an eyebrow and coughed through a chuckle. "Yeah. What—is that?" He coughed. It looked like a futuristic torture device.

"Uh," Timrekka said, "it's one of my failed inventions called a stem cell injection, really only intended for a single use because I didn't have a surplus of stem cells stored away from what I stole from Trollop's stash, but the way I made the injector is why I think it could help. See, when it's stabbed in, I—"

"Hmm." Gideon chuckled as best he could manage. "*Stabbed* in?"

"Mhm." Timrekka nodded, confused by Gideon's hesitance. "After it's stabbed in, the tip splays out with needle-thin metal prongs like a grappling hook, each intended to spread the distribution of the stem cells more efficiently in any one area of the body; like I said, not my best work, and I've never found anyone brave enough to test it, although, I mean, I think the stem cells could come in handy at some point, but I digress."

Izzy wasn't so sure. "You think stem cells will help Gideon's ribs?"

"No," Timrekka said. "I mean maybe, but I'm actually thinking we use the prongs to catch underneath his ribs and pull them out enough to release some of the pressure from his lungs, but you have more of a medicinal background than I do, so I was wondering if you think that'd work, and if you would know the best spot to stab it." His casually repetitive delivery of the word "stab" had Gideon shaking his head.

Izzy nodded as his creative juices surged. "Oh, I like that! Umm." He thought. "There's no guarantee it'll be an effective fix, but it could set them until we can light jump somewhere."

Traveler walked over. "I'll hold him down."

Dumakleiza realized she could help, too. "Take one arm, Diviner. I shall take his other."

Gideon rolled his eyes and smiled as they moved into position. He took a few shallow breaths. He'd experienced more than his fair share of pain, but this one sounded more like torture.

Timrekka roughly patted around Gideon's ribs. "Where would be best?"

Gideon lurched in their grip. "Whoa, easy with the goods."

Izzy reached forward and felt around with a softer touch. It wasn't hard to tell where the worst of the injury was. He wiggled his finger near Gideon's floating rib and nodded. Gideon took as deep of a breath as he could. He was about to say something snarky, but before he could get a word in, Timrekka jabbed the injector into his body. Gideon's eyes shot open. His own screams barely registered in his ears as he felt the prongs splay out. Traveler and Dumakleiza held tight as Gideon involuntarily thrashed. The pain was immediately mitigated by the strange sensation from whatever alien stem cells were spreading through his side. They felt warm and prickly. They did nothing to relieve the pressure, but the sensation was distracting.

Timrekka pulled, popping Gideon's ribs away from his lungs with an audible crunch. Gideon grunted. The pain was too intense and fast to yell, but as it subsided a little, he managed a full breath. A fit of violent coughing forced him to draw the first deep inhalations since waking. He winced as Timrekka hit a button that retracted the prongs and then pulled it out.

"Ow!" Gideon yelled and laughed as the pain flared again.

Izzy leaned in with a rag and wiped away the blood dribbling down Gideon's suit. Traveler reached down and cauterized the wound with the same implant he'd cut Gideon's shoulder with.

Everyone stepped back, allowing Gideon some space. He was still in pain, but it had at least allowed him to breathe.

Gideon took another deep breath, relishing in oxygen's luxury. "Thank you, guys. That sucked." He chuckled. "That reallysucked. Not gonna lie."

Timrekka looked him over, satisfied with his handiwork. "How are you feeling? Can you breathe?"

Gideon nodded. "Yes, I'm good. Thanks, Timmy. Don't know what we'd do without you." He coughed and then looked at Traveler. "Enough about me. What's the plan?"

Traveler's expression died as he was thrust back into Abdabriel's betrayal. "I don't know. We're too late to go back to Whewliss and warn them."

Gideon nodded as he sat up a little. "What did Abdabriel mean when he said something about doing something to Lord Coyzle?"

Traveler shrugged, trying to not draw his own conclusions. "I don't know. But maybe we could go back and —"

"No," Master Brawd said without looking away from the floor. "Abdabriel's gone back to Whewliss, which means he has control of the gelatin. We'd be vaporized or imprisoned as soon as we were processed through."

Dumakleiza was on board with any vengeful course of action. "Why do we not simply jump to another location on your world of Whewliss?"

"Because," Traveler answered for Master Brawd, "our greatest defense has now become our biggest hindrance: the fractal gas being constantly pumped and recycled through our atmosphere's outer layer. Millions of microscopic two-way mirrors per every square foot that reflect and direct any body of light directly toward and into the gelatin." He sighed. "It's a funneling system we developed to prevent exactly what we want to do now. Nobody lands on Whewliss without our knowledge. The underside is clear, so exiting the planet is simple, and breaking in is impossible. It's very efficient."

"Well." Gideon puzzled. "How do you keep a worldwide amount of reflective dust in the atmosphere aimed in a single direction?"

Traveler nodded, expecting the question. "The top layer is coated reflectively, and the bottom is coated with a magnetic spray. Whewliss's magnetic pull does the work naturally. That's how we decided where to establish EBOO in the first place."

"Damn." Gideon smiled. "Aside from that being reallycool, that is a problem." He shook his head and tilted it back against the wall. "And Whewliss has enough to cover the entire planet?"

Traveler nodded. "Think of the area that smoke from a single volcano can cover."

Gideon thought back to some of Earth's volcanic eruptions. "Fair. Okay, next plan?"

"Uh." Traveler racked his mind. "If Abdabriel has recruited as many soldiers as he says, and he's launching his plan's first phase as we speak, we have no idea which planets are safe right now. Oh!" He perked up a little. "I can go outside and look at the space forecast. Every LOLA-abiding planet has a distress call. I can check which ones, if any, have sent one out. We can go to any that haven't and try to formulate a plan with their military to prepare for when—"

"It won't work," Master Brawd said. "I already checked. The forecast has stopped. Lady Skorric isn't updating the IPOK. She's either in Abdabriel's custody or he's killed her."

"No." Traveler blinked a few times, refusing to consider either possibility. "He wouldn't have done that, would he?" He lowered his head, feeling hopeless. "They're both council members. He wouldn't—how could—"

"So, the forecast is gone?" Izzy asked, worried about the implications. He was fascinated by the Wall, but he didn't want to be stuck there.

"No," Traveler said, trying to force himself to keep talking. "It means we can still see planetary locations and the updates of moving celestial bodies, but we have no idea what's happening with the people on any world. We have full knowledge still of where we're going, but we're going in blind, reference the conditions of each planet's inhabitants."

Timrekka quietly muttered, "Maybe we should just stay here and focus on exploring the fourth phase."

Master Brawd shook his head, keeping his eyes on the floor. "We have to take swift and immediate action, or there's a probability that none of us will have home worlds to return to—at least none that welcome us. Abdabriel intends to make sure of that. Anywhere we go would be under his rule following his invasion. He spared us once. He won't again."

"Okay." Gideon brainstormed out loud. "He said he's recruited somewhere around fourteen million soldiers, right? That's a lot for one world, but across the universe, that's a marginal force against a potential resistance of trillions or quadrillions. Why don't we just go do some recruiting of our own and create a badass army to kick his ass?"

Master Brawd flexed his jaw. "It could work, but it would take years to reach enough worlds and amass a formidable force. Plus Abdabriel has been planning this for who knows how long, and he's recruited only from the most advanced planets. The intricacy required for a successful execution of his plan requires—" He angrily grunted as his fist tightened and released. "I can't believe we didn't see the danger right under our chins!" He looked up. "Timrekka, Izzy, can you conceive anything capable of blasting through the fractal gas? If I can just get my hands on Abdabriel, I can cut this invasion's heart out, and its body will die off."

Timrekka and Izzy looked at each other. They had no idea how to tackle the requested task, but they started mulling over ideas. Inventing and creating were their favorite activities, but they had no experience with fractal gas, so it was all theoretical.

"Well, I suppose we could try to — "

"And even if I can't get ahold of Abdabriel directly, if I can at least reach the soldiers under my command, I could organize a defensive assault with the Whewlight army," Master Brawd said. "They wouldn't surrender to him."

"I hope you're right," Traveler said, struggling to see a positive outcome.

Dumakleiza tickled under Cooby's chin, looking adoringly into his big, beady eyes. "If I may, before any course of action is taken, I must first remove the dead man from our camp outside. On Cul, I buried the body of every man I cut down. Regardless of the monsters they were, I always — "

"That's it!" Timrekka yelled out. "Oh, sorry, Dumakleiza, I didn't mean to interrupt, but that man's body, that could be the solution. Traveler, Mister Brawd, er, *Master* Brawd, sorry, but are his cells still compatible with light postmortem?"

Traveler grimaced, put off by the morbid question. "I, uh, don't know. I've never heard of any attempt at jumping a dead body."

Master Brawd finally looked up, glancing at Timrekka. "What's your idea?"

"Well." Timrekka's eyes buzzed around as his idea flew through his head faster than he could voice it. "When glass burns, it melts. I've never melted a mirror, but I'm assuming it's similar, if not exact, so if Whewliss is encased in micro-mirrors, theoretically we could blast a wave of heat hot enough to melt glass right through it, which would create a brief window, ironically named, that we could jump through if we follow immediately behind it before the surrounding fractal gas fills the void."

He threw his hands up, his heart racing with excitement. "The hotter the blast, the bigger the window."

"Yeah!" Izzy yelled out as his eyes matched Timrekka's enthusiasm. "I see where you're going with this idea."

Master Brawd tensed. "How are you going to do that?"

"Oh." Izzy's energy came down as he looked at Timrekka. "Yeah, what does —? Hmm."

"Easy," Timrekka boasted. "I'm assuming you're always careful and precise about how tightly you wind light's elasticity for the sake of our safety, but this is an opportunity to test its full power and pull that elasticity back as far as you can."

"I think Isee what you're getting at," Gideon said with less pain as his eyes lit up. The realization brought new breath to his lungs. He turned to Traveler. "You explained this to me after the Roaring Valley." Traveler gave him a confused expression, so Gideon elaborated. "You said if someone is shot too fast, they become a laser and literally dig their own grave into the ground." Gideon looked to Timrekka to see if he was on the right path. Timrekka motioned for him to continue. Gideon nodded and went on. "Besides," he said and glanced at Dumakleiza, "the dead guy *does* need to be buried."

Master Brawd leaned forward, growing more interested. "It could work," he said with an almost hopeful tone, "but without the IPOK, there's no way of knowing if where we shoot him will be clear of life. If anyone's in the line of fire, they'll be vaporized at those speeds."

"A risk." Timrekka nodded. "This is why I suggested, and still suggest, we just stay here and focus on the fourth phase." He smiled, trying to sell the safer idea. The looks on everyone's faces demanded they focus on Abdabriel. Timrekka sighed. "But since you all want to go, it's the only way I can think of to break through the fractal gas, and that's only if it's possible to shoot a corpse, so you'll have to plan a location that's predictably and statistically the safest for us to arrive at, launch him as fast as you think will do the trick, prepare to jump immediately after, and all of that has to be done with two chariot jumps." Even he realized how crazy and perilous his plan was, but he was still proud of having conceived it.

"Well." Gideon shrugged. "I mean we could be starting the zombie apocalypse by jumping a dead body."

Master Brawd slowly nodded. "I've never heard of anything like this." He sighed in nervous apprehension. "There's no time. It will have to do." His eyes oscillated as he calculated the steps necessary to pull it off. "It's going to require two separate jumps to take place in *immediate* succession, so, Four Zero, you will shoot the corpse, and I will jump everyone else directly after. For this to work, you will have to shoot the corpse and only then grab onto one of us within a second after launching him. Any longer of a delay and we risk the window closing and us ending up in the gelatin." Traveler tensely nodded as Master Brawd went on. "Additionally, you need to launch him fast, and I mean *fast,* because we have to hit the *exact* same spot or, once again, we will end up in the gelatin. There has to be nofractal remaining in the window we aim for or this plan fails and Abdabriel will have us."

Though he was still in a considerable amount of pain, Gideon smiled, excited for the risk. "Supposing this bit of joyous insanity works, what's your plan for after?"

Master Brawd chewed on the inside of his bottom lip as he turned to Gideon. "Find as many of my soldiers as are still alive, assemble a team, and then execute Abdabriel and his zealots. My army hasn't prepared for this scenario, but we've prepared for invasions. They are courageous, and they are resolute. We will kill him before his plan gets any more traction."

"Well, shit." Gideon nodded. "Let's do this."

Master Brawd turned to Timrekka. "I understand your fear, and I do not blame you. Nor do I expect you to fight a battle for Whewliss. If you wish to remain behind, I relieve you of any guilt and encourage you to study the fourth phase in our absence. Should we survive, we will come for you after."

"No," Timrekka said almost instantly. "I'm scared, but I'm coming with you; I'm not hiding here all by myself."

Master Brawd turned to the rest of the group. "If anyone wishes to stay behind, do so with my support. Everyone else, let's go." With that, he turned and marched out of the Wall Post. Everyone followed, Gideon wincing as he struggled to keep the pace.

Traveler quickly made his way to the dead man and squatted down next to him. He tried not to let the eerie feeling of death distract him from his job, but seeing the lifeless body made his stomach uneasy. He grabbed the man's limp wrist and reached up with his other hand. He held his fingers open, waiting to see what the starlight would allow. His peripherals begged him to stare at the bloody bark protruding from the man's throat, but he kept his eyes on the sky. He smiled.

"He's not too far gone, but I'm guessing we don't have long." He closed his fist and held on.

Master Brawd wasted no time as he reached a hand up, trying to get a grip on as much starlight as he could. "Everyone, grab on." He stared intently into the vastness of space. "Four Zero, aim for the exact center of Dreamland."

Traveler nodded. "Yes, master."

As everyone formed a chain of held hands, Gideon piped up. "What's Dreamland?"

Traveler narrowed his eyes, trying to acquire enough light while simultaneously aiming with absolute precision. "It's the largest garden in EBOO. A work of art consisting of every color. About two-hundred-thousand-square-feet." Sweat began beading on his forehead as he focused his aim and held the light longer than he was comfortable with. The elastic power had to be more than enough. He had to be absolutely sure. "It is forbidden to walk in Dreamland in order to preserve it. So the only people we might hit shouldn't be in there in the first place." He squinted more narrowly as he held perfectly still.

Master Brawd did the same thing. "Four Zero, on your mark."

Traveler could feel new warmth taking hold of the corpse as the buzzing energy of overflowing light made the dead vibrate. There was almost a glow to it. The recruits all stared wide-eyed. Finally, the subtlest of smiles appeared on his face.

"It'll be a shame to see the flowers burn." With that, he opened his fist, and the corpse vanished. Traveler leapt for Izzy's hand.

Gideon cracked a smile. "Badass line, Spaceman."

Master Brawd opened his hand, and everyone was consumed by white light.

19

"Of course this happened to me." Jasss's foggy voice echoed in Gideon's mind as he came to. Had they made it? Were they in Dreamland, or had they been redirected to the gelatin?

A strong smell of burning plants filled his nostrils. The scent was cast aside as glowing light flooded his vision. It was daytime on Whewliss, nearing the evening by the looks of it. His dreamy state faded, along with the remaining whiteness from his eyes. Gideon shook his head and looked around at everyone else to make sure they'd all made it together. It was a pleasant surprise to land during the day after however long they had been bathed in the Wall's darkness.

Gideon looked beyond and was instantly taken aback by the beauty surrounding them. Lush flowers and plants spanned in every direction. They'd landed smack-dab in the center of the most awe-inspiring cornucopia of foreign florae he'd ever seen. He felt like he was standing in a rainbow that crashed to the ground.

Jasss's hushed griping turned his attention back. "Will someone pull me out of here?"

Gideon smirked at Jasss climbing out of a hole about four by two feet in the dirt. It was inundated in cooling embers and ashen plants. Small flames danced around as others devoured stems and petals, sending floating ash into the air.

Master Brawd offered his hand and pulled Jasss up. She brushed off some burning dirt and shook her head.

"Well that was just—"

"Get down," Traveler sharply whispered. At his command, everyone dropped to their knees or bellies, eyes alert and hearts racing. The heavy foliage easily concealed them beneath opulent, kaleidoscopic waves. They looked around, trying to see whatever he had. They managed to spot two women and a man, all wearing the same suits as Abdabriel's cronies. They were walking down one of EBOO's many sidewalks in the distance. Traveler narrowed his eyes, looking to see if there were any more of them nearby. "What's next?"

Master Brawd held perfectly still, controlling his huffing as he watched the three walk away. "I need to get to Panoply Hall and gather as many Whewlights as I can, take them to the City of Light, and gather a more formidable force."

Traveler nodded. "I can light whip us there."

"No. We can't risk getting caught during the recovery from the whip. We need to be alert. Follow my lead. We're going to walk there."

"Hey," Gideon whispered with guttural tone. "I don't mean to interrupt, but if you want a tactical advantage, wouldn't it be more strategic to get to the gelatin and overtake whatever force is there, so that no more of Abdabriel's soldiers can show up to help him?"

Master Brawd nodded. "It's closer, as well."

Dumakleiza held Cooby close and whispered into his perked ears. "Coobs, we must be without voice until we are safe from the false pretty god."

Timrekka was shaking, but he couldn't help squinting at her. "Is that what you're calling Master N'kowsky?" Dumakleiza nodded. Timrekka blinked. "It's a complimentary title. I'm surprised you didn't think of a meaner name than 'pretty.'"

"He remains pretty, regardless of his vile soul," Dumakleiza said with a snarl. "I feel no pity watching pretty things die." She motioned to the burning flowers. "False gods fall the hardest, and I shall bask in the warmth of his burning bones."

Timrekka's eyes widened as he stared at her. "I just want to clarify, there's nothing you're mad at me for, right? Like we're doing good, right?"

Master Brawd brought his hand down from his ear after whispering something only he could hear. Frustration festered as he looked around, struggling to galvanize his fragmented focus.

"I can't get ahold of Lord Coyzle or my lieutenants." He looked up at Whewliss's sun. It was about an hour from twilight, and he wanted to use the darkness to their advantage. He nodded to himself and focused as he looked around for any other signs of life. The normally busy sidewalks were void of EBOO workers, and the air, vacant of conversation. Luckily, however, there weren't any more soldiers visible.

"We were lucky to land during the day. They would have spotted this fire at night." Master Brawd glanced around a bit more. "I'm assuming if Abdabriel is still here that he's gone to the City of Light for a more efficient takeover. He's probably left a small contingent here to guard the gelatin and keep EBOO quiet. There shouldn't be too many of them. As it gets darker, we'll work our way to the gelatin and discretely dispose of any members of this army of light along the way." He looked back at the group and assessed what assets he had at his disposal. "Dumakleiza, Jasss, you two are the smallest, most nimble, and familiar with skulking. Work your way through Dreamland and post up near its edge in that direction. Keep us updated with any movement, and if you find yourselves in trouble, double back." He pointed toward what looked to them like just another part of the city of EBOO. "Gideon, Timrekka, to that edge." He pointed to the adjacent side of Dreamland. "Four Zero, Izzy, that one." He motioned a third side of the square garden. "And I'll take that one. Your translators double as communication devices if you plug the ear, they're in with your index finger and hold your thumb from the same hand against your lips, like so." As he demonstrated, Traveler looked at him in disbelief.

"How long have they been able to do that?"

"Forever. It's a military secret. Every translator is programmed for it. Opens up a secure channel. Only Lord Coyzle, my lieutenants, and myself know of the function. Abdabriel and his soldiers shouldn't be able to trace any of our communications." He moved past everyone's amazement and continued. "We don't have time to waste. Let's go. Report any movement you see." At his command, they got lower and crawled under the tall flowers toward the edges of Dreamland.

✳

As the sun set, a few whispers were reported of other soldiers patrolling around EBOO, but none had spotted the recruits hiding in Dreamland. After an hour and a half of minimal communication, the group gathered outside of the massive garden, hiding in shadows. Night was upon them, and they had to move fast. It appeared that Master Brawd's theory of minimal security had been correct.

Master Brawd quietly motioned with his hand. "This way."

"Wait," Timrekka whispered. "Will one of you cut Gideon's shoulder? Because he hasn't been himself since we landed."

Gideon rolled his eyes. "There's no time. Let's just go." The rest of the group instantly felt his irritability. Gideon didn't care. He was getting more impatient with every passing second. "I'm not a priority right now," he growled. "Let's just go."

Traveler stepped forward and firmly grabbed his left arm. "Don't move," he whispered. There was enough on his mind. Soldiers would inevitably walk by soon. There was no time for a debate. He held on tightly as Gideon resisted. In times past, he'd tried to burn a perfect line from the top of Gideon's shoulder to the bottom, but they had to hurry. Everyone impatiently watched as Traveler focused his laser implant and cauterized a burn down Gideon's shoulder. His normally straight line was emotional and jagged, but it got the job done. After nodding to Master Brawd, he dragged Gideon the first couple steps to force him to walk.

They moved as a unit through the well-lit city. It was normally bubbling with crickets chirping, workers walking between buildings, activity flowing around the clock. Oftentimes there were even musicians hired to keep everyone's energy high and upbeat. This time it was silent. There were no people aside from the random soldiers, and even the insects had gone still. The group repeatedly prepared themselves for violence or scattered bodies in Abdabriel's wake, but the eerie quiet and lack of life was even more off putting.

A soldier rounded a corner right in front of the group, but before he could register what he was seeing, Dumakleiza leapt at him. Cooby barked but quieted as he buried his fangs into the man's neck. Dumakleiza simultaneously swept his legs and dropped him to the ground. Even Master Brawd was impressed. The kill was swift, and the body placed down silently. Dumakleiza was in her element. With Cooby wrapped around her, she was back to attacking anything that moved. Whewliss had never felt so much like home.

Gideon was torn between shock and an erection, so his body went with both.

It only took a few brisk minutes to reach the massive gelatin structure, but every second felt like they were moving in slow motion. The recruits' first time on Whewliss, they had been too distracted and excited to pay much attention to the sheer size of the building. This time they took in its full magnitude. It stretched up like a skyscraper, but each wall was at least a mile across. Gideon couldn't help thinking it looked like the largest airport he'd ever seen. Even in the darkness of night, the designs and colors on the outer walls were intricate and beautiful.

The sightseeing was cut short as Master Brawd ushered them through a secret side door. Once they were inside, the uneasiness increased. There was no way of knowing how many soldiers Abdabriel would have posted up with the gelatin, so they had to be prepared for more rather than less.

Master Brawd knew exactly where he was going, and with the lack of signs of life, he'd thrown caution to the wind. He sped through the halls and rooms with both hands out. It was still strange for Gideon to see someone aggressively holding finger guns out like children playing cops and robbers.

A soldier nonchalantly turned a corner and froze when she saw them. "Hey, what are you all—" *Fft.* A trail of smoke led to a burn on the wall behind her. No blood spilled out of the cauterized hole in her head as she fell to the ground. Master Brawd's aimed fingers followed as he searched for anyone who may have accompanied her. The rest of the group was frozen in surprise behind him. They hadn't seen Whewlight weapons actually fired before, and the lightning fast efficiency was scary. Master Brawd waited but saw no movement. He walked forward again with the others close behind.

After a few long hallways and stressful turns, Master Brawd paused at a doorway and peered around the corner into the gelatin's control room.

Gideon was too curious to wait behind Master Brawd like the rest of the group. He leaned forward and glanced around Master Brawd's thick body, trying to get a look for himself. Amid the sincerity of the moment, he took a second to appreciate the unexpected simplicity of the space. It was a well-lit control room made of white walls, a colorful floor that matched that of Prism Hall, and a wall-sized window that allowed the controller to see into the arrival pad. He'd expected to see more buttons and knobs than the cockpit of a jumbo jet, but it was quite the opposite. There was one large desk, about the size of a grand piano, and a chair with a man in it. Otherwise, the spacious room consisted of a couple of fancy couches and some paintings on the walls. The desk appeared to be a touch screen, just like the window. Gideon wanted to get his hands on it and see how it worked, but he knew that was a rodeo for another time.

Master Brawd glared at the man in the chair. He was donning one of the same unfamiliar gelatin suits and had dirty-blond shoulder-length hair. Whoever he was, he wasn't Lady Melodeen, and that was enough to warrant him a death sentence in Master Brawd's eyes.

Master Brawd turned the corner with his right hand aimed directly at the unsuspecting stranger and walked forward. As soon as he was in the room, he slipped up behind the man and placed his index finger against the back of his head. The man spun around to see Master Brawd's finger right in his face. He froze, his blue eyes panicking as he looked up.

"Who are you?" the soldier asked.

Master Brawd growled, "Your suit reads your pulse. If you lie to me, I will kill you. Do you understand?" He didn't need to elaborate threats. His words were enough. The soldier nodded and gulped as he resisted the urge to raise his own hand and fight back. Master Brawd kept his finger aimed at the man's right eye. "I have three questions. Where is Abdabriel? What is your plan for overthrowing Whewliss? And where is —"

"Master...Brawd..." a woman's weak voice called from behind. Someone was tucked away between a couch and the wall. Master Brawd leaned to get a better look, seeing blood stains on the floor. More injuries became visible as he recognized Lady Melodeen. She groaned through a battered face as she looked back and forth between Master Brawd and the man in the chair.

Master Brawd's eyes didn't flicker, though the fire behind them exploded. He turned back to the man and squatted down, smoothly lowering his finger's aim from the man's head to his crotch. He leaned in as the man leaned back.

"Please don't. Please don't do that," the soldier begged, squirming in his seat.

"Don't talk," Master Brawd instructed. "Recruits, tend to Lady Melodeen. Get her on the couch." He stared at the man and listened to the recruits entering the room. They gasped at the sight of Lady Melodeen beaten and bloodied, and then assisted her. Once Master Brawd heard her groan on the padded seat, he spoke. "Lady Melodeen, are you in any condition to explain what happened?"

"Yes," Lady Melodeen whimpered through labored breaths. "They're using…arachniblasts."

As soon as she said "arachniblasts," Master Brawd aimed his index finger up at the man's head and tapped his thumb against it. *Fft.* An ashy hole burned up through his jaw and out the top of his head. He went limp in the chair with no blood spray.

"What'd you kill him for?" Traveler couldn't help his outburst. "He could have given us vital information."

"Not worth the risk," Master Brawd calmly replied before turning around to see Lady Melodeen. "Arachniblasts are top-secret implants that were outlawed after they were deemed inhumane."

"What do they do?" Traveler asked, wondering what kind of implant could be so dangerous as to be above his paygrade. He'd heard of some dangerous implants but none that even the military had disbanded.

"They react to body heat. Once fired, they instantly kill the target, regardless of where on the body they hit, boiling the blood until it vaporizes. Simultaneously, they trigger a chain reaction with up to eight other bodies of heat within an eight-foot radius, hence their name. It can kill up to nine people with a single shot, regardless of how poor the aim—more than enough to kill all of us, given the opportunity. Doesn't matter what he knew. If he decided to be a martyr, we'd all be dead." Master Brawd flexed his jaw and looked at Lady Melodeen. He reached out and took her feeble hand, feeling how weak she was. "We will get you lit as soon as we can. Tell me what happened."

She nodded and coughed up blood onto her chin. "Master N'kowsky arrived in the gelatin." She took some labored breaths. "After I let him through, he greeted the assistants and myself and then arrested them all. He assured me that he wouldn't kill me——that I would understand soon and that I would come to see the light." Tears streamed down her face as she stared into Master Brawd's eyes. "He told that man——" She pointed at the corpse in the chair. "——to keep me alive. But not to let me interfere with…approving his soldiers through the gelatin." Rage burned through her tears. "I did my best to not make his job easy."

Master Brawd nodded. "You did well." He caressed her hand. "Abdabriel went to the City of Light, didn't he? I assume to kill Lord Coyzle and then broadcast his terms to the rest of Whewliss?"

More tears slid down Lady Melodeen's face. "Yes. He's going to the City of Light. But Lord Coyzle was here in EBOO when Master N'kowsky arrived."

Master Brawd's stone expression flickered. He closed his eyes and steamed as he prolonged the inevitable question. He opened his eyes and looked into Lady Melodeen's.

"Where's his body?"

Lady Melodeen took a few breaths, fighting more tears. "He's not dead. He's——" She struggled to gulp. Gideon and Izzy tilted her head up a little higher. "Master N'kowsky's mercenaries killed every Whewlight soldier stationed in EBOO. He shot their bodies aimlessly into space. And then——"

Master Brawd's veins raced. "He is no master, and we must stop recognizing him as such." He wanted to hit something, to beat something, to destroy something. His soldiers were being slaughtered, and he couldn't even bury their bodies. The image of Candelle floating away flashed before his eyes. He ground his teeth and forced himself to focus. "Where is Lord Coyzle?" he asked as calmly as he could, trying not to scream it.

"He's in——" Lady Melodeen stifled a breath. "——the Winkloh Star."

A cold silence came over the room. Even with their limited understanding, the recruits knew what fate Lord Coyzle was condemned to: an unconscious eternity of spinning around with capital criminals.

Master Brawd slowly slipped his hands away from Lady Melodeen's and clasped them under his chin as he stared off. He tried to think of a course of action, but he looked hopeless, rage and loss clouding above him. The recruits looked at one another, wanting to find some sort of guidance, but the problem was beyond their expertise. Gideon knew there was nothing in his vocabulary or backpack that could help the moment, so he leaned over to Dumakleiza.

"Duma, there's no one I would trust to pray for this group more than you."

She nodded, seeing Gideon's rare solemnity. "Sir Gideon, there's no one for whom I'd rather pray." She stared at him a moment longer, letting his face linger in her mind before she closed her eyes and started whispering under her breath.

Traveler considered a solution with a shaky voice. "We could break the glass."

Master Brawd shook his head. "Depending on the condition of Master Keevind, we may not even have access to the Winkloh Star. If we got in and broke the glass, we would release Lord Coyzle and fourteen criminals at the same time, eleven of which are Daemoaniks. With only you and me having implants, we'd all be dead before we could save Lord Coyzle."

Traveler nodded. "I thought of that. Get the recruits our most lethal implants and deputize them. Between all of us, we can easily contain the—"

"If Abdabriel gained access to arachniblasts, then he hacked our military system. Between that and him deactivating the IPOK, I guarantee you that means he's put new security on our databases and locked everyone out but himself. No one will be able to access implants other than him."

Lady Melodeen weakly nodded. "It's true." She coughed. "He did it here." She lifted a finger and pointed toward the control table.

Master Brawd blew steam through his nostrils and closed his eyes. "That means we can't access the weapons necessary to defend ourselves against eleven Daemoaniks, let alone Abdabriel's armies." He squeezed his fists. "If this were ever to happen, Abdabriel was the one most qualified to fix it. We never suspected that *he'd* be the one to betray us."

Traveler racked his mind for other options, but nothing had any promise. "That also means he probably removed the implant safeguards, which means that all implants are functional on all planets. That is a very dangerous reality for worlds less advanced." He felt lost. "What do we do now?"

"I don't know."

"Where do we go?"

"I don't know!" Master Brawd slammed his fist into the ground. "I don't know! We're not prepared for this!" Everyone leaned away as his maelstrom of rage erupted. "We have no army! We have *two* weapons! You and me! And you're not even a soldier. There's nowhere we can go where his army can't find us. There's nowhere we can go that we can even prepare for without the IPOK. Our Lord is stuck in purgatory with monsters. Our adversary is armed with banned weaponry, and he's the most knowledgeable person about the entire universe *in* the entire universe!" He released his fists as his chest deflated and shoulders slumped. "I don't know what to do. I don't know where to go."

Everyone sat in silence. None of them had any idea how to save the day. Rescuing one planet was becoming an impossible task. The idea of stopping Abdabriel from invading all their worlds was even more so. Only Lady Melodeen made any noise with her raspy breathing, and even Cooby could feel the tension as he buried his face in Dumakleiza's neck.

Gideon sighed. "Abdabriel was right about one thing. We are unorganized." He ignored the expected glares and looks of confusion. "I've been in many situations that have felt hopeless." He adjusted his cupping of Lady Melodeen's head as she coughed. "In those moments, I relied on my recklessness. I count my lucky stars that it paid off every time, but this is different." He looked at Master Brawd. "I'm willing to put my recklessness aside right now if you'll do the same."

Master Brawd's impatient eyes glazed over at Gideon's vagueness. "What do you mean?"

"We go against our natures," Gideon simply stated as his energy shined through a mischievous smile. "I was part of a recovery heist with some monks once." He realized the other recruits may not know what monks are. "Basically, I was helping these five righteous dudes get some holy relics back that had been stolen by bandits. It was wild." Gideon grinned as he reminisced. "But they couldn't get themselves organized. The first attempt got one of the monks killed, and that only fueled the others. After two more failed attempts to sneak into the bandits' camp, they realized that they were playing everything too close to the chest, too cautiously, too familiar with their own methodology. Basically, they were being monks. Finally, one of them suggested they betray their natures in order to think outside the box." He shook his head. "Long story short, two cross-dressed monks, one toting a gun, and one disguised as a bandit later, and they fought off the bandits and secured their relics." Gideon looked around at everyone. "What do we have to lose? Let's try a new approach. We all come from verydifferent backgrounds, worlds apart. Working together is something every human being is capable of, but we've proven is not in *our* nature. We're all loners. So, here's what I propose: Four Zero here leads the charge with the most dangerous idea he can think of instead of playing anything safe, Duma fights *beside* us instead of charging in on her own, Timrekka invents weapons with the sole purpose of hurting others, Jasss commits to fighting with us instead of instinctually running away or hiding, Izzy—" He squinted and cocked his head to the side. "Dude, I don't know. Just try something different." He chuckled. "I don't know you that well yet." He smiled. "And you, Master Brawd, there has got to be something top-secret in our giant universe, something that you've been sworn to secrecy over——something that you know of that could help us."

Master Brawd looked up at him with a scared look in his eyes. Everyone saw it. The rage and helplessness vanished, and something else had taken its place. If it was enough to drain the color from Master Brawd, it was enough to make the rest of them uneasy.

Gideon smiled and nodded. "I'm right, aren't I?" His smile grew as Master Brawd's face went paler. "Oh, I'm onto something."

Traveler recognized Master Brawd's distinct fear. "H.P."

20

Master Brawd shook his head, silencing Traveler with a single look. "Not an option, Four Zero. You know better than to even mention that around aliens."

Gideon watched the exchange of fearful glares between them. He wanted to say something but figured it wiser to let it play out. Whatever was on the forbidden planet was bad enough to have Master Brawd and the rest of Whewliss spooked. They'd divulged the fourth phase but still had secrets that the recruits weren't allowed to know.

Traveler blinked a few times and summoned the courage to challenge his superior. "With all due respect, master, I don't believe rank or alien intelligence matters right now. Gideon's right." He shrugged. "We're running out of options, and more importantly, we're running out of time. We have to think of a solution that Abdabriel hasn't already taken preventative measures against, and we both know he's thought of everything." Traveler waited. "I'm open to literally any other option if you have one."

Master Brawd glared at him as he racked his mind for alternatives. He was willing to die for the safety of Whewliss's future, but the cost of Traveler's suggestion was infinitely more than just his life. Admitting that it might be the only course of action was something he refused to surrender to. After coming up blank, he turned his glare to the floor.

Lady Melodeen coughed some blood onto her lips and looked at Master Brawd. "Mackel, if the light has betrayed us, perhaps it is time we turn to the dark." Her words sent goosebumps down Gideon's back. He couldn't hold his question in any longer.

"Master Brawd, what isH.P.?"

Master Brawd closed his eyes and bunched his lips as a cold sweat started dripping down his face. Even with Lady Melodeen's encouragement, he didn't want to answer the question. Hollow heartbeats drummed in his ears as he finally shook his head. Opening his eyelids felt like peeling skin from bones.

"All right, Gideon." He tried to stop the words from leaving his mouth as his chest tightened. "What I'm about to tell you is nothing more than a rumor. It's just a story that was told to us by the last surviving Daemoaniks before we condemned them to the Winkloh Stars. We have no way of confirming its validity. However, the legend it has created is dangerous enough to be classified so far beyond top-secret that it's—it's—" He ground his teeth. "It's only because of Abdabriel that you're being told. Even mentioning H.P. to an alien is treason."

"Mackel," Lady Melodeen weakly muttered, "I know you're afraid." She looked at him as sternly as her tired eyes could. "Just tell them." She tilted her head back, relaxing it into Gideon's hands. "There's no such thing as top-secret anymore."

Master Brawd deflated. "The Daemoaniks told us that during the ULW, after Shadowmaker executed our planetary leaders of the resistance, King Slaughtvike betrayed and captured him. No loose ends. Shadowmaker was imprisoned in a maximum-security facility designed specifically to contain him. King Slaughtvike assigned more than two-hundred-Daemonic-soldiers to guard it for Shadowmaker's life sentence."

"Oh, wow. That's a plot twist." Gideon leaned forward. "Is that what H.P. is? A prison planet?"

Master Brawd shook his head as his eyes trailed off. "The prison was on Daemoana. The Daemoaniks told us that Shadowmaker was there for less than a day before he broke out." Master Brawd's haunted tone deepened. "Guess how many Daemoaniks he killed during his escape?"

"All two-hundred-soldiers," Gideon said before Master Brawd finished his question.

Master Brawd slowly turned his gaze up until his eyes met Gideon's. They stared at each other as Master Brawd struggled to answer. He had to force an inhale as he maintained eerily steady eye contact with Gideon.

"Upon his escape, Shadowmaker killed over five billion."

Gideon immediately chuckled at the absurd response, but as he stared at Master Brawd's expression, his laughter died. Master Brawd was horrified, as if death itself was looming over his shoulder. There was no doubt in his eyes, no sarcasm on his lips, no joke in his voice.

Gideon looked to Traveler for a brief second to see if there were any answers in his familiar face. Traveler stared back with fear and then turned away. Gideon's expression went flat as he gave Master Brawd his full attention. He only had one guess.

"The planet that collided with Daemoana—"

Master Brawd didn't budge. "Before we imprisoned the last Daemoaniks, they warned us that no world is safe from Shadowmaker, that he destroyed Daemoana, and that he could destroy Whewliss or any other planet if he wanted to. Nowhere is safe. The last thing they said: Nowhere is safe."

"Wait." Gideon's brain was smoking. "How did he make a planet hit another planet? How is that even possible?"

Master Brawd looked up at him. "We don't know. The Daemoaniks didn't have an answer to that question either, but every single one of them *knew* it was him. They believed in their blackened souls that Shadowmaker found a way to kill them all, that he'd managed to bend the heavens to unleash hell." Sweat poured down his face. "After their world was destroyed, everything changed. The Daemoaniks all but welcomed their fates in the Winkloh Stars just to be able to hide from Shadowmaker, or at least be unconscious when his terror came for them."

Dumakleiza couldn't help joining. "Your legend claims that the Maker of Shadows was betrayed by his own people? And in the fires of vengeance, that he destroyed his own world?" It was an impossible story, and she was concerned that she didn't understand it correctly.

Master Brawd slowly nodded. "Like I said, we cannot confirm any of it."

Gideon looked from Master Brawd to Lady Melodeen and then to Traveler. All three Whewlights were visibly losing their grip on the moment. He could see that they believed the legend down to their bones. There were no ifs, maybes, or buts, only fear and silent reverence for the mythical monster. None of them looked at anyone or anything. Their eyes trailed off through the floor and walls as fear toyed with their sanities.

"So." Dumakleiza tried to tie the story off. "The Maker of Shadows died with his world?"

"No," Gideon said as he started seeing how the puzzle pieces fit together. "He's on H.P., isn't he?" Master Brawd and Traveler looked at him with silent horror that gave more than enough of an answer. Gideon's eyes widened. "And Lord Coyzle was telling the truth when he dismissed it, wasn't he? A world encased in such thick, gaseous clouds that it's impossible to see beyond its atmosphere. The perfect place for Shadowmaker to hide."

Traveler gulped down enough dread to nearly choke on. "Shadowmaker is not a man who needs to hide. There's no one for him to hide from. But it's a perfect place for him to wait."

"Wait for what?" Gideon's eyebrows were as high as they could go.

"I don't know. I don't want to know."

"This is amazing." Gideon's curiosity was bubbling more than he'd ever felt before. "What does H.P. stand for?"

Master Brawd turned his eyes back to the floor as he wiped sweat from his face. "Horror Planet."

"Holy spirit." Gideon couldn't help smiling. "Horror Planet? Are you serious? You named an entire planet based off a legend of an assassin that *might* be there?"

"No," Master Brawd responded. "Horror Planet is named for its atmosphere and what else it could contain. It's capable of sustaining life. That's all we know for sure. The entire world is saturated in darkness every day and every night. There is no sunlight that breaks through." His pulse wasn't slowing down. "That means that if anything lives there — plant life, animal life, human life — it is all nocturnal. Whatever exists beneath the black clouds covering H.P. has lived in darkness its entire life, and if what has proven true on every other world is consistent, the majority of nocturnal creatures are predators."

Timrekka finally stopped biting his hesitant tongue. "But there's also a chance that nothing lives there — no animals, no people — and that everything the Daemoaniks told you is fabricated and that maybe

Daemoana was destroyed by random natural forces and not by Shadowmaker and that Shadowmaker is actually dead?" He nodded, hoping that the answer would be an overwhelming yes after they considered all possibilities with common sense.

Master Brawd nodded. "All of that is possible."

Gideon blinked a few times as he tried to process everything. He dipped his head and mulled it over. There was so much more added to his understanding of the universe, and he was dying for confirmation. The answers were out there. He looked over at Traveler and cocked his head to the side.

"So, what's your idea, Spaceman?" He had a feeling he knew what Traveler was going to propose.

Traveler looked back and forth between Gideon and Master Brawd a few times before answering. "We go. See if he's alive. And beg him to help us."

"Yes!" Gideon threw his free hand in the air. "Oh, sorry, Lady Melodeen." He brought his hand down and coddled her neck.

Master Brawd closed his eyes and dropped his head. He silently prayed to anything or anyone who would listen. There had to be another option. There had to be a better way. All his hardened military callous was crumbling behind his eyes. What Four Zero was suggesting was his definition of madness, of suicide. His greatest nightmare was materializing in the waking world, and even the brightness of the room they were in couldn't save him.

Traveler took a few panicky breaths as he realized he'd suggested searching for Shadowmaker out loud. He half-wished he could suck his words back into his mouth and swallow the suggestion, but something wild felt freed. He, a cowardly Whewlight, had actually suggested they go try and find Shadowmaker on the most dangerous world they knew of.

Gideon looked around at the other recruits, all avoiding looking at him as they considered the plan. "What do you guys say?"

Dumakleiza slowly nodded. "Sir Gideon, this plan is mad." She looked around at the other recruits. "To kill a man who proclaims himself a god, we seek aid from a devil, and through this inversion, save the innocent." A sly smile curled up one side of her mouth. "Thatis a purpose I will bleed for."

She looked at Gideon and narrowed her eyes. "By Grim's grace and guidance, we commit to this course of action." Her dragon eye all but flared fire as she scratched Cooby's chin over her shoulder. "You are not alone, Sir Gideon. Cooby and I will proudly stand by your side." She smiled. "Besides," she said and thwapped him on the back, "who would keep you alive if not us?"

Jasss rolled her eyes and groaned. "This is the mostsenseless, rashest, stupidest idea I've ever heard. It'd be less foolish to hand myself back over to the slavers on Ojīptian."

Gideon saw the struggle in her eyes. "So, you're definitely coming."

"Of course I am," she growled as she stood to her feet. She wasn't upset with the prospect of death, but rather struggled admitting how excited the idea actually made her.

"Hold on, hold on, hold on." Timrekka waved his hands. "We don't even know if Shadowmaker is alive, and we don't know what kind of climate or location we'd be jumping into because there's no way to see beyond H.P.'s atmosphere, supposing we even survive the jump, and it's a dark world and potentially filled with nocturnal predators of who knows what species or variety, and if we don't die from them, we're looking for the most notorious killer in the history of mankind, who can kill people with coinsfrom galaxies away and even supposedly make *worlds collide*, and he has noreason to help us and instead will likely kill us. Literally every single step of this 'plan' is a death sentence."

"Yes." Gideon nodded "I know it sounds —"

"Oh," Timrekka interrupted, "and I just realized, how are we going to land at all. If the clouds are thick enough to keep light out, then we are going to materialize when our light hits the clouds, at least a mile above the planet's surface, essentially falling to our deaths there, and we have the same problem with our escape because even if we live and we find Shadowmaker, even if we convince him to join our cause, we're still trapped in the dark with no light available for a jump off H.P. There are far too many risks, and there's no way we're lucky enough for everything to go our way on this one, I'm sorry."

Gideon looked to Traveler and Master Brawd. "What if we pull the same double-jump we used to get here? Burn a hole through the clouds and jump through it before they close?"

Master Brawd shook his head. "The clouds are too thick for that."

"See?" Timrekka threw his hands out. "This can't work."

"Oh, come on," Gideon said as his mischievous grin returned. "Don't be so negative. That's why we need you, Tim. Unless conceiving a way to make parachutes trigger upon cloud arrival is too complicated for your scientific mind. And I know you hate invention challenges, but you couldn't possibly conceive anything to solve the darkness jumping issue, could you? Nah." He waved his hand. "You're right. Probably not your cup of tea."

Traveler chuckled as Timrekka sulked in silence. "He's right. This is perfectly fitting for your skillset. Gideon's just throwing a hairball at you."

Gideon pinched the bridge of his nose. "*Curve*ball." He laughed. "Come on, Tim-the-science-man-Tailor. This will be fun for you nerds to bond over."

Izzy begrudgingly agreed. "If we're guaranteed to fail should we not go, we may as well try. I'd rather die for something than for nothing."

"Classic line." Gideon nodded while looking at Timrekka. His smile maintained as he patted the Thamioshling's broad back. "Listen, Timmy, honestly, I'm not going to try and pressure you into going. If this adventure's not for you, I get it. I really do. It's just that you are an invaluable badass and an even better friend."

"I'll go, I'll go!" Timrekka erratically spat out in a frenzy of nerves. "I don't have any other friends and I can't let you die, especially knowing that I could have helped." He shook his head. "But I'm not happy about this plan, it's a bad plan, we're going to die, it's a horrible plan."

"Yes, it is." Gideon smiled, happy that everyone was on board.

Lady Melodeen took a few breaths and then spoke as loud as she could. "We have...parachutes in a...stockroom...here." She coughed. "With some minor adjustments...they could work."

"No kidding?" Gideon smiled. "That's perfect." He turned. "Master Brawd?"

After more brooding silence, Master Brawd finally looked up at him. "We can't leave Lord Coyzle here with Abdabriel. I swore to protect him at all costs."

Gideon tilted his head. "With our current circumstances, I think he's in the safest place he can be. No one's going to hurt him while he's——no offense——powering EBOO. If we make it back safely, we break him out. If we fail and die, then he's still safer there than if we break him out now."

Traveler nodded. "I agree."

"No," Master Brawd insisted. "We do not leave our Lord in a Winkloh Star. Mentioning H.P. is treason. Going there without his authorization is unforgivable, no matter how dire the situation or heroic the intention." He looked from Traveler to Gideon. "If you wish to do this, it must be sanctioned by Lord Coyzle."

Gideon puffed out his bottom lip. "Okay, fine. How do we go about freeing him from the Winkloh Star then?"

"I don't know," Master Brawd said. "It's never been done."

Timrekka leaned forward. "No one's everbeen freed from a Winkloh Star?"

"No. They are alternatives to death sentences. They're not designed to be exited. Ever. The condemned aren't meant to leave."

Lady Melodeen coughed up more blood and groaned as she felt her limbs growing weaker. "I don't have...much time." Her words barely formed a whisper. "I need light."

Master Brawd looked at her. "We will find somewhere to jump you. That's the first priority." He held her hand. "Do you know where Master Keevind is?"

"Dead." Lady Melodeen's feeble eyes teared up.

Jasss sighed. "Fist me. Then how are we going to get to the Winkloh Star?"

"I—" Lady Melodeen held her emotions in as best she could. "I have access."

Gideon's eyes shot open. "I have an idea! None of you are going to like it, but I think it'll kill a lot of birds with a single stone. Actually, that's pretty literal."

Traveler brought his head back. "I don't like when you use that tone."

Gideon chuckled. "Well, you're *definitely* not going to like this."

21

After obtaining parachutes from the stockroom, Timrekka took a few minutes to tamper with their release triggers. He'd set them to open at a certain velocity in order to save them during comatose freefall. It was an easier task than he'd expected, and he was almost disappointed with how little had to do, but at least their survival was marginally more promising.

Master Brawd peered outside from the secret door they'd entered through, searching for movement. The building with the Winkloh Star was only about five-hundred-feet-away. They could run to it with Lady Melodeen in tow in less than a minute.

Master Brawd saw that more soldiers had accumulated. The invaders didn't appear to be tipped off about their being there, and he didn't want to alert them with any sudden movement, but their chances of easily reaching the Winkloh Star had just declined. A quick headcount put their adversaries at around twenty soldiers patrolling. Master Brawd kept looking around. They had to get to the Winkloh Star, bring Lady Melodeen with them, and have her in good enough condition to access the security doors, heal her, and then do something truly mad. Each step sounded more challenging than the last.

Everyone else was gathered behind Master Brawd, unable to see around him as he took up the entire doorway. They all wanted to see what they were dealing with, but they had to wait for his instruction.

"Why do we delay?" Dumakleiza asked. "Should we not charge and fight our way there?"

"There are too many of them," Master Brawd said with a tone that was clearly meant to hush her. "We need a diversion."

Gideon squatted down, catching a small glimpse from under Master Brawd's thick torso. "Timmy, how's your throwing arm?"

Timrekka awkwardly adjusted his goggles at the mere mentioning of getting involved. "I have never been athletic," he whispered. "But I know that you know that and that it won't deter whatever idea you're concocting," he said with a slump.

"You're our resident superhero." Gideon looked at him and raised an eyebrow. "Throw one of the decorative rocks by the door at any building within a mile." He knew the instruction was a bit of an exaggeration, but the general concept might work.

Without questioning the haphazard idea, Master Brawd bent down while keeping his eyes on the patrol. He grabbed what felt like maybe a ten-pound stone. It was smooth and polished, ornamental in design, and he handed it backward. It was the only stone in reach, and it was probably too heavy, but it was worth a shot. It was passed until it reached Timrekka, who took it and immediately started sweating. He hated being put on the spot.

"You've got this, Timmy," Gideon whispered, punching Timrekka in the arm. He retracted what instantly felt like a jammed wrist. "Yeah, you've got this." He shook his hand out.

Master Brawd and everyone else got out of the way so Timrekka could step into the doorway. He stood there, wide-eyed and terrified, trembling with the large stone easily cupped in his gargantuan hand. He blinked at it a few times, trying to think through the proper form for throwing anything. Back on Thamiosh, he'd lacked strength, coordination, grace, and skill. Now everyone was relying on him to do what they couldn't. He almost vomited as he stepped out and faced the nearest building. He awkwardly brought his arm back and whipped the stone forward, nearly tripping from his own force.

His amplified strength overpowered his inexperience, hurling the stone like a bullet. It flew through the night sky so fast that he immediately lost sight of it. They waited until they heard the roof of Prism Hall shatter.

"Sorry," Timrekka stammered and then shuffled backward until he was inside the doorway. They listened to the falling debris in Prism Hall, every sound making Timrekka wince. He felt bad for breaking such a beautiful building. As more crumbling and crashing went on, they heard soldiers yelling.

Master Brawd peered out again. "Huh." He was surprised by how impressed he was. "It's working. Let's go. Now."

They followed close behind him as he ran out into the open. Timrekka scooped up Lady Melodeen and jogged, easily keeping pace with the others. They watched as every soldier ran toward Prism Hall. If even one saw them, they'd be compromised and have to fight for their lives. They all prayed under their breath as they closed the short distance. Master Brawd and Traveler had index fingers out, ready to fire at anyone. The minute felt like an hour, but they made it to the Winkloh Star's enclosure incident free. There was no time to celebrate the small victory. They had to get inside and out of sight.

"Lady Melodeen." Master Brawd ushered Timrekka to bring her to the door scanner. He and Traveler stood on the outside of the group and kept a lookout as everyone else formed a protective perimeter around Lady Melodeen. In her battered state, they worried that the security measures wouldn't allow her in. Master Keevind's explanation of blood pressure, stress, fear, and all the other inhibitors preventing access raced through their minds.

Sure enough, a loud beep announced that access had been denied due to Lady Melodeen's stress levels. They started to panic. They were out in the open, and it'd only be a minute or two until the soldiers searched all of Prism Hall and found no one. They had to hurry.

Izzy stepped over to Lady Melodeen and placed one hand on the back of her frail neck. With the other, he applied compression to both sides of her temple. He gently rubbed specific pressure points, massaging and nodding.

"Try again."

Lady Melodeen barely even heard him as the much-needed relaxation brought her to the brink of sleep. She went through the motions again as the rest of the group sweated thick globs of doubt. Izzy kept digging his fingers into her neck, calmly releasing knots as her strength ebbed.

The door opened. They turned with wide eyes, surprised by the success. Izzy shrugged and smiled as everyone rushed inside. "Didn't actually
know if that was going to work." Once everyone was in, he closed the
door behind them as quietly as he could.

They dimmed their optical implants and entered the blinding room
after Lady Melodeen barely managed to access the second security door.
They shielded their eyes, struggling to see much of anything.

Lady Melodeen went completely limp in Timrekka's arms. "Launch...
me..."

Master Brawd stepped over to her and placed his hand on her arm.
"It's going to be okay. You'll be out soon." His words didn't even register.
He watched her eyes roll back in her head, so he pulled her from Tim-
rekka and laid her on the ground. He closed one hand toward the
Winkloh Star while keeping the other on her wrist. With a hesitant
breath, he opened his fist. Lady Melodeen vanished, and the Winkloh
Star glowed a little brighter.

Everyone watched in silence. Most of them had never witnessed someone committed to Winkloh Star before, and seeing a body vanish without
immediately reappearing was still a bit farfetched. It didn't make sense to
the eye, even with the understanding of how it worked. They stared into
the brightness and felt the intensity of knowing Lady Melodeen was swirling at unimaginable speeds along with Lord Coyzle and Daemoaniks.

Master Brawd composed himself and got to his feet. "Okay, Gideon,
what is your plan?"

"Well." Gideon stared at the glowing glass. "As soon as we smash a
hole in it, people are going to shooting out and materialize, right?"

Traveler nodded as the reality began setting in. "That's what I'm guessing."

Master Brawd grew defensive. "And we will kill as many Daemoaniks
as we can as fast as we can before they recover. Dumakleiza, Timrekka,
Four Zero, and myself will handle any that retaliate. That's protocol,
should the star ever break."

"No. No. No." Gideon said. "As capable as I'm sure you all are, I
think it'd be better if we pretend that all of us have the implants and hold
finger guns aimed at them. Because of our actual unpreparedness, we

should ask them about Shadowmaker and see what other information we can get before we go."

Timrekka looked at him and stepped back a little. "But what if they—"

"Who are you more scared of?" Gideon asked. "A handful of Daemoaniks or Shadowmaker?" The following silence was the answer he knew to be true. "Exactly. And I personally would prefer to know more about the devil before we go looking for him in hell." No one else objected, though they all wanted to.

"And then what?" Master Brawd asked, his teeth on edge.

Traveler smirked. "Then he's going to ask them if they want to come with us."

"No," Master Brawd barked louder than he'd intended.

Gideon nodded. "You're getting to know me too well, Spaceman. I'm going to have to change my game up to keep you on your—" He trailed off to see how Traveler would muck up the Earthling quote.

"Horses?"

"Close enough," Gideon chuckled.

"No," Master Brawd repeated himself.

"Hey." Gideon raised his hands. "Another saying we have back on Earth is 'The enemy of my enemy is my friend.' Though, I don't exactly know who's all an enemy in this messy pickle. But luck favors the prepared. Who knows how the Daemoaniks could help. They have no home, no allegiance anymore, no purpose, and they're not even in the same time that they remember. They know more about Shadowmaker than any of you and certainly more than any of us. May as well pick their brains. Why not offer them a purpose?"

He recognized the absolute position that Master Brawd had taken. There was no convincing him. Gideon smiled and went for one last try anyway.

"Listen. The greatest leader that Earthever had lived a few centuries ago. He abolished my country's slavery and oversaw some of our worst times, bringing us from the darkness of war to the horizon of a bright future." He glanced at Jasss and then looked back to Master Brawd. "He said many of my favorite quotes, but one that's always stood out to me is 'Have I not destroyed my enemies by making friends of them?'"

Master Brawd's expression didn't change. "It doesn't matter their potential usefulness, they do not possess the ability to even resemble friends of one another, let alone you and me." Regardless of his hatred of them, he understood the benefit of the Daemoaniks' insights. "Offer them your invitation, and when they turn on you, I will try to save you, but should I fail, just know — right before they tear your body apart — I warned you." He looked at the Winkloh Star. "Lord Coyzle will know what to do. First priority after breaking the glass is separating him and Lady Melodeen from the Daemoaniks." He took a deep breath and then looked at Timrekka, exhaling as he prepared for what was about to happen. "Timrekka, punch a hole in a lower portion of the glass and then get behind me." He held his finger out, aiming it in tactical anticipation for what might happen. Traveler stood next to him with his fingers aimed, as well. Dumakleiza stepped up and prepared to attack with her hands and feet. Gideon, Izzy, and Jasss all stood behind them, ready to run if need be.

Timrekka slowly approached the Winkloh Star. He was scared for a plethora of reasons, and it took everything to make his feet move. He took a few nervous breaths and then felt around the sphere's underbelly. Wherever he punched had to be aimed toward the ground, or else people would reassemble and then fall, likely breaking their legs.

"Here?" He pointed at the under curve of the massive sphere. Master Brawd nodded. Timrekka groaned and then wound back. He squealed and closed his eyes as he swung with amateur form. *Smash!* The instant he felt impact, he yelped and dove backward, getting behind the others as fast as he could.

Sounds of shattering glass raining onto the floor were barely noticeable as bodies began appearing where the broken hole aimed the light. Indistinct people materialized against the corner of the room, stacked against and on top of one another in comatose flaccidity. The group knew there were going to be sixteen bodies total that came out of the Winkloh Star, but in the hysteria of people appearing all over the small room, it seemed like there were more. As soon as the Winkloh Star emptied, the room went dark.

"Oh, no, no, no, no, no, no, no," Timrekka rattled in dread. Dim red lights turned on in the ceiling, backups should something ever go wrong with the Winkloh Star. The light glow ominously lit the bodies coming to.

In the midst of the heap, Master Brawd saw Lord Coyzle. He lurched forward and grabbed him under the arms, yanking his comatose body back behind the recruits. Master Brawd was ready to sacrifice every single one of them before he allowed his lord to die. As soon as he'd placed Lord Coyzle far from the rest, he returned and fished out Lady Melodeen. She appeared fully healed. Master Brawd placed her in the back next to Lord Coyzle and then returned to the front of the recruits with his fingers at the ready.

Light groans and indistinct mumbling from the prisoners susurrated through the room like a whispering chill. It was normal after a light jump, but the kind of people making them had the recruits' neck hair on end. The harsh transition from the Winkloh Star's blinding light to the red glow was difficult for their eyes to adjust to. They held their fingers out and aimed at the bodies slowly getting to their feet. They hoped they looked convincing with their suggested implants and that the Daemoaniks would react accordingly.

Gideon squinted, curious what the mutilated monsters of men looked like. The way Lady Skorric had described them in Dark to Light Hall could only paint a mental picture so vivid in its horror. Gideon wanted to see just what lengths mankind had gone to for universal conquest. Finally, his eyes adjusted enough to see the Daemoaniks in the limited light.

As they started regaining composure, the Daemoaniks stood tall, their eyes rolling forward from incapacitated decades. Their skin looked pale and sickly, like thick plastic sheets stretched tightly over white marble, spider webs of multicolored veins sprawling underneath. Their cheekbones, jaws, foreheads, elbows, shoulders, every joint in their hands, and all visible curvatures of their bodies were jutted and protruding. Every normally overlooked bone structure was accentuated in grotesque exaggeration, tortured, unnaturally forced and expanded in sharp angles. Their fingers made even Gideon's skin crawl. They'd shaven down the flesh and bones of each digit, filing them into points. The skin faded down each fingertip until all that remained were mutilated claws. Gideon's stomach twisted at the pain they'd put themselves through. They had no hair on their heads, nor eyebrows or any of the fine hairs that normally spanned across human skin.

Gideon couldn't stop staring at the sharp angles of their faces. Their horrifying appearances alone made him understand why the Whewlights and other worlds had reacted with shock. They looked like monsters. There was no other way to describe them. He could barely see anything resembling humanity. For the first time since he'd met Traveler, the term "aliens" felt chillingly real.

Along with the eleven Daemoaniks, two men and a woman with normal, human appearances had been freed from the Winkloh Star. The recruits overlooked the nonthreatening Whewlights. The three convicts looked around at their cellmates and shrunk down, realizing their circumstance. One of the Whewlight prisoners started urinating as he shook in place, fear trickling down his leg.

Master Brawd glanced at the recruits, making sure their fingers were aimed at the Daemoaniks, who were finally taking in their surroundings. Fingers were up, and demeanors were as convincing as they were going to get. He turned his eyes to the freed criminals and spoke directly.

"Due to extenuating circumstances from an interstellar threat, you have been temporarily released." He watched as the Daemoaniks stared at him with black eyes. They'd understood him perfectly, yet they'd begun posturing themselves to strike. The recruits tried their hardest to keep their fingers from wavering. The illusion of being armed was working but only as long as they believed it, too. The instant they cowered and ran, the Daemoaniks would know the truth. They had to hold still with stern expressions to match. Master Brawd's heart was racing. It had been decades since he'd last laid eyes on Daemoaniks. Old scars were bleeding through.

"I'm going to speak with our lord. If any of you make any sudden movements, these soldiers will not hesitate to execute you." With that, he turned and walked back to Lord Coyzle. He couldn't linger. His confidence in the threat had to be absolute.

The recruits stared in sullen silence as the Daemoaniks ravenously eyed them up and down like predators watching soft, tender infants. There was no fear in the Daemoaniks' soulless eyes, only an understanding. It was more than evident that at the first opportunity, they would slaughter the recruits.

Gideon was trying his hardest not to smile. His face naturally wanted to express his giddiness at seeing actual monsters, but he forced a glare. He didn't see any emotions behind the Daemoaniks' pupils, only an animalistic desire to feed. It was as if they didn't care that they'd woken up in a new era, that their world was gone, that they were completely unaware of the circumstances. They were nothing but hunger and hatred, fangs and claws.

Dumakleiza's glare was sincere. She thought holding a measly finger toward the devilish aliens was childish, but it was keeping them in place. She wanted a chance to face off against one and see how menacing they truly were. Her own savagery yearned to drive a blade through one of their skulls and demonstrate their mortality. Cooby, on the other hand, ducked his head behind her neck. His instincts recognized the true nature of the Daemoaniks.

Timrekka was petrified beyond the point of fear. Trembling wasn't even an option, and neither was moving. He wanted to gulp, but he couldn't. He wanted to cry, but even his tears were hiding. With his finger aimed at one of the Daemoaniks, he prepared himself for what seemed like inevitable death——presumably excruciating but quick.

One of the Daemoaniks cracked an eerie smile at them, exposing filed fangs. Gideon couldn't help smiling back. He couldn't even tell if it was a male or female.

Lord Coyzle looked from Lady Melodeen to Master Brawd. "What is happening?" The sight of the Daemoaniks alarmed him even more than Abdabriel's betrayal. "How long was I in the Star?"

Lady Melodeen's rejuvenated eyes were glued to the monsters. "Three days."

Her answer didn't take Lord Coyzle's attention away from Master Brawd. "Has Abdabriel been stopped?"

Master Brawd shook his head. "He has EBOO. It's only a matter of time until they realize the Winkloh Star's been deactivated and we're found in here."

"Then—" Lord Coyzle tried to wrap his mind around what was happening. "—what is the plan? And—" He lowered his voice. "—why did you not execute the Daemoaniks immediately? That's protocol. You know that."

Master Brawd glanced back at them. "Because——we might need them."

"*What*?" Lord Coyzle roared, unconcerned with the Daemoaniks hearing him. He wanted them to know that their fates were sealed, and he'd be the one to seal them. "I will *never* work alongside the Daemoaniks!" He looked past Master Brawd, hoping the monsters were watching him. None of them looked away from the recruits. Lord Coyzle turned back to Master Brawd. "Kill them."

"We have a plan. You're not going to like it, but it's the only one we have." Master Brawd firmly stated, knowing how difficult the conversation was about to get. "If we kill them, it's likely that we will lose Whewliss to Abdabriel's rule, and all other worlds will follow our fate."

While they quietly discussed Gideon and Traveler's plan, Traveler and the recruits held steady at their posts. The dead silence of the standoff was haunting. They weren't sure what they'd expected, but watching the Daemoaniks stare back with cracked smiles and unwavering eyes was worse than their nightmares. The Daemoaniks' imminent executions did nothing to intimidate or scare them. In fact, their breathing was quickening. Even if the recruits did have the lethal implants, there weren't enough of them to fend off eleven monsters.

One of the Whewlight criminals whimpered as he felt cold fingers press against the back of his neck. No one saw what was happening. He was completely alone in a crowded room. The sharpened bone fingertips gently squeezed, feeling his warmth. The Whewlight trembled in the clutches of the beast. He didn't dare move or flinch. If he gave into the Daemoanik's taunting, his spine would be suddenly rendered free from his body. It didn't matter how many finger lasers were aimed at them. The world he'd awoken to was a hell he couldn't escape, literal bone fingers playfully dragging down his back.

Gideon was the first to notice. He watched for a while, wondering what was going to happen, but his curiosity surpassed his patience.

"Hey, you three *not* scary people." He smiled cordially and waved with his "unarmed" hand. "What'd you do to get locked up with these folks?" He motioned at the Daemoaniks. None of the monsters acknowledged him as the woman summoned the courage to speak. She nervously cleared her throat, tears streaming down her trembling cheeks.

"M——m——murder. I——I killed three people." There was no point in lying. She whimpered as her confession released more tears. She could feel the Daemoaniks' perverse pleasure, soaking up her fear like lizards in the sun.

The urine-coated man nodded, hoping that confessing would somehow grant him mercy. "Twelve. Twelve. I killed twelve people, and I'm sorry." He shook in place after exhausting his bladder. "I'm so sorry."

"Kids." The man with the Daemoanik's hand on his back barely managed a whisper. "I killed kids." The hand caressing his back didn't speed up or slow down at the appalling admission. It just continued touching him like a lover, unwavering, uncaring, undaunted, playful.

"Wow." Gideon slowly nodded, ignoring his own judgments. "I guess that's basically the prerequisite for joining the Winkloh club. Never thought you'd be standing with a bunch of Daemoaniks, did ya?" Gideon didn't feel much pity for them. Their circumstance seemed more than deserved. None of them answered as they simply stood still and cried. Gideon glanced around at the Daemoaniks. "If I ever make it home, I'm dressing up as one of you for Halloween."

Finally, Master Brawd and Lord Coyzle walked out in front of them, staring down the Daemoaniks. Master Brawd's hands were out with both index fingers aimed and ready to fire. Lord Coyzle was struggling to accept their predicament. His face was twisted with a sour expression of indecision. After more frustrated silence, he looked up at the Daemoaniks.

"As much as I despise your people, your knowledge could be invaluable." Even addressing them made his stomach churn. He fought the urge to vomit as he knowingly betrayed everything he stood for. "One of our own is attempting a hostile takeover of the known universe, something you are familiar with." His words tasted bitter. He turned to Gideon. "You have my approval for what you request, but I cannot continue speaking to filth." He turned and glared at the Daemoaniks, every fiber of his being wanting them dead on the floor.

Gideon nodded. "I got it." He grinned at the Daemoaniks. "So, here's the deal. I know we don't scare you. That's clear as day. However—" He paused for dramatic flare. "—we seek help from the one guy who does."

The room's energy instantly shifted. The Daemoaniks' soulless demeanor melted away, exposing something deeper, something darker. Their sinister smirks disappeared, and their eyes widened as they realized what Gideon meant. Even the heartless monsters could feel fear. Their sickly, pale skin turned whiter as what little blood they possessed retreated to the inner confines of their tortured bodies.

Gideon nodded. "Good, I have your attention." He popped his neck to the side, enjoying the monsters' terror. "So, all we need from you are insights about Shadowmaker."

"Don't say that name!" a terrifyingly unnatural voice roared out from one of the Daemoaniks. It sounded like a swarm of nails tearing through a chalkboard. Before anyone could respond to the outburst, the monster reached up and plunged its bony claws into its own throat. It simultaneously grabbed its head with the other and violently ripped it around. Blood poured from its neck as its head went limp and the beast fell dead to the floor.

The three Whewlight criminals shrieked in horror as four more Daemoaniks followed, viciously taking their own lives at the mere mentioning of Shadowmaker. They were quicker to kill themselves than to live in a room where his name was spoken. The recruits struggled to keep their positions. Even Dumakleiza was wide-eyed. Five dead and twitching Daemoanik bodies bled on the floor, and the remaining six monsters looked dangerously close to following the dead. One of them looked at Gideon and brought a shaved finger to its lips, whispering with an eerie voice.

"Do not say the name."

"Um." Gideon tried to recover. "We've said his name many times, and nothing's happened to us, but, uh, okay." He swallowed hard. "I won't say it. We just—" He shook his head, trying to regain a fraction of his composure. "Um, we're going to the world you claim he's hiding at. I won't say his name, but what can you tell us about him that might help us?"

The same Daemoanik ushered him to lower his voice as it leaned in a little, more afraid of what it was about to say than it was of the implants. "He will not aid you. If you go there, he will kill you. There is nothing you can do to stop him."

Gideon nodded. "Are you're sure that he went to Horror Planet? You're sure that he's alive?"

The Daemoanik's hollow eyes flickered. "What time has passed?"

"Uh." Gideon turned to the Whewlights.

Traveler cleared his throat, struggling to breathe. "About one-hundred-Whewliss-years."

The Daemoanik mulled over the answer, his dark eyes flickering at the news. "He's everywhere."

Gideon narrowed his eyes. "You claim that he destroyed Daemoana. How?"

At the mentioning of their dead home world, the Daemoaniks grew visibly upset.

The one speaking on the others' behalf glared at Gideon. "You will be his. Better to die here. It would be faster."

"We'll take our chances with him," Gideon said with an overly confident grin. "In fact, I think I know the answer, but you're more than welcome to join us if you'd like. Better than a prison here."

The Daemoaniks looked at him in disbelief. He actually invited them to Horror Planet to help find Shadowmaker. The idea was so insane that they were momentarily taken aback.

"Oh." Gideon remembered something as he turned to Lord Coyzle. "We haven't discussed this, but this is as close to a Make A Wish Foundation as I can imagine. Why don't you come with us?"

"What?" Lord Coyzle was caught completely off guard.

"No," Master Brawd reactively answered.

"Well." Gideon shrugged. "You want to explore other worlds, but you're always too busy running Whewliss. This is the wildest adventure you could go on, and you're useless here right now. Sorry. No offense. Just saying. But, you know, you're the boss and all."

Lord Coyzle wasn't sure what to say.

"No," Master Brawd repeated himself as he stared at the monsters.

The Daemoanik caressing the Whewlight's back bore holes through Gideon as he studied the situation. "The enemy is outside." His grating voice expressed how obvious it was that they were hiding in the prison.

Gideon nodded. "Yes. Soldiers that we have to avoid before we make the jump to H.P."

"How many?" the Daemoanik asked with newfound excitement.

Gideon cracked a smile. "We're not sure exactly how many, but we're outnumbered." He watched as the answer made the six Daemoaniks grin with fanged delight.

"Nothing will make us join you in finding—him," the Daemoanik responded with a deep growl. "But we can create a distraction. Then you can jump to your deaths." The other Daemoaniks drooled as they nodded, savoring the flavors to come.

Gideon cocked his head to the side and then turned his eyes to Lord Coyzle. "What do you say, boss? Let them run rampant through EBOO and surprise Abdabriel's soldiers? Your call."

Lord Coyzle blinked rapidly. There were too many decisions to make, too much hysteria to control. He took a deep breath and then looked to Lady Melodeen.

"Are there any survivors in the city?"

Lady Melodeen shook her head. "I was the only one they left behind. All other survivors were taken to the City of Light as examples to be made."

Lord Coyzle swallowed the news whole as he tried to think through anger. "You will get to the panic room in Interstellar Port. Even if they—" He looked sickeningly at the Daemoaniks. "—survive, they won't be able to reach you in there. Don't let anyone in." Lady Melodeen nodded as Lord Coyzle turned his full attention to the Daemoaniks. "If you do this for us, I will forgive your crimes and—" He couldn't believe what he was about to say. "—if we return and any of you are still alive, I will personally send you to an uninhabited world, where you can live out the rest of your lives however you see fit."

The Daemoaniks seemed uninterested in Lord Coyzle's mercy and more fixated on the upcoming bloodshed.

Gideon tried not to jump up and down from excitement. "What about you, Lord Coyzle?"

"A peace offering will mean more coming from me than it would from you." Lord Coyzle turned to face Gideon. "I'm going."

"So am I." A crackled voice surprised everyone as one of the Daemoaniks took a bold step forward. The mutilated creature had a twisted smile on its face, staring straight at Gideon. "You are a crazy man. You're not afraid of him." The Daemoanik's smile grew. "I want to see what happens when he finds you."

Dumakleiza glared at the beast. "When we find him."

The Daemoanik shook its head. "When he finds you."

The other five were dumbfounded by their cellmate's insanity. They felt the closest thing to concern that they could, knowing that it was going to be subjected to something more terrifying than death.

"Well," Gideon said and chuckled, unable to contain it, "good thing we brought some extra parachutes." He glanced at the other recruits, who hadn't budged or said anything. They were all slack-jawed, staring at the Daemoaniks. "Izzy," Gideon ushered.

Izzy snapped into the moment and grabbed two of the parachutes off the floor. He handed one to Lord Coyzle and hesitantly tossed the second to the Daemoanik. They both slipped the harnesses around their bodies, staring at each other while they did. Lord Coyzle didn't know how he felt about everything happening, but he couldn't think of a better course of action.

Two blood-curdling screams turned everyone's attention to the Whewlight criminals. All three of them fell dead to the floor as the Daemoaniks standing behind them stared deadpan at Gideon. They had severed spinal cords in their hands and blood pooling around their feet. The three Whewlights were unnaturally crumpled on the ground, their backs ripped open. The woman was bent backward, the back of her head touching her heels, and one of the men's necks was missing. It had all happened instantaneously, and everyone, including Gideon, was frozen in horror. They had but a small taste of what Whewliss experienced when Daemoana invaded.

One of the Daemoaniks chuckled as it wiped the blood on its ragged clothes. "Had to make sure we still knew how." The other Daemoaniks laughed along. The beast glared at Gideon and Lord Coyzle. "Do you want to talk more, or do you want to open that door and let us out?"

22

Everyone's muscles were tense, afraid, and ready. They had to be ready. Every single hair was raised like wire. Heavy breathing marinated their otherwise silent dread for the simple plan. The doors would open, Daemoaniks would lead the charge, and do what they did best. Then everyone going to H.P. would gather in an open spot, where Master Brawd would perform the riskiest chariot jump in Whewlight history, and someone was going to have to hold the hand of the Daemoanik going with them. They knew it was going to be Gideon, and as excited as he was to have the honor, even Gideon was hesitant. He was curious how its skin would feel, and keenly aware that it could turn on him at any point.

Abdabriel's soldiers were oblivious, and they were particularly unaware of the Daemoaniks being freed. Soon the monsters would get the delicious privilege of ripping into flesh. Nonchalant patrolling had the soldiers meandering through EBOO, lost in conversation with one another. The city had been swept and cleared. They were waiting until Abdabriel conquered the City of Light so they could get their next instruction. It was an honor to be a part of such an immeasurable undertaking, and they knew they'd have authoritative positions of power in the future. Life was good.

Inside the closed doors of the Winkloh structure, the Daemoaniks had been ushered to the front at finger point, corralled like cattle so they'd be the first to emerge. Everyone else hung back to wait.

"Before you do this, there are two things you need to be aware of," Master Brawd said to the Daemoaniks. "The enemy is dressed in shimmering white suits. Kill only them. That's all that should be out there, but should anyone else surprise us, you are not to harm them, or *I* will kill you." He allowed a brief second of silence to ensure they believed him. "Secondly, the enemy is wielding arachniblasts, a weapon that, if successfully fired at one of you, will in turn kill any others within eight-foot proximities. The only tactical advice I have is to spread out. The closer you are together, the less of them you'll kill before they slaughter you." It was disgusting to be leading a small team of Daemoaniks against one of his own, but in a small way, a way that he'd never admit out loud, Master Brawd was excited to unleash them.

The Daemoanik going with them cracked a morbid grin and chuckled under its steaming breath. "I'm sad I will not be helping devour them." Its foot was tapping as if it was enjoying some music, and its fingertips were clawing against its own thigh.

Lord Coyzle closed his eyes, savoring the closest to normalcy he was going to experience for a while. It felt like swollen serpents were writhing in his guts, and he couldn't stop questioning their plan. He opened his eyes and nodded. There was no going back.

"Go."

At his instruction, the Daemoaniks opened the front door. The cool night air briskly blew in and rushed through everyone. Subtle glows showed nothing threatening or sinister outside, just the beauty of EBOO's quietness. The five Daemoaniks slipped out, three going left, two going right, disappearing in silence. The recruits had expected them to go out screaming and roaring like wild beasts on a carnivorous rampage. The stillness left after their exit made it almost seem like a bad dream had passed, like they'd never been there at all.

Keeping the sixth Daemoanik out front at finger point, Master Brawd marched forward enough to be able to peer out of the door. There hadn't been any screams or yells from unsuspecting soldiers, and the quiet was distressing. He and the Daemoanik looked out from either side of the doorway. A cool smirk was on the Daemoanik's face. It clearly had confidence in its team. It gave Master Brawd a sour cocktail of uneasiness and reminding of their destructive abilities. He searched the darkness while adjusting his optical implant to enhance his vision. Still, he saw nothing. There were no enemies in sight, and the Daemoaniks had vanished.

"Where are they?" he whispered to the sixth.

"Do not cry," the Daemoanik cackled. "They are playing."

Suddenly, one of the other Daemoaniks ran around the side of the building, stopping in front of them. Blood was smeared all over its hands and face, and its smile glowed from ear to ear.

"You said there was a small army. We only found four."

Master Brawd slowly exhaled as he looked about. "There were more. I'm assuming those four soldiers you found are dead?"

A simple, disappointed glance from the bloodied monster for even asking answered his question. Master Brawd nodded, focused on the objective. It was unsettling that he hadn't heard even a yelp from the soldiers they'd just killed in under a minute.

The bloody Daemoanik looked around and then motioned for them to exit the Winkloh Star. "Now is your chance." Its insidious voice sounded treacherous, but they didn't have another choice.

Master Brawd nodded. He had to trust the monster. Keeping the sixth Daemoanik with him, he led everyone out and into the open. Their exposure was immediately demoralizing. There wouldn't be a location with a better vantage point. They just needed to be outside where they could see the stars. They looked around for more of Abdabriel's goons. They were out there somewhere, probably patrolling out of sight, but they'd be back. As soon as even one soldier saw them, the entire force would be called. It was even more disconcerting seeing none of them. The unknown was an infinitely darker place than visible adversaries.

Master Brawd had both index fingers out and ready. "Four Zero," he uttered quietly, "lead the jump. I will stand guard." Traveler obeyed, reaching up and harnessing as much starlight as he could as he aimed for the one place he'd been instructed to never even look at. Master Brawd stayed concentrated. "Lady Melodeen." He looked at her, praying he'd see her again. "Run." Abdabriel's soldiers were somewhere close, four Daemoaniks were hunting nearby, and she had to run through an uncovered five-hundred-feet to return to Interstellar Port. Master Brawd looked deep into her eyes as she fearfully glanced back and forth between the distance and him. She leaned up and planted one long kiss on his lips and then ran.

Gideon brought his head back with furrowed brows as he whispered to Traveler. "Were they—?"

"Second wife," Traveler quietly responded as he aimed the chariot jump.

"Huh." Gideon smiled. "Mackelis full of surprises."

A loud scream broke the tense silence like exploding glass. Everyone turned and looked into the darkness. One of the Daemoaniks emerged, covered in blood, a satisfied smile bearing glistening fangs. Whoever had screamed was gutted, but the alarm had been sounded.

Within seconds, soldiers appeared in the distance, running toward them. Everyone's eyes shot open. There were somewhere between ten and fifteen hustling in their direction, and they were sure more were coming.

Master Brawd focused, ready to assist the Daemoaniks in protecting the rest of the group. "Four Zero, how much time?" There was no point in quiet anymore. He glanced at Lady Melodeen to see her halfway to the door. She had to make it. She had to. She was running as fast as her recovered legs could carry her.

Traveler flexed his jaw as sweat beaded on his forehead. "I'm not ready!"

Fft.Fft.Fft. Laser burns exploded in the grass around them and against the walls of the Winkloh enclosure. The soldiers were getting close enough to fire, and their poor aims would improve with each step. A loud roar caught one of the running men off guard as a Daemoanik leapt out from some bushes. The beast disemboweled him with a single swipe of its hand, spraying the man through the air. Two more soldiers saw it happen but didn't believe their eyes. Before they could comprehend that they were facing Daemoaniks, another burst from the shadows and tackled them.

Traveler winced, trying to focus as fear rose around him like floodwaters. "Everyone, grab hold!" He didn't even care if the accompanying Daemoanik latched onto his arm. He was ready to go.

They obeyed, reaching for any bare skin. Gideon grabbed his wrist. *Fft.Fft.* The soldiers' shots were getting closer. Dumakleiza gripped Gideon's hand over Traveler, interlocking their fingers as she searched for any opportunity to assist in killing the enemy. The accompanying Daemoanik clasped its filed fingers around Gideon's other wrist while eagerly watching the violence unfold around them. Lord Coyzle, Timrekka, Jasss, and Izzy formed a tightly bunched chain as they, too, grabbed hold. All they were missing was Master Brawd, busy firing back.

One of the panic-ridden soldiers finally managed to land a shot at a Daemoanik's face in a moment of desperation. She'd used a different implanted weapon because the Daemoanik's head exploded. It wasn't an arachniblast. It was something else that she had pulled out after realizing what kind of force they were facing. Her victory was short lived, as her nervous chuckle was sideswiped by another Daemoanik leaping out from behind a tree. It ripped out her stomach with one swift claw.

Fft.Fft. Master Brawd dove and rolled. He narrowly avoided an arachniblast and fired back. *Fft.* His superior combative training and expertise aimed his finger true. *Fft.* He saw the flaring glow of his shot blast through a soldier's chest.

"Mackel!" The shrill scream turned him to see Lady Melodeen on the ground a few feet shy of the door. Two soldiers had her at finger point, and a third restrained her hands behind her back.

Master Brawd's eyes flared as he spun his hand to fire at them. *Fft.* Another shot caught him in the stomach and knocked him off his feet. He tumbled backward until he came to a stop. His body violently pulsed as electric currents surged through him. He was immobilized. The electric pain was excruciating, like needles stabbing into every part of him, but all he could think about was Lady Melodeen.

Fft.Fft.Fft.Fft. Timrekka and Jasss flew back and tumbled along the grass, also shaking in electric seizures. Timrekka landed fifteen-feet back while the Jasss rolled farther. The nearest combatants were closing in fast. A Daemoanik snagged two soldiers in the rear of their assault, ripping out one's throat and thrashing the other from behind until his spine ripped from his body like cooked bones from soggy meat.

"Master Brawd!" Traveler yelled. "Master Brawd! I'm ready! Get up! Get up! I'm ready!"

"You can make it!" Lord Coyzle yelled as he ducked, dodging a similar blow. He felt powerless watching his friend writhe in the grass. The shot didn't kill him, which meant that the soldiers were going to bring him to Abdabriel. Lord Coyzle's eyes burned with helpless rage. "Mackel Brawd!"

Master Brawd couldn't move amid paralyzing convulsions. "G—g—go!" was all he could muster. "No...time!"

Traveler looked at Mackel, Timrekka, and Jasss. He wanted to grab them. He wanted to pull them in and then open his hand, but Master Brawd was right.

"We'll come back for you! I promise!" Traveler yelled. He knew he was promising a fool's dream.

Fft.Fft. Before anyone could say or do anything else, Traveler opened his hand, and all they saw was white.

23

As soon as Gideon's mind snapped into consciousness, he felt cold wind battering his weightless body. His eyes hadn't opened, but he recognized the velocity of free fall. He was all too familiar with it after numerous skydives and cliff and bungee jumps. His limbs lifelessly flailed with unconscious apathy, and his numb fingers and hair were whipping about in the tornadic wind. He smelled metallic ion in the air, like tasting electricity. As soon as the scent made sense in his mind, he heard deafening thunder explode near him. The powerful jolt was strong enough to expedite his recovery and open his eyes. Tears immediately flooded as the cold air stung his vision and nostrils. He couldn't see. Everything was dark with random blurs of lightning flashes.

It wasn't difficult to guess that he was falling through the clouds on H.P. No one had any idea how thick they were or what to expect below them. Gideon's shoot hadn't opened, and he assumed it was because he hadn't reached enough speed yet. Maybe the planet's gravity wasn't strong enough to pull him that fast. He'd have to pull it himself if he didn't speed up. He couldn't see any of the others, and the rushing wind was too loud to hear each other.

He was surprised when the first thing his mind went to was Dumakleiza's safety. He knew he cared about her. Of course. But the thought of losing her suddenly tore at him in a way that even the Daemoaniks' claws never could. When did that happen? The "L" word planted itself at the forefront of his mind, but he tried to swallow it. He wasn't ready, but he needed to know if she was okay. As he waited for any visibility, he held on tighter, preparing to react to whatever Horror Planet had in store.

Flash. Crack! The air was so thick with electric currents that the hair on Gideon's arms had little bursts of light zapping between them. His already surging energy spiked, and his pulse went into overdrive. The burning adrenaline made the memory of everything that had just happened come flying back, and it was colder than the wind he was falling through. Timrekka, Master Brawd, Jasss, and Lady Melodeen had been captured. There was no way of contacting them or finding out if they were okay.

Gideon knew that everyone who hadmade it to H.P. was probably going to die there, but it would feel like more of a success if they could die together. He could only hope and pray that the rest of his team would survive the jump and that they could eventually return to see the others again.

Finally, the dark clouds disappeared. Gideon wiped some spit trailing up his face as Horror Planet became visible, or at least as visible as it could be. Really, there was nothing to see. He stared downward. It felt like he was skydiving at night over uninhabited ground. There were no lights, no cities, no fires, nothing. Only darkness. He adjusted his optical implant to the brightest setting and looked around through teary eyes fighting to stay open amid the torrents. He managed to make out other falling bodies. They were only silhouettes illuminated by flashes, but they were recognizable. He looked around, counting all six of his teammates falling with him. Good. He couldn't tell if they were awake or still recovering, but the limited light at least confirmed that they'd made it that far. He looked back down. He couldn't gauge how high they were or how long until they would splat against whatever kind of ground waited below.

"Hey!" Gideon yelled as loud as he could, trying to reach any of them. "We should pull our shoots now!"

No one responded, or maybe they did. He couldn't tell. He couldn't even hear himself over the wind and random blasts of thunder. In a helpless panic, he found himself torn between trying to aim his body toward theirs to pull their shoots in case they were still unconscious or pulling his right away. If they were nearing the ground, and the parachutes weren't activated themselves, he would have to pull his and continue the mission. There was no point in everyone dying. On the other hand, if they still had a long distance to fall, it was imperative that he try to aim himself and save as many as he could. In the darkness, there was no way of knowing. "Traveler! Duma!" He screamed at the top of his lungs, but once again, he couldn't even hear his own desperate pleas.

Flash! Two seconds. *Boom!* Bright lightning illuminated everything below for a brief second and then it was gone. It was enough. They were maybe half a mile from the ground and closing fast. There was no time. Gideon's eyes shot open as he scrambled, suddenly realizing that he had no idea how to operate the alien parachute.

"Duma!" he yelled as his hands urgently searched for any kind of lever or handle. "Duma!" He couldn't find anything. There was no obvious trigger like he was used to back on Earth.

Beep! Beep! Beep! Something flashed on the harness wrapped around his chest and then *boof!* The parachute shot out, instantly yanking against his armpits and inner thighs. Gideon's ears popped with a light ringing as his legs swung back and forth from the sudden midair jolt. He coughed and wheezed, looking around as everything slowed to a gentle descent. Everyone else's shoots had apparently activated at the same time. They were all falling at the same pace around him, though he still couldn't tell their silhouetted conditions.

"Duma!" Gideon yelled again as he opened and closed his mouth, trying to get his ears to pop. He pinched his nostrils and blew pressure into them. It worked. His eyes fluttered as sounds of distant thunder grew clear and sharp.

"I am in good health, Sir Gideon!" Dumakleiza's relieving voice yelled from a ways away. Her response triggered, in turn, a loud howl from Cooby as he coasted around Dumakleiza in circles. His long arms were out, and he was boasting how easily he could coast on his own without any need for a parachute. He was accustomed to quick leaps, but this was a treat for his skin flaps.

Gideon smiled as his growing anxiety seemed a little less dim. "Thank God." He looked around, still struggling to see the others as he rubbed his smooth shoulder. "How's everyone else doing?"

"Alive," Lord Coyzle reported. "I'm not sure if this was a good idea." He groaned a failed attempt at a chuckle. His first jump away from

Whewliss was to Horror Planet. The decision was instantly regretted. It had seemed like a courageous decision at the time, but feeling powerless exposure to an alien world saturated in darkness had him feeling the cold fingers of death. Goose bumps were protruding out of his skin like miniature horns, and it wasn't even cold anymore.

Traveler yelled from a bit farther away. "I'm not sure if this is better or worse than Roaring Valley." He held onto the parachute straps with a death grip as he searched below for any hint of visibility. Ground had to be approaching them soon. "Also, I think I'm going to trade my gubernaculum for a new one." He laughed, expecting to hear Gideon laugh with him, but only silence responded. He rolled his eyes. It meant Gideon was grumpy because of his shoulder, and Traveler was getting tired of fixing something that didn't even seem broken. He wanted to know the secret locked away in the impenetrable vault buried in Gideon's mind. He groaned, annoyed. That would have to wait. He pointed all his fingers downward, bunching them together like flowers waiting to blossom. A bright glow shone from them as his implants activated a high-powered flashlight.

"Four Zero," Lord Coyzle urgently said. "Not now. We don't want our position given away." His fear-driven instruction was still law, so Traveler spread his fingers, and everything returned to black.

"Yeah, hi," Izzy said as concerns flooded his mind. "I'm okay, I guess. Where is the ground? Does anyone see it? *Is* there ground?"

"It should be soon!" Gideon yelled, remembering how close they'd been before their shoots deployed. He peered down, desperate for any indication as he prepared his legs for a surprise impact.

Flash! Lightning, which had been blinding as they fell through the clouds, brightened everything below. The ground was directly beneath them. Everyone's eyes shot open in a freaked moment of forced preparation. The lightning had flashed just in time, exposing marshy wetlands.

Splash! They landed in seemingly black water, luckily only waist deep. There was a putrid scent, like sulfur and salty smoke, thick and clinging. Random bunches of trees stuck out of the black water like islands desperate to exist above the surface. They had hanging leaves that looked more like seaweed. The whole location reminded Gideon of gator-infested swamplands.

Lord Coyzle was the only one to lose his footing and fall beneath the surface. He jumped up, waving his arms and clawing water out of his eyes.

"Oh, that is just awful." He shuddered as it dripped off him. "Is that water? It doesn't feel like water." He gagged. "It certainly doesn't taste like water."

Cooby squalled and screamed as he splashed around, struggling to stay above the surface. His body kept sinking and dunking his face as all six arms fought for stability. Dumakleiza found her footing and snatched him up so he could hold onto her back, his wet fur trembling. They were both suddenly wrapped up in Gideon's arms as he rushed over.

"You're okay. You're okay," he said in a low voice, his vulnerability not making any attempt to hide itself. Gideon didn't even realize he was going to kiss Dumakleiza until after his lips parted from hers. His hastened pulse slowed as he closed his eyes and allowed himself to breathe. "You're okay."

Dumakleiza smiled and placed a strong hand on his healed shoulder. "As are you, Sir Gideon. Do not fret on our behalf." She stared dotingly into his troubled eyes and nodded. "It would take more than a pair-of-shooting to part me from you." Her version of "parachute" brought the faintest smile to Gideon's lips.

Traveler assisted Lord Coyzle with standing and then looked around. "I've got you, my lord. Everyone else okay?" He did a quick headcount. It was easier to see now that they had landed. Random glimpses of bright flashes helped from the storm clouds above, and there was just enough light on Horror Planet for their optical implants to utilize. As Traveler finished ensuring everyone had made it, the Daemoanik squared off against him about ten feet away. Traveler froze as his heart threatened to stop. The beast inhaled and then spoke in a low tone.

"Remove your implants." Its deep voice made everyone cringe.

"W—what?" Traveler asked.

"Your implants," it said again. "If he's here, he knows we are, too. Remove your weapons."

"It doesn't matter where he is," Lord Coyzle muttered with authority. "We both know that our weapons are useless against him, and so does he. There's no point removing them."

"He will see them as a threat," the Daemoanik growled as it took one step toward him with its claws splayed out.

Lord Coyzle didn't back down. "He won't see us at all if we don't survive long enough to find him."

Traveler pointed at the Daemoanik, threatening the monster's life despite his fear of it. "Stay back." He wanted to yell the instruction but had barely found the courage to speak.

"You do not scare me," the Daemoanik said without blinking. It even mimicked Traveler's head motions, twisting, turning, keeping him in its gaze. "I will tear the implants from you myself, and you will thank me as you bleed into the water."

"No." Lord Coyzle glared the monster down. "If you attempt anything, we will kill you. And even if you manage to overpower and kill all of us, you will die here alone. *Shadowmaker*—" He emphasized the name to ensure that the Daemoanik would listen. "—hated your people—*his* people—enough to destroy Daemoana." The monster cowered at the name, glancing around the dark. Lord Coyzle tried to posture himself taller amid the slippery footing. "Your only chance at survival is us. If he finds you alone, he will kill you without a second thought." Lord Coyzle looked around, more aware of the unknown dangers. "We don't know what lives here, and because of that, it's better if we're armed. You can surrender to my supremacy and join us, you can go off on your own and take your chances with Horror Planet, or we can kill you now. Make your choice." The Daemoanik glared at him, aching to tear into his stomach or maybe his throat, but ultimately chose neither.

As the confrontation slowly diffused, Gideon looked at Traveler and Lord Coyzle. "If we don't find Shadowmaker, Abdabriel is going to kill the others. He's going to kill Timrekka."

The Daemoanik spun and roared, "Don't say that name!"

"Get over yourself," Gideon scoffed. "He knows we're here. Saying his name isn't going to make a damn difference, ya spineless piece of shit." His response made the monster tilt its head to the side. It thought it had a good read on Gideon after the first impression at the Winkloh Star, but the sudden aggression was unexpected, and it found it strangely amusing.

Traveler grunted, "Gideon, get ahold of yourself. We don't have time." He didn't have patience for Gideon's neediness on Horror Planet. There were muchbigger issues to worry about.

Gideon's eyes flared as he brought his head back. "Me get ahold of *my*self?" he scoffed.

"Sir Gideon." Dumakleiza hoped to sway his emotional state, but Gideon had already taken a step toward the Daemoanik.

"If we're able to get past our fears of you, Horror Planet, and *Shadowmaker*, I think it's time you dug deep and found your balls if you haven't already cut them off with your clawed hand while jerking o—"

"Enough!" Traveler yelled out. The Daemoanik smiled at Gideon's rage. Dumakleiza didn't have any weapons, but she was ready to at least try to tackle the Daemoanik if it attacked Gideon. She knew Gideon wouldn't stand a chance against it without her. Really, she wasn't sure how well they'd do together. The creature looked capable of killing all of them. Traveler shook his head. "If you're so desperate to cut into something, cut Gideon's left shoulder. One line from top to bottom."

The monster took his eyes off Gideon and looked at Traveler, not sure if he'd meant it or not. It was a strange thing to instruct for such a soft-minded Whewlight. Traveler motioned for them to hurry up. "I'm not joking. Cut him. He won't stop you."

Lord Coyzle narrowed his eyes. "Four Zero, what do you think you are doi—"

"You saw my optical recordings, Lord Coyzle," Traveler said while maintaining eye contact with the Daemoanik. "Gideon needs this." He shook his head and yelled at the monster, who still hadn't moved. "Cut him! I need the twoof you on your best behavior, and right now you are both endangering us all. *Cut. Him.*"

The Daemoanik grinned and stepped toward Gideon, expecting him to scream, fight back, or maybe run. It's what every previous victim of the mutilated killer had done. To its surprise, Gideon held still as it approached, staring unwaveringly into its dark eyes. The Daemoanik leaned in, inches from his face, daring him to scream or flinch, wanting him to. It longed for the satisfaction of inflicting terror with nothing more than its presence. Once again, Gideon surprised it. Instead of retracting, he leaned forward, touching his forehead to the Daemoanik's. He could smell the monster's skin, and every detail of its tortured eyes was exposed.

"Are your ears too melted to hear?" Gideon asked through his flexed jaw. "Spaceman said to cut my shoulder. Not too much for you, is it?"

The Daemoanik's grin grew into a smile as it placed its carved index finger against the soft, rosy skin atop Gideon's left shoulder. It slowly pressed until the filed bone pierced through. Gideon didn't react. He just matched the monster's glare. The Daemoanik was amused. It pulled down ever-so slowly, savoring each sensation of Gideon's skin splitting open. It was the first blood it had gotten since before the Winkloh Star, and the warmth reinforced its reason for living.

The physical satisfaction was less intoxicating than the beast's curiosity about Gideon. The Earthling was truly unafraid. It wasn't just an act. The Daemoanik had seen people pretend to be unafraid, but when it finally came down to it, everyone cracked and cried out.

The Daemoanik retracted its filed finger and brought it to its lips. It licked the blood off, but Gideon paid no attention to its intimidation attempt. Rather, he groaned with closed eyes. He was no longer paying any attention to the Daemoanik. He tilted his head back and exhaled, his shoulders slumping at the relief. Everyone watched as he collected himself through the pain, appreciating the sting of it. The Daemoanik couldn't even relish the taste of blood. It was too interested in what Gideon was going to do next. Only distant thunder broke the silence.

Gideon shivered and cracked a genuine smile as his eyes opened. He took a couple breaths as his heart slowed. He wiped the dripping blood off his arm, smearing it on his torso as he looked at the confused Daemoanik.

"What's your name?" He wasn't his energetic self yet, but his boldness had acquired some charm. The Daemoanik licked the remaining blood from its sharpened teeth and studied Gideon. The question caught it off guard, and it had to think about how to respond. It had been a while since it had heard or even thought about its own name, let alone even thinking of itself as a gender. It was a he. That much was easy to recall, and of course, obvious, even though it had been tortured into thinking of itself as nothing but a weapon.

"Vorlak," it said with a subtle dip in confidence. The name didn't even feel right coming out. "Vorlak," he said again, gaining belief in the name as lost memories crept back.

Gideon nodded as his smile grew. "Nice to meet you, Vorlak. Thanks for helping with that." He sighed again, feeling repeated relief from his shoulder. Vorlak steadily gazed at him, unsure of how he wanted to react. Gideon's chest deflated a little more. "We haven't actually met. I'm Gideon." He extended his hand, knowing Vorlak probably didn't understand the custom or what to do with it.

"Gideon." The confused Daemoanik tasted the name as he stared at Gideon's hand. "Crazy man."

Cooby screamed and clung to Dumakleiza's shoulders, grabbing everyone's attention. They looked as he tried to climb higher, but there was nowhere to go. His frantic monkey hands scrambled Dumakleiza's face as he barked at something in the water.

Dumakleiza brushed his paws out of her face as he caught her lip and scratched her nose. "Coobs, what troubles you?" She grabbed two of his legs and held them still.

They all saw it. It was barely noticeable in the dark, but something moved beneath the placid surface. They lurched backward. Shimmering ripples indicated something large swimming between them.

"What forbidding creatures prowl these waters?" Dumakleiza muttered under her breath. "Grim, your loyal daughter calls upon you." Her pulse raced as she shared Cooby's desperation for higher ground.

Izzy stepped backward with heightened awareness of every sensation in the water. "Thick marshland." He shivered, looking for whatever had slipped by. "It's likely reptilian." He gulped as the water became still. "My guess is it's lying in wait, evaluating us while it decides."

"Decides what?" Lord Coyzle asked, trembling.

"Who to eat," was all Izzy could get out before heavy water erupted from something bursting through the surface. They screamed and turned to shield their eyes. A loud smack echoed out as something slapped the surface and disappeared beneath it.

"Where is it?" Lord Coyzle yelled.

"Where's Vorlak?" Gideon asked. Everyone looked around. They were all accounted for, except the Daemoanik.

The moment of stillness was short lived. Violent splashes returned as the surface broke a second time. They spun. Traveler shone his fingertips in its direction, hoping to blind whatever was coming at them.

They stopped as they saw Vorlak. His torso was encased in rows of fangs, his arms pinned against his sides. He was sideways in the air, lifted above the surface and splashed back below over and over in the creature's instinctive attempt to drown and throttle him. The massive reptile was similar to an alligator but with a rounded mouth rather than an extended snout. It was gnawing around Vorlak's waist, trying to rip him in half. Quick glimpses amid the violent thrashing exposed a head about three quarters the size of Vorlak's entire frame and a body at least twenty feet long. Vorlak was alive and laughing with every breath he could get. His hardened skin was proving difficult for the cold-blooded carnivore to bite through. Only a few puncture wounds were visible.

Traveler acted quickly, pointing his right index finger at the blur of scales, teeth, flesh, and water. It was impossible to get an easy shot in the dark mess. If he shot and killed Vorlak, he wouldn't care, but he was going to keep him alive as long as he could. He wiped spraying drops of water from his eyes with his free hand and aimed. It was the best shot he was going to get. *Fft.*

Vorlak fell into the water. The massive reptile flipped backward, exposing its full underbelly with only its tail still beneath the water. It roared a breathy growl and fell over itself. It smacked against the water with curled feet aimed skyward. As the waves stilled, the long creature floated belly-up, a glowing circle in its abdomen. After a few twitches, Traveler fired two more times into its head.

Vorlak stood with a grin, black water washing down his face as he emerged with calm elegance. Everyone turned to see if he was okay, but his eyes were still on the reptile. Traveler's light shone on his blood trickling into the water from the punctures in his stomach.

"Oh, no," Traveler said as he then turned the light to show more blood dripping down Gideon's shoulder. He had no time to explain and then act. They had to be simultaneous. He stepped over to Gideon and grabbed his arm.

"What?" Gideon asked.

"Don't move." Traveler focused the light and cauterized the slice down his shoulder. As soon as it was done, he turned. "Vorlak, your turn." He used the toughest voice he could force. "Please don't eat me." He made his way over to the Daemoanik, still staring intently at the dead animal. There was no time for caution. He reached out and cauterized the gashes in Vorlak's stomach, expecting to get clawed in the face. Vorlak didn't move. Traveler stepped back and looked around to make sure that everyone was still there. "If there are more of those things, they heard us, or they'll smell the blood. We have to move."

They looked around. There was no obvious direction to go, as everything in their limited sight looked like continuing swamplands. The little bouquets of trees wouldn't be enough to provide shelter, and everywhere else was black water.

"Where?" Lord Coyzle asked, not seeing any options. He looked up at the sky. "We should go back to Whewliss."

"We can't," Traveler said, knowing that Lord Coyzle was more than aware. "We have to get somewhere safer."

"Where?" Lord Coyzle yelled, his voice shaking.

"Well," Izzy said, trying to focus on what limited Horror Planet he understood. "The trees are more tightly bunched in that direction." Traveler's light followed his pointed finger and showed that the small islands of trees were in fact closer in proximity. Izzy nodded, confident in his observation. "There's more likely dry land that way." He wasn't sure if that would mean more or less danger.

Subtle splashes spun Traveler's light around behind them. He saw distant ripples in the water moving toward them. There was more than one this time. It looked like there were three or four bodies beneath the water, and they were swimming quickly.

"Then, that's where we'll go!" Traveler said. "Run!"

Everyone saw what he was looking at. Predators had clearly smelled them and were closing in for food. They ran, pushing through the thick water as fast as they could. Their legs trudged in slow motion. Running through black molasses was a nightmare in itself. Traveler feared where the bigger nightmare awaited: behind them or ahead.

24

Fft.Fft. EBOO went quiet after a few more shots. The unexpected Daemoaniks lay motionless in the grass with cauterized holes bored through them. The onslaught of arriving soldiers had been given the instruction "overkill."

The incapacitated recruits were still twitching as the electric currents slowed. Dead bodies were strewn about the well-lit city, and the surviving soldiers were dumbstruck. Monsters they'd thought lost to history had resurfaced and torn through them like knives through warm butter.

"Well, this was unexpected." Abdabriel almost sounded excited as he walked over to Master Brawd and the recruits, tased in the grass. Thirty handpicked soldiers followed closely behind him, ready to kill anything that threatened their god.

One of the soldiers who had been stationed in EBOO approached. He was grunting, cut open in a few places, blood trailing behind his feet.

"I'm sorry, Holy One," he wheezed through aching muscles. His gelatin suit was helping keep him conscious, but he needed a light jump. "I apologize for calling you back from the City of Light." The soldier was worried there would be punishment. "They—came out of nowhere." Three more soldiers who had fought with him stepped up and nodded as they, too, compressed their wounds.

"No." Abdabriel looked around at the carnage. "They came from the Winkloh Star." He smirked as he stared at one of the dead Daemoaniks. "I left you in charge," he said with a disappointed headshake. "You were given a simple instruction. Guard the gelatin and prevent anything like, oh, I don't know, *this* from happening." He chuckled and ran his hand down his chin, exhaling in frustration. "I hold my soldiers to a higher standard, as you will set the first example for a brighter future. I can't tolerate this kind of ineptitude." He looked at the soldiers, pitying them with heartbroken disappointment. "You understand." With that, he lifted a finger and shot the soldier in the stomach. *Fft.* A pop and sizzle released steam from the soldier's orifices, simultaneously zapping the others next to him. All four dried out like grapes cooked to raisins. Abdabriel shook his head and turned after unleashing the arachniblast.

"*They*, however—" He motioned to Master Brawd, Timrekka, and Jasss. "—did *not* come from the Winkloh Star." He turned to the contingent he'd brought with him. "They didn't come through the gelatin either."

"No, Holy One," a woman answered. "The gelatin hasn't been breached, but the guard placed at it is dead."

"Hmm." Abdabriel mulled over the inconvenient puzzle. "Then how did they get here? Even I had to come through the gelatin when I returned." He looked around as everyone awaited his instruction. "Get them up. And her." He pointed at Lady Melodeen. "Put blackout cuffs on their hands. Can't have them light jumping away."

"Holy One." One of the soldiers bowed. "You don't want them executed for their crimes against the light?"

Abdabriel slowly shook his head with bunched lips. "No, I can't find it in myself to execute a fellow council member, no matter how much they've earned it." He stared down at Master Brawd. "They will come around once they see. They simply do not understand yet."

"And the others?" the same soldier prodded, curious why his fellow soldiers had been executed but some of Abdabriel's enemies were being shown mercy.

Abdabriel understood. "The others are some of the bravest souls in the entire universe." He looked at Timrekka and Jasss with genuine admiration. "They have a much larger role to play in my vision. For all of us." He motioned for the soldiers to get them up and cuffed. "Besides, if they finally refuse after seeing the light, then I would rather kill them in front of billions. I would rather broadcast the punishment of resistance to all worlds. Lessons aren't learned if there's no one to witness."

"Yes, Holy One," the soldier replied.

Abdabriel watched as the four intruders were stood up and placed in blackout cuffs. The restraints clasped fully around both hands behind the back, encasing them in black metal that prevented any contact with light. Abdabriel nodded as soon as they were restrained. They still hadn't recovered enough to speak or move on their own.

"Add extra binds and magnet-clamps to that one." He pointed at Timrekka. "Thamioshlings are very strong. In fact, I don't think I've ever seen one off Thamiosh, so let's not assume our cuffs alone will hold him." At his command, the soldiers added extra restraints to his arms until they looked like they were cocooned in steel spider webs. Abdabriel shook his head, embarrassed by his own modesty. "You know what? Let's bind his feet, as well. Ah." He playfully waved his hand. "Full body. Restrain his full body. It's his mind I want." He chuckled, almost wanting to see Timrekka break free and kill some his soldiers before putting him down. "Could you imagine if—" His words trailed off. His soldiers wouldn't appreciate his amusement at their fighting the Thamioshling. "Never mind."

"He's awake," said one of the soldiers restraining Timrekka.

"Oh?" Abdabriel was impressed. "I guess that makes sense with his strength and all." He stepped over. "Timrekka, how are you feeling?"

Timrekka groaned, his large eyes rolling around in his goggles as he came to. "Master, uh, N'kowsky?" His mind hadn't recovered enough to remember much.

"Abdabriel," Abdabriel corrected. "How did you get here? I'm dying to know."

Timrekka gulped a fuzzy taste down and shook his head as memories came flooding back. "I won't tell you, I won't help you, I—" He groaned. "You're just another Trollop."

Abdabriel nodded. "Timrekka, I wish I had time for a back and forth. I'd enjoy one, but I just don't have the time in this exact moment. I've got to return to the City of Light, and you know what's exciting? You're coming with me." He smiled, hoping to see the same eagerness on Timrekka's face. It wasn't there. "However, I don't know if Mackel here will be joining us. That's up to you."

Timrekka looked up through strained eyes. "What do you mean it's up to me?"

"I mean," Abdabriel said while pointing a finger gun at Master Brawd, "you can tell me how you managed to get past the gelatin. Or Mackel can be buried alongside Daemoaniks."

Timrekka's eyes flared. "Okay, okay, okay, okay." He nodded. "Dumakleiza killed one of your men on the Wall and then—" He winced, afraid that Abdabriel would kill him out of punishment. "—we shot him through the fractal gas at amplified speeds and then jumped through the hole before it closed," he whimpered. He wanted to keep his friends safe, but it came at the cost of incriminating himself. "It was my idea. Please don't hurt Master Brawd. It was my idea. It was my fault." He scrunched his face, bracing for death.

Abdabriel waited and then chuckled, bringing his hand to his side. "Wow, I feel like a child!" he laughed. "That's brilliant. We never planned for that. Wow." He stood back in amazement, looking at his soldiers as his laughter grew. They slowly joined him, only some of them understanding Timrekka's explanation. Abdabriel shook his head. "That's really impressive ingenuity. Your problem solving is, well, I never would have thought of that."

"Please just kill me and get it over with," Timrekka said with all the courage he could scrape up.

"Kill you?" Abdabriel's laughter subsided. "Are you joking? You're incredible. I would have never thought of that. I want you with me!" he yelled out, proclaiming his admiration to anyone in earshot. "Once the universe is safe, you are going to help me provide it with technologies beyond anything we have now. Galaxies will bow down before you, and they will love you for the life you give them. You will pioneer mankind into a bright future, void of murder, hunger, darkness. You and I will create a glorious tomorrow without want. No longer will the underprivileged be underprivileged." Abdabriel stepped forward and placed both hands on Timrekka's shoulders. "I want to unleash your brilliant mind and provide you with limitless resources, so you can invent, experiment, and create everything your dazzling brain can envisage. I will provide you with teams of millions of the brightest minds, the most promising scientists from every world, and they will follow your guidance. They will do what you tell them to do, work tirelessly on projects you assign, create what you tell them to create. You've worked so long on your own. Can you imagine what you could do with an army of scientists doing your bidding? Can you imagine what you will be capable of creating?" He laughed out of pure excitement. "I understand you're having trouble accepting the transition right now. Change is painful. I empathize. Truly I do. Noneof this has been easy for me." A pained look glimmered in his beautiful eyes but quickly disappeared. "I can't wait to unleash all of your potential." He shook his head, unable to contain himself. "Gah, I can't believe you thought of a way through the fractal gas. That's so *fourth phase recruit* of you." He chuckled and looked around at his soldiers. "Remember when I said all we needed was a few soldiers here to keep things peaceful? Wow, was I wrong." He chuckled louder. "You know—" He looked at Timrekka. "—we have defensive countermeasure drones that could have been patrolling overhead along with the soldiers I stationed here. We haven't needed them for decades, but I plan on using them on other worlds until we establish fractal gas there. I thought them pointless here." He shook his head, embarrassed. "I feel foolish. However, I'm glad I didn't have them operating or else you'd all be dead and then I wouldn't have you." He shook his head and looked around. "Well, you got me in a back and forth, even though I don't have time. You're so impressive!"

Timrekka was silent. He couldn't help admitting that Abdabriel's offer was tempting. His scientific mind was abuzz with possibilities. There were so many dismissed ideas he'd thought impossible due to the lack of support, resources, and manpower. The temptations were exponentially appealing.

"Oh." Abdabriel's tone grew solemn. "Two questions before we go to the City of Light. What happened to Tsuna? And where did Gideon and the others go?" Though he'd been abundantly kind and welcoming just moments before, Timrekka knew that the answers could earn punishment. It wasn't in his nature to lie, but telling the truth about hunting down Shadowmaker could be dangerous.

"Uh, Master Brawd dropped Tsuna down the hole after he killed Candelle."

Abdabriel scoffed. "Really? Well, hopefully the fourth phase isn't hell." He winked. "I'm a little disappointed, but Tsuna was the least impressive recruit, so I guess that's forgivable." His smile disappeared again. "And where are the others?"

"They," Master Brawd's twitching voice answered, "returned to the Wall."

Abdabriel turned, surprised to hear Master Brawd awake. "Good morning, old friend. How are you feeling?" His kind words were met by a hateful expression on Master Brawd's pained face. Abdabriel nodded. "I know it'll be a while before you and I can reconcile. I truly am sorry about what had to be done. Candelle was a good woman."

Master Brawd wanted to tear Abdabriel apart. He believed in efficiency, only killing with precise execution, but with Abdabriel, he wanted to take his time. He wanted to savor the pain, the suffering, and the pleas for mercy before he finally silenced him forever.

"They rescued Lord Coyzle from you, so you couldn't hurt him."

Abdabriel rolled his eyes. "He was in the Winkloh Star. I wasn't going to hurt him. I preserved him." He shook his head. "I'm sorry, I'm interrupting. Go on."

"He's safer in the unknown of the fourth phase than he is at your 'mercy.'"

Abdabriel shook his head and rolled his eyes. "As ridiculous as that dramatic sentiment is, I'm glad he's getting to pursue his dreams. I guess we all win. I get to save humanity from itself, and LordCoyzle gets to go play in a hole at the edge of space."

"What now?" Master Brawd asked through a clenched jaw, expecting to be executed on the spot.

"Now," Abdabriel said with childlike excitement, "we go to the City of Light and address Whewliss after my army finishes purging the dark."

Master Brawd shook his head in disgust. "You're slaughtering every Whewlight soldier? Every man and woman who enlisted to keep us safe? They admired you. Many joined *because* of our efforts in the ULW, and you're just killing them like Daemoaniks."

"No, of course not." Abdabriel brought his head back, offended by the accusation. "I give every one of them the opportunity to join me. I only have to kill those who resist. It's regrettable but necessary."

Master Brawd ignored him and looked over to see Lady Melodeen unconscious and in restraints. "What about Lady Melodeen?"

"Old friend, I have no intention of killing my fellow council members. We've been through too much together. I wish only to show you the future before I accept your final acceptance or dismissal of my invitation. Of course you don't see my vision now. Soon you will see how much brighter it is."

"You killed Lady Skorric and Master Keevind."

"*I* didn't," Abdabriel said with genuine anger. "Two soldiers who disobeyed my supreme instruction to spare them did. They've since been punished, shot into the darkness of space. I regret Lady Skorric and Master Keevind's deaths. They haunt me. I want them beside me, as well."

"I'm going to kill you."

Abdabriel nodded. "There you are. Honestly, I'd be skeptical if you didn't threaten me. Wouldn't be you." He turned to his soldiers. "I want twenty of you to stay here. And please, please do a better job. Oh, and let's get those drones up and going now. I don't think anyone else will be brave enough to show up, but I'd rather be safe than sorry." He turned to Master Brawd and Timrekka. "Well, shall we be on our way?"

Master Brawd peeled his fuming eyes from Abdabriel and stared deep into the night sky. His gut twisted at the mere thought of Shadowmaker, but if it would avenge the dead, he was willing to hope in darkness.

25

Splashes and lasers disrupted the still swamp in a hurricane of madness. Everyone ran through black water, desperate to get away from the giant reptiles. Traveler continued firing aimlessly behind them. For all they knew, they were running straight into another danger, into the claws of another predator. Horror Planet was likely riddled with them. There was no promise of safety, and fleeing blindly only heightened their growing list of fears.

"We need to find land fast!" Traveler yelled, his legs aching. "I don't have much energy left, and I won't be able to shoot soon."

There was no time to explain that, without a light source, his implant operated off his own energy, and he was almost out. If they didn't find land, he'd fatigue and collapse, leaving them vulnerable. He'd managed to kill two of the reptilians with blind shots, but the more they ran, the more animals they attracted. Every time Traveler looked over his shoulder, more had amassed.

"The water's getting shallower!" Gideon yelled. "I think we're going in the right direction." The water was only up to his knees, making it easier to run. Still, the grueling escape was taking its toll.

Cooby squalled, roaring at the beasts pursuing them. He knew he was too small to handle even one of them, but his instincts insisted he protect Dumakleiza. He clawed the air, barking threats and warnings.

Lord Coyzle was in shock as he struggled to keep his footing. He was a brilliant politician who'd led Whewliss out of despair. He was celebrated as the greatest leader in the planet's history, revered by most, loved by more, but his survival skills were nonexistent, and Horror Planet did not allow a learning curve. He was unaccustomed to feeling death coming for him. Even when Abdabriel had arrived and started slaughtering Whewlights, he'd at least been able to communicate with the enemy. But now Lord Coyzle was terrified of actual monsters. There was no reasoning, no debating, no civilized way of handling the situation. He was running for his life, fleeing the unknown on a world where he couldn't even see where he was going.

"You're enjoying this, aren't you?" he yelled at Gideon, finally understanding why Four Zero loved and hated him.

Gideon gave a short laugh as he fought for breath amid the ceaseless cardio and disruptive splashing. "You said you wanted to get out more," he chuckled and coughed water out. "Are you not having fun playing hide-and-seek with alien crocodiles?"

Lord Coyzle shook his head. "Four Zero, you are truly the maddest Whewlight I know. You and Gideon are of the same breed."

"I am unsure whether that is a compliment or insult!" Traveler yelled as he fired more shots behind them. *Fft.Fft.*

"So am I!"

"Land!" Izzy yelled, pointing ahead.

They felt a sliver of hope as the water continued getting shallower. Their feet rose above the surface with each stride. A second wind of hope surged through them. They ran faster as they finally found themselves free of the soup. Their feet hit mud, the godsend of a beach making some of them laugh. They made it a good distance onto solid ground before Traveler stopped and spun around. He was ready to face off against any of the reptiles following them out of the water. Everyone else gathered behind him, wheezing and coughing. Dumakleiza and Vorlak joined Traveler, ready to fight.

Loud hissing followed as only one crocodile decided to leave the safety of water. It crawled at capable speed, almost slithering, as its short legs carried it. Seeing it fully exposed made it slightly less intimidating, except for the daggers lining its mouth.

Fft.Fft. Traveler fired straight into its throat, burning deep, cauterized holes that burst out the back of its head. The creature collapsed to its belly, a gurgling gasp seething out as its teeth clamped shut.

"Good shot!" Lord Coyzle exclaimed. "Well done, Four Zero." He bent over and put his hands on his knees.

They took a moment to gather themselves. It was hot and humid on the dark world, which at least made it easier to take deep inhalations. Their lungs were starved, their muscles were tired, their legs were on the verge of giving out, and their gelatin suits were no longer catering to their needs so far from Whewliss.

Dumakleiza tentatively glared at the smiling Daemoanik, whose eyes were glued to the dead animal. "Vorlak of Daemoana," she said with scathing authority, "accompany me to its corpse." Vorlak didn't move, but Dumakleiza's audacity got his attention. He glanced at her with emotionless eyes. Cooby was in immediate disagreement with her invitation, and he had no problem expressing it. He growled, hiding his face behind Dumakleiza's neck and hair. His hissing continued as Vorlak cracked an eerie smile. Duma rolled her eyes. "I ask for your assistance not out of desire for friendship. I simply require your aid in ripping the beast's teeth from its mouth, a task which I assume you to be capable of." With that, she started toward the dead reptile. Whether or not Vorlak would help her, she was going to arm herself with something, and the fangs would have to suffice. To her surprise, Vorlak followed.

Gideon turned his attention to Traveler and Lord Coyzle while keeping his eyes on Dumakleiza, praying that Vorlak wouldn't try anything.

Lord Coyzle finally caught his breath enough to express a few of his compiling concerns. "What now? Do you have a plan for how to find Shadowmaker?"

Traveler sighed. He had an idea, but it wasn't one he actually wanted to put into motion. He took a few more breaths and looked around, failing to see anything. "Well." He shone his light in every direction, getting a feel for their surroundings. The world seemed untouched, untampered with, raw in every way. Everything he saw was either foreign trees or more swampland. Even the foliage on Horror Planet was menacing in nature. The trees curled and bowed like figures stretching in the dark. Only in the light was their innocuous shape exposed. A misty fog lightly blew through them like ghosts in a dream.

Traveler blinked a few times, trying to focus on Lord Coyzle's question. "Sorry, this place creeps me out. Um, well, if Shadowmaker is here, he knows we are, too. We're intruding on his world. There's no way we'll manage to scour an entire planet between the six of us."

Lord Coyzle blew some air through tight lips. "I don't like that plan." He didn't have a better one, but he still wasn't comfortable being bait. "And that's all only if he's still alive."

Gideon squinted. "Why wouldn't he be? Do you think something here might've killed him?"

"Time," Traveler answered. "If he came here, then he's been trapped in darkness for nearly one-hundred-years."

"—with no light to jump with." Gideon understood, slumping at the disheartening realization. "Knowing that much, why did we even come here? Even if he was born on this world and lived a long life, he'd be a feeble, old man now."

Traveler shrugged. "Nobody understands that man. He's a history mystery." He smirked. "Thought you'd enjoy that." He cleared his throat, hacking up more black water. "I wouldn't put it past him to have found a way to survive, even if he is an old man now."

Izzy frowned. "I'm disappointed in myself for not considering all that." He looked around. Everything was dark. The minimal lighting breaking through the dense clouds above them gave, at best, similar visibility to that of a moon. "We're stuck here, aren't we? Or is there something else you're not telling us about Shadowmaker?"

"There are no more secrets," Traveler answered. "You know what we know about him. I'm just going on faith. Or hope. Whatever you want to call it. I've heard of numerous gods, goddesses, spirits, deities, and in-finite other kinds of higher powers in my travels. I don't know what I believe in, but I have been praying to whomever. There has to be a way to defeat Abdabriel, and this is the only thing I can think of." He sighed. "And who knows, maybe Shadowmaker isdead. Maybe we're never get-ting off this world. Maybe someone else will eventually dethrone

Abdabriel after he's dominated every planet for hundreds of years. I don't know. But I'd rather die trying to find a solution than give up."

"Agreed." Gideon nodded, still recovering from the news. "Well, what's the next step in searching for our geriatric antihero?"

"I think we should get much farther away from the water," Lord Coyzle answered as fast as he could. "And we should build a fire."

Izzy shook his head. "Won't that draw attention to us? I'm not sure if that's what we want."

"Actually," Gideon said with a smile, "that's exactly what we want. May as well make it easy for Shadowmaker to find us."

"What about the wildlife?"

"Uh," Gideon chuckled. "They live in darkness. Something tells me they've never seen fire or even light other than lightning. Fire will probably scare the shit out of them. Besides —" His stomach gurgled. "We need to eat. How does barbequed gator sound to you guys?" He nodded toward the reptile Dumakleiza and Vorlak were cutting up.

Lord Coyzle's eyebrow rose. "You want to eatthat thing?"

"Unless you know of a better five-star restaurant around here. Hell, I'd take a two-star."

"What?"

"Nothing." Gideon smiled. "Figure we cut off its legs and its tail. We could carry that a safe distance from the water to cook up some grub." He smiled, excited by the prospect.

"You really think it's safe to eat?" Lord Coyzle asked.

"Actually," Izzy said as he thought about it, "it should be. Reptilian meat can be a bit tougher than mammalian, but it'll suffice while we look for a better food source. Maybe it's good?" He shrugged.

"Maybe what is good?" Dumakleiza asked.

The others turned to look at her in Traveler's light. She had fashioned a makeshift belt out of her treasure sack's strap. Her treasure was securely fastened to her left hip and tucked into her belt were eight reptile fangs. The jagged teeth and her hands were drenched in blood, but the pirate princess was glowing with happiness. She had weapons again. Vorlak was standing a few feet from her with blood coating his entire body. He'd clearly had just as much fun but was less objective during their fang retrieval.

"Um" Gideon laughed at the sight. "We were just talking about removing the gator's legs and tail so we could carry it inland and cook it over a fire."

"Okay." Vorlak turned right around to return to the carcass.

Traveler shook his head. "Well, Gideon, you were right about giving them a purpose. Maybe he'll settle down one day as the local butcher."

Gideon nodded with a smile as they all heard tissue ripping apart. "He seems as happy as a kid in a candy store over there." Everyone watched as Vorlak ripped through the beast's scales, skin, soft tissues, and bone until he dismembered one of its legs. Blood spilled on the beach, and they heard him giggle and hum to himself. Gideon laughed. "I take that back. *Happier*. He's happierthan a kid in a candy store." He couldn't help feeling a strange sense of delight watching Vorlak contribute. The Daemoanik was being helpful, whether or not that was his reason for mutilating the giant reptile, and it gave Gideon hope for the monster.

Vorlak perked up his blood-drenched head. "Come get it!" his gravelly voice yelled. Just the sight of his demonically shaped features covered in thick red made Traveler and Lord Coyzle furious. They had to keep reminding themselves of his usefulness. Vorlak walked to the water's edge and dipped his head beneath it, drinking hearty gulps of the soupy marsh.

Everyone walked over and grabbed a disarticulated limb. Lord Coyzle gagged at the smell, but he put his lordship aside and helped. Even Cooby carried the smaller half of the lizard's large tail, immediately sinking his teeth into the severed portion.

"All right," Traveler said as he tossed one of the bloody stumps over his shoulder. "Let's go inland." They followed as he walked away from the water, lighting the darkness with his finger.

Gideon sped to walk beside him. "While we're walking aimlessly, wanna play your favorite game? It's been a while."

"Sure," Traveler said, welcoming the distraction amid the dark.

"Score." Gideon glanced at the others, all staying close as they moved through the unknown. "Feel free to join in." He cleared his throat. "All right, I'll start. *What if* Shadowmaker is dead and we're stuck here? We clearly will have no way of getting off this spooky rock and will be oblivious to Abdabriel's whereabouts and whether or not he's successfully conquering the universe. In fact, it'll be of little consequence to us because we'll be here. So, what on Earth will we do with ourselves here on Horror Planet?"

Before Traveler could think of a response, Izzy piped in. "Well, I'm pretty sure that's where my expertise would be of value." He took a moment to ponder the possibility. "I imagine we would explore much of this world, figuring out where the most fruitful soil is, and where the safest location would be from weather and wildlife. I would study the plant-life, the terrain, and seasonal differentiation. I would want to have as comprehensive an understanding of H.P. as I could before we settled somewhere. Then, while structures are being built, I would focus on planting gardens to provide food." He couldn't help getting a little excited about the idea. "I would find a way to create basic necessities. I would calculate what elements are available here and see how many technologies from our worlds I could recreate. It would be a hefty challenge, but it might be kind of fun."

"Perfect," Gideon said, smiling at the scientist. "I'm curious how much you could recreate from scratch."

Izzy nodded. "It'd certainly be easier with Timrekka here. His genius was, well, it outshined mine."

Everyone other than Vorlak nodded, saddened by the reminder of those they'd lost.

Traveler picked up the conversation so they wouldn't dwell on depressing truths. "My guess is that the three of us—" He motioned to Gideon and Lord Coyzle. "—would probably be in charge of building a shelter. I'm not sure what other special skills we have that would be helpful here."

"I'm definitely not the survival type like the rest of you," Lord Coyzle said, agreeing with Four Zero's assumption. "I've never built anything. It's an archaic skill back on Whewliss. We have machines and robotics that take care of home building."

"It'd be some good bonding time," Gideon said. "Roll up our sleeves and get our hands dirty in the dark. We'd live by firelight." He thought about it. "That's probably what I'd like the least: Never seeing the sun again—or any star for that matter."

"I would be the hunter," Dumakleiza said. "Cooby and I would provide wild game for sustenance."

"Me, too," Vorlak stated, knowing he didn't have much else to do.

"Actually," Gideon said and smiled, "Vorlak, I envision you catching a baby gator and raising it as your own. In this new life of yours, I'd peg you as one of those guys who bonds with a baby monster and raises it as a pet."

Traveler laughed. "Only you, Gideon."

"I can't tell if you're being sincere," Lord Coyzle commented, glancing back and forth between Gideon and Vorlak. "Do you really believe a Daemoanik could find a place in a civilized world?"

"No," Gideon answered honestly. "But H.P. is the furthest thing from a civilized world. Furthest? Farthest? Both." He chuckled. "Who knows what he could make of himself here?" Gideon grinned at Vorlak, who was intently staring ahead, obviously lost in his own thought.

Vorlak had never considered what kind of life he would lead post-destruction of Daemoana. Before being shot into the Winkloh Star, he'd accepted the reality that he'd be comatose until freed and executed. Waking to a new world in a new time without any of his familiarities provided a blank slate.

Gideon smiled again. "He could go kill dangerous wildlife, keeping that bloodlust fed, and eventually, who knows, maybe join us for games of chess while smoking a pipe." He chuckled as everyone looked at him, confused by his statement. "I think he's a fun addition to the group."

They took a moment to mull over the real possibility: They might be stuck on H.P. Only sounds of distant critters and a light breeze played the soundtrack to their footsteps through the dark.

26

It was a pristine morning in the City of Light. Whewliss's sun was shining with only handfuls of wispy clouds in the distant sky. Warm temperatures provided full breaths of clean air, and indigenous birds wrought friendly songs. On any other day, it would have been perfect settings in the planet's capital.

White light faded from Timrekka's eyes after they landed. He wasn't sure what to expect as he recovered from the jump. He had plenty of built-up curiosity about Whewliss's capital, but with Abdabriel in command of the tour, he was prepared to meet its grandeur with a bitter taste. Before his eyes could adjust, he felt multiple soldiers grab his arms. They were marching him somewhere, but he had no idea where. He blinked a few times as his feet moved. Wherever they were in the city, it was beautiful. The first thing he noticed was difficult to make sense of. They'd landed in a large park, mostly comprised of open grass and random gardens around sculptures of famous Whewlights. But what had Timrekka mesmerized was a building at the far end of the park. At least, he assumed it was a building.

"How does—" He tried to make sense of it. Floating a head above a broad, metal platform was an enormous glass sphere. Timrekka couldn't tell exactly, but it looked to be somewhere around two-hundred-feet in diameter. The bottom third of the sphere was solid metal, smooth, and flawless in its chrome. He assumed the metal bottom was magnetically responding to what must be a repelling platform to keep the gargantuan glass ball suspended in the air. It didn't look real. It was like a magic trick of impossible proportions.

The top two thirds of the sphere were clear, revealing an entire inner community of rooms and halls. From the distance, Timrekka could see Abdabriel's soldiers working on advanced computers, patrolling hallways, and standing guard inside of it. For a moment, he forgot about how villainous they were. He simply wanted to go up into the floating building and take a tour. Its interior was decorated with striking flowers also hovering above smaller magnetic platforms. Vibrant colors exquisitely complimented each other with masterful interior decorating. And to top it all off, the entire sphere was slowly rotating in the air, granting any worker within a three-hundred-and-sixty-degree-view of the city.

The spectacle dazzled Timrekka, momentarily taking his breath away. He forgot that he was in restraints, simply appreciating the illustriousness of it. He turned to look at more of the city. His smile grew as he saw there were many more floating spheres around the City of Light, all filled with what looked like smaller cities within. Each was intricately designed, looking to serve unique and separate purposes. Atop each one were digitally projected names of businesses. Some were banks, some implant centers, celebrated restaurants, lavish salons, stores of various sorts, and many more too far away from Timrekka to read.

He looked down to see what existed below the seemingly endless ocean of floating buildings. At first he'd thought they'd landed in a city park and that was why there was such a large flatness of grass, but as he took in his full surroundings, he realized that it spread across the city as far as he could tell. All the buildings were in the air, so the ground was nothing more than sidewalks and decorations. More commemorative statues were ornamentally placed, gardens purposefully located for maximum wow factor, and light pads on every sidewalk corner. The sidewalks were more than simple cement, stone, or tile; they were lit with what looked like electronic response sensors. Every time someone walked on one, the ground reacted to their footprints. Colors and texts responded to each step, recognizing the person, and addressing their personal needs and interests.

For the most part, the city was occupied by Abdabriel's soldiers, so the sidewalk had no record of the aliens from other worlds, but there were still Whewlights walking about. Timrekka blinked a few times, unsure if he was seeing them right. He was. There were still Whewlights populating the city. He assumed they must have put up no resistance and maybe even joined Abdabriel's cause. They'd been allowed to continue their daily routines and were the most interesting to watch interact with the sidewalks. They spoke as they walked, confirming appointments that electronic projections double-checked, booked new ones, and responded to advertisements popping up on the ground in front of them.

Soft whirring directed Timrekka's attention upward. In the sky, along with brightly colored birds, were drones flying around. They weren't intimidating with their tiny size, but Timrekka had a feeling they were capable of devastating responses to threats. Unfortunately, it was one of Whewlight's own who'd slipped by their defenses and then hacked their systems. Now the drones were in Abdabriel's control, patrolling in accordance with his design.

"It's a little different than Thamiosh, isn't it?" Abdabriel asked as he joined Timrekka, taking in the sight like it was his first visit.

Timrekka nodded. "It's beautiful, and the magnetically repelling orbs are brilliant, but is there any purpose, or are they simply because Whewlights can make such things?"

"There are a few environmental perks to the skydrops, as they're called, but for the most part, they simply represent what we're capable of."

"They're incredible," Timrekka said with a shimmer in his eyes. He was amazed and taken aback by the overwhelming aura of the City of Light. It took a moment for him to focus back on what mattered. He shook his head and looked around. Jasss was being walked up behind them. She looked calm and patient, suppressing her agitation. He assumed she was familiar with restraints and the demeaning treatment that came along with them. "Where are Master Brawd and Lady Melodeen?" he asked Abdabriel, his voice shaking as he tried to muster courage.

"They're alive and safe," Abdabriel reassured. "They've been committed to the City of Light's Winkloh Star." He saw Timrekka's disheartened expression. "Oh, don't worry. I have no interest in hurting them. I've expressed that many times. Eventually, the truth of it will sink in." He patted Timrekka's shoulders as his soldier marched him forward. "I want to establish my vision in its entirety here on Whewliss before I free them and demonstrate what a peaceful future I'm creating. Until then, I expect they'll cling to their old ways and try to resist. Once they see how smoothly our plan runs, however, I believe they'll relinquish their fears."

"So, why are Jasss and me not in Winkloh Stars, as we have no interest in joining you, but you still have us in chains, so are you planning on executing us publicly or something?" Timrekka asked, immediately regretting it. What if voicing his thoughts inspired Abdabriel's actions.

"Because—" Abdabriel flashed his dazzling smile. "—you're more open-minded than they are. You're both younger, less than one-hundred-years-old, and that makes new ideas less terrifying to you. They are so stuck in the past that they can't accept the future. I don't necessarily blame them. It's a lot to handle. But you——*you*, Timrekka, are brilliant, and you're no fool. Of course you're going to question me, my motives, and my methods. I don't blame you. Really, I don't. That's why I want to show you the light before it's turned on. Because I know you won't respond out of fear but of understanding. Wouldn't you rather make an educated decision than a fear-driven denial of progress?"

Timrekka thought for a moment. "Where are all of the Whewlights?"

"Well—" Abdabriel looked around at the pristine cityscape. "—those who resisted when we arrived——well, you know what happened to them. I don't like to talk about it because I never wanted it to happen in the first place. But their bodies have been honored and removed with the utmost respect. I don't mean to demonstrate my authority with violence. I want a bright future, so they've been disposed of humanely." He smiled as he turned to a more positive topic. "And other than a handful I've deemed promising enough to continue their day-to-day jobs, everyone else is being housed in pristine facilities until the big unveiling. Thousands will be gathered in a few days after the city has been fully swept, and my army has successfully gained control of every city across the globe. At that time, I will present my plan to the planet, and they will see the light. I will be broadcast to billions of Whewlights all over this world, and together, we will unite." He gleamed with pride. "Then I will establish my downline, creating a strong hierarchy beneath me here before moving on to the next world. I will establish peace one planet at a time. Only then will weprovide technology, intelligence, and tools to help each world flourish." He looked at Timrekka, ready for his speech's finale. "Can you imagine how Thamiosh will react when we finally unite every territory? Can you imagine how peaceful and beautiful your home world will be when we provide them with Whewlight technology and bring them from a state of civil war to a one of prosperity, united, happy? No more war. No more violence. No more fighting for scraps. Every single Thamioshling will have more than they've ever dreamed of, none of them wishing for what their neighbor possesses. They'll be given the best education, teaching them Whewlight knowledge, bringing them out of the darkness and into the light. Can you see it, Timrekka? Can you see my vision?"

Timrekka was silent. He wanted to argue, to rebuke Abdabriel's madness. He wanted to deny that it made any sense, but the picture Abdabriel had just painted in his mind was a welcomed one. He could lie out loud, but he couldn't lie to himself. It sounded like a dream, one he'd had for as long as he could remember. The idea of feeling proud of his world seemed so farfetched that it was an impossibility, but what Abdabriel was proposing could make it real. Timrekka's ethics and morals warred in his head at the cost of a few million lives. He knew that it was too much to pay, but weren't the people of Thamiosh killing each other anyway?

As Timrekka lost himself in deliberation, Abdabriel smiled and turned to Jasss. "And, Jasss, while I know you currently agree with the rest of the recruits, abhorring me, unable to see my revelation, viewing me as a villain, I have to ask you—" He stared into her withdrawn eyes. "—does it not seem ludicrous to you that Ojīptian still practices slavery?" He allowed his intro to sink in. "Your home world is merely a century or two behind Whewliss in technological advancement and yet they still enslave each other—an archaic act that Whewliss abolished so long ago that it feels like a poorly written joke in our history." He scoffed and shook his head as he couldn't help laughing. "The fact that we, as a people, have known of your suffering, and yet done nothing due to ethical debates about interference with another planet's freedom to live however it wants, disgusts me. It's preposterous. It has been irresponsible of us to sit back and watch your people suffer unnecessarily. Surely *you* can see the benefit of my vision on Ojīptian." He saw her eyes flinch. She was listening. "Can you imagine worldwide peace there? Can you picture every single slave freed and given equality? In fact, more than that. We would eradicate the slavers. Any Ojīptian that fights for slavery would be executed. How is that a bad thing?" He saw no point in waiting for a response to the rhetorical question. "Justice would be brought to those who oppress you. Your people would be freed, empowered, and given Whewlight-level technology. Once again, no more fear, no more fighting, no more slavery, no more hunger, no more wanting. Ojīptian would thrive, and again, I offer it to you to protect and oversee. Not only would you be done running for the rest of your life, but you would be given power—enough power to ensure that your people never again experience anything other than the light."

While Jasss shared Timrekka's need to digest the vision painted in her head, she had one thing to say. "Your end goal is something I want more than anything," she admitted. "But how you plan on reaching it scares me. If it didn't come at the cost, I would join you in a heartbeat."

"Me, too," Timrekka quietly said as he walked forward, his eyes staring through the grass.

Abdabriel nodded. "I understand. There's something I want to show the both of you." After a few more steps, he stopped and looked around at the soldiers escorting the two recruits. He nodded graciously. "I can handle them from here. Remove their restraints." He watched a bird flying around while every cuff, bind, and manacle was undone. The soldiers obeyed his command without question, though they thought it unwise.

Timrekka and Jasss stared at Abdabriel, unsure of what their next move should be. Would it be wise to run? Jasss was fond of that option. Should they try and kill Abdabriel with their bare hands? Timrekka knew he could probably do it, but then they'd be executed immediately, or even worse, tortured.

Jasss rubbed her wrists, wasting no time expressing her thoughts. "What makes you think we won't run or kill you?"

Abdabriel puffed out his bottom lip and looked around. "Running would be pointless. Even if you made it out of the city, which you wouldn't, there's no place on Whewliss that you could hide where our drones wouldn't find you." He delivered the response with such calm confidence that she assumed he was right. "And as for killing me—" Abdabriel chuckled. "—Timrekka, I invite you to punch me as hard as you can."

Timrekka brought his head back, confused. "I don't want to." It was a lie. He did want to, but the safer course of action was to lie. "I want you to stop what you're doing, and I want you to stop killing people, but I don't want to hit you."

Abdabriel's eyes fluttered as he nodded with a smirk. "Let's not pretend to be what we aren't. I know I haven't convinced you of the light, and I know you want to hit me. Here on Whewliss, you're a force to be reckoned with, too. I bet you could remove a Whewlight's head with half your strength. Come on, give me one-hundred-percent." He arched his chin up to provide an easier target. "You won't be punished. My soldiers won't retaliate. I give you my word."

Timrekka shook his head. "I don't want to." The scientist had gone from upset to scared. He didn't trust Abdabriel, and there were more than enough soldiers around to put him in the ground. "I don't want to," he repeated, hoping Abdabriel would drop the issue. "I won't hit you, I promise, and I have no interest in trying to run away because I know that I would die in either scenario."

Abdabriel rolled his eyes and lifted his index finger at Timrekka. "Does this help?" It was aimed directly between Timrekka's goggle lenses. Timrekka's already magnified eyes grew wider. Jasss wasn't sure what to do. Should she help? She had a feeling that any sudden movement would get them both killed. Timrekka was shaking. Abdabriel nodded. "In order for us to establish any understanding, there has to be respect. You can't respect what you doubt, and right now the two of you doubt my ability to handle myself without bodyguards. That simply will not do if I want your undivided attention when I'm showing you the light." His friendly tone vanished. "Now hit me. I'll make it an easy choice by killing you if you don't." His eyes burned with demand. "Punching me in self-defense sounds justified, doesn't it? I think so. Now, kill me if you want to live."

Timrekka whimpered. He winced every time Abdabriel spoke. Each threat rendered him immobile. He brought his giant fist back and swung at Abdabriel's face as hard as he could.

An inch before his punch could make contact, his fist slipped and flung backward over his own shoulder as something unseen caught and threw it. He stumbled back a few steps and fell onto his butt, his hand ultimately slamming wrist deep into the soft, grassy ground. He yelped in surprised discomfort, immediately bringing his other hand to his shoulder. It felt like he'd strained the soft tissue, and his fist was throbbing. His strength had prevented him from feeling much pain ever since leaving Thamiosh, but he felt it now.

Abdabriel chuckled. "Well done, Timrekka. You *are* strong! That would have easily killed me." He laughed while reveling in Timrekka's power. His soldiers joined him in amused jeering. After enjoying the moment long enough for Timrekka's cheeks to flush with embarrassment and anger, two soldiers walked over and helped him to his feet. He timidly brushed himself off and looked at Abdabriel, whose smile shone brightly. As upset as he was, Timrekka wanted to understand what just happened.

"What was that?" he asked under his breath.

"State-of-the-art reflection suit," Abdabriel said proudly. "It's a precautionary measure that took years to perfect. If I recall correctly, Lord Coyzle showed you his, right?" Timrekka didn't give much of a response as he irritably listened. Abdabriel smiled. "His was the only one, but I made one in secret. I'm not the scientist you are, so bear with my crass explanation." He ran his hands over the arms of his suit, admiring its function. "Through some process that I don't understand, it basically recognizes any hostile action or projectile, including fluids and gases, and deflects them with equal force or something like that. So, the harder you hit, the more powerfully you'll be thrown back, as you're now aware." He chuckled. "I don't remember exactly how much it can take, but it's a lot. Like *a lot* a lot." He beamed at Timrekka and Jasss. "We invented it a long time ago to protect Lord Coyzle from what happened to his father. Theoretically, it should deflect any coins shooting down from the sky. Shadowmaker himself couldn't get to me. However—" Abdabriel looked up at the clear, blue sky. "—now that Lord Coyzle's gone to the Wall, his won't function there. It only works on Whewliss, something I plan on extending to every world I bring peace to." He flashed his beautiful smile. "I will be invulnerable wherever I go."

Timrekka lowered his eyes, losing hope in any solution. He wanted to know if Gideon, Traveler, and Dumakleiza had survived their jump.

He wanted to believe that they had and that they would find a way to help, but he was losing confidence. They were worlds away on a planet that, for all he knew, killed them the moment they arrived. He glanced up at Abdabriel.

"What do you want to show us?"

"Aw, don't despair," Abdabriel said, recognizing the despondence in Timrekka's voice. "In time you will look back and laugh at how hesitant you were to join a future that will ultimately make you happier than you've ever been. I guarantee it." He smiled and patted Timrekka on the shoulder. "The suit allows for kind interactions, just not violence. If that's not the future, I don't know what is. Now," he rubbed his hands together, "for what I want to show you."

They approached one of the massive skydrops. Abdabriel led them right up to its magnetic base. The large, black platform was a solid metal circle. At first, it appeared perfectly flat, but as they stepped up onto it, they noticed it dipped down in the center like a shallow bowl in order to ensure that the sphere stayed centered over it.

Timrekka and Jasss looked up, overwhelmed and worried as they found themselves in the shadow of the floating building. The looming sphere was surreal in its architecture and greatly more intimidating up close. Standing beneath it made them dizzy as they watched it turn. They felt like it was going to fall and crush them at any second. There was a vibrating hum from the magnetic field surrounding them.

Abdabriel walked them toward the center, where two small circles were built side by side into the base of the platform. One of the circles was lit, while the second was an artistically painted pad without any light. It wasn't hard to decipher what they were for. Abdabriel politely stood next to the lit circle and motioned for them to individually step onto it. It was off-putting for him to courteously insist they go first. The mixed signal of kindness juxtaposed with his agenda kept them unsure what his next move would be. They couldn't help worrying that he may be tricking them into launching themselves into space or something.

"After you." Abdabriel graciously motioned for them to step onto the bright circle.

After quick deliberation, Jasss went first. She stepped onto the light pad and vanished. Abdabriel smiled and then nodded to Timrekka, insisting that he follow. Timrekka gulped down his anxiety and stepped onto the pad.

Bright light illuminated Timrekka's sight before his vision was restored. He looked around to find himself standing by Jasss on an elaborate balcony. With quick glances, he realized it wasn't a balcony but a railed bridge arching over something within the skydrop. He looked around, staring in awe. The spherical windowed wall of the skydrop presented a magnificent view of the City of Light. From their vantage point, they could almost see over the other skydrops spanning out for many miles, and the view of the ground beneath them was incredible. They could see Army of Light soldiers wandering below like ants in the distance, and they couldn't help feeling the superiority that came along with the view.

"Welcome to one of our experimental farms," Abdabriel said as he stepped up to the railing next to them. There were no soldiers accompanying them. They were alone together, and Abdabriel thrived on the fact that he remained untouchable.

Timrekka livened up at the comment and then looked down. Sure enough, the skydrop's four floors beneath them had different kinds of crops. A hollow core provided a full view of each floor lining the perimeter all the way to the bottom. There was a recognizable strain of corn growing on the top floor, purple pears on the third, Timrekka guessed Whewlight versions of carrots on the second, and then a floor of wheat at the bottom. What was especially odd about the crops was how aesthetically even and beautiful they all were. There was no variation with unique quality or shape from one vegetable to the next. They looked copied and pasted. Every single product on all four floors looked perfect, exact according to optimal specification.

"They're perfect," Timrekka gasped, unable to hide how rapt he was.

"Yes, they *really* are," Abdabriel confirmed as Jasss stood by without speaking. "They are more perfect than any crops on any farms on any world. Even unpopulated worlds that haven't been ruined by mankind fall short because nature allows flaws." He smiled down at the floating farm. "Here on Whewliss, we have mutated, crossbred, genetically engineered, and spliced plant DNA into our crops until they reached perfection." There was no perversion or diabolical tone in his explanation. He simply sounded proud of his people's accomplishment, and it was oddly contagious. "By digitally programming and monitoring the seedlings, we manipulate and control each plant's growth. I don't understand it all, but I know that we get warnings of sickly plants, we can modify the speed of growth to ensure they all mature at the same rates, and many other things." As he spoke, he saw Timrekka's eyes buzzing. The Thamioshling was enthralled. It made Abdabriel smile. "Here, inside the skydrops, we create the perfect atmosphere for each kind of produce. It protects them from outdoor elements, such as cold, heat, insects, wild animals, etcetera. We've reached a point where we can keep harvesting year-round, and each skydrop farm can produce enough food to feed more than one-hundred-families every single month. Their efficiency is unprecedented."

Timrekka was amazed by the feat, his eyes tracing every detail of the crops. Jasss, on the other hand, turned her gaze to Abdabriel.

"You show us this as a metaphor. An example of what our worlds could be—how our people could thrive."

"Yes," Abdabriel stated plainly.

"You think you can create a glass wall to protect us. You want to contain us, keep us from danger, provide the perfect environment for us to thrive inside of, so we can flourish into our definitive potential."

"Yes. With all my heart," Abdabriel warmly said.

"And what of any sickly strains or branches that don't produce?"

Abdabriel looked down at the crops. "A sickly strain is a virus that will infect others. Unproductive branches bear no fruit or vegetables. To inhibit the progress of others is to selfishly diminish future with overcrowding and parasites."

Jasss scoffed and shook her head. "I think you're missing a large part of—"

"I believe I can predict your argument," Abdabriel calmly interrupted. "Life is about experiencing mistakes. Through tribulations and trials, we familiarize ourselves with triumph and find life's deepest lessons carved in our souls. By waging wars, man can appreciate the liberation of peace and harmony. Only through loss and starvation can we understand plenteousness. And of course, death is how we appreciate life." He nodded. "They are lessons truer than the blood running through our veins, but they are lessons as old as time itself. That being said, why must we continue relearning the same lessons over and over and over? Why must we repeatedly familiarize ourselves with the same morals? Why do we repeat the mistakes our forefathers made, or that we made ourselves?" He postured himself. "Jasss. Mankind was given the gift of free will and intelligence. Using those tools, we can *choose* to abolish whatever we want. Your people think it asinine to eradicate slavery, just as you lack the vision to see what other possibilities exist in a future where we relieve ourselves of trivial fear. We Whewlights, eradicated sickness with light. We created perfect food supplies with technology. Abolishing slavery was rudimentary in comparison. How is it so impossible to foresee a future where we've abolished war?" His eyes burned with passion that he could barely contain.

Silence befell the skydrop. Abdabriel's words echoed to stillness, and there was no response from Timrekka or Jasss. They stood in silence as the palpable tension in the air refused to dissipate.

Timrekka brought his eyes up and glanced at Abdabriel. "I don't want to return to Thamiosh ever again, at least not the way that it was, and I don't want to oversee it if—whenyou're finished with it, and I don't know if I'll ever see my friends again, and that scares me; everything scares me. I don't agree with your methods, but I doagree with your end goal." He choked back tears as he felt Jasss's glare slowly turn toward him. "If you give me a reflection suit like yours, so I don't have to be afraid of everything, give me a lab where I can work and leave me alone with your instructions, as long as what I invent isn't used to cause harm, I will stop resisting."

27

After what felt like hours of walking inland, the group found themselves hiking through a canyon, sheer walls on both sides, too high to see the top of. To Gideon, it felt like they'd gone from Louisiana marshes to a dark hike through the Rocky Mountains. The terrain smelled of pine, pungent minerals, and electricity as lightning randomly cracked above. It provided brief glimpses of the top of the canyon, illuminating tall mountains like evil beings looking down the drop, watching, mocking, betting on their survival. Their feet were starting to ache after the gauntlet of obstacles and holes in the dark.

The stench of open flesh permeated the air. The dismembered reptile limbs they carried held no appeal, though their stomachs were empty. They hoped cooking them would improve the smell and make it palatable. Cooby and Vorlak were drooling as they'd already snuck bites of the carcass.

Traveler's light was the only visibility they had aside from the random flashes. Horror Planet was bringing the "horror" of its title to life as they clung to the circle of light aimed in front of them. Whenever their conversation would die down, they heard strange sounds in the blackness. Sometimes it sounded like footsteps, though they rarely caught glimpses of the source. Other times the noises sounded like animals squawking, roaring, or hissing. Dumakleiza swore she heard whispering, but she couldn't see anything.

"There's water," Traveler said. His light exposed a stream ahead. It was strange seeing familiarities encircled in light amid the eerie darkness.

Everywhere felt like something was breathing on the backs of their necks until Traveler illuminated something that felt like home.

"Oh, thank god," Gideon jogged ahead until he reached the cool water running along the canyon floor. He unslung his backpack and squatted down next to where the stream flowed into an underground canal. He scooped up messy mouthfuls and drank. As he continued slurping, the others joined him on either side, drinking their fills.

Lord Coyzle looked around, feeling vulnerable in the darkness. "Let's make a fire."

"That's what I was thinking," Traveler said.

"Near the only water source?" Vorlak asked while looking around.

"Of course," Lord Coyzle answered, irritated by the Daemoanik questioning him.

"Others will come," Vorlak said with an expectant grin.

"Others who? What others?"

Vorlak shrugged and then drank from the stream. His comment rotted in Lord Coyzle's mind. The esteemed Whewlight suddenly found himself aware of every sound in the distance.

Gideon groaned as excess water dribbled down his chin. "So much better than swamp soup." He gasped a grateful breath. "Okay, let's collect firewood. Did anyone bring marshmallows?"

After collecting branches, long grass, and twigs, they gathered around the pile of assorted kindling. It was a few paces from the babbling stream, so they could get a drink if need be. The pile was large, fifteen feet across and three feet high. If they were going to make themselves noticeable, it was going to be a declarative statement to anything or anyone in eyeshot.

Traveler aimed a finger at the base of the pile, where they'd stuffed most of the smaller grass and sticks. He squinted and focused his light, shrinking it down to a concentrated laser. Aside from the blinding dot, everything around them became darker. Their flashlight was temporarily gone, and they were immersed in silence. They could smell smoke in the blackness. A light glow appeared as the laser rendered an infant flame.

Traveler maintained his aim until the fire grew, consuming some grass and a few branches. Comforting aromas of burning wood and leaves filled their nostrils. Soon it was large enough to shine a warm, yellow glow on the group. Crackling sounds brought smiles to their faces. The fire had taken, and Traveler was finally able to relax.

"That'll do nicely, Spaceman," Gideon said as he plopped his butt on the ground in front of the fire. "That. Feels. Amazing." Just taking weight off his feet had him ready for a nap. He stared into the flames, appreciating the old friend that looked familiar on any world.

Savory smells began perforating the air as the reptile meat cooked on top of stones in the fire. They'd put the culinary rocks around the edges so their primitive barbeque would be easily accessed when ready. Gideon began to respond to the aromas. His appetite was suddenly at the forefront of his mind, and the horrors of the dark world were replaced by an anxious belly.

"Do you think Shadowmaker can see us?" Izzy asked, uneasy about the fire in the dark. His comment made Vorlak tense.

"If he's here, yes," Lord Coyzle said. "He is absolutely aware of our presence."

Izzy nodded as he stared out into the night. "Do you think he can hear what we're saying? Like, can he hear me asking you this right now?"

Lord Coyzle joined him in searching their surroundings. "I'm not sure." The question made him uncomfortable enough to whisper just in case.

"'Sup, Shadowmaker?" Gideon yelled out. His voice echoed through the canyon, making everyone jump.

Traveler slowly closed his eyes and then opened them. "I'm not even going to get you a muzzle. I'm just going to get you put down."

Vorlak's eyes were peeled open, staring in disgusted disbelief at Gideon. "What planet are you from?"

"Earth," Gideon said with a smile, still waiting for any response from the darkness. "You should visit sometime."

"No." Vorlak shook his head and then stared into the fire, its bright glow exposing the ghostly veins sprawled through his wide eyes. He didn't want to look at Gideon, just in case the Earthling was contagious.

Horror Planet wasn't cold, but the heat was still comforting. The circle of unlikely friends stared at the hypnotic flames, all afraid to relax the way Gideon had. They thought it wiser to stay on high alert in case anything surprised them. Gideon, on the other hand, looked cozy and peaceful. His eyes were closed, and there was a content look on his face. He was perfectly happy right where he was. Horror Planet didn't seem to bother him, and it maddened Vorlak how nervous that made him.

"What happened to our suits?" Izzy asked, looking at his. The others glanced at theirs. Their suits had lost their colors and patterns, now a dull white. It looked like they were wearing battered onesies with water stains and wear from their swampland exodus.

"There's no light on H.P.," Lord Coyzle said, still recovering from Gideon's outburst. "They will react a little to the fire, but without a sun, they lose their functionality. Just another reason I don't like this world."

"Huh." Gideon smiled. "Solar powered. You Whewlights and your lights."

Dumakleiza walked over behind Gideon and started playing with his hair, her fierce eyes fixed on the flames. She didn't care about her suit. Gideon smiled as her strong fingers massaged his scalp.

"I do not fear this Maker of Shadows, and if he hears me saying that and kills me, I will find honor in my death," Duma said. "I will not censor my tongue out of fear. It matters not how dangerous he is." Her features were amplified in the warm light. "Grimleck hears *everything*, even the Maker of Shadows, and he is the only one whose judgment I concern myself with."

"Actually, I have a question about that, Duma," Traveler said as he stretched his tired legs by the flames. "Grimleck, like deities from many similar religions, sees everything, correct?" Dumakleiza nodded, preparing herself for a confrontational debate. Traveler took a deep breath. "Why then is it necessary to pray and ask him for help? Doesn't he see the danger you're in without you having to get his attention?"

Crackling wood filled the silence as Dumakleiza thought about his question. She didn't stop rubbing Gideon's head. In fact, her hands relaxed a little, as if the question freed some tension. She turned to Traveler.

"Surrender is my answer," she said as the fire danced in her eyes. "Of course he is aware of any troubles we stumble into. However, it is in our nature to save ourselves. We wish not to admit struggle or defeat. Rather, our minds seek the ability to prove that we need no god."

Gideon slowly nodded, trying keep Dumakleiza's fingers going. "Yeah, I've always seen God, Jesus, Grim-like figures as being like a father. It's easiest for me to understand spirituality with family metaphors." He smiled and giggled as one of Dumakleiza's soft strokes caught his ear. "I imagine God watching us like a protective but coaching dad. He sees us struggling but allows us to try and figure it out on our own. Sometimes we can, but he's happy to just watch over us and enjoy our growing process. Other times we struggle and can't overcome obstacles on our own. He waits until we ask for help. It not only allows him to step in without upsetting us, but it shows our spiritual maturity when we *surrender* to him."

"Yes," Dumakleiza said, looking down at Gideon's relaxed face. "Prayer is not intended to acquire the attention of a distant deity. It is telling my father, who is always near and always watching, that I surrender to his wisdom and guidance, that I need him, that I trust him, and that I believe he will handle my life better than I."

Traveler slowly nodded as he thought about it. "I can internalize that without a stomach ache." He smiled. "*What if—*"

"Uh oh," Gideon said with obvious excitement.

Traveler chuckled. "What if there is only one god, and before I continue, I'm not aiming for a religious debate, but what if there's only one and he put us all on different worlds as an experiment?"

Gideon puffed out his bottom lip. "I would say that's probably not too farfetched. Kind of like when I was a kid, I used to fill different mason jars with dirt and then put a bunch of ants in each just to see how they'd act. In some I'd put sticks and leaves, and in others I'd put nothing. One time I even flipped the container upside down." He chuckled. "I wondered if they'd die underneath the heavy sand, or if they'd find a way to survive. I was actually quite impressed when most of them tunneled to the surface and then started digging new homes."

"You would make a monster of a god," Dumakleiza jokingly said as she grabbed a fistful of his hair and pulled.

"Ow!" Gideon winced. "I would be nice to *you*." He winked at her. "But yeah, it was interesting to see how differently they'd act in separate ant farms."

"But, like—" Traveler's energy was returning to normal. "—what if we were never meant to discover light travel? What if our interacting, or Abdabriel attempting to unite every world, ultimately leads to our extinction?"

"How would that lead to our extinction?" Lord Coyzle asked.

"I don't know." Traveler smirked. "It's a what-ifconversation. Maybe we eventually discover a disease that's transmitted between worlds simply by our alien interactions. Maybe the war that Abdabriel claims is inevitable actually happens, and we all destroy each other. Maybe whatever deities exist rain fire down from the heavens and obliterate every habitable world when they decide we are destructive beings. Just some thoughts." He glanced at the group. "Look around. We have the strangest group of people I can imagine. It just makes me curious about certain aspects of life."

"Right now I'm questioning many things," Lord Coyzle said as he allowed himself to get lost in the flames.

"Hey," Gideon said with some energy, "did you guys hear the one where an Earthling, a Culite, a Juraelean, two Whewlights, and a Daemoanik walk into a bar?"

"What?" Lord Coyzle asked, completely lost.

"They decided to break up because they needed some *space*." Gideon gave a cheesy smile, knowing they probably wouldn't get it. Vorlak was the only to roar and heehaw at the joke. He leapt to his feet, and without any modesty, continued laughing while peeing into the dirt.

Traveler averted his eyes as he scoffed a chuckle toward Gideon. "You're the worst."

"I do not understand," Dumakleiza said. Cooby climbed off her and purred closer to the warmth. "What broke up with whom?"

"Nothing," Gideon sniggered. "This just *is* an eclectic group, and I love it. I'm glad we've visited different anthills and dragged each other through the paint of our home worlds." He looked at Traveler. "I don't think our interactions will lead to our demise. I truly believe that, as you say, our interacting is meant to parachute our minds and help us become more understanding, enlightened beings."

"I admit I'm uncomfortable leaving Whewliss," Lord Coyzle said. "I've been a politician for so long that expressing my dream for leaving has become more of a rehearsed relatability than a real desire. Actually being on another world is a helpless feeling. I'm accustomed to being in absolute control of everything."

Gideon nodded and smiled at him. "I can imagine that going from the most highly regarded world leader to camping on H.P. is a radical change."

"It really is." Lord Coyzle grinned as he thought about it. "I've spent a lifetime developing the City of Light, protecting Whewliss. I've had light technology at my fingertips, *in* my fingertips, and been protected by armed guards ever since the ULW. I've never felt so — "

"Scared?" Traveler guessed.

"Free, actually," Lord Coyzle said. "I mean, yes, I'm quite scared. But I, I don't know. Everything around us right now is real. There are no electronics, no technology, no screens or projections. Our suits have stopped functioning. There isn't even any paved ground. Everything is just, uh, wild and raw." He smiled. "I think I might be enjoying myself."

"Oh, no." Gideon winked. "We can't have that."

"I know it's not a vacation, but there's a part of me secretly experiencing it as such."

"You know what I think the scariest reality is here?" Izzy asked. "We don't have light, so we have to heal at a normal rate. We have to use actual medicine and remedies. No instant healing with light jumps."

Lord Coyzle blinked a few times as he considered the handicap. "Oh, I don't like that."

"Yes," Izzy continued. "Injuries on H.P. are going to be actual injuries. They'll require time and result in scars."

Gideon laughed, "How long has it been since any of you had scars?"

"Not since I was a child," Traveler said. "And even then, we had scar minimizing surgeries before the Daemoaniks introduced us to light travel." He glanced briefly at Vorlak, who was preoccupied with holding his hand in some flames.

Dumakleiza looked herself up and down. "I still struggle to accept that I've lost mine. My body is missing the memories that told my tales."

Gideon swooned as he looked at her. "Your scars were beautiful. And now you are a blank canvas, ready for a new story."

They smiled at each other.

Lord Coyzle tried to conceal a cringe. "I wish I wasn't so scared when it comes to pain. I'm just unfamiliar with experiencing it. I can't recall any of mine. They never last long enough to remember."

Gideon turned to him. "As someone who specializes in scars, I would recommend looking at any you get as failure trophies."

"What do you mean?" Lord Coyzle was hesitant to be anything like Gideon.

"I mean that scars only come from moments that have technically gone wrong. Mistakes, if you will." Gideon smiled bigger. "They're failure trophies."

Vorlak leaned forward, his deformed face casting harsh shadows in the fire's light. "Would you speak of scars with such devotion if I didn't split your shoulder open?"

Gideon grinned back before looking at his shoulder. It had stopped bleeding, but the jagged slice was still fresh and clotting. He took a deep breath and then turned to Vorlak while the others listened.

"Every mistake we make walks hand in hand with a lesson to be learned." He leaned forward, so his shoulder was the visual focus. "It's in these lessons that we find experience. Now, experience will come to us whether we want it or not, but it's entirely up to us to form wisdom from it."

Traveler stood up and grabbed a girthy stick. He walked around the fire, using it to rotate the gator meat, doing his best to keep everything cooking evenly. He enjoyed the silence, marinating in the mesmerizing flames. He thought over Gideon's words and absorbed the delectable smells. After he made it all the way around, he sat back down in the dirt and groaned. He was surprised with how much he was enjoying the comradery around the bonfire.

"That's beautiful. I can't tell if that is something from your heart or your bag."

Gideon smiled. "As much as I'd like to take credit for that one — " He sat forward, pulling his backpack in front of himself. He pilfered through the random items within. "It was ironically in a situation pretty close to this one. You see — " He grinned as his hands fished through the clunky pack. "I was passing through Detroit, and through a series of events, found myself at a meeting between a Grand Dragon, the leader of a white supremacy group we have called the KKK, and a leader of a group who could be considered quite the opposite, called the Black Panthers." Gideon withdrew two white bandanas tied together at their ends. They were dirty and worn. He held them up, showing the pictures on each. "On this one, you see a black panther, and on this one, a white cross encircled in red. I heard that quote when — "

"Question," Traveler interrupted. "While I'm sure this story is good, I just realized that I haven't seen you take any keepsakes from the many people we've met together. Have you, or is that something you only did on Earth?"

Gideon smirked at the question, returning the bandanas to his backpack. "Oh, Spaceman." He removed another buried item. "Does this look familiar?" In his hand was a dirty rock covered in dried blood.

Traveler smiled. "Is that — I thought you left that there?"

"What's the significance of the rock?" Izzy wondered out loud.

Traveler glanced at him and then looked at Gideon with an approving nod. "It's one of the first impressions I ever got of our Earthling. He insisted on introducing himself to some Neanderthals *in the nude.*" Gideon chuckled as Traveler continued. "A female almost raped him, and the jealous male tried to bash his skull in with *that.*" Traveler pointed at the rock.

"Really?" Izzy smiled. "What happened then?"

"Well," Traveler continued, "Gideon was Gideon and became best friends with them." Traveler got a sassy look in his eyes. "I bet even the male would have mated with him." Gideon burst out laughing. Traveler's chuckling slowed down a little. "What kind of situation would you use that one in? Or what kind of little moment would you use it for?"

"Well." Gideon tilted his head side to side as he thought. "I'd use it to explain that you don't need to be able to communicate with words to sort out differences and create friendship." He shoved his hand back into his backpack and pulled out a leather-bound handle with what looked like a broken blade. "This is one of the items that the monkeys offered us on the Isle of Beasts on Cul." Without waiting for comments, Gideon reached into his backpack and pulled out two pencils bound by a rubber band. "These are the pencils Timrekka had me look at with the chameleon contacts."

Traveler nodded with approval. "Across every world I've been to, most people are locked doors. But you've continually proven to be a human boner key."

Everyone turned and looked at Traveler with perplexed expressions and stifled laughter. They weren't sure if it was an inside joke between him and Gideon, but it sounded like a mistake.

Gideon blinked with a blank expression as he tried to make sense of it. "What?"

Traveler's eyebrows lowered. "I didn't mess thatone up, did I?" He looked around at the awkward expressions. "You know, a key that can open any door."

Gideon laughed so hard that he fell in the dirt. "A *skeleton* key!" Tears welled in his eyes. "Boner key! Holy spirit."

Traveler chuckled a frustrated belly laugh and rolled his eyes. "Anyways." He waited for the noise to die down. "What I meant was, ugh, I swear I'm done using Earthling quotes."

"No!" Gideon yelled out. "Never give up. It's not your style." He smiled. "Okay, sorry, go on." He rubbed the smile out of his cheeks.

"I've just never seen someone able to so easily connect with anyone from anywhere. It's incredible. It's as mysterious to me as the fourth phase."

"Ah, we haven't talked about thatfor a while," Gideon said as the scent of cooking meat smelled ready. Steam filled the dark air. He stood up and walked over to the fire's edge, grabbing a stick and poking the closest member of gator. A piece slid off, exposing tender, red flesh. The rest of the limb had raw spots that needed further cooking, but they could at least begin gnawing on what was ready. Gideon glanced at Vorlak, who was visibly drooling with anticipation. "Yo, Vorlak, I'm assuming your marble skin probably isn't as sensitive as my soft, plump chicken fingers."

He winked and summoned his southern accent. "Wanna help me serve everyone up some gator?"

"Yes," Vorlak answered out of hunger for his own portion. He leapt to his feet and sped over to Gideon. Without waiting for instruction or consideration, he plunged his arm through the flames and grabbed the gator leg. His sharpened fingers tore through the cooked flesh, filling his grasp with a handful of meat. He didn't wince at the intense heat. Food was all that mattered. He pulled until the chunk ripped free and tossed it to Dumakleiza first. She caught it and dropped it to the dirt. It was too hot to handle. Vorlak continued ripping off cooked bits of reptile and tossing them to everyone around the fire. With his other hand, he grabbed a fistful of raw gator and stuffed it into his mouth, loud smacking and chomping spilling down his chin.

Gideon tentatively pulled a piece of steaming meat from the handful he'd been thrown and blew on it. "Anyway, speaking of mysterious, there's still a secret you haven't told me."

"What's that?" Traveler asked.

"The very first time we met on top of Auyantepui Mountain, there was a question I asked you that you *still* haven't answered." After another stumped look from Traveler, Gideon smiled. "What's your name?" His question made Dumakleiza and Izzy nod with shared curiosity.

Traveler smiled and took a bite of his food, chewing slowly as he tried to appreciate the gamy flavor. "I'll make a deal with you, Gideon Green." He masticated with some peculiar expressions and then swallowed. "If you tell us the story of your shoulder, I'll tell you my name."

The air grew tense as everyone stopped eating. It was a question they all wanted to know but never knew if there was an okay time to ask. It seemed forbidden. Traveler was the only one to continue eating, unafraid of digging too deep. He shrugged and took another bite as Gideon struggled to respond.

"It was—" Gideon flexed his jaw and lowered his eyes as darkness weighed on him. He slowly shook his head. "I'm sorry. It's something I've never told anyone, and I—I just don't want to."

"Really?" Traveler asked, a little aggravated. "We're going to die here, whether it's now or later—probably soon. You have the strangest group of people I've ever heard of, and we're chatting around a fire. Knowing you as well as I do, I'd say this is literally theperfect time."

Lord Coyzle didn't allow Gideon's shift in emotion to affect him. "I know Four Zero's real name."

Gideon's eyes peered into Traveler's, pleading with him. "What's the plan when we find Shadowmaker? What if I can't boner key him?"

Traveler glared up at the thunder clouds and then back down. "One day, Gideon. One day we're going to find the *skeleton* key to unlock you. That will mean more to me than exploring the fourth phase." He took another bite and chewed in silence. Gideon's question was an important one, one that affected all their fates, their lives, their chances at success against an extragalactic tyrant, and yet they were still focused on his shoulder. It would have to wait. Traveler scoffed. "If youdie before telling me, I'm bringing you back to life just to kill you again." He shook his head and groaned as he refocused. "If we can't convince Shadowmaker to join us, the best chance we have is offering him whatever he wants— as long as it's nothing worse than what Abdabriel has planned."

"I have an offering," Dumakleiza said, seeing an opportunity to con-tribute. They looked at her as she untied her belt. "I will offer the Maker of Shadows my family's holy treasure."

"Really?" Gideon asked. "I know what that would mean to you, Duma."

"Yes," Dumakleiza said with confidence as she looked at her sack of gold and assorted jewels. "It can be used only for holy purpose. I can think of no purpose more righteous than saving innocents from the pretty god."

Traveler was starting to adore Dumakleiza's naïve purity. He assumed Shadowmaker would have no need for her offering, but he loved her gen-uine heart.

"That is quite noble," Lord Coyzle said, understanding that it was more of an emotional sacrifice than physical. "And it might work. I'm not sure what price the Daemoaniks offered him to kill my father. I as-sume it was a substantial amount of Daemoanik currency." He did nothing to hide his glare as he turned to Vorlak. "How much was it?"

Vorlak shrugged, nose deep in meat. "Don't know" was all he managed to say before returning to the mangled bite.

Lord Coyzle turned to Dumakleiza. "You already have my gratitude for your risks and sacrifices, but if your payment sways the mind of Shadowmaker, resulting in his aid—I don't know. I will be indebted to you for all time. All of humanity would be. Even if we fail, you are saintly in your martyrdom. The light has—" He choked on his own words and shook his head. "For the first time in my life, I don't want to give light any credit for guiding or protecting us." He turned to Gideon. "What's that thing you say?"

"May death not find you sleeping?"

Lord Coyzle slowly nodded as he digested the words more than the meat. "That is a mantra that I'm beginning to understand." He earnestly looked into Gideon's eyes. "I humbly ask your permission to adopt it."

"Oh, I would be honored," Gideon said with a smile. "You've demonstrated more courage and integrity than any politician I've ever known."

"Thank you, Gideon." Lord Coyzle relaxed and looked into the fire. "I need that wisdom right now."

"Hey," Izzy said, "not to interrupt, but I was just thinking about what kind of trees and plant life could exist on H.P., and I realized something. There shouldn't be any. At least not like this." He waited as everyone looked at him, unsure of what he meant. "There's no light breaking through the clouds. There's no photosynthesis."

"Hmm." Gideon looked around in the darkness. "That's kind of neat. I hadn't thought about that."

"Dumakleiza," Izzy said, "between your dragon eye and the optical implant in it, you should be able to see more than all of us. How would you describe the trees?"

"Oh." Dumakleiza brought her head back. "It slipped my mind that I am capable of using science to make my eyes like night creatures." She looked upward and winked her right eye until her already amplified vision was heightened as much as it could be. H.P. was brightened to the level of a full moon's light through her dragon eye. She smiled as she stared through illuminated vision at the thick clouds above them, flowing and bursting with electric currents. "The sky here reflects my soul. It is truly untamed." She brought her eyes down to look at the trees. "The trees appear as —" She froze. Her throat tightened and her muscles instinctively flexed. Her expression alone made the chewing stop.

"What is it?" Lord Coyzle asked in a lowered voice.

Dumakleiza didn't respond. She stared into the distance, where only she could see pale figures staring at them from behind trees and boulders. Her heart raced. The forms were difficult to see, but they appeared human, or at least she guessed they were. Ghostly white skin made up the naked, crouching bodies. The creatures hunched, moving around on all fours, staring at them in silence. Gangly, malnourished limbs resembled human arms and legs with knobby joints. Long black hair was unkempt and wild, pouring out of their heads like branches. There were too many of them to count as they swarmed a safe distance from the light. Dumakleiza couldn't be sure from far away, but their eyes looked large and reflected fire's light like nocturnal animals. It looked like they were communicating, murmuring, whispering to each other, and motioning with crude sign language as they studied the group of strangers around the fire.

Dumakleiza turned and looked in the other direction as she withdrew two of the reptilian fangs. With the possible threat, she simmered and calmed, switching to a mindset of readiness. More of the lurking beings amassed, large eyes shining with the interest of wild scavengers. Their ears looked larger than normal, and their faces had a strange combination of hunger and curiosity.

"What do you see?" Lord Coyzle asked more urgently.

"We're surrounded." Dumakleiza's answer shot everyone to their feet. The tension in the air made Cooby bark into the darkness. He hadn't picked up on the creatures' scents. He'd been too distracted with his meal, but the intruders suddenly had his full attention. His food hit the ground as he scurried up Dumakleiza's back and held on, screeching out at what he couldn't see.

"What are we surrounded by?" Gideon asked. "More of those monsters?"

Dumakleiza shook her head. "People." The unexpected answer made the group pause. Their eyes strained more earnestly in the darkness, curious what the people of Horror Planet might look like.

Gideon squinted, trying to understand. "Do they have weapons? Do they look like they want to hurt us?"

"I cannot tell," Dumakleiza answered. "Nor can I determine how many there are, but they surround us on every side."

Vorlak grinned with sinister excitement.

28

After exiting the farm, Abdabriel brought Timrekka and Jasss a ways through the City of Light. A meager handful of soldiers accompanied them, while most had been dismissed for other tasks. Finally, they stopped at the metal base of a new skydrop. From beneath it, neither Timrekka nor Jasss had any idea what function it had or what was contained inside. Abdabriel looked from the looming sphere down to Timrekka.

"I will have a suit brought to you by the end of the day at the soonest." He motioned to his own. "This is the only one in existence aside from Lord Coyzle's, so please be patient while I have another made for you."

Timrekka slowly nodded with heaviness behind his eyes. "Thank you, Master N'k—um, Abdabriel."

"Call me Holy One." Abdabriel smirked. "Actually, that is for my soldiers. I prefer our informality. Abdabriel will be a name I reserve for those I favor above the masses. Such as yourself." He looked upward. "This is where I will leave you for the time being. I would enjoy learning more about you and hearing your thoughts, but now that you've seen a glimmer of the light, I want you to submerge yourself in it and see just how incredible life is going to be. Marinate in the possibilities if you will." He patted Timrekka's firm shoulder. "This skydrop is one of our leading labs." He noticed Timrekka trying to conceal some excitement. It made him smile. "There are two Whewlight scientists I've allowed to continue their work in there. Unfortunately, the rest had to be removed upon my arrival, but the two who cooperated with the transition have been informed of you and the authority I've endowed you with. Feel free to make yourself at home and learn all you want about our world and our technology." He winked at him. "And of course, get your hands dirty and experiment away. The two resident scientists will help however you'd like."

Timrekka took a deep breath and nodded. "Okay."

"It should be fun," Abdabriel said with childlike eagerness. "Of course, should there be any problems with them or if you need any supplies, tell one of my soldiers and they will take care of it. You can also have them bring you food or whatever. I don't know what all a man like you requires." He chuckled. "You understand what I'm saying. Now, get in there. I want to take a walk with Jasss."

Timrekka shot an apprehensive glance at Jasss, whose calloused glare didn't budge. He'd expected her to express the same fear of being alone with Abdabriel that he would have if their positions were switched. Jasss just breathed, calculating, plotting. On one hand, Timrekka didn't want to leave her, but at the same time, he knew that his presence wouldn't prevent any hostility Abdabriel had planned. Abdabriel was following through with his promises so far. Timrekka thought of Dumakleiza, knowing that she would be praying. He missed her strength. He made a silent prayer of his own, hoping that his friends were alive, though he was losing faith in the possibility. Finally, after a constricted exhale, he nodded and walked over to the light pad. With one last glance at his fellow recruit, he stepped onto it and vanished.

Abdabriel watched until Timrekka disappeared. "His hair is going to turn even whiter when he sees all the toys in there." He turned to Jasss. "It's going to be fun to see what he comes up with. I can only imagine." Abdabriel glowed with pride.

Jasss wasn't in the mood for a conversation filled with lavish words and fancy promises.

"I hope you're not planning on wasting your time trying to convince me to join your cause with more 'guarantees of greatness and peace.'"

"What would convince you?" Abdabriel asked.

"Why do you care?" Jasss scoffed, raising her hands. "I'm not a politician. I'm certainly not a leader. I'm not a warrior of any kind. I'm not even a scientist. I have nothing to contribute to your *amazing* cause." She shrugged, almost laughing at the absurdity of him pursuing her. "I'm a runaway slave. I've spent my entire life spreading my legs so my bones wouldn't be broken. What do you want from me?"

A smile slowly appeared on Abdabriel's face. He looked to the soldiers standing beside Jasss and then nodded at one of them.

"How long ago did I recruit you?"

It took the soldier a moment to realize he was being addressed. "Um, three Whewliss years ago."

Abdabriel nodded. "And what have I said about fourth phase recruits ever since you very first met me?"

"That if there ever were any, they would be the bravest people in the universe, Holy One. That even you would pale in comparison to the courage they'd possess."

Abdabriel pointed a finger at him while looking at Jasss. "Exactly. *Exactly.* I have revered you before I even knew who any of you were. Your past doesn't matter. Your character has displayed more." He looked up as the right words eluded him. "Listen, on a world of sheep, every golden tiger is feared. It doesn't matter if it's been told that it's a sheep its entire life, eventually it will realize it's a golden tiger. You may not have come from a position of title or power, but how could you have? You were a slave. You were imprisoned. You were beaten. You were owned." He paused. "But then what happened? You escaped. You liberated as many of your own people as you could, keeping them safe in secret. You protected numerous other slaves from their captors—even killing a few slavers, if I heard correctly. You are a golden tiger. Once I free your world from itself, your people will look to you as theexample, thesymbol of freedom."

"Words," Jasss spat back, unimpressed. "My entire life I've heard promises of liberation. You're no different. Every elected leader, every politician, every king, every ruler of every kind. Gag me with a fist." She scoffed again. "They *all* promised things would be different under their reign. But every single hollow word would collapse in on itself once they rose to power. Slavery was never abolished. It would only grow stronger with illusions of padded shackles. Freedom was always on the horizon. It was dangled in front of us to keep us moving forward, working tirelessly every single day, thinking that tomorrow—tomorrow would be the day." She leaned in closer to Abdabriel's sparkling eyes. "But it was only ever words." She spat on the ground and glared at him. "You are no different than them. In fact, you're even more pathetic because you're making a campaign from worlds away. So, don't patronize me with words. I don't care about your promises of 'soon'or 'eventually.' You can shove your words sideways up your holyurethra."

The soldiers brought their heads back, bracing themselves for Abdabriel's wrath. Surely, there was no way he would tolerate such blatant and crude insolence. They knew he would executethem on the spot if they were ever stupid enough to speak to him like that.

Abdabriel studied Jasss's fiery eyes. He didn't smile. He didn't glare. He simply thought over her response. "You—you are bursting with passion." His stern expression contained a brewing idea. "I am not yet ready to visit Ojīptian. It's a ways down my list of worlds, and while I willbring peace there eventually, it will not be soon enough to convince you of my sincerity." He thought for a moment as Jasss returned an unmoved stare. "You fourth phase recruits are heroes in my eyes. I've imagined you for many years, dreaming of the legends you would one day become. Lord Coyzle, the council, all of EBOO held you all in such high regard without ever even meeting you." He took a deep breath and then nodded. "No more words. No more promises. You require something tangible. You require action. You require respect forged in blood." He smiled. "This goes against my plan, but I'm willing to amend my methodology if it will earn your cooperation." He postured himself taller and then looked to the soldiers, who were completely baffled by his handling of the situation. "Assemble a team of fifty that are currently doing the least and bring them to me."

Jasss squinted, a little confused by the instruction. The soldiers, too, stared at Abdabriel, perplexed.

Abdabriel raised his voice. "Were my instructions imprecise?"

"No, Holy One," one of the soldiers said. He was a larger man with red hair, appearing as strong as any man Jasss had ever seen. He looked tough enough to handle himself in dangerous situations, with a demeanor that suggested he'd spent much of his life doing just that. He had a bit of a heftier belly, but it did nothing to soften his appearance. "Holy One," he said with some sour displeasure, "I don't mean any disrespect, but don't we have more important things to focus on than appealing to the likes of a brattish girl—one who has disrespected you?"

Abdabriel paused. "What is your name, soldier?"

"Zykel."

"How old are you?"

"Forty-eight."

"Ah." Abdabriel nodded. "And how many worlds do you know?"

The soldier noticed the others inching away from him. "I, uh—" He looked at Abdabriel. "Whewliss is the first world I've visited, aside from my own planet."

"Uh-huh." Abdabriel clicked his tongue with elegant disdain. "You're less than a century old, and you have been to two worlds." He took a step toward the soldier, who was growing nervous. "So, what you're telling me is, compared to my age and knowledge, you are a child and you know nothing. You lack my experience of the universe, of every world, and therefore, in comparison to the grand vision I've invited you to help create, your eyes are closed. Does that sum everything up rather well?"

Zykel lowered his gaze, his heart racing as he considered his responses. "I apologize, Holy One."

Abdabriel nodded. "Look at me."

Zykel was trembling as he forced some words. "Holy One, I am not worthy. I should keep my eyes down, as they lack vision."

Abdabriel nodded. "Yes, they do. But I insist. Look at me, Zykel."

Zykel slowly looked up at Abdabriel. "Yes, Holy One."

"That's better." Abdabriel smiled. "You are afraid. I appreciate that. I can see your fear, and it is necessary." He sighed. "I'm assuming you are afraid that I am going to kill you to make an example of those who question my judgment. Is that an accurate guess?" Zykel slowly nodded as Abdabriel did, too. "I could. But your fear is enough for me. You can breathe. I'm not going to kill you." He chuckled. "But if you ever question me again, I will fill your mouth with flesh-eating insects and then seal your lips together so you can't even scream while they feed on your throat and into your stomach." Zykel froze at the threat. Abdabriel maintained his smile as he leaned over where Zykel's eyes had wandered. "Do we understand one another?"

"Yes, Holy One," Zykel answered as quickly as he could, gulping his pooling saliva.

"Great," Abdabriel sighed. "And do me a favor? Don't keep this conversation a secret." He winked at Zykel.

"Yes, Holy One." Zykel nodded and cleared his throat. "So, you want fifty soldiers brought to you?"

"As soon as possible." Abdabriel smiled. "Thank you, Zykel. I enjoyed our talk."

Zykel and the other soldiers walked away, leaving Abdabriel and Jasss alone. Even as the distance between them increased, the tension lingered for a while. Abdabriel shook his head and looked at Jasss with wide eyes.

"I'm sorry, Jasss. That got a little out of hand." He shook his head and scoffed. "I had two children in my younger years—two daughters, and they never required that strong of a hand to keep them in line."

Jasss turned her head a little as her eyebrows lowered. "Where are they now?"

"Pylillis always dreamed of being an observer." Abdabriel's eyes sparkled at the memory. "Always wanted to see other worlds and protect our way of life." His expression died down, turning blank, emotionless. "But she was caught in the crossfire of a war on the third world she visited. I still feel her lips on my cheek." His hand went to his face and his eyes went dark. "She was the light that guided me."

Jasss stared blankly at him. The story's twist was no different than her everyday way of life, but she listened regardless.

"And your other daughter?"

Abdabriel's eyes went down and then bounced back up as he forced the strength to finish his story. "Faydreigh killed herself after learning of her sister's murder."

Jasss nodded, understanding Abdabriel's motivation for his cause. "I see."

"I know nothing I do will bring them back, but if I can end all other wars by waging one last one now, eventually stories like theirs will only be found in museums and history books."

"But what about the families of those you kill to reach that goal?"

"I'm not doing what I'm doing for current generations. All current pain will fade. I'm doing this for the future of mankind. Generations to come will not experience such heartache, and they will have me to thank for that mercy."

For a moment, they both were quiet. Abdabriel had to suppress his emotions. He had to cauterize healed scars that had been reopened. It was something he'd become better at over time. Jasss waited in silence, unsure of what to say. She didn't really care about his dead children, not out of spite, but because it was only a taste of the anguish he'd already caused others. Regardless of her apathy toward his suffering, she waited in silence while he regrouped himself.

"I'm sorry, Jasss. I'm just bleeding more words at your feet." He cleared his throat and then fully composed himself in an instant, as if by magic. "No more words or promises. I will give you a tangible gift." He smiled. "I will give you one of the best suits we have. You will be given the most advanced and efficient implants we offer. The fifty soldiers being assembled will be placed under your command, and together, the fifty-one of you will go to Ojīptian." Jasss was taken aback. She wasn't sure how to respond. Abdabriel went on. "What you do there is entirely up to you. You know the planet better than I do, so any assault you desire will be cleaner and more efficient. If you wish to grant mercy to the slavers for the sakes of their families, so be it. If you wish to open the jugular of every slaver andtheir family, so be it." He smiled at her. "No more words. It is time for action."

29

"How far away are they?" Lord Coyzle asked. He was trying not to panic as his eyes strained in the darkness.

"By my guess—" Dumakleiza stared out. "—eighty paces."

"Hello!" Gideon shouted out to the beings he couldn't yet see. "We come in peace. Take us to your leader!" He snickered at the others. "I've always wanted to say that."

Traveler's eyes were fixated on the blackness. "We've never studied their language. Our translators are useless with them." He wanted to shine his light out where Dumakleiza was looking, but he was worried it might be mistaken as a threat. Until they knew more about the indigenous of the planet, he wanted to interact as little as possible.

The firelight only made the night seem darker, creating unknown horrors in the blackness. Everyone went silent, waiting for Dumakleiza's updates.

Lord Coyzle was inching closer to the fire, trying to stay within its perimeter of visibility. There was nowhere to hide. He was on their world, and whoever *they* were, he feared that they would not be receptive of aliens. He was longing for the reassurance of daylight and the confidence provided by bodyguards and technology. More than anything, he longed for a functioning reflection suit.

Izzy stepped over next to Dumakleiza. "What do they look like?"

"I told you," Dumakleiza said under her breath. "They are human."

Izzy nodded. "Right, but do they have any unique features, or do they look just like us?"

Dumakleiza stared out at the pale figures prowling behind bushes and trees on all fours, whispering to each other too quietly for her to hear. They looked so nimble and agile with their animalistic movements. It bothered her. They were close enough that she should be able to hear their footsteps.

"Uh. They possess no clothing. Their eyes are abnormally sized."

"How so?"

"They are large and reflective, like that of a nighttime hunter. They have black hair. Their bodies are white in color, and their ears seem — " She bunched her lips as she thought of how best to describe them. " — bigger and oddly shaped. Like those of a bat."

Izzy nodded and tried to follow her gaze. "Wild, nocturnal homo sapiens. That's a significant discovery." He knew it was not something to focus on in the moment, but he couldn't help it.

"What are we going to do?" Lord Coyzle asked.

"Well." Traveler tried to think rationally. "We should stay calm. Perhaps they don't want to hurt us. They might just be curious about who we are. That's what we, as a species, tend to do: pursue curiosity." He held his finger tight by his side, refraining from lifting it. "They're keeping their distance, which probably means they don't like the fire—possibly don't even know what it is. It'll likely deter them for a while due to their nocturnal nature. However, should they turn aggressive, our wisest move would be to grab torches and warn them off."

Gideon nodded. "What if we — "

"You're not going to go introduce yourself to them," Traveler said. "Not yet, at least."

Gideon slumped down a little. "Fine."

Lord Coyzle was over being in the unknown. "Four Zero, shine your light out. I want to see them."

"My lord, I don't believe that's the wisest idea. It could scare them and perhaps cause a frenzy of some sort. We have no idea how they will react or what they're capable of, especially in large numbers."

"Good," Lord Coyzle said, his voice on the verge of breaking. "I *want* them to be afraid of us. We won't hurt them if they don't attack us first, but they should know not to. It'll be a friendly warning." After his opinion was met with further hesitation, he turned authoritative. "Four Zero, shine your light. That's a command."

Traveler nodded, raised his finger, and adjusted his thumb. He paused as no light appeared. He aimed his finger more urgently, repeating the same motion.

Nothing happened.

"It's not working." He brought his hand down and then up, repeating the familiar process. Nothing. He knew he was doing it right. After all, he was an expert in Whewlight technology.

"What do you mean it's not working?" Lord Coyzle asked with loud nerves. "Try it again."

"I am," Traveler muttered under his breath, baffled by his own inability to use a simple tool.

Gideon and Izzy watched Traveler's finger. It had worked just minutes before when he'd ignited the fire. Dumakleiza and Vorlak kept their eyes on the darkness, waiting, preparing.

Lord Coyzle couldn't handle it. "What other implants do you have, Four Zero?"

"None of them are working," Traveler said. "Gideon?"

"What?" Gideon shrugged. "You know I don't have any implants."

"Hmm," Traveler said. "I know. I was checking to see if our translators are working. If we were completely out of energy, all our implants, including translators, would be failing. Why are my finger implants not working but our translators are?"

"I don't like this," Lord Coyzle said. The blackness kept getting darker as they ran out of options or answers. They'd been reduced to animals, technology out of reach, and hope dwindling. "Four Zero, do something."

"I've never heard of this happening," Traveler puzzled. "What's going on?" He looked up and down, simultaneously blinking his right eye. His aperture adjusted normally. Only the implants in his hands had stopped functioning. "I have no idea why —"

"Darkness," an unfamiliar voice said.

Everyone turned to see who had spoken. The voice was strangely calm. Sitting close to the fire, only a few feet from Vorlak, was a man. An earthy, brown cloak prevented them from seeing his face. His posture was completely unconcerned about the darkness or the swarming indige-nous. He sat cross-legged, staring into the flames. No one had seen or heard him approach.

Vorlak leaned forward, his sharp fingers ready to disembowel. The man didn't acknowledge him. Before anyone could ask who he was, he spoke again.

"Why are you here?" He didn't look away from the fire, and his voice remained calm. There was no threat or urgency.

Gideon squinted with a curious grin. "Who are you, stranger?"

"A student," the man responded and looked up, exposing his face in the firelight. Gideon thought he looked to be in his early-to-mid-forties. His skin was a smooth olive tan, and his bright hazel eyes reflected the flames with the intensity of a lion's. A perfectly trimmed beard blanketed the bottom of his face.

Vorlak screamed, his legs nearly giving out. The Daemoanik monster leapt away, throwing himself into the fire. Embers and sparks burst into the air as he disrupted the settling wood, crunching and staggering across. He struggled, unable to get footing, but his eyes didn't leave the man. Vorlak yelled as he scrambled out of the other side of the flames. Without checking to see if he was on fire, he dove behind Gideon and cowered on the ground, moaning in terror. Thick, weeping screams poured into the black air. He didn't try to conceal anything as he shook violently enough to nearly dislocate his shoulder.

Gideon slowly turned with a gaping mouth. "You can't be — " He stud-ied the stranger's middle-aged appearance. "You're too young," he said in disbelief. Vorlak's reaction had goosebumps flying down Gideon's arms, but the stranger didn't look threatening.

"Too young?" the stranger asked.

Lord Coyzle's eyes were wide open. For a moment, he forgot about the surrounding horde. "Are you...Shadowmaker?"

The man looked back into the fire, appreciating the simplicity of it. "I believed that title swallowed by history. Now I know who I am to you. Who you are to me remains to be explained. Why are you here?"

Izzy's ears itched with nerves. "You're alive."

Traveler's jaw moved up and down before he managed words. "Are you Shadowmaker? You're too young."

Dumakleiza turned her gaze to the cloaked stranger. "You said darkness was to blame for the Diviner's failing science. Are you speaking of dark magic?" For the first time, Dumakleiza's archaic fears were shared by the others.

The man maintained his fixation with the flames. "By questioning my age, I assume you think I'm stuck on Fayde." He held his hands out to warm them. "That means that you arestuck here."

Traveler's eyes darted around as he tried to breathe. "You can leave? How do you leave?"

Gideon smiled. "Is that H.P.'s actual name? Fayde? Like, what the people here have named it?"

"Yes. You are fortunate I wasn't elsewhere when you chose to come after me. And there is no such thing as magic anywhere in this universe," Shadowmaker responded. "Darkness is simply the absence of light. It's mathematic. I subtracted your ability to process light with your implants. They are unfair against a world that has thus far been untampered with."

Traveler was going numb with fear. "My implants —"

" —are deactivated. As are your cells. You will not be jumping anywhere. I leave you only your eyes and your ears for us to have this conversation. Why are you here? I have asked three times now." Shadowmaker didn't look away from the fire, and his voice didn't fluctuate.

Silence followed as everyone stared at him, unsure how to react. He looked normal, unsuspecting, and arguably approachable by the fire. He had no scary features, no Daemoanik appearance, and even his clothing was quaint——barbaric even. While no one had ever had any reason to assume his form, they'd expected a demon of a man. But he wasn't a giant with an overabundance of muscle or a monster with deformations. In fact, if they didn't know who he was, they would have thought he was nothing but a rugged stranger.

Gideon finally managed to break his eyes away long enough to look at the two Whewlights. "Do you guys want me to tell him?" He was trying not to explode with excitement. They were in the presence of

Shadowmaker—the one and only Shadowmaker. With a barely noticeable nod from the petrified Lord Coyzle, Gideon brought his hands to his face like a child. "Okay!" He couldn't help trying to take a step toward Shadowmaker, but his legs wouldn't move. No matter how hard he tried to walk, his muscles didn't respond to his commands. He assumed it was because of something Shadowmaker had done, which only made him more in awe. "Whewliss's LOLA ambassador betrayed us and is trying to conquer every habited plant, er, planet. We are here to humbly request your help in stopping him because we totally can't."

They waited as Shadowmaker's eyes remained on the fire. Gideon had laid out their intentions rather bluntly, and they could only hope that was the best way to reach Shadowmaker's sympathies.

Only Vorlak's whimpering broke the quiet.

Shadowmaker gave a single nod. "Okay," he said without looking away from the fire. "It will cost you something real."

Everyone slowly took their eyes off him and looked at each other, confused by his immediate agreement. Again, they weren't sure what they'd been expecting, but it seemed too easy. They'd anticipated a lengthy debate, and if they were honest, they'd been prepared to beg.

"Understood," Lord Coyzle finally said. "Name your price."

"Something real," Shadowmaker repeated himself.

"Oh, Maker of Shadows." Dumakleiza proudly stepped toward him, untying the treasure sack from her waist. "I humbly offer you the holy treasure of Yagūl as payment for your contract." She tossed the sack of gold and treasure to the ground next to him. It spilled open, jewels of all colors pouring into the dirt. They reflected the fiery light in vibrant elegance while Dumakleiza stood confident with her hands on her hips.

Shadowmaker's eyes didn't leave the flames. "I have no need for currency of any denomination from any world. My services will cost something real."

Dumakleiza's eyebrows bunched. Her shoulders dropped. She was speechless. Amid everything happening around her, she was heartbroken. She'd spent her entire life defending her treasure, protecting it from those who sought to steal it, but now she'd finally chosen to give it away, and it was unwanted.

"What do you mean by 'real?'" Gideon asked.

Cooby dropped off Dumakleiza's shoulders and crawled toward Shadowmaker. Dumakleiza blinked a few times before she realized he'd left her.

"Coobs! *Cooby!* Come here!"

Cooby ignored her and crawled right up to Shadowmaker, smelling his arm. Dumakleiza watched, nauseated by Cooby's inevitable death. He cooed at Shadowmaker's scent and then pawed at him.

"Coobs!" Dumakleiza gasped. She tried to run after him, but she couldn't move. She looked down and saw nothing out of the ordinary. She squinted. There was a metal ball the size of the tip of her pinky on the dirt between her feet. Whatever it was, it seemed responsible for her inability to move her legs. It didn't hurt, and she could still feel every sensation in her legs, but she couldn't control them. She had no idea when Shadowmaker had placed the ball there, and her incomprehension was instantly infuriating. "What devilry is this?"

Shadowmaker turned and cracked a smile as he took Cooby onto his lap. Cooby purred and sat down, licking Shadowmaker's face. Dumakleiza's mouth hung open in dread as she was stuck watching. Shadowmaker scratched Cooby's chin.

"It's been decades since I last held a tanion," he said. "Magnificent creatures and companions." He smiled as Cooby licked all over his face.

For the first time, Dumakleiza sacrificed her pride and pleaded, "Please, Maker of Shadows, do not hurt my Coobs!"

Shadowmaker stared deep into Cooby's beady eyes. "The tanion is the only one of your party that is guaranteed safety on this world."

Traveler couldn't help himself. "How did you send the coins through space?" He'd puzzled over the mystery his entire life.

Shadowmaker didn't take his eyes off Cooby as they playfully batted at each other. "Clothes and small items jump with us due to our DNA on them, but that extension of ourselves is limited and temporary. For an inanimate object to be sent alone, it must be coated in DNA: skin, saliva, urine, semen, or blood. The coins were coated in blood. My blood. That is the price I paid for the lives they claimed."

Lord Coyzle and Traveler looked at each other as they digested his answer. Gideon considered a whole slew of philosophical what-if questions.

"For that act alone—" Lord Coyzle said with surfacing anger. "—you owe us your help as—as—as a debt." He glared at Shadowmaker with breaking emotions, but Shadowmaker paid him no mind. The lack of visible response only further angered Lord Coyzle.

Shadowmaker caressed Cooby's ears, making the tanion's eyes roll back. He then kissed Cooby's forehead and placed him on the ground. As Cooby jaunted back to Dumakleiza, Shadowmaker's eyes returned to the fire.

"I killed your father," he said to Lord Coyzle with no anger, regret, or pride.

Lord Coyzle refrained from glaring. "How do you know who I am?"

"I killed all your resistance leaders, along with many others in the ULW. I then destroyed Daemoana and brought my own people to the edge of extinction, saving you all. My debt to you has long been paid."

Lord Coyzle wanted to argueeven though there was no argument to be made. He stared at the man nonchalantly joining them by the fire. He wanted nothing more than to scream into his face. It didn't make sense. This wasn't how it was supposed to be when he found Shadowmaker.

"But—"

"You are at peace with your father's death. It is apparent. Your attempt to use it as leverage against me is nothing more than an act of desperation."

"How dare you sa—"

"I know who all of you are, or at least where you're from," Shadowmaker said with absolute indifference. "I've visited Whewliss many times since the war. Your gelatin keeper unknowingly granted me access on multiple occasions."

Lord Coyzle felt violated by the answer, as if everything he'd ever believed had suddenly been exposed as a lie. "How? How did you—"

"It does an excellent job. You truly are one of the most advanced peoples." He didn't scoff or use a derogatory tone, but his comment alone made Lord Coyzle and Traveler feel small. "I do admire your Winkloh Stars. Brilliant engineering and manipulation of light. I enjoyed learning about them during my last visit." As everyone listened, Shadowmaker stood with powerful elegance, using only his feet from his cross-legged position. With the same motion, he slid the hood over his head and onto his back, exposing a buzzed head of short hair. Between the ferocity of his hazel eyes and the simplicity of his hairstyle, he came off as purely tactical.

"Why?" Lord Coyzle fumbled the question out. "Why did you come to Whewliss? Are you—" He gulped. "—planning another invasion?"

"No," Shadowmaker stated, still looking into the flames. "That has never been my intent. As I said earlier, I am a student. I visited Whewliss to learn."

"Learn what?" Lord Coyzle asked, needing to know why.

"Everything." Without looking away, Shadowmaker pointed at Gideon. "The last time I visited Earth, I studied your submarines. My people never focused on learning what lay beneath our waters. It pains me that we will never know what aquatic life existed before I regrettably eradicated it. Exploring your oceans made me feel like a child. It was eye-opening and beautiful." He pointed to Dumakleiza. "During my last visit to Cul, I learned a new form of meditation that frees the spirit in a way that most of the more advanced worlds have yet to discover. It taught me how to read the subtlest shifts in the air's vibration, allowing me to fine-tune predictions and defenses. Remarkable relaxation from a blind shaman." He pointed to Izzy. "Some of the best poetry I've ever heard was on Jurael. It was not what I expected to study during my visit there, and I am grateful for its surprise." He lowered his hand, clasping his fingers together in front of his waist. "Do not worry, Albei Coyzle, I have not unveiled my identity on any world. I do not want the attention." His knowledge of the classified name made Lord Coyzle feel even more desecrated and inferior. "I wish only to be an anonymous face, visiting in secret for the sole purpose of learning. I am no threat. I am a student."

"So," Gideon said, grinning at the unexpected, "you've basically visited every world and become a master of, well, everything."

"I am not a master of anything," Shadowmaker said. "There is always more to learn."

"But, like—" Gideon looked up as he tried to wrap his mind around it. "—you've spent the last couple-hundred-years just learning? Like, each planet's history, scientific discoveries, mathematics, languages, martial arts, meditation, construction styles, *music*, poetry, um—" He tried to think of more categories. "Stuff like that?"

"Longer than that but yes," Shadowmaker said with a subtle nod. "Stuff like that." He disrobed his cloak, smoothly slipping it off his shoulders and arms. Beneath it he wore nothing, and in his nudity, he showed no fear of the dangerous planet around him. His body was lean. He may not have been a gigantic man with bulging muscles, but he was well-defined. Gideon half expected to see tattoos spanning across Shadowmaker's body, but alas, his sharp musculature was the same olive tone as his face, and he had only one tattoo. Over his left pectoral was a simple black outline of what looked to Gideon like a long, pointy eared teddy bear head. He couldn't help wondering aloud.

"Is that a—"

"You have one day," Shadowmaker said to all of them. "At that time, I will be leaving Fayde. Should you survive 'til then, I will visit you before my departure to receive your payment."

Lord Coyzle's eyes darted back and forth in a panic. "We don't know what you mean by 'something real.' What do you mean?" His urgent tone shifted to frantic. "We will give you whatever you want! I swear it on my father's grave."

"If you do not give me what I require, I will not kill you as you fear, but I will remove every implant you have and leave you to your fates on Fayde."

"No!" Traveler's outburst was involuntary. "If we fail, at least send us back to Whewliss. We will leave you alone. We all promise."

Shadowmaker stared peacefully into the fire, watching as it waned. "Your knowledge of my location compromises this unscathed sanctuary. Provide me with something real by this time tomorrow, or I will remove the remaining implants from your eyes and ears, and you will have the same chance at survival as any other living creature on Fayde." He pointed at Vorlak. "Except for the Daemoanik. Him, I will kill should you fail. I have not yet decided if he will live should you succeed."

They were suddenly overly aware of the pale people lurking in the distance. Traveler's implants were deactivated. He had no technological weapons. They had their hands and whatever they could wield, but that would only delay the inevitable fangs and claws of the creatures outnumbering them on the foreign world. If Shadowmaker deactivated their optical implants and their translators, they would wander blind and alone in the darkness, unable to communicate with each other. Fear swarmed Traveler like rising waters, consuming him, taunting him, promising inescapable death.

"But," Lord Coyzle pleaded, "we have done nothing to —"

"The tanion I will take with me now. Cooby." Shadowmaker tried the name.

"I will kill you if you take my Coobs." Dumakleiza's threat made zero impact.

"Cooby. Cooby." Once Shadowmaker was satisfied with his understanding of the name, he continued. "Should you give me what I want tomorrow, he will be returned to you. But should you not, he deserves better than a life in darkness."

"Do not separate me from my Coobs!" Dumakleiza roared.

"Would you prefer him eaten alongside you?"

"I wish no harm to ever come to him!" Dumakleiza yelled, tears burning in her eyes.

"Then be grateful he will be spared that fate."

Dumakleiza shook with hysteric rage. "You mercilessly leave us to fend for ourselves against those monsters?" She pointed out at the swarming indigenous, still whispering to each other in the blackness. They were inching closer as the firelight dimmed.

"The Fayded are less monsters than any of you," Shadowmaker corrected. "In fact, they are more animal than human, driven by primal instinct over selfish desire. While they do kill out of hunger and self-defense, they do not kill for personal gain."

"Then they won't eat *us*, right?" Izzy asked in a last-ditch effort to establish hope. "After all, we're humans. Just like them. So, they won't want to kill us."

"If they go long enough without food, I've seen them resort to cannibalism." Shadowmaker's response made everyone's throat tighten.

They were running out of time and light. The fire hadn't been stoked, and none of them could move to add more wood.

Shadowmaker stepped back from the flames with his cloak draped over his right arm. "The Fayded are not whom you should concern yourselves with. They possess limited threat and are not the dominant species in this canyon."

"What is?" Traveler asked, suddenly even more terrified of the unknown in the night.

"The darkness is home to much more dangerous creatures," Shadowmaker said as he tossed his cloak onto the fire. The instant it landed, it broke apart, disintegrating over the remaining flames and embers. Whatever the material was, it devoured the remaining fire, choking it, depriving it of oxygen. One large burst of smoke billowed up as the light died. Lord Coyzle and Izzy gasped as Vorlak's whimpering cries grew louder. Shadowmaker's eyes reflected the last few embers as they burned out. "If the Fayded retreat to their homes underground, it's for a good reason. I'd suggest you follow them."

With that, the remaining flames died. Even the burning coals went cold and black. Everything was still, and aside from Vorlak, everything was silent. They were all able to move again, as if a trance had just been lifted. Their legs were free, but they couldn't see anything. The sobering blackness of the night closed in with claustrophobic constriction. Traveler couldn't start another fire. His implant was deactivated. There was no more light, and they could hear soft footsteps approaching from all around. The Fayded no longer needed to sneak around the firelight. They were in their element: heavy darkness, where the light-starved aliens were easy prey.

Vorlak was still screaming like a stuck pig, shaking in utter fear. The Daemoanik had been broken.

"Shadowmaker?" Lord Coyzle quietly called, actually hoping to hear a response from the man who'd plagued his nightmares since childhood. There was no response. It was real. Shadowmaker had left them. Without light, without weapons, and without Cooby, Shadowmaker had left them. They were alone, surrounded by nocturnal creatures, and the footsteps were getting closer.

30

Timrekka had all but forgotten about the other recruits as he indulged in the skydrop laboratory. It had been hours since Abdabriel had dropped him off, but he felt like he'd barely seen anything. The layout was the same as the farm. There were four levels within the floating sphere, each filled with desks containing centuries of documented experiments and discoveries. A hollow center to the building, along with an arching bridge, allowed a full view of each floor from anywhere inside. Mysterious objects, machines, tools, devices, and drawings with unknown purposes and functions were neatly organized throughout the entire skydrop. Holograms and screens displayed flashing updates and moving pieces controlled by the Whewlights. Of all of the numerous items, Timrekka was only able to correctly guess what three of them were. The rest needed to be explained, and he loved not being in the know. There was so much to learn and explore.

"This is an obsolete prototype," said Doctor Moybo, a taller, bald Whewlight with dark skin. He pointed to a glass case displayed on a table, containing small electrodes with bird symbols on them. "It's called a brain pigeon."

"What does it do?" Timrekka leaned in as close as he could without marking the glass.

"The idea was to help paraplegics and quadriplegics overcome their handicap. When the brain cannot communicate with parts of the body, those parts no longer function."

"Of course, of course—how was this supposed to fix that?"

"Well." Doctor Moybo was enjoying teaching the man he was ultimately instructed to kneel to. "It wasn't meant to fix it, as much as bypass it. If you think of muscles, tendons, bones, nerves, and every part of the body as needing wiring from the brain, constantly processing instructions through electrical impulses, then imagine a wire cutter severing the flow. Suddenly legs won't receive instruction. Now—" His voice grew excited to share an old invention. "—imagine that we place this—" He pointed to the largest electrode. "—in the patient's brain, and these—" He pointed at two smaller electrodes. "—inside the patient's legs." He cleared his throat and joined Timrekka leaning in close, staring through the glass.

"Radio transmission of brainwaves, sending instructions from the mind to the body, wirelessly enabling a paraplegic to walk again," Timrekka said as if his eyes just opened for the first time.

Moybo nodded. "Precisely. However, once the healing properties of light were discovered to be superior, we shelved many promising medical breakthroughs. They just weren't necessary anymore."

"I wish we had never discovered light," said the second scientist, Doctor Minkel, a heavier-set woman with wide, narrow eyes. "Or I guess I wish the Daemoaniks had never forced its knowledge upon us. I mean, it has propelled us beyond what we thought we'd never reach, but it's made much of our old research a waste." She shrugged. "I know I'm alone in my distaste for light's gifts, but I feel like it's made so much of our history, well, laughable. It's almost made *us* unnecessary."

Timrekka couldn't look away from the brain pigeon. "Do you two mind if I tinker with this? I have some ideas, and I want to understand it, and maybe I can find a use for it."

Moybo and Minkel looked at each other before turning to Timrekka.

"You don't have to ask permission for anything," Minkel said, wondering if Timrekka only asked to test their loyalty. "Anything." She shrugged. "Abdabriel said we are to follow your every instruction. You're the boss here."

Timrekka blinked a few times. It still wasn't registering. He especially didn't want to admit that he liked the paradigm shift.

"Um." He looked at the two faces waiting for his instruction. "Well, I, um, I've never been in charge of anyone else before, so I don't know how to go about it if I'm being honest because I still want to hear your thoughts and input, and I guess I'd rather treat you as colleagues than boss you around. Is that weird or the wrong way to handle things? I don't know; I'm used to working alone, and I'm sorry, I'm rambling, and I probably sound like a crazy person."

Moybo chuckled, "You sound like a man who's better with study than interaction. I'm guessing you usually get so lost in your work that you have trouble finding your way back to the rest of humanity."

Timrekka nodded with a sheepish head dip. "Yes, science is easy. People are difficult."

"I think you'll do just fine," Moybo said. "What would you like now? We can continue showing you around. There's enough of a tour left to keep us busy for a few days. Or we can get to work on anything you'd like."

Timrekka's eyes darted around. He had exponentially multiplying ideas bottlenecking in his overloaded brain. He smiled, trying to prioritize them. A little chuckle escaped his lips.

"Uh, would you two mind showing me the different implants available and tell me how they work because we don't have them on my world, and I'm fascinated by the options therein."

"Oh, wow," Minkel scoffed. "What kind are we talking about? There are hundreds of kinds of implants and thousands upon thousands of apps that can be coded into each one. More are being invented every day." She walked over to a transparent glass screen floating above a desk. "We can look through them, even the top-secret apps, thanks to the Holy One." The circular glass screen lit up when she touched it. It came alive with brightly colored buttons and words in a language foreign to Timrekka. His optical implants instantly translated them into his language. Minkel hit a few buttons and swiped the screen until a diagram of a human body appeared.

"What kind of implant are we looking for?" Minkel asked. Red lights lit up across the diagram, indicating diverse options available throughout the body. She zoomed in, displaying implants for the cranium, eyes, forehead, ears, nose, mouth, facial skin, jawline, neck, and more. She zoomed out and then in again, showing all the options within the torso, then the arms and hands, then the legs and feet, genitals, and everywhere in between.

"As you can see, they come in all shapes and sizes, customizable to your wildest dreams." She looked over to see Timrekka's wide eyes. "Though, technically you're the only one in here that's had dreams recently." Timrekka didn't hear her sleep joke as he devoured the information like a dry sponge. Minkel and Moybo chuckled as she went on. "Now we can browse implant apps. Do you want to look at apps for games, business and finance, education, holographic entertainment, stuff for kids, health and fitness, military, including offensive and defensive, medical, aesthetic, navigational, utilities, cosmetic..." Minkel kept reading categories, but Timrekka was already singing songs of potential in his head as he studied every option flashing before his eyes.

"This is incredible."

"A little different than Thamiosh, I'm guessing," Moybo said with a big smile. "You are really going to love our—"

"How's the tour going?" Abdabriel's eager voice surprised them from behind. He was standing a level above them on the skydrop's bridge. He smiled down as the scientists looked up to see him accompanied by four soldiers.

"Holy One," Moybo and Minkel said in unison.

"How are my two second favorite scientists doing? I'm sure you've both made Timrekka feel welcome."

"Yes, of course," Moybo said as they both nodded.

"Timrekka?" Abdabriel focused on him. "Everything going okay?"

"Yes." Timrekka nodded, keeping his eyes down.

"Oh, Timrekka." Abdabriel chuckled. "I hope I've proven that I want only good things for you. You really can relax. You're not a slave or anything." He chuckled a wink. "Speaking of which, Jasss has seen the light. Can you believe it?" He did a little dance to emphasize his excitement. "She's on Ojīptian as we speak, leading mysoldiers to liberate her people. Rather exciting stuff if you ask me." He smiled as he saw Timrekka processing. "So, stop acting like I'm going to hurt you."

Timrekka nodded right away. "Okay."

Abdabriel rolled his eyes and shook his head before turning to the other two. "I apologize for interrupting. I will leave promptly so you three can continue your, uh, science fun." He shrugged as more eloquent words eluded him. "I simply need my requested implant."

"Of course, Holy One," Moybo said as he concealed his hesitance.

Timrekka watched as Moybo hit a few buttons. A thumb implant appeared on the screen, accompanied by an app description and sensual advertising videos for it. Timrekka squinted. Erotically posed men and woman writhed with bright colors coursing through their bodies in waves. Light moaning played, along with an emitted scent from somewhere around the computer. The delightful aroma immediately aroused Timrekka. He was intrigued by Whewliss's clear use of pheromones and scents in their advertising. Moybo hit a few more buttons and then stepped away from the screen, turning his eyes up to Abdabriel and his soldiers.

"It's ready."

"Great," Abdabriel said. He led the four soldiers down. "These are the brave warriors I've selected. They are the privileged that I've deemed worthy of my personal detail." He showed them off proudly. The two largest men were bald twins with menacing tattoos covering their faces. Permanent snarls expressed disgust for the inventors. One female soldier was the most heavily muscled out of the four. She looked capable of snapping a grown man in half. But the worst of them, at least in Timrekka's opinion, was the thinnest. He was tall and slender, nearly skeletal, with pale skin. What really made him threatening was his lack of eyes. They'd been removed, gouged out, leaving smoothly healed sockets. The two holes in his face left him soulless and unhuman.

"Hi," was all Timrekka could squeak out.

"True patriots to the cause. They are, without doubt, the most effective, highly trained, and lethal soldiers under my command—and thusly in the entire universe," Abdabriel bragged. "Hired killers from other worlds, previously without purpose. But now—" He smiled at the four. "Now their skills will be redirected and honed to help protect the light." He motioned to the massive woman. "This is Mosh Elle. She's the most prolific assassin from her home planet, Dyfruh." As Abdabriel spoke, Mosh Elle growled at Timrekka without flinching her expression. "She feeds off the fear of others, so keep your chin up." Abdabriel chuckled before he continued. "She crushes people with her arms. Like a large serpent. Their final moments of thrashing are apparently more rewarding than anything I can pay her." He dismissed the violence with a shrug. "Hoping I never have to witness it, but I'd rather be safe than sorry."

The three scientists stared at her like exposed prey would a carnivore.

"And these two handsome gentlemen," Abdabriel said, pointing at the two enormous men, towering a head taller than him, "are the brothers Diabelicoff." Timrekka stared at their broad shoulders, thick arms, intimidating scowls, and tattoos. They were even wider than he was. Abdabriel smiled at them like treasured possessions. "I recruited them on Eowa, a brooding world filled with territorial gangs. Much like yours, Timrekka. You would probably have a lot to talk about with them." Abdabriel smiled. "They are no exception to their planet's infatuation with violence. In fact, they are known planet-wide on Eowa as the two men solely responsible for assassinating six world leaders in order to pave the way for their family's fruitful takeover of an entire continent. Impressive if you ask me. During their excursions, they cut a bloody path through bodyguards, armies—men, women, and children. I'm not proud of that last part, but it tells me they'll do whatever's necessary for the cause." Abdabriel chuckled. "In fact, when I went to hire them, they killed twelve of my soldiers before I could say anything. I think they even ate a guy?"

The scientists gave subservient bows to acknowledge the introductions. They didn't know what else to do.

"And this," Abdabriel said, pointing to the eyeless man, "is Greaper. He is from a world unknown to most. Only I knew where it was located, and I still don't know the name of it. Private people. When I first visited it to introduce them to LOLA, I saw such potential that I decided not to report anything back to Lord Coyzle at the time. Figured it was a secret just for me. Anyways, I hired Greaper out of horrified respect for the warrior that he is." Abdabriel grinned at his most esteemed bodyguard. "Greaper's people ritualistically carve out their own eyes at puberty in order to hone their other senses. They were the only world I ever visited that came close to Daemoana's atrocious transformations, but they did it for a promising purpose: self-betterment." Abdabriel nodded with approval. "And Greaper was their most celebrated warrior. I have no idea how many people he's killed, but according to little pieces I've picked up along the way, I've decided I probably don't want to know." He chuckled before his tone turned serious. "Greaper's methods are fascinating, and they never fail him. You see, his people based all their combative tactics and training off the hunting techniques of spiders. The ways they trap, poise, and leap into action too quickly and accurately to be stopped. His hands are always too fast for his victims to even notice until it's too late. It's fascinating to watch. You can barely see it happen. I know I shouldn't, but I love it." He stared in adoration at his bodyguards. "These four are the only soldiers in the Army of Light that I respectfully fear. They are the reason I will never take off my reflection suit unless they were on a separate world than me." He chuckled again. "They're scarier than Shadowmaker ever was."

Timrekka bit his tongue as he glanced up and then back down. He couldn't deny the terror they evoked within him.

Abdabriel thought while rubbing his chin. "Though, we're going to have to do something to make them less daunting in appearance. Maybe a makeover of sorts." He nodded with a hand on the muscular woman's back. "Can't have them scaring people before I can unify them." He chuckled and waved through the air. "Anyways, I'm sorry. I promised I'd make this quick. I was just excited to introduce my bodyguards to a fourth phase recruit. It's so exciting!" He shook his fists in the air. "But I digress. Please give them the implants, and we'll leave you to your lab stuff."

Moybo nodded. "Yes, Holy One." He kept his head down and placed a metallic, cubed rectangle on the table beneath the screen. The chrome device was smooth on all edges, except for one end, which had a hole in it. Moybo motioned to it. "One at a time, if you will." The soldiers silently stepped up. The first stuck his thumb inside. Once it was in, Moybo tapped the screen. There was a high whirring sound and then a light indicating completion. Moybo motioned for the next soldier. "You're ready." One by one, the other three completed the process until all four of them had the implant.

"Well, that was easy," Abdabriel said. "Thank you." He turned to walk back up the stairs to the exit pad. "Oh!" He paused before the top step. "Timrekka, here it is," he said as he pointed to a black sealed bag draped over the railing. "Your reflection suit. Ahead of schedule, I might add." He winked.

Timrekka glanced up and then brought his eyes back down as he nodded. "Thank you."

"Of course." Abdabriel smiled, resuming his walk to the exit pad. "Be careful putting it on. Any aggressive motions before it's completely applied and they—get testy. Meh, what am I saying? You'll figure it out. Carry on, you three." With that, he stepped onto the pad and disappeared, followed by his bodyguards.

The instant they were gone, Timrekka turned to Moybo and Minkel. "What's the implant do?"

Minkel sighed and shook her head. "It was originally a pleasure app. If you have it, you press your thumb anywhere on someone's body, and it activates the entire nervous system. The body feels waves of ecstasy and pleasure coursing through it. Supposedly it can even make people climax. I've never tried it. I prefer the real thing."

Timrekka shook away a blush and studied their aggrieved faces. "And now?"

"Well, the app's original design had limited settings, safeguards, so no one could overstimulate someone else. Even pleasure, if turned too high, will become pain. If *pain* is turned too high—"

"Torture." Timrekka understood. "He had you remove the safeguards."

Moybo nodded. "Not only remove it. Increase its capability." He blew stressed air through tight lips. "Whoever they touch will feel searing pain throughout their entire body. Every nerve will fire to its highest capability. It shouldn't kill them, but if my calculations are correct, they'll wish they were dead. They'll wish for it more than anything."

Minkel scrunched her eyebrows and then exhaled with a head slump. "I'm guessing they're for interrogations. Everything Abdabriel does supposedly has a reason. I don't think he'll just hurt people for the tickle of it." She shook her head and rubbed her eyes. "Anyways, where were we? Apps?"

As they turned to return to business as usual, some muffled yells caught Timrekka's attention. "What's that?"

"If it's anything like what it has been the last few days, you don't want to know," Minkel said as she arbitrarily leafed through items on a separate desk, refusing to acknowledge the sounds.

Timrekka walked over to the clear wall of the skydrop and peered down. Through the glass, he saw Abdabriel and his bodyguards outside on the grass. They were standing over a group of Whewlights on their knees before Abdabriel, who was addressing them, but Timrekka couldn't make out what he was saying.

"Is there any way to hear from up here?"

"Why do you want to?" Minkel asked. "Does watching people die tickle you?"

Timrekka shook his head while keeping his eyes on everyone below them. "No, I just don't want to lose myself in an illusion."

Moybo sighed and walked over next to Timrekka. He extended one hand outward, aiming it toward Abdabriel, about seventy feet away. He spread his fingers and rotated his hand. Timrekka jerked his head back as he heard Abdabriel's voice. It was being projected through Moybo's open mouth.

"How does —"

Minkel begrudgingly walked over to them. "It reads sounds up to one-hundred-feet away. Then the vocal chords are tricked into mimicking them. Did you know that our vocal chords can even mimic animals and machines? It's pretty coo—" Timrekka held a finger up, shushing her so he could listen.

"…was unfortunately necessary," Abdabriel said. Timrekka could hear some of the Whewlights weeping. "Now, I've told you all this already. I do not want to hurt anyof you." He sighed, frustrated and impatient. "So please, please just tell me where the rest of you are hiding so I can talk to them." More crying. "I can't invite them into the light when I can't even talk to them."

After more whimpering and noncompliance, Abdabriel shook his head and motioned for Greaper to step forward. The hollow-eyed man walked up to one of the women, who was clutching two children in her arms. She yelled, telling him to leave them alone, that she'd tear him apart if he touched her children. He ignored her and grabbed one of the kids, a boy, who looked to be about twelve. Both the mother and boy burst into tears as he was ripped from her. They reached for each other, yelling indistinct hysterics, but Abdabriel's soldiers held her in place. Timrekka's blood ran cold as he watched Greaper place his thumb on the son's forehead. Almost immediately, the boy convulsed, a contorted expression of inescapable anguish wrenching his face. Greaper held him in place, keeping his thumb on the boy's head. The eyeless assassin stared into the distance, cold and numb to what he was inflicting.

Abdabriel watched the mother. "This will continue until you tell me where they are, or your boy dies. Your choice. You're killing him."

"Stop!" she screamed. "Okay, okay, okay! I'll tell you!" Her blabbering pleas made the surrounding soldiers chuckle.

"What's that?" Abdabriel leaned in.

"I'll tell you!" the mother yelled as the other captors begged her not to.

After waiting a moment longer, Abdabriel motioned for Greaper to let the boy go. The child fell to the ground, convulsions still pulsing throughout his body. The mother crawled over and pulled him into her arms, slowly rocking him as he stared unresponsive into the sky.

Abdabriel stepped over to her and leaned down. He was willing to allow her to betray her people in confidence. It was too quiet for Timrekka to hear as she whimpered into Abdabriel's ear. Tears laced the last of her words before Abdabriel nodded and stepped back.

"See? That's all I wanted, and it could have been completely painless. Next time I ask for information, just tell—"

Fft. Fft. Two shots bounced off Ababriel's reflection suit, ricocheting away from the side of his head. The Whewlights, along with some of the soldiers, jumped back. Everyone looked around for the shooter.

Abdabriel chuckled and looked at the gathered Whewlights. "Is that why you were so easy to apprehend? An assassination attempt? You were the set up to get me into the open?" He shook his head, disappointed and heartbroken.

"No, I swear we didn't —"

Fft. Abdabriel silenced a pleading man by burning a hole through his forehead. He sighed and turned to his soldiers.

"Find who it was."

"We already have," a soldier said, pointing to more soldiers escorting someone their way.

Minkel, who'd been uninterested in the action down below, stepped over next to Timrekka, "Someone tried to kill him?"

Timrekka nodded. "Looks like a Whewlight soldier."

"Oh, god," Minkel sniveled, dreading another execution. She looked away, returning to her work. "I can't watch this."

Timrekka's face scrunched as he watched, listening to Abdabriel's voice projected through Moybo's mouth.

"I know you," Abdabriel said with surprised delight. "You're —" He tapped his chin, trying to think of the name as his soldiers forced the shooter before him. "I know I know this," he puzzled. "Oh! Dycitz. Rauphel Dycitz? That's it. Wow, you're *the* Rauphel Dycitz." He smiled at his soldiers and the Whewlights on the ground. The soldiers gave a blank expression as the name triggered no memory. Everyone kneeling before him was too emotional to share his exuberance, though they were intimately familiar with the stories surrounding Rauphel Dycitz. Abdabriel looked back and forth between the two groups. "Do any of you know who this is?"

Nobody answered as his soldiers threw Rauphel on the ground next to the others. He was a broad man with dark skin almost appearing red. A wiry beard was shaved down to a point, and his suit had random blood spatters. Abdabriel assumed Rauphel had left a red trail on his hunt for him.

"Traitor!" Rauphel stood with bloodshot eyes. "I kneel only before Lord Coyzle. I will kill you for what you've done to him."

Minkel returned to Timrekka's side and placed a hand on his shoulder as her heavy eyes looked down. "Oh, no, it *is* Rauphel Dycitz."

"Who is he?" Timrekka asked.

Minkel responded with despondent silence.

Abdabriel nodded at Rauphel. "I'm sure you *would* kill me, given the opportunity. Pretty sure your shot would have hit me directly between the eyes. I've heard you've never missed." He looked around. "Seriously? No one knows this man? He's a war hero. Acclaimed and praised for saving a group of, what was it, thirty? I think thirty Whewlight soldiers—using only his hands. His hand-to-hand skills are—" Abdabriel blew air through his lips. "He's someone I would *never* want to be on the wrong side of. If it wasn't for this suit, I'd be evacuating my bowels as we speak." He chuckled. "In fact, I remember Master Brawd mentioning him a few times, something about Rauphel being one of the only soldiers who was his better in combat. Saved his life a couple times." He turned to Rauphel. "I've admired you for a while now. I know I should be mad at you for, well, trying to kill me, but I can't help my excitement meeting you." Abdabriel composed himself and stood a little taller. "I'll ignore your attempt on my life if you'll sit down with me over some food so we can have a talk."

"You can go rape yourself," Rauphel spat at Abdabriel, his saliva thrown back from the reflection suit. Every soldier instantly raised their hands, aiming armed fingers at him.

"Whoa!" Abdabriel ushered them to lower their weapons. "Calm down. He's upset. Our entire mission is going to be met with a lot of opposition. Can't be too quick to execute *everyone*." He stared in admiration at the famed warrior glaring back at him. "I'll ask one more time out of respect for you. Not everyone gets repeat invitations, so consider yourself lucky. Though, I think I'm really the lucky one right now. *The* Rauphel Dycitz, I can't get over it." He smiled. "Now will you sit down with me and talk? That's all I'm asking."

"I would rather die," Rauphel stated with his head held high.

Abdabriel rolled his eyes. "Fine," he sighed and motioned for one of the two giant brothers to kill him. "Wait!" He waved his hands. "I can't. I can't just have you put down like an animal. It won't rest well with me." He clicked his tongue as an idea struck him. "I'll at least let you go out with honor." He looked around at his soldiers. "Rauphel Dycitz is a warrior we should hold high. If he wishes for death, he's earned it to be in combat. He deserves that. Do any of you want to fight him? No implants, mind you. Hand-to-hand only. And remember, he's skilled, so only step up if you are, too."

The soldiers looked at each other. Three hands went up. Abdabriel motioned for the volunteers to step forward. As they did, Rauphel studied them with burning eyes and a clenched jaw. They all looked gritty and experienced, but Rauphel didn't appear to care. He turned to Abdabriel.

"You betrayed your own people. You betrayed your lord, and I will not fight for your entertainment."

"Entertaining or not, you should fight if you want to live. But if you've been listening, I don't want you fighting at all right now." Abdabriel shrugged. "Seriously, I'll call them off if you calm down and talk with me. The meal will be my treat. I know a great restaurant near here that serves —"

"Stop being a coward," Rauphel growled. "Fight me yourself. Lead your army by example, Master N'kowsky."

"Eh, that would be over quickly," Abdabriel said, shaking his head. "I've heard what Master Brawd said about you. You kill with such effectiveness that the dead may as well have been shadowed without even jumping." He smiled at Rauphel in admiration. "Last chance. I'm begging you."

Rauphel glared back. He turned and accepted his fate, squaring off against the three soldiers circling him.

"This will not end well for any of you," he said with cool reserve. "Abandon this mutiny."

Abdabriel sighed, "All right. Enough." He sounded distraught, his eyes struggling to watch. "Get it over with."

The instant he gave permission, the soldiers charged Rauphel from different directions, eager to demonstrate their lethality to the Holy One. One dove for his legs, one went for an upper body tackle, and the third swung at his face.

Rauphel spun, kicking the diver's jaw, simultaneously moving out of the way of the tackler, and head butting the third man's fist. The first soldier clutched at his neck. Rauphel sprang into action as the second man regained his footing. The third retracted his hand, immediately sending his other fist. Rauphel caught it, spun it out of the way, and shoved his free palm up into the man's nose, smashing bone and cartilage into his brain, killing him instantly.

"Oh, wow, that fast! Blech!" Abdabriel winced as the man fell to the grass.

The second, smaller soldier caught Rauphel off guard with an elbow to the back of his head. Rauphel spun around, reacting in time to avoid the soldier's heel connecting to his face. He ducked, caught the foot, pivoted, and swept the soldier's planted foot. There was no time to finish him off as the third re-engaged. He grabbed Rauphel from behind, wrapping his arms around him. Rauphel reactively found one of the man's pinkies and snapped it backward, nearly ripping it out of the skin. The man screamed as Rauphel grabbed his arm and flipped him around. With two fluid movements, he slammed the screaming soldier to the ground and drove his heel into the other's throat. He immediately dropped to his knees, grabbed both sides of the yelping soldier's head, and snapped it around. The flowing tears immediately stopped.

It was only once the three soldiers went silent that Rauphel heard cheering from those watching. He ignored them and turned to Abdabriel.

"How many more of your soldiers do you want me to kill before you end this?" he asked, a little out of breath. "Just end it. We both know that's what's going to happen."

"That. Was. Impressive," Abdabriel said. "You have no idea how happy I am to have gotten to witness you in action with my own eyes." He smiled. "I'm still willing to talk with you. Maybe that exercise gave you a chance to simmer down?" Spit bounced off his suit before he finished his offer. He raised his eyebrows, offended. "Fine. I'm not wasting any more time on you. Greaper." He looked at the hollow-eyed man. "Make it quick."

Greaper stepped forward, his tall, slender body gliding like a spirit underwater. He walked into the middle of the crowd, facing Rauphel, seemingly staring at him with his sockets. He smiled as if he could see Rauphel's rage, as if he could appreciate it, savor it. Without rushing, he walked toward his prey and reached for Rauphel's face. Rauphel powerfully swatted the emaciated hand out of the way, spinning to snap Greaper's arm, but the eyeless man easily weaved out of the way and threw his other hand forward too quickly to stop. He collapsed Rauphel's trachea and immediately clasped his long, bony fingers around Rauphel's face. His wide palm smothered Rauphel's nose and mouth, cutting off his gasping. Rauphel spun, expertly swinging his hands, trying to chop Greaper's arm, snap an elbow, or at least push him back. Greaper gracefully moved his arm around, avoiding every hit, almost psychically. As Rauphel fought for breath, he grabbed Greaper's wrist and pulled, trying to accomplish the simple task of removing the suffocating hand from his face. Greaper grabbed his right arm and held it away as he waited, squeezing Rauphel's face harder. Muffled screams and gasps for air led to twitching limbs.

Abdabriel looked at his other bodyguards. "Kill the rest." He pointed at the Whewlights on the ground. He ignored the immediate begging pleas. "They tried to have me killed. They cannot be reasoned with. They cannot be saved." Abdabriel stared at the screaming children before turning to his soldiers. "We know where the other Whewlights are hiding. Bring them here. Hopefully they are more promising than these."

Rauphel finally stopped twitching as the slaughter began.

Timrekka looked away as he saw one of the bald brothers crush a man's head with a clap. He closed his eyes and put his hands over his ears as the cries grew louder.

"Stop, stop, stop, stop, stop, stop, stop!" he yelled, shaking his head and dropping down to a squat.

Moybo's hand fell to his side, and his mouth closed. "This is how it's been," he solemnly said as his normal voice returned.

"We should get back to work." Minkel barely managed to keep her composure as tears welled in her eyes. She took a few shaky breaths and then looked to Timrekka, who was still swaying on the ground. "What do you want us to do?" No response. "Timrekka!" she yelled, losing herself. "What do you want us to do?"

Timrekka looked from Moybo to Minkel and back again. He trembled, trying to make sense of anything. After some deliberation, he looked up to the skydrop bridge where Abdabriel had been standing.

"I want to put on my suit."

31

"Cooby!" Dumakleiza yelled into the darkness. "Cooby, come back to me!" She would have been unafraid of the creatures around them, but without Cooby, she felt vulnerable and alone. "Coobs!"

As Vorlak continued his fetal hysterics, Traveler tried to remain calm. "Everyone, turn your optics as bright as they can go." He looked around, finally catching glimpses of the incoming Fayded. The creeping, gangly figures crawling toward them made his breath falter. They looked like a swarm of insects, pale and unreachable with words. Amid the Daemoanik cries, he could hear soft whispering susurrating around them.

"They're everywhere." Lord Coyzle shook. "What do we do? What do we do?"

"They look weak," Izzy observed, trying to keep his cool. "And if what Shadowmaker said was true, about them being more animal than human, they're going to go for our throats. It's instinct. Protect your throats."

Duma shook her head. "I have bared witness to beasts devouring bellies while the prey lives."

Gideon hurried over to Vorlak and grabbed under his armpits. "Come on, Vorlak, you've gotta get up." He hoisted, but the Daemoanik was too heavy. "We're going to die if we don't protect ourselves. Get up." It was no use. Vorlak was lost in madness. Gideon let go and looked around at the swarming Fayded, now only about thirty feet away on every side. "Screw it." He shook his head, wondering why he'd allowed his true nature to get lost in the collective fear. "Spaceman, hold my backpack." He tossed his bag to Traveler and turned to the extinguished fire.

"Gideon, no!" Traveler yelled. "Don't do this. We've got to stick together."

"They're here for food," Gideon said, focused on his task as he walked over to the ashes. "My mama always told me that aggressive personalities are usually just empty bellies." He grabbed a gator leg and one of the tail halves. With both in tow, he turned and headed toward the nearest Fayded. He assumed they had animalistic instincts, reactive to energies, so he smiled and moved briskly, hoping he'd come off as nonthreatening.

"Sir Gideon," Dumakleiza sharply whispered.

Gideon stopped a few feet shy, squatting down and extending the meat for them to approach on their own terms. He knew he had their attention. Even those on the other side of his group were watching. Large, glassy eyes stared, flashing up and down between Gideon and the food. Their ears perked up with tilted heads, and their noses were abuzz, sniffing as they picked up the savory scents. Gideon was accustomed to seeing people well-fed and filled out, but it made sense seeing scrawny limbs and sucked in cheeks on the Fayded. They were more of an indigenous herd than community, so food was likely scarce. He admitted they looked nightmarish, but that was just appearance. Their eerie whispering loudened as they discussed what to do.

"It's okay," Gideon said with a smile. "Don't be scared." He spoke slow and quiet. Even his tone needed to be nonthreatening. He couldn't stop his throat from tightening as one of the Fayded scurried toward him, its arms and legs moving over the ground almost silently while keeping its hungry eyes on him. Gideon's pulse quickened, the hair on his neck stiffening, but he maintained his smile. It was a male. Gideon couldn't distinguish their genders from a distance, but as the male approached, it comforted Gideon to see the protective nature of what he guessed might be an alpha.

Traveler's jaw was flexed so tight that his teeth hurt. "Come on, Gideon."

"He's insane," Lord Coyzle whispered with wide eyes. "Completely insane."

"Yes, he is, but he just might be able to pull this off." Traveler pleaded with fate, hope, and to any deity watching through Horror Planet's clouds.

Gideon extended the meat a little farther, trying to bridge the remaining foot between the male and himself. "It's okay, bat man. Come take it. It's yummy." He smiled bigger, watching the Fayded's curious nose twitch. Its placid eyes were unnerving—haunting even, but its mannerisms suggested nothing more than hunger. It whispered something and then lurched forward, snatching the cooked chunk of tail from Gideon's hand. Gideon jumped at the speed of its bony movements but grinned once he realized what it was doing. It scampered back to the other Fayded, whispering something to each other. Gideon watched as they tore it apart and devoured the gator. The indigenous on the other side were whispering louder. They weren't patient in their need for feedback, and their jealous bellies were growling.

After the gator tail was eaten all the way down to the bone, some of the bone included, the fed Fayded began hooting. But even their celebrating was quiet, hushed, as if withheld. It made the hair on the visitors' necks stand. They didn't want to undermine what little rapport Gideon had made with the natives, but the Fayded's delight sounded hesitant, as if there was something they didn't want to hear them.

Gideon slowly looked back at his group. "What are you guys waiting for? Offer them the rest."

Dumakleiza stood guard while the others obeyed, curious why they hadn't started as soon as they'd seen it working. Dumakleiza refused to lower her weapons, just in case. Izzy and Traveler turned to grab chunks of meat. Lord Coyzle exhaled compounding nerves and grabbed some, too. They squatted down in a circle around the doused fire, facing outward. They extended their hands, offering the gator, waiting, hoping, doubting.

More male Fayded crawled over on all fours and accepted the food. They returned it to the herd, offering it to the females to eat with them. Gideon thought of them like hairless monkeys, wrinkled and deformed. On the faces of those closest, he recognized primitive expressions of fright, inquisitiveness, and hunger. He hoped that offering food would create enough of a bond to spare their lives.

Once all the gator had been devoured, the entire herd closed in, crawling toward the group with raised expectation. They whispered atthem instead of to each other, presumably demanding more.

Gideon slowly walked backward, returning to the group as he shook his head. "That's all we've got." He knew they didn't understand him, but he figured it was like talking to a dog. Maybe they'd at least understand his intent or be able to read his vocal inflections. "No more food. We have no more food." Still, the Fayded continued crawling toward them, whispering, sniffing.

The visitors scooted backward until they reached each other. They stared at the encroaching Fayded, who were within reaching distance on all sides. The whispering grew louder, and faces expressed unsatisfied appetites. They'd had a taste, but there hadn't been enough to go around. One of them sniffed and poked Vorlak, still trembling on the ground. His crying instantly stopped at bony fingers prodding him.

"Don't touch me!" he roared, lashing upward without looking. His claws caught one Fayded's face and another's shoulder, his raging strength sending them yelping through the air. They screamed like vultures, crashing into others and falling to the ground. Vorlak was up and swinging wildly as fear blinded him. Shadowmaker was hunting him. Nowhere was safe.

"Vorlak! Stop!" Gideon's cry was too late.

The Fayded broke into a frantic frenzy, scrambling with violent desperation. Their whispers erupted into shrill screams as they bound around, galloping and clawing at everything, including each other. Those closest to Gideon and the others attacked, climbing over the visitors' bodies like insects, biting, growling, and scratching. Gideon and Traveler fell to the ground first as numbers blanketed them.

Vorlak tore through bodies with hysteric rage. Clawed hand after clawed hand ripped the Fayded apart, easily tossing them away. He recklessly roared and ran. Many of the Fayded reacted defensively, trying to tackle him and bite his skin.

"Don't touch me!" he screamed, his monstrous voice breaking.

Gideon didn't want to fight the Fayded. He didn't want to undermine what little connection he'd established, but they were tearing into him. Their fingernails were jagged and sharp, swarming over his skin like hornets. He cried out in pain as he felt chomping teeth all over his body. He was stronger than they were, but there were too many for it to matter. A sharp gash tore across his face. All he could see from underneath the frenzy were glimpses of flashing sky, illuminating twisted faces. The shrill screeches and whispers drowned out the cries of his friends.

Traveler struggled to block all the mouths and hands lusting to open his throat. He kept aiming his fingers and moving his thumb to trigger the laser implant, but nothing happened. In the midst of terror, he couldn't help reacting with dead weapons. Savagery was his only option as primal instinct kicked in. Every impact hurt, but the effectiveness outweighed the pain. He couldn't fend them off well enough to get to his feet.

Izzy and Lord Coyzle were next to each other in a full-fledged panic. The pale beasts clawed at Lord Coyzle's stomach, trying to disembowel him. He yelped in terror, struggling backwards, pushing against the dirt, trying to escape. All that mattered was surviving.

With swift and precise swings of her gator teeth, Dumakleiza opened four arteries and leapt to her feet. There was a moment of regret for defending herself so viciously against people who were simply spooked, but she had to survive if she wanted to see her Cooby again. She couldn't die without him on her back, fighting alongside her. If one of them was to die, they were both dying together. Tears welled in her eyes as she cut deep gashes into two, three, four, five Fayded. She managed to catch glimpses of what was happening around her. She saw endless Fayded in every direction, all lost in a herd-wide frenzy. They'd flooded the canyon. Her enhanced dragon eye could only see Vorlak running through them. Everyone else was buried beneath teeming waves of pale bodies.

"Cooby!" she wept out to the darkness. Her breaking heart wanted to protect Sir Gideon, as well, but her focus was shattered. She opened a jugular while simultaneously severing the tendons behind a knee. She'd been robbed of her tanion, and she was losing faith in ever finding him. Her head perked up. Faith. She needed more faith. Of course!

"Grim!" she yelled out boldly, shouting over the maelstrom of bodies. "My god! My lord! Your servant Dumakleiza of the family Yagūl needs you now!" She ducked and opened a stomach, spilling innards into the dirt. "Grim, I plead with you! I plead with you! Send your winged warriors of mighty strength to aid us in our time of dire need! I *beg* you! Unite me with my Coobs once more!"

Vorlak ran directionless. Enough Fayded witnessed his strength and lethality for those in his path to move. They scattered from him, scurrying away on all fours, diving into holes that led underground or climbing up trees. Vorlak was done screaming, entering blind survival. He was unaware of every Fayded he'd torn through. Every impact of flesh and bone felt like a bar on the cage that locked him in with Shadowmaker. Heavy breathing led frantic feet until Vorlak tripped. Something large obstructed his path, sending him forward, tumbling to a stop in the dirt. He jumped to his feet and spun around, ready to attack whatever had gotten in his way.

"I said don't touch m—" He stopped. Amid his fear, Vorlak was puzzled by what he saw at his feet. Even with the sea of whispers and screams around him in the canyon, he stared, confused. At first all he saw were bones. Human bones. But then he looked closer. Bones didn't make sense. He knew bones to be hard and coarse and whatever had tripped him had felt soft and squishy. He reached out and touched it. Human bones were balled up, encased in a dark brown, spongy substance. He pulled up his hand and smelled the brown slime that had smudged off. He brought his nose back, intrigued. The rancid aroma reminded him of stomach bile, another smell he was intimately familiar with. He took a step back and looked at the full object he'd fallen over. It was about eight feet long and three feet thick. His eyes slowly widened as he realized exactly what it was. Gooey brown bile, black hair, protruding bones, and branches made up the thickly bunched glop. Vorlak stepped back from it, his fear shifting and aiming toward the dark sky. The regurgitated pellet was larger than his entire body, which meant one thing.

Flash! The lightning was no different than every other burst, but this time Vorlak was looking for something specific. The brief glimpse of bright light made his calloused heart stop. Darkness had already resumed, but the flash left an image frozen in his mind. Perched on the cliff overlooking the canyon had been a massive silhouette of a creature—an enormous owl. He hadn't been able to make out its details, but it stood twice as tall as the trees it was perched next to. The residually flashing image exposed a gigantic, round head with sunken eyes. They were too dark to see, but it had been facing down, watching them. Vorlak growled, preparing to attack it if it flew down at him. He hadn't been afraid of the large reptiles in the marsh, but from how it looked from a distance, the perched beast looked to dwarf the gators. The mad Daemoanik refused to show any fear to the looming predator as he bared his fangs to the darkness.

Flash! Lightning illuminated the canyon again. Vorlak lurched back. The silhouette was gone. He looked around, but he couldn't see anything in the blackness. He could barely see the nearest Fayded, let alone anything far above. He knew what was hunting them. He recalled his own people's history. The Daemoaniks had studied every predator they could to best equip themselves for invasions, and he knew the silence with which owls snatched their prey. His pulse raced as the cries of every human around him went silent in his ears. He was listening for something specific, something no one else knew was coming. He squatted down next to the pellet to hide himself visibly and aromatically. He closed his eyes and slowed his breathing, focusing only on his ears.

A sudden rush of wind dipped down and returned to the sky. Vorlak's eyes shot open. He was the only one focused enough to distinguish the cry of the Fayded being ripped away into the sky. He leapt to his feet and looked up. He couldn't see it anywhere. The stealthy silence of the owl was impressive with its size. It made him wonder how many of them it took before he'd noticed it. He thought quickly and then turned. The crazy man would know what to do. He rushed toward where his travel companions were buried, running into the thick of it, and plowing through Fayded.

Dumakleiza was still the only one on her feet. Thick blood was sprayed over her entire body and flinging through the air with every swing of her weapons. The monotonous strikes against jugulars and specific kill spots were becoming tedious. Her body ached. She'd never had to fight more than a handful of invading men on the island of Yagūl, and it never lasted long. Even worse, she hadn't had to fight without her Cooby for as far back as her memory went. Battling an entire herd of agitated Fayded was too much. There wasn't enough energy or rage to keep her going much longer. Her primary goal was to make it to Sir Gideon and protect him, but she was having enough trouble staying standing where she was.

Gideon, too, was exhausted. Unlike Dumakleiza, his weariness was taking a violent toll. Claw marks scratched across his face and neck, most of which were bleeding. His body felt like it had been whipped through a glass hurricane, cuts and sores stinging, exposed in the night air. His energy was depleted, leaving nothing but flailing hands without any strength behind them.

"Crazy man!" Vorlak roared as he effortlessly tossed some of the Fayded aside. He grabbed Gideon's arms. All Gideon sensed was a blurred haze of screams and pain. Vorlak shook him. "Crazy man! Owl! There is an owl!"

Gideon's eyes rolled around in his skull, teetering on delirium. It took a moment for Vorlak's presence to register. The Daemoanik continued shaking Gideon, and the roughly jolted motions weren't helping.

"Vorlak. What are you —"

Flash! Lightning shot Gideon's eyes open. The sight of an elephant-sized owl sobered up his disorientation in an instant. The lightning flashed just in time to expose the giant bird swooping down above them. Its feet were extended and open, sharp talons larger than Gideon's legs reaching for its target. He'd barely caught enough of a glimpse to see much more before it silently wrapped its talons around a Fayded woman's entire torso. Only the top half of her face and the bottoms of her feet were visible. Before she realized what was happening, she had been ripped up into the sky, her screams lost to the darkness.

This time, everyone saw the bird. For one split second, the entire canyon went silent. It took a moment to process the creature hunting them. Then, in an ear shattering panic, the mass hysteria exploded. This time the Fayded scattered, jumping off the invading humans. Their screams grew louder as they recognized the beast. Gideon and the others watched as the indigenous ran, screams ricocheting off the canyon walls as they sought shelter from the giant owl.

Dumakleiza looked up, realizing she was the only one who could still see it. "Oh, Grim, this is not what I meant by winged warriors." Her eyes widened as she saw the owl swallowing the Fayded woman whole, midair. She'd seen owls before, but never one that would eat mid-flight and then return for more. It would take many bodies to satiate the aerial denizen. Without savoring its kill, the owl spun in the sky and aimed its gargantuan body back down toward the ground.

Dumakleiza bellowed, "Run!" Her instruction was loud and clear. She sprinted to Gideon and Vorlak. With swift and adamant motions, she grabbed Gideon's arm and ran, following the closest Fayded wherever they were going. She trusted their knowledge of the canyon. Gideon stumbled behind her, his legs giving out. Dumakleiza didn't care as she dragged him as fast as she could. "We must follow the instructions given by the Maker of Shadows!" As they ran after the pale people galloping, Dumakleiza saw that they were headed toward one of the canyon walls. She could see holes in the rock face that the Fayded were crawling into. As they continued disappearing into underground tunnels, Dumakleiza glanced over her shoulder. The owl was closing in. "Run!"

The others were close behind, moving as fast as they could while frantically glancing back. They couldn't see anything in the black skies, and their panic-stricken hearts were beating out of their chests.

Whoosh! Just before they reached the canyon wall, what felt like four powerful arms wrapped around Dumakleiza's entire body, squeezing so hard that she immediately felt her ribs compress. The impact of the embrace knocked the wind out of her, instantly ripping her off her feet. It was so jarring that she couldn't think. Whiplash tore at her neck, and cold wind hit her face. She faintly heard the sounds of claws galloping up the canyon wall as she was carried upward. She saw Vorlak leap off the rock toward her. The sight of him sinking his fangs into one of the owl's talons was a blur. The loud screech of the owl, devastating, deep, and hollow, rang in her ears like a distant dream. Suddenly she was free-falling. She slipped in and out of consciousness, blinking heavily as she felt a heavy impact and passed out.

As Vorlak dragged Dumakleiza by her ankle, he roared, "Into the caves!"

32

Once the captured Whewlights were executed and their bodies done away with, Abdabriel sent a team of his soldiers to find and retrieve those still in hiding. Maybe those Whewlights could be saved from their blindness.

Abdabriel retired to the City of Light's capital skydrop. It was more than twice the size of the others, standing out in its magnificence and architectural accomplishment. Gaudy beauty and grandeur decoratively designed accents about its exterior, but the splendor was dull to Abdabriel. He walked under the looming giant that normally inspired hope and pride in the Whewlight people, hanging his head in exhaustion. He wasn't even in the mood for a rejuvenating light jump around Whewliss to get his head on straight. Normally that would be the exact prescription for such sluggish ailment, but the old Whewlight saying was true: "Light heals the body, not the mind."

He felt the need to wallow in his frustration with the Whewlight population. Many of them had submitted to his rule but those who tried his patience with ignorant naivety, pleading for their lives when they could be joining him, dampened his spirit. He honestly didn't know why so many couldn't see the logic in his vision. Why were their eyes so stubbornly closed? He needed to collect his thoughts and meditate. Dwelling on frustrations forced solutions to surface. He normally worked well under pressure, but the pressure was breaking him. He instructed his four bodyguards to wait outside. They were to prevent anyone from disturbing him while he took time to reflect. He walked under the capital's shadow and vanished.

Inside, he walked through lavish hallways decorated with paintings and vast technologies available for his convenience. Beautiful plants and patterned walls came off as dismal. Soothing scents of indigenous flowers from aromatherapy machines in every room he walked past smelled rotten. Every profligate luxury in the capital was lost on him as he puzzled over bland solutions. He'd spent the better part of his life as an ambassador, talking to peoples of every nationality of every world. Kings, lords, presidents, monarchs, nobles, aristocrats, chiefs, and leaders of every kind had peacefully and happilyagreed to his terms in times past. He'd always had an easy time swaying them when discussing LOLA. His vision for an even brighter future should be met with even more enthusiasm. It should be embraced with open arms, warring worlds graciously thanking him for ending their bloodshed. It didn't make sense.

Abdabriel sighed and walked through the skydrop, ready to sit and think in Lord Coyzle's office. It was his office now. He walked up the final staircase to the grand chamber and paused. The room was at the top of the sphere, overlooking the other skydrops in the City of Light. The rounded glass ceiling was kept in pristine condition, regularly maintained to create the illusion of being outdoors while also feeling safely enclosed. Its entire floor was a digital mural, constantly transitioning through images of iconic historical Whewlight figures and moments. It was all meant to inspire whoever was in the office, reminding them that others had paved their path before them. Aside from the one desk made of swirling silver and glass, there was a large chair where Lord Coyzle would sit, a smaller chair for visitors, a couple cabinets, and bookshelves filled with Whewlight laws, histories of Whewliss and other planets, interstellar knowledge, and some of Lord Coyzle's favorite literature. Additionally, the only decoration was a digitally projected poster of the originally signed LOLA.

Abdabriel was puzzled as he stared into the room. Nothing was out of the ordinary. However, sitting in the smaller chair, facing away from him, was a cloaked figure. The stranger didn't turn as Abdabriel entered the room with intentionally loud footsteps. The lack of reaction intrigued him further.

"Who are you?"

"A student," the mysterious man responded without moving.

Abdabriel squinted at the back of the stranger's head as he walked around, still keeping his distance. "A student?" He couldn't help a weird unease in his gut. "A student of what?"

"Everything." The stranger's calm responses were instant, as if he knew what Abdabriel was going to say before he said it.

"Okay." Abdabriel was thrown off from his charismatic confidence, and he knew it. He cleared his throat and straightened his posture. His plaguing frustrations were momentarily put aside as he studied the man in the chair. The man didn't say anything while Abdabriel took time to compose his thoughts. He was clearly waiting for Abdabriel to steer the conversation. That was something Abdabriel could do.

"Are you here to kill me?" Abdabriel had confidence in his ability to survive any assault, but knowing intent was imperative.

"I'm here to talk with you," the hooded stranger said. Abdabriel took a second to study him before responding. The man sat in the smaller chair, not assuming any arrogance by taking Abdabriel's seat. That was a good sign. It indicated submission. Abdabriel liked that.

"Who are you?" Abdabriel asked as he walked a wide angle to his chair, cautiously keeping his distance. He had to see the man's face.

"A student," the cloaked figure repeated himself.

Abdabriel finally reached his chair, stumbling a little as he kept his eyes glued to the stranger. He finally saw the face beneath the hood. The man didn't look threatening, though there was an undeniable intensity in his hazel eyes. He looked to be of average size. His hands were each placed palms down on his knees, and once Abdabriel sat, the man looked directly at him without any emotional shift. Abdabriel smiled with narrowing eyes.

"I think you're here to kill me," he said, exaggerating his relaxing lean back in the chair. "You appear as an assassin, though I can't place your home world. Where are you from?"

The man didn't blink as he stared back, clearly waiting for Abdabriel to ask a more pertinent question. Abdabriel felt a flare of irritation but suppressed it, choosing rather to play the stranger's game. He leaned forward, trying to match calmness as he smiled again.

"Just in case I'm right, I feel I should warn you, you'll fail. My suit is—"

"Impressive," the stranger finished for him with a flare of curiosity. "Unlike any defensive measure I've seen before." The compliment made Abdabriel smile sincerely as the stranger went on. "Not impervious though."

Abdabriel's smile died. "How is it not?"

"I do not yet know," the stranger responded, his eyes unwavering and unblinking. "Deflecting physical force is impressive but only truly keeps you safe from the mindless. It is merely a puzzle to a tactician. However, I am not here to kill you. I am here to talk with you. I am a student. I have told you three times now."

Abdabriel was intrigued by the stranger's ambiguity. He'd been to nearly every world and was knowledgeable about each planet's people, but for the life of him, he couldn't place the hooded man.

"Okay." He nodded, surrendering to the mystery. "I give up. Let's talk." He chuckled, releasing some pent-up stress. "I apologize for my hesitance. I've just been dealing with closed-minded people for a while and meeting someone willing to have a civil conversation is a refreshing surprise." He sighed, shaking the rest of his nerves free. "Anyways, anyways, anyways. For starters, how on Whewliss did you get in here without alarming any of my soldiers or drones?"

"I hear you are attempting a takeover of inhabited worlds."

Abdabriel subtly cocked his head to the side. "I prefer the truth of bringing peace to all inhabited worlds. Whom did you hear this from?"

"Your Lord Coyzle," the stranger stated as simple fact.

Abdabriel's expression disappeared. "What?" He blinked a couple of times. "On the Wall?" The cloaked man didn't respond. He had Abdabriel's full attention. "Are you from the Wall?" He leaned in as his pulse sped up and gooseflesh spread over his body. "Are you from the fourth phase?" He sounded terrified and excited.

The hooded stranger's eyebrow twitched, showing an elusive flicker of interest. "The fourth phase? I'm not familiar with this place. What is it?"

Abdabriel squinted narrower and nodded. "What's your name?"

The stranger paused. "I've come a long way to hear about your plan. Tell me what it is."

Abdabriel smiled. "Oh, no, you don't get to remain clandestine while expecting me to divulge my plans. It doesn't work like that. You've got to give to receive." He offered his signature wink.

The stranger didn't falter as he asked, "Is it because of your daughters' deaths?"

Abdabriel swallowed a wave of pain. "I would like to know how you learned of that. Was that also Lord Coyzle?" Abdabriel shook his head, closing his eyes. "Yes." He gulped some nerves and focused. "I had seen warring worlds long before that. For years I wanted to do something about it. For decades and decades, I pitched viable solutions to Lord Coyzle, and he always turned them down. He clung to his cowardice disguised as 'leaving other worlds to their own fates.' I obeyed, keeping my vision to myself, focusing, rather, on my ambassadorial duties." He cleared his throat and took a sip of water from a glass on the desk. His eyes darkened. "It wasn't until Pylillis and Faydreigh's deaths that I realized I must do something myself." He looked up. "They were the final addition of tears into a raging ocean of mourning."

"I see," the hooded man said. "I assume thatversion of their eulogy renders understanding when you tell it."

The comment instantly offended Abdabriel. "What are you insinuating?"

"I insinuate nothing. I am impressed with the circumstantial narrative you've so delicately weaved." The stranger's tone had no aggression or hostility, though his words carried much of both.

"If I were you, I would choose my next words very caref—"

"Pylillis was the daughter you never wanted, dashing your dreams of the son you always wished her to be," the stranger said. His comment silenced Abdabriel just long enough to finish. "Strange to me that you would cling to such resentment toward a child when you possess the technology to have another child and decide the gender. Pylillis never had any interest in being one of Whewliss's observers. My research tells me she wanted to be a musician. In fact, she had social anxiety, so observing would have been an unrealistic occupation for her. One day you saw an opportunity, and as the opportunist that you are, seized it. You, her own father, grabbed her unsuspecting arm and launched her to a warring world, sending her into the most dangerous part of the fighting. You expected she'd be killed and that it would weave the beginning of a web of lies you could build off. With that, you could manipulate the emotions of those you wished to understand your motive. Pain and death unite humanity, so their sympathies would bridge misunderstandings and help you attain control over inhabited worlds. I assume you intend to use an even more embellished version of the story when you address each planet. It would certainly help your cause."

Abdabriel was dumbfounded. A maelstrom of rage, hatred, exposed fear, and vulnerability was expressed through sudden sweat. His suit reactively cooled as he furrowed his brows.

"I lovedmy daughter. Istill do. How dare y—"

"Drop the charade. You know the truth. I know the truth. I have no need for proof or exposure of any of this. I know what you are, and that's all that matters in this moment."

Abdabriel had had enough. Without warning, he lifted his hand as fast as he could. *Fft.Fft.* He double took as he saw his shots burning holes in the wall behind the stranger. His eyes had barely processed how quickly the hooded man had moved his head out of the way. They were inhuman reflexes.

The man's expression barely shifted. "I wouldn't recommend destroying your office in a futile attempt to kill me."

Abdabriel gulped and glared at the man whose patience was beginning to terrify him. "I just sent out a distress call to my bodyguards. This conversation is over."

"No, it's not," the man said just as patiently as he had the entire discussion. "Your distress call never made it, and they can't get into the skydrop." He waited while Abdabriel digested the news. "As I've told you enough times for a simpleton to understand, I am not here to kill you. I am a student. I'm here to talk with you and learn about your plan."

"Who are you?" Abdabriel begged as anger-fueled tears welled in his eyes. "Are you just here to insult me? To threaten me? Because you will regret that. If you say one more thing about my daughters, I swear I will—"

"Actions are the only indication of intent that I believe," the man said. "Threats are whispers in the wind that even a child can muster."

"Then what do you — "

"I believe you loved your other daughter, Faydreigh. She was the favorite." The hooded stranger's words struck a chord in Abdabriel. "Her portion of the story is true. You hadn't counted on her emotional attachment to Pylillis taking such a toll, so when the news of Pylillis's tragic and untimely death triggered Faydreigh to take her own life, you truly were motivated."

After stunned silence, Abdabriel stammered, "H — h — how do you know any of this?" He was exposed like a bleeding nerve, and it was taking everything within him to not break. Rage was his greatest crutch. "How do you know this?"

"I am a demander of truth. Anyone who wishes to know the truth need only look for it. Most will settle for what they're told. Doing one's own research is a lost art, and you, Abdabriel N'kowsky, were good at covering up your hatred of Pylillis with your weaved narrative. I must compliment the difficulty you provided in my hunt for the truth. However, deleted security footage from your drones and erased files are still capable of being dug up." He allowed Abdabriel to consider a response, but silence was all that fell between them. "I understand the inconsolable father motive, even if it is only for one of two dead daughters. May I have that glass of water?"

"Uh." Abdabriel almost missed the request as he blankly stared at the man who knew his most intimate secrets. He twitched and wiped a tear from his eye before numbly reaching forward and sliding the glass of water across the desk. He watched with wide, blinking eyes as the man took a small sip and then placed the glass down.

"Thank you," the stranger said. "I admire your plan. That is, if I understand it correctly." He watched as Abdabriel's frantic eyes struggled to focus. "I agree more than you probably think I do at this point. I have seen more wars and death than you, and I agree that a strong hand should dictate humanity's fate, as people simply cannot govern themselves. The cost of millions of lives to save billions is inarguably logical. The potential cost of billions to save trillions, even more so. I would go as far as to say that killing the majority, if need be, would even be a worthwhile sacrifice for a peaceful existence of the minimal survivors. Even if one percent of all people were all that remained after you purge the stars, that would be enough to begin a new era of peace, where every child would be raised under your rule. They could then be instructed and guided in your light, eventually repopulating the universe without the staining scourge of war. Future generations would look back, grateful to you for the sacrifice you gave for their sake."

Abdabriel couldn't stop nodding as the stranger unexpectedly spoke the vision he wished more could understand. "Exactly." He was confused by the hooded man's juxtaposed conversational dynamics, but if the ultimate goal was to side with him, he'd recover. "Finally, someone who understands. You are the first person to so clearly see the light on this world, and I can't tell you how invigorating it is to have—"

"Unfortunate," the stranger said.

"What? Wait." Abdabriel blinked, even more confused. "What?"

"That approach doesn't always work," the man said. "But more often than not, it does. If I am speaking with someone flirting with lunacy, I can often regurgitate their plan back at them with exaggerated absurdity. They will then, in turn, hear how foolish their own idea sounds when coming from someone else." The man's tone didn't fluctuate. "You're not flirting with lunacy. It's already seduced you, and now you are a slave to its will. Your greatest illusion is believing the roles are the other way around."

"But I—" Abdabriel wasn't sure what to say. His regularly smooth confidence was lodged in his throat.

"You have expired, Abdabriel N'kowsky. Since the discovery of light travel, the purpose of an individual life has shifted. We are no longer driven by the desire to make ourselves matter within a natural lifetime. We have lost the appreciation of the pursuit of happiness, of a career, of love. We still experience those desires, but they fade as we live beyond the time we were intended to. On a grander scale, those purposes are lost."

"And," Abdabriel quietly spoke as he stared helplessly at the stranger, "what should our purpose be now?"

"I do not know," the stranger said. "I am in constant pursuit of the answer to that question. It eludes me. However, I believe that anyone who reaches a point where they claim to have all the answers and then condemn those who oppose them—" The stranger paused and leaned a little closer, making Abdabriel retreat back in his chair. "They are expired and more lost than those they wish to lead. No matter how long we live, if we have the arrogance to think we've transcended beyond others into godhood, death will come for us, and no speed of light can save us from it." He stared deep into Abdabriel's shattered self. "That is no threat. That is chaos inevitably returning to order."

It took a while for Abdabriel to be able to say anything. Every considered response felt like a trap that would ensnare and maim him. He was normally the sharp-witted one, silencing anyone who opposed him with a silver tongue, but the hooded stranger had become his greatest fear in the manner of minutes. He tried to swallow, but his mouth was dry.

"I—" He was afraid to say what he wanted to say. "I just want you to go away." He mumbled, immediately feeling ashamed, pathetic, and childish. He slumped, realizing how uncharacteristic his wish had sounded.

The stranger nodded. "That is the first honesty you've shared with me. The one thing your impervious suit cannot repel is the truth." With that, he stood to his feet, keeping his hood over his head. "Thank you for speaking with me. I enjoyed learning about who you truly are." The cloaked man turned and started toward the staircase leading down from the office. "Your bodyguards have been trying to contact you for a few minutes now but not out of concern for your safety." His peculiar comment made Abdabriel's eyebrows shakily rise.

"W—what?"

"I'm assuming they want to tell you that your soldiers did not find the Whewlights hiding from you. They might even want to inform you that those soldiers are dead. I wouldn't waste your time looking for the Whewlights. They are safe, and you will not find them." He walked down the stairs and out of sight.

Abdabriel blinked in disbelief. The instant the hooded stranger was gone, he heard footsteps running through the skydrop. They grew louder until Mosh Elle, his monstrous, female bodyguard burst up the staircase and into the office.

"Holy One!" she yelled. "The soldiers you sent to find the hiding Whewlights are—"

"Dead," Abdabriel muttered, staring through her. His correct assumption stumped her. Abdabriel asked a question he already knew the answer to. "Where did the cloaked assassin go?"

"What? What man?" Mosh Elle looked around. All she saw were the two burning holes in the glass from Abdabriel's missed shots. "What man?"

33

Inside the canyon cave, it felt as though days had passed, but there was no way to know. Nobody even knew what Fayde's rotation or orbit was, so waiting for "a day" was a waste. Additionally, the marginal difference in visibility between Fayde's day and night was difficult to notice. It all felt like darkness. Every so often, loud hooting would echo through the canyon, vibrating the walls. The enormous owl's hoots were laden with bass and a guttural snarl. Everyone's home worlds had their own version of owls, but none compared to the leviathan waiting for them out in the night. It remained above, ever watchful for someone to wander out.

The cave was spacious for being dug out. There was no way to know if the Fayded had used their hands or tools to create homes in the rock or if some other creature had created the tunnels prior. There wasn't enough room to stand, something that was befitting of the quadrupedal indigenous, but made it difficult for the bipedal aliens. Sitting or crawling were the only options. However, the inner width of the canals and tunnels allowed for more movement. Most of the Fayded had disappeared into passageways leading farther into the canyon wall, but a few remained behind to ensure that the intruders wouldn't venture too far into their homes.

With the violent frenzy lingering only in the minds of the advanced humans, the Fayded had returned to their innocuous and quizzical natures. Curious approaches periodically brought them face-to-face before the Fayded would whisper and scamper off. They were even more difficult to see without lightning or the little glow breaking through stormy clouds, but everyone's eyes had adjusted to the darkness as much as they were going to.

Dumakleiza was in the worst condition. She was lying on the ground, wheezing for breath with her head limp on Gideon's lap. The owl's grip had crushed her ribcage and likely hemorrhaged organs. She hadn't been able to mutter more than a few sentences, and even those were incoherent. She'd called out for Cooby more than once, struggling to remember anything in her delirium.

Even with his plethora of scratches and gouges, Gideon hadn't left her side. He was in more pain than he would admit, but he was far better off than Duma. Just the pressure of his back against the rock irritated the fingernail gashes from the Fayded. Gideon had removed a vile of African violet oil from his bag and applied it under Dumakleiza's nose. The aroma soothed her aching body by relaxing her mind. Gideon clung to a sliver of hope, but it was waning.

Traveler, Lord Coyzle, and Izzy shared the same injuries. Their entire bodies stung, making it impossible to get comfortable or relax. Most of their wounds had stopped bleeding, but the more serious cuts and gashes were still leaking. There was no healing light and no medicinal implants to aid them. Traveler and Izzy passed out several times. Exhaustion was relentless. But as soon as any comfort swooped in, shooting pains or resonating hoots from the monster owl roused them back into the waking darkness.

Vorlak spent hours patrolling on all fours, growling at the Fayded, keeping them away with foul threats of disembowelment. There had been no physical contact since entering the cave, and he made sure it stayed that way. He didn't have any injuries, and his fear of Shadowmaker and the owl had kept him jumpy. However, as time in the darkness dragged on and on, he finally succumbed. The Daemoanik warrior curled up on the rock floor, loud snores pouring out of him as he slept.

Lord Coyzle stubbornly fought sleep, though his eyelids were heavier than they'd ever been. He wanted to remain alert and on the lookout. The Fayded were near, the owl lurked outside, and who knew what other unknown creatures could smell their bleeding bodies. Lord Coyzle was avoiding the discussion of how long they probably had. He was dying for the taste of water or the relief of food. The desperation that Shadow-maker had told them the Fayded resorted to in times of hunger was beginning to make sense.

Conversations rose and fell as everyone accepted their fate in their own way. The thought of Shadowmaker showing up was beginning to feel comical in its impossibility. Even if he did arrive, would he help them? Could he? They had nothing "real" to offer him. The prospect of him executing all of them began to sound like mercy. It would be better than the slow deaths they were decaying toward.

"My lord," Traveler said with a cough.

Lord Coyzle slowly turned to face him, wincing from cuts in his neck. "Yes, Four Zero?"

"You should...get some sleep," Traveler said.

Lord Coyzle groaned as he shook his throbbing head. "I can't." He closed his eyes, gasping for air as he spoke. "I've not slept since...I was a child."

Gideon slowly turned to look at him. "Not even once?"

"No. What is...it like?" Lord Coyzle asked. "I don't remember."

Gideon's laugh hurt his throat. "You've been awake since puberty?" He smiled. "Well, you've probably forgotten, uh, what dreaming is like." His breath was heavy, too. "I bet it'll feel like a...hallucination to you. But it'll be a nice escape."

"Well," Lord Coyzle said with a small smile, "that sounds pretty nice." He tilted his head back against the wall and closed his bloodshot eyes. Almost instantly, he started twitching, deep, slow breaths carrying him away.

Gideon chuckled, but it turned into a rough coughing fit, small sprays of blood hitting his hand.

"Look." Izzy pointed a shaky finger. Three Fayded women had snuck up on them, and they were all carrying human skulls, likely from their own people. The skulls had been smashed in half, and the craniums were filled with water. Izzy smiled as they extended the skulls as offerings. "Primitive use of tools." Even in his dying state, he was amazed, witnessing the Fayded's early stage of development.

Everyone lacked the energy to express their nervousness. They watched as the Fayded tentatively approached and whispered while offering the water. They either had no recollection of the earlier frenzy or were just accustomed to the extreme ups and downs.

Gideon smiled and took one while whispering, "Thank you." As soon as he had the broken skull, the female whispered something back and scampered off into the darkness. The same thing happened when Traveler and Izzy accepted the other two. Once the Fayded were gone, Gideon lowered the skull to Dumakleiza's mumbling lips. He gently poured some into her mouth while tilting her head up to help her swallow. Amid her weakened state, she managed to sip, emptying three quarters of the skull. She gasped and leaned her head back on Gideon's leg, giving him a subtle smile.

"I am grateful for you, Sir Gideon." Her dragon eye stung red and trailed tears down her cheek.

Gideon smiled back down. "And I, you, my beautiful pirate princess." After letting their eyes linger a moment longer, he lifted the skull and drank what little was left. There were no words to describe how good the water felt spreading through his marred body. It didn't matter how filthy drinking from an unwashed skull was. They would have resorted to drinking their own urine if they had any. Gideon slowly brought his eyes back down to look at Dumakleiza. She was asleep, her eyes fluttering.

After Traveler finished his skull, he groaned, fighting back tears. He took a few breaths and collected himself enough to address the others.

"I want you all to know —" He took a couple labored breaths. "— how privileged I feel to have gotten to know you." He could feel the life leaving his legs as they continued bleeding into the rocks.

Dumakleiza was too weak to respond. She barely even heard what he said. Izzy, too, had fallen asleep after drinking the skull water.

Gideon smiled at Traveler, tears of his own beginning to slip down his cheeks. "Spaceman, thank you." He went to reach for his backpack but then paused. He managed a weak smile as he looked at Traveler. "There is nothing in there worthy of you, man." His vulnerability made Traveler well up as they faced their end. Gideon scoffed an emotional smile and grabbed the backpack. He stared at it for a moment while Dumakleiza groaned on his lap. "But I tell you what, you alien best friend of mine." He took more strenuous breaths. "I want to give you my most treasured possession because of how much you have affected my life."

Traveler exhaled phlegm as his lungs failed to fill. "What is your most treasured possession?" Amid his fading consciousness, he became incredibly curious about what item Gideon favored above all others.

Gideon gave as big of a smile as his pained face could muster as he scooted the entire bag across the ground. "My backpack."

Traveler stared at it for a moment, unsure of how to react. He'd never thought about the backpack itself, but he suddenly realized how priceless it was to Gideon. Slow blinks released more tears as Traveler looked up at Gideon.

"Gideon, I—I can't take that."

Gideon shrugged and leaned his head back, his eyes needing to close. "Sure you can, Spaceman." He stared at the backpack. "The Sonder Sack needs a good home."

"Sonder Sack?" Traveler coughed a blood-filled smile. "Your backpack is named Sonder?" His face calmed as it made sense. "Other people's stories."

"Yup." Gideon finally managed a deep inhale. He looked from the backpack to Traveler, who'd stopped fighting back tears. "You are the... bravest man I've ever met. Ever." He stared sincerely at Traveler. "If these are our...final moments, I want you to look back on your life...and your dreams of overcoming your fears and be proud because you did. Sonder is the greatest gift I have to give to honor that success."

Traveler broke, thick tears streaming down his face as his eyes squeezed shut. He was speechless, lost in the gravity of the moment. After a heavy, trembling sigh, he nodded.

"Thank you, Gideon." He stared at the backpack. "I'm not sure what to say." He grabbed a feeble handful of the backpack's exterior, feeling the worn texture of it. He knew there were countless memories and secrets the backpack held. Gideon's soul may as well be nestled within it. Traveler's fragile grin grew as he looked up at Gideon. "Regardless of our failure with this mission—" He thought for a moment. "—dying next to you in a cave, after everything we've been through—" He smiled. "I guess this is pretty cool, too. Is that how Earthlings say it? Cool?"

Gideon coughed a smile and nodded. "I feel the same way, Spaceman." He surrendered to the pain, relaxing his body as he looked at his best friend. "We should get some rest."

"If we do that, there's a good chance we won't wake up." Traveler chuckled. "And then death *would* find us sleeping."

They both laughed and coughed together as their bodies grew colder. They were shivering, but Gideon couldn't stop smiling at Traveler's comment.

"Then my whole life would be a lie." He managed to form a small smile as his eyes stared at their cramped surroundings. "We probably are going to die here though." He couldn't even muster a nod. "One of my favorite quotes from Earth is, 'I hope to arrive to my death late, in love, and a little drunk.'" Gideon expressed a smile without needing his mouth. "I suppose two out of three isn't bad."

"I don't know." Traveler looked sincerely at Gideon. "I believe you have all three."

"Oh?"

"Light has made us all late to our deaths." Traveler coughed, his limbs feeling numb. "And you seem drunk *on* love. Even if it is with a pirate."

A full smile appeared on Gideon's face as he looked down at Dumakleiza, fast asleep. "Aye, aye." He winced as he lifted his head to look at Traveler. "*What if*...we find each other again on the other side?"

Traveler whispered a chuckle, trying to avoid another coughing fit. "We'd better. Or I'll never know the story behind everything in here." He clutched the backpack.

"Yeah." Gideon nodded as his eyes involuntarily rolled back. "If only there was...something *real* in there."

"Right," Traveler scoffed and leaned his head back with closed eyes. "I don't think anythingwould convince Shadowmaker to help us."

"Something real would," an unexpected voice came from the darkness.

Gideon and Traveler looked in its direction as a warm glow appeared. They covered their eyes with twisted expressions of discomfort. The glow became a small fire too bright for them to handle. After adjusting their optical implants to darker settings, they were able to process what they were seeing. Sitting cross-legged before them was Shadowmaker. He had a silver plate on the ground between them with a simple candle burning in its center. It was enough to create visibility in the tunnels.

"Oh, good." Gideon fought anger as he leaned his head back again. "You didn't get lost."

The others were sleeping too deeply to be roused by the light or Shadowmaker's voice. Their snores echoed through the cave, lost in better places. Shadowmaker had a new cloak exactly like the one he'd thrown on the fire. He looked at Gideon and Traveler, unconcerned about the others unconscious around him.

"I'm impressed you survived the night. I did not predict all of you would."

"Well," Gideon smirked. "The owl was a hoot." Traveler smiled at the joke that he normally would have scoffed at. Gideon raised an eyebrow at Shadowmaker. "Was that fun to watch?"

"The owl is Qua, a feared deity of the Fayded, and I wasn't watching," Shadowmaker said. "I was elsewhere, learning. I see the Fayded showed you hospitality. Now you understand they're not monsters after all."

"Yes, the skull water." Gideon looked at their injuries, visible in the firelight. Traveler was doing the same. He was less invested in the pointless conversation and more interested in how bad their wounds were. He'd hoped the light would reveal that they weren't as bad as they felt, but unfortunately they were worse. They sat in settled pools of their own blood. It was obvious that they wouldn't last another day. He sneered a dry exhale.

"It's the least they could do after condemning us to slow deaths in this cave," Traveler said, bitter and heavy.

Shadowmaker looked between the dying people before him. "A fascinating fact about the Fayded is they innately host a disease unique to their species. It is found in rare cases on other worlds but not planet-wide with other forms of Homo sapiens."

Gideon and Traveler had no idea what he was getting at or why it mattered. Maybe he just wanted to teach them something he'd learned. It was irritating that he would talk to them about something inconsequential in their last moments, but they had no choice but to listen.

"It's an evolved strain of photodermatitis, a disorder where skin reacts to sunlight with boils and rashes. However, the aggressive strain in the Fayded's genetics is lethal. I call it Fayded Light. I've never found a cure, though they don't need one. They are safe here on Fayde. But if they were to light jump, it wouldn't heal them as it does us. It would injure them. Light jumping more than once would likely kill them. What cures the rest of us is a lethal gamble for the Fayded. As the first aliens to Fayde aside from myself, I wanted to share that with you." Shadowmaker looked up at Gideon and Traveler. "Yes, your time is limited here in the darkness. You will bleed out soon. You have one opportunity for survival. Give me my payment."

Gideon chuckled helplessly. "We don't know the answer to your riddle. We must not have anything real in our pockets." He managed a weak shrug.

"Disappointing," Shadowmaker said. "Then I will leave you to your fates."

Traveler turned away, hot tears welling as he looked at Lord Coyzle sleeping against the wall. "I'm sorry, my lord. We failed you. We failed Whewliss."

Gideon glanced down at Dumakleiza before turning back to Shadowmaker. "If that is your decision, could you at least end it now? I don't want her to feel any more pain. And I don't want to slowly bleed out."

Shadowmaker stared at him, mulling over the request. "I will honor that. Look at her. She can be the image you carry into whatever comes next."

Traveler sniffled before exhaling his failure through tight lips. "Gideon, I almost—" He coughed. "—wish your shoulder wasn't cut, so you could appreciate what is happening. Tell me that story tomorrow." He closed his eyes, every second leading up to death feeling longer and longer. The anticipation had his heart racing. It was too much. He opened his eyes and looked at Shadowmaker, who was staring at Gideon.

"What does that mean?" Shadowmaker asked.

Gideon wasn't paying any attention. He stared lovingly at Dumakleiza, tears dropping onto her face as he caressed it.

Traveler blinked, thick globs bunching between his eyelids. "It —" His heart wasn't sure if it should keep beating or give up. "It's —" Words eluded him. *The* Shadowmaker was supposed to be executing them. Traveler's emotions were struggling to keep up. "Uh, Gideon's left shoulder has to be cut whenever we light jump. Or a, uh — a, uh, a darkness overcomes him." He coughed more blood onto his chin. "I don't know why. He won't tell me."

Gideon didn't hear them as he requested one last detail. "Please make it painless, at least for Duma. I don't want her to feel it."

"Tell me about your shoulder," Shadowmaker said.

Gideon slowly looked up at him, realizing what was being discussed. "What are you—how does that matter at all right now?" He saw only Shadowmaker's patient expression in response. "I haven't even told Traveler about that." He paused as Shadowmaker pulled a small metal device from under his cloak.

Without waiting, Shadowmaker aimed it at Gideon. A pure, white line shone from it like a flashlight. Gideon winced, bracing for pain. He glanced down to see it focused on his shoulder. At first, he assumed Shadowmaker was getting a better look for himself, but as he squinted, he saw what was really happening. All the claw marks, gashes, and wounds in the light were healing as the instrument galvanized the light cells in his shoulder. They reacted the same way they did during light jumps. Shadowmaker turned the device off and returned it beneath his robe.

As soon as his eyes adjusted to the darker firelight, Gideon recognized his perfectly restored shoulder. The injuries from the frenzy were gone, and more specifically, the cut from Vorlak's claw.

Traveler resituated as intrigue reinvigorated him. Shadowmaker's curiosity would not go unsatisfied.

Gideon blinked a few times. As he stared at his shoulder, his gut imploded with rage. No one had earned the right to know, least of all a stranger, and even with the myriad of legends, that's all Shadowmaker was. Gideon's past was no one's business except his own, and even he tried to avoid it since the original injury. Gideon flexed his jaw and glared at the cloaked man.

"Stop toying with me." A different kind of tears steamed in his eyes. "Just kill us."

Shadowmaker's patient eyes flickered in the firelight as he noticed the shift in Gideon's energy. "Interesting." He waited. "Tell me about your shoulder."

"Why?" Gideon asked as his eyes widened. "Why do you care?" he growled as the little blood he still had boiled. "Even if I told you, you're just going to kill us after."

Traveler reached up and wiped his eyes as he observed. Even if Shadowmaker *was* going to execute them, maybe Traveler would at least get to hear about Gideon's secret beforehand.

Shadowmaker patiently stared back as Gideon's eyes darkened. "Tell me about your shoulder. I've said this three times now."

"Say it again," Gideon snarled, jostling Dumakleiza as his stomach tensed. "Say it *four* times. *Five* times. Six, seven, eight, I don't give a shit!" He coughed once, forcing his phlegm down. Everyone aside from Vorlak started waking up.

Shadowmaker cracked a grin. "I'm intrigued. Thank you for that." He stared at Gideon, fascinated by his rage. He studied the Earthling. This was a pure moment, a rare moment, and he wasn't in any hurry. "Perhaps you're merely a masochist," Shadowmaker dismissed with a sour sting. "Maybe the cut on your shoulder means nothing after all, and the pain is purely sexual."

"Stop." Gideon pleaded with livid groans. "Just stop."

Dumakleiza managed to look up at him, unsure of what was happening.

"I doubt it has any meaning," Shadowmaker said to Traveler. "I believe the Earthling suffers from a perverse addiction to pain. I have met many people with scars containing personal meaning. This is not that. This is simple."

Traveler coughed as Shadowmaker's stare made him feel small. "No. No, there's more to it than that." He turned and looked at Gideon's chest heaving. "There has to be."

"There isn't," Shadowmaker calmly stated. "The Earthling possesses no great mystery. He is —"

"Stop it!" Gideon yelled, squeezing his eyes closed. He reached up and covered his ears.

"He is of weak constitution and sanity," Shadowmaker said. "He is a masochist relying on pain to function, or else he would resort to something worse and hurt those closest to him."

"I don't want to hurt *anyone*!" Gideon cried, slow wails ebbing from his lips.

Shadowmaker studied Gideon's reaction. "You attacked someone."

"Stop!"

"You killed someone."

"*No!*" Gideon slammed his head back against the rocks—hoping to end his consciousness—or more.

Traveler lurched away as much as he could manage. He hadn't seen Gideon completely lose control before, and it scared him.

Shadowmaker didn't budge. "Who did you kill?"

"Shut the *fuck up!* I didn't kill anyone!" Gideon burst into tears as his dam shattered. He held his face, whacking his head against the rock again and again. Loud wails echoed through the tunnels like wicked ghosts. Gideon was broken. His body convulsed, shaking Dumakleiza's head as she stared up at him, tears welling in her own eyes. She was barely awake, but it wasn't hard to piece together what was happening.

Izzy and Lord Coyzle stared in exhaustion as they, too, awoke. Vorlak slowly opened his eyes and looked around. The instant he saw Shadowmaker, he launched from the floor and backed away, pressing his body tightly up against a wall. He didn't scream. His pleasant dream of cannibalistic bloodshed had transformed into a waking nightmare, and even he was too exhausted to react with anything more than trembling. The only sound filling the tunnels was Gideon.

Shadowmaker asked again. "Who did you kill?"

Gideon didn't lash out or yell. He just cried. His mind was gone, sinking beneath the depths of someplace far away. Whatever prison his scar usually kept locked had been ripped open, and his demons were free.

Dumakleiza touched Gideon's shivering arm. "Sir Gideon?"

Everyone, including Shadowmaker, waited as Gideon's crying faded into swollen silence. He didn't look up. He didn't move. He didn't say anything.

Finally, he lifted his head, leaning it back against the rocks with a twisted expression of loss. He stared up at the ceiling as sputtering breaths shook saliva from his lips.

"My mother was a saint. I heard that my entire childhood." Gideon's words didn't sound like his own. "She used to bring me with her—to help at homeless shelters when I was a kid." He whimpered some breaths. "She would volunteer as much of her time as she could. Sometimes she skipped sleep. Her weekdays were dedicated to the homeless, school programs, charities, and whatnot." He grunted as a cough clawed at his throat. "She was always sick. My entire life, she was sick. She said she had a disease. She would never tell me what it was. Just that 'mommy was sick.' It didn't matter though. She still devoted every second that wasn't for me to everyone but herself. When I was old enough, she brought me with to meet who the other half of her heart belonged to." Gideon squeezed his eyes shut, forcing thick sludge out. "It was a prison. We went there, and she told me it was where she would, uh, talk with the inmates. She kept in contact with most of them, writing them letters throughout the weeks and visiting them on weekends." Gideon's tears stopped as he stared through the floor. "She would read to them. Sometimes the Bible. Sometimes other books. She laughed with them, cried with them, and listened, just giving them someone to talk to. Even the warden and the guards would use her as a makeshift therapist sometimes. She had a way with people that surpassed anyone else I've ever known." He paused to breathe.

"I remember asking her who the inmates were, and why she volunteered at a prison of all places." He almost smiled for a second, but it disappeared as he stared further into nothingness. "She said it was because they were people. That even people the courts deemed as bad, even people who have made mistakes, should be shown kindness. She loved to say that kindness was a universal language—one that every person understands." He took a few more slow breaths. "My mother and I, we were each other's entire family, and I treasured her." He sniffled and coughed.

"I was shy, homeschooled for most of my life. I was bad at making friends, so I went with my mom everywhere she would let me. She was my best friend. My only friend, really." He blinked a few times as he managed to focus. "When I first met the inmates, they told me that my mom was a saint, and I agreed. I'd heard it a thousand times before." He sighed, his shoulders slumping. "I wanted to go with her and help. At first—at first, she wouldn't let me. She said it was a bad idea. Dangerous for a kid. But I wanted to be just like her. I wanted to help people the way she did. I wanted to learn how to treat people in a way that would have them saying I was a saint." Gideon coughed as a small smile graced the edges of his mouth. "Finally, I think she realized how much it meant to me, so she let me. We went every weekend. I came to like many of them. They became my first friends, and I looked forward to seeing them and catching up. I talked their ears off all the time, telling them about my week and things I was excited about." Gideon went silent as his thoughts trailed off.

Traveler stared at him, finally seeing him torn open.

Dumakleiza softly touched Gideon's face. "Your mother sounds honorable, Sir Gideon."

Shadowmaker listened without saying anything.

After a deep breath, Gideon resumed. "It went on for a little over a year until—" He paused, his eyelids lowering. He cleared his throat. "My mother insisted that I could only join her at the prison if the inmates agreed not to tell me what crimes they had committed. 'That's not why we go there,' she would say. But I got curious. So, one day I started digging. I looked through old newspapers and prison records. I wanted to know more about my friends. I didn't understand why the men I thought were cool, funny, and nice were in cages. I needed to know. But what I found—was—" Gideon grew visibly tense and red. "I dug too deep."

Traveler and Shadowmaker listened in silence, but Dumakleiza was impatient. "What did you find?"

Gideon stared through the rock, the floor, through everything. It took him a moment to speak.

"The reason my mom devoted her entire being to helping people was because, uh, I used to have an older brother. His name was Aiden." Saying the name took a visible toll on Gideon. "My mom never told me about him. I never knew that I had a brother." Gideon stopped to breathe. "Through a series of bad decisions, he went to juvie, jail, spent time in and out of halfway houses, and ultimately earned a ten-year sentence in that same prison." Gideon's face went limp. "My mom visited him regularly but—" Gideon flickered between sadness and anger. "But—there was a prison riot during visiting hours. And—" Gideon stopped breathing. Traveler saw the color of Gideon's eyes change right in front of him. Gideon flexed his jaw since his hands were too weak to clench into fists. He moaned a hateful exhale. "All the inmates that were in on it began attacking everyone. The guards, the other inmates, the visitors, everyone." His voice shifted into a murderous growl. "Three people were killed. Nine others, including my mom, were hospitalized." Gideon's voice tremored. "The hospital records said that they—" The veins in his neck all but burst. "—that the inmates…had their way with her." He heaved with every breath. "Those animals…took turns with her. I don't know how many of them. The records just said 'multiple.'"

Traveler watched Gideon with a twisted gut.

Gideon's lividness made his wounds bleed again. "Three things resulted from the riot: Aiden was murdered. My mom got the disease that was slowly killing her. And the third thing was…me."

The cave felt colder. There was an awkward presence. Traveler and Dumakleiza ached for Gideon, while Shadowmaker's regular stare had transitioned into patient fixation. He was giving Gideon his full attention.

"My mother was a saint," Gideon repeated. "She kept me. No one would have blamed her if she didn't. *I* wouldn't have blamed her, but she did. She kept me. Even though every time she looked at me, I know she saw—" He closed his eyes, taking a moment. "And still, *still*, she went back to visit them. To show *them* kindness." The word "kindness" spat from his mouth like rotten food. "She forgave the men who did that to her. Immediately. She returned to help them, to try to save them from…from whatever. So pathetic. Stupid. Weak."

The tears weren't even coming, and his fists were too heavy to swing. Gideon was trapped within himself, caged by reopened wounds. His eyes narrowed into such a hatefully grotesque expression that Traveler didn't recognize him. It wasn't Gideon anymore. He was someone else.

Gideon's tone lowered. "I kept my discoveries to myself. I continued visiting the prison with my mom, biding my time while I studied the security and the guards' protocols. I did my research and narrowed the list of inmates down to five. They were the only ones who had been there since before the riot. They were my targets. It took me two months before I made my move." Steam hissed off Gideon's body. "During one of our visits, I broke into an unguarded area using a tool I snuck in using a hollowed-out insole inside my shoe. I was going to kill them with it. It didn't matter if they were the ones who did it or not. They were my only suspects, and my mother deserved vengeance." Gideon's eyes went black. "I snuck up on the first of them I saw and stabbed him in the back. It went deep. I'd never stabbed someone before. I'd never hurt anyone before. There was so much blood. Right away. I was too shocked to think to stab him again, and before I could, he grabbed me and threw me down. Before I knew what was going on, him and some other inmates were kicking me. I don't know how long I was on the ground before the guards stopped them."

Gideon reached over and held his left shoulder. "I spent eleven days in the hospital. I had two fractured ribs, my face was beaten to shit— purple and red and black, and I had a laceration on my left shoulder." He glared at the floor. "My mom didn't leave my side, but I wouldn't speak to her. I wouldn't even look at her." Tears streamed down his face. "I couldn't believe that she would just...overlook what they'd done to her and to my brother. I hated them for it. I—I...I hated her." Gideon shook his head as much as his fading strength would permit. "When I was released from the hospital, I asked my mom one question." Gideon's anger subsided for a moment, replaced by something missing. "I asked her if she knew who my father was." His bottom lip tightened up. "She said no. She said she didn't know and that she didn't want to know. She never told them that—that the, uh, the—the riot." He took a shaky breath. "That she got pregnant from it. They just thought I was her kid. Simply that. She said she'd forgiven them, and that if she could, I should, too." Gideon closed his eyes as his face bunched. "How could I forgive them? How could she? I—I knew that no matter what I did, she was stillgoing to go back there, even after they almost killed me," Gideon wheezed, wanting to scream, to punch the stone walls until his knuckles split and his bones cracked. "I told her that I would never forgive them, and that if she did, that I hated her. I said that she deserved to be in there with them." Gideon went silent for a few shallow breaths. "I wouldn't look at her. I couldn't. She was weak. She was pathetic." There were no more tears to cry, but Gideon's anguish twisted tighter in his stomach.

Tears streamed down Traveler's face. He looked at Shadowmaker, whose expression hadn't changed.

Gideon took a deep breath. "I left. I ran away and followed in Aiden's footsteps. I lost myself in drugs, theft, arson, blah, blah, blah. Until I heard that the disease had killed my mom." He went quiet as the memory gutted him. He slammed his head against the wall again, numb to it. "The last thing I said to her — " He couldn't finish. He just stared off, directionless, haunted by the unsaid. "The first time I saw her since my hospitalization was the last time. She had an open casket. There were so many people attending her funeral, people from all over, whose lives she'd touched. The church couldn't hold all of them. Among them, the warden had granted permission to the five inmates to join him in attending under armed guard. It was weird to see." Gideon's breathing released as his chest deflated. "So many people took turns talking about what my mom had done for them. The service lasted for hours. So many testimonies and tears of gratitude." Gideon took a deep breath. "At the end, the inmates were escorted to the pulpit one at a time to share how my mom affected their lives. And—and it was incredible." Gideon's mouth quivered a smile. "Their stories were painful and honest, and they confessed to everything they'd done, followed by my mom's undying love — her undeserved forgiveness after the horrors they'd done to her."

"Wow," Traveler said under his breath.

"I hid in the back," Gideon said. "I didn't give a testimony." He closed his eyes. "After the funeral—once everyone else had left, the inmates asked to speak with me. I don't know why I agreed to, but I did." Gideon tried to gulp with his dry mouth. "They told me that my mom loved me more than anything—that she told them about how proud she was of me every time she visited. Then they, uh, they told me not to waste my life as they had done with theirs. They were doomed to die, sleeping in cells. They said that they hoped after everything, that I would be set free from any anger or guilt, and that I could live my life in fearless memory of my mother. Lastly, they asked me to forgive them." Gideon smiled as he finally looked directly into Shadowmaker's eyes. "Something happened in that moment. I can't explain it. I hated them, and I wanted nothing more than for them to suffer and die just like my mother and brother had. But I don't know. It was as if something took over my body, like a light overcame me. A weightlessness. Without hesitation, I forgave them. I forgave each of them." Fresh tears streamed down Gideon's cheeks. "I asked them to forgive me, and they did. They forgave me and told me I needed to leave — leave my hometown, where I'd spent my entire life, and see the world." Gideon's lips continued trembling, but his face finally relaxed, a peacefulness settling over it. "That was the single most defining moment of my entire life. It changed everything." He exhaled in relief. "Ever since that day, I've been…living. I had no family and no other friends to leave behind. I've just been in the wind."

He sighed as his pulse slowed and the pain crept back in.

"My scar, it reminds me of my mom. It reminds me of her strength and compassion, and ability to see the good in the worst places." Gideon's cough returned. "It reminds me of who I am, and more importantly, who I could have been. Hate that I never want to feel again." Gideon caressed his left shoulder as he stared at Shadowmaker. He lowered his eyebrows and exhaled. "The end. Now you know."

Shadowmaker didn't say anything as he processed Gideon's story.

Dumakleiza squeezed Gideon's arm with fading strength. "Your mother would take pride in the man you are."

Tears poured down Traveler's face as he stared at Gideon.

Finally, Shadowmaker gave a subtle nod. "I have received numerous requests for assistance throughout my travels. Evil plagues every world. There are no exceptions. There will always be man turned to monster, and there will always be victims praying for liberation. If I am to involve myself, I want to see the depths of those I'm saving. I want to see the person I am keeping alive by killing another. Riches are lost upon me, and gifts, like all things physical, fade, decay, and rot. I have no interest or need. My price, which I cherish above all things, is a glimpse into the character of those whose lives would go on. There is no point in saving those who have nothing real to offer this life." Shadowmaker's emotionless manner transformed. "Gideon, I look forward to seeing more than a glimpse after I help you with Abdabriel N'kowsky. I accept your payment."

34

Shadowmaker removed the flashlight from his pocket and took his time closing the worst of everyone's cuts. They were all quiet. They needed food, water, and rest. Healing their wounds wouldn't be enough. The flashlight didn't generate blood to make up for what they'd lost. It didn't heal them internally as they digested contaminated water. It didn't fill their stomachs with food. It only allowed them the ability to go find the necessary components for survival.

"I have an additional question about your story, Earthling," Shadowmaker said.

Gideon's shoulder still wasn't cut. Sharing his story for the first time had purged his soul, but he still needed the scar to function. He paused before looking up.

"What?"

"Was your mother's disease passed along to you congenitally?"

Gideon slowly nodded, uninterested in trying to conceal any more secrets. "Yes." He was physically and emotionally depleted, and the relief from confessing his darkness only exhausted him further.

Traveler, who was helping Lord Coyzle sit up, looked at Gideon. "Wait." It made sense finally. "Is that why you don't care about dying?"

Gideon gave a hollow nod. "Yeah. There was no point hiding from it. Why not challenge it instead?"

Traveler squinted. "But the first light jump healed you. You knew that it did." He swallowed. "You haven't changed, though. You're still just as insane." He looked around at their circumstances. "If not more so."

Gideon helped Dumakleiza sit up for Shadowmaker to shine his light on. "What's that Whewlight saying? Light heals the body."

Traveler slowly nodded. "Not the mind."

Gideon gave a half-assed smile as he tried to cheer up. "So, Shadow-maker. I have a few questions of my own, if you don't mind."

"About what?" Shadowmaker asked.

"You, of course," Gideon said with a shrug. "What else would I be curious about?"

"Knowing more about me will not benefit your cause."

"Oh, come on." Gideon rolled his eyes. "Humor me. From one student to another."

Shadowmaker paused. "Ask your questions."

"Score. Okay, awesome." Gideon collected his thoughts. "Um, well, before coming here, we all thought you were the bogeyman, but we're seeing a bit more. So, I guess I just want to understand who you really are. Kind of like you did with us." Gideon cleared his throat. "I'm curious why you hate your own kind so much. You nearly killed Vorlak just for breathing when we showed up." Vorlak trembled, still clutching the wall, confused by Gideon addressing Shadowmaker without shitting himself. "Why is that? And reference your history, I have a couple questions. How did the Daemoaniks capture you? In fact, what did they pay you to kill the resistance leaders in the first place? Did it cost King Slaughtvike something 'real?'" Gideon coughed as the questions poured out of him. "Of course, I'm supercurious about the big one: How the hell did you make two planets collide? That seems impossible. And—" Gideon cocked his head to the side as a realization hit him. "—now that we know you aren't stuck on Fayde, why do you even come here? You're clearly not hiding from anyone. What's here for you?"

Shadowmaker continued moving the flashlight over Dumakleiza's cuts, undistracted by the questions. Everyone stared at him, hoping he'd answer at least some.

"I will answer your questions if you agree to three conditions. First, once they have all been addressed, you must answer one that I have," Shadowmaker said to Lord Coyzle.

Lord Coyzle clammed up. "What question?"

"Secondly, you must stop referring to the Daemoaniks as my people. They lost that privilege," Shadowmaker said. "Thirdly, you will address me by my name."

Gideon cracked a smile. "Which is?"

"Cassiak."

Lord Coyzle, Traveler, and Izzy looked at him with wide eyes. Their jaws all but hit the floor as Traveler asked what they all wanted to know.

"Cassiak *Stagvayne*? The Daemoanik who first discovered light travel?"

Shadowmaker gave a subtle nod.

"Impossible," Traveler said. "That would make you a-thousand-years-old. Or older. How old are you?" His question was only answered by a glance from Shadowmaker.

"Whoa." Gideon resituated on his butt, intrigue distracting him from his uncut shoulder. "Plot twist. Okay, Cassiak, agreed."

Cassiak looked to Lord Coyzle, waiting for his agreement, as well. Lord Coyzle gulped. He couldn't imagine what question meant enough to Shadowmaker for the discussion to hinge upon.

"I will try to answer your question."

"The terms are set," Cassiak said. "I answer your questions only to clarify the atrocities linked to my name, though some are true." He didn't look away from his work as he spoke. "When I discovered the capabilities of light, I soon thereafter found another inhabitable world. It was the first of many. I spent years developing and perfecting light travel before attempting it. I never publicly apply what I have not privately mastered. I visited the new world and studied much of what there was to learn there. I was instantly addicted. Their cultures were vastly different from my own, and I realized how much there was in the universe that I didn't know. I spent eight of their years there. I blended in and learned how to camouflage myself as one of their own. I was never found out. I learned their scientific and technological differences and discoveries. I studied their combative advancements and weaponry. I learned a few of their languages, practiced their architectural styles. I studied everything. I was insatiable, and they were beautiful in their differences. I was in awe of what they knew that we didn't. New knowledge is a delicacy." He almost smiled. "When I returned to Daemoana, I told one of my close friends, Daris Slaughtvike, about my discoveries. He was the president of my homeland, the Daemoanik country, Klipestave. He, too, shared my hunger for learning about other worlds, though, at the time, I did not know the depths his hunger would sink to. The excitable naivety of my youth was the seed of calamity, and I was too blind to see its trajectory." He paused. "Due to the overwhelming evidence I provided, the world leaders of Daemoana met and created the first world government. They voted Daris in as the first planetary leader: *King* Slaughtvike. I joined in the planetary celebration."

Traveler blinked a few times as he absorbed. "Our history books lack allof this."

Cassiak went on. "I was richly rewarded for my discoveries and inventions. My status among my people was elevated. I bought a simple home, married a woman named Daylucia, and we spent our lives visiting other worlds together. For many years, I was blissfully unaware of King Slaughtvike's secret agenda. Daylucia and I were too in love with our own search for knowledge, and our romantic obsession with traveling the stars together." The subtle shifts in his tonal nuances spoke explicit volumes. "King Slaughtvike slowly poisoned the minds of those in power beneath him, manipulating their pride, greed, and desire for more. I was young and hadn't yet learned the significance of keeping careful watch of my world's government. I assumed Daris would rule Daemoana with benevolence and wisdom. I trusted him, and his position stemmed from my discovery."

Cassiak finished mending as many of Dumakleiza's wounds as he deemed necessary for travel and moved on to Lord Coyzle. "By the time I learned of what was happening worldwide on Daemoana — the mutilations and misanthropic plans to overthrow all other worlds — Daylucia had given birth to my son, Helethro, a name not of Daemoana, but that I'd heard on another world. Helethro Stagvayne." A wave of anger flared on his face but vanished as quickly as it appeared. "I moved them to a desolate island on Daemoana. It was uninhabited and relatively unknown. I assumed we would be safe from the pandemonium there——at least long enough." He paused to blink away the memories. "Reflecting on my history is a no-holds-barred judgment of my own ignorance."

Everyone had a rather good idea of where the story was going as Cassiak continued. "King Slaughtvike waged his war, and we stayed far from it. I was appalled to hear that nearly every single man, woman, andchild was being forced to undergo——that." Cassiak pointed at Vorlak without looking at him. "I focused on my family. We prepared a defensive onslaught of weaponry around our home in case Slaughtvike should decide to come looking for me. It was an unlikely scenario, but I was the only Daemoanik who continued to learn as the rest of that wretched world descended into hell. I assumed it would be easy to fend off any of my own people. They had thrown their humanity away, and as you said, they preferred feeling death in their hands, so they would be easy to kill if need be." He retold his story with haunted callous, like a bone that healed the wrong way. "Eventually, Daylucia and I decided we would be safer on another world, so I ventured out to find the best option while she remained behind to watch over Helethro. After visiting and selecting a new home world, I returned to find Daylucia and Helethro gone. Instead, King Slaughtvike was waiting for me in my own home. He had two-hun-dred-and-eleven-guards with him. I didn't recognize him. Along with the rest of Daemoana, he had tortured himself into an unnatural creature of hatred and lust. He informed me that my family was safe, but they would be executed if I brought any harm to him or his soldiers. He said that if I ever wanted to see them again, I would help him end the resistance. To my everlasting shame, your history books know what happened next."

"Jesus," Gideon said, captivated but heartbroken for Shadowmaker.

"When I returned to Daemoana, I had disbanded the resistance, and King Slaughtvike had resumed his conquering at the price of my soul. I just wanted my wife and son back. In the ever-expanding vastness of the universe, they were all that mattered. King Slaughtvike told me I could find my family in a facility where they had been kept during my instructed assassinations."

"The prison," Traveler whispered under his breath.

"Yes," Cassiak said without looking away from his work. "The facility was built into the ground, eight floors deep. At the lowest level, I was shown to the room where my wife and son were waiting for me. They were ripped apart. The cell was painted with them." He went silent, though he didn't slow with the flashlight as he moved on to Izzy. "The Daemoaniks locked me in with their remains. I still hear the guards laughing as they shut the door. For hours I screamed into the blood-soaked walls. My wife had been torn into too many pieces for me to hold anything but meat, but I held what remained of my son that night. Their voices haunted me in the blackness, begging me to save them, wondering why I hadn't been there to protect them."

Cassiak closed his eyes and then continued, "When I broke out, I killed the guards assigned to keep me there. I found King Slaughtvike and brought him to Fayde. Once here, I planned my vengeance. Daemoana was a pestilential cesspool, containing nothing but wretched, murderous filth, and there was no saving it. Rather, I would cleanse the universe by removing the infection that stemmed from my mistakes. I studied the stars, designing an algorithm for the interacting physics of spacetime and the bodies of mass therein. It took weeks until my opportunity arrived. I sent an object, just as I had to assassinate the resistance leaders. With precise calculations, it hit a small asteroid with exactly the right amount of force to shift its direction, sending it into the path of a larger meteor. Three bodies of mass in my designed chain reaction later, and the nearest planet to Daemoana, Trikkit, was hit by a three-hundred-billion-ton-asteroid, changing its trajectory just enough to send it careening into Daemoana's orbital path."

The cave went silent as Cassiak continued with the flashlight. "I've changed my mind. Never have I discussed this since its origination. I will allow my birth name to be forgotten by history. I want no connection to the Daemoaniks. Call me by the title given to me since. Call me Shadowmaker."

Gideon's eyebrows were as high as they could go. "Please tell me King Slaughtvike was the object you launched through space to begin the chain reaction. That would be so badass."

"Oh. Uh. Oh!" Gideon exclaimed. "One of your signature coins?"

"No," Shadowmaker said without emotion. "I sent a stone that fit in my hand. It possessed the required mass to change the trajectory upon its collision. Using Slaughtvike would have been inefficient in accomplishing planetary destruction."

Gideon slowly nodded, trying to usher focus to the unanswered question. "Then, how did you kill Slaughtvike? You strike me as someone who wouldn't pass up the opportunity for flare—especially with vengeance—and especially with him."

Shadowmaker looked directly at him, the intensity in his eyes making Gideon shrink away. "Every world has thousands of theories of what happens after death. Most involve the continuation of existence. Out of those, the majority believe in a version of heaven, paradise, utopia, and an antithesis: a hell, underworld, an abyss. I wanted to condemn Daris Slaughtvike to the darkest hell I could, but there was no evidence anywhere of such a place. I needed to know without any doubt. There is no proof that he would receive the eternal punishment he deserved for his countless crimes. In fact, many of the beliefs I've studied theorize that the afterlife is the very lack of existence. And if that was the truth, I would be granting Slaughtvike mercy by ending his life. That is a potential sympathy I could not allow. The unknown was intolerable. If there was a god, he would not judge as harshly as I would, and if there was a devil, he would not punish as severely as I hungered to."

Gideon's eyes slowly peeled open. He wasn't sure if he understood what Shadowmaker was alluding to correctly, but if he was, the idea was far worse than death.

"Wh—wha—one-hundred-years." He blinked a few times. "That's why you still come to Fayde."

Lord Coyzle, Traveler, and Izzy felt the darkness thicken like smoke as they, too, realized what Shadowmaker was saying.

"Daris Slaughtvike, along with one-thousand Daemoanik soldiers, still live," Shadowmaker said. "They are individually locked in cells inside of a prison of my own design here on Fayde. It is in a place safe from the wildlife and the Fayded. It is unfindable by anyone aside from myself." Everyone's pulses raced in newfound fear of Shadowmaker's wrath as he continued. "Their health is monitored, and their lives are regulated by light that shines upon them at all times. They cannot escape, and they are bound in every way to prevent them from killing themselves. I have ensured that they are conscious and preserved, unable to sleep. I release a single Daemoanik every Fayded year. I give them one week to run and find refuge on Fayde before I hunt them with tactics acquired on one of my travels. I use only newly learned methods during the hunt to ensure I have mastered them. It allows brief moments of hope for each Daemoanik soldier, and then I snuff it out when the hunt concludes." Shadowmaker's tone didn't shift or darken, though his words became more and more terrifying. "Once our business is concluded on Whewliss, I will return to Fayde and finish the hunt I came here for before your interruption."

"And?" Traveler almost vomited as he forced the words out of his mouth. "And what about Slaughtvike?"

"Slaughtvike's mind has drifted into inescapable madness. He is confined in loneliness with only his thoughts, the true parasites of sanity. He only feels physical pain during my visits. Out of memory of the damage he inflicted upon billions, I use my hands to deliver him to the doorstep of death. I then revive him, leaving him in blinding, healing light, unable to move, unable to sleep, to escape, to die. He stopped screaming nearly eighty years ago. The time will come when he cannot be revived, or he dies of the incurable disease: age. At that point, he will move on to whatever hell awaits him in the afterlife, if there is one. Until then, at least I will know he suffered in this life."

Everyone was silent. None of them knew what to say. Newfound fears of Shadowmaker rooted themselves deep in their bowels. He was capable of unthinkable tortures, and they knew that their minds would do no better than Slaughtvike's if they were in his position. They didn't want to try to understand how much misery he'd experienced, but they couldn't help it as their thoughts wandered.

Lord Coyzle broke the silence. "I——I have hated King Slaughtvike my entire life." He stared despondently into the floor. "But he should have died a long time ago, along with my hatred. He should have died with yours. How——how can you continue living this way?" He looked at Shadowmaker, terrified, confused. "After hearing Gideon's story of forgiveness, don't you want to end this?"

"Be careful, Albei Coyzle," Shadowmaker warned. "You are in danger of sounding like Abdabriel N'kowsky."

Lord Coyzle brought his head back. "What? How? When did you speak to—"

"To insist that one person should learn a life lesson from the experience of another is as arrogant as saying that a drowning man should take a deep breath because he can see someone breathing above the surface. Is that not the very belief that motivates Abdabriel?"

Lord Coyzle didn't know what to say. King Slaughtvike, the man he'd loathed since childhood, the man he despised even more than Shadowmaker, was still alive, and yet he felt a swell of pity for him.

"I—I don't believe anyone should be tortured like that."

"If it is any consolation," Shadowmaker said, "I will grant one act of forgiveness. I will spare the life of the Daemoanik you brought with you. Do not ask for more, or I will kill him, too."

Again, everyone went silent. Gideon felt like they were all suddenly walking on eggshells, so even he kept his mouth shut. Vorlak had resumed his audible whimpering, knowing that Shadowmaker would follow through on his promise.

Outside in the open, the feeble group huddled together as Shadowmaker reached a hand toward the storming clouds. Dumakleiza still wasn't able to stand, but she held onto Gideon's hand while sitting against his legs. The others were searching their surroundings for any signs of the owl. They assumed Shadowmaker was aware of where it was, and that if it attacked, he had a plan, but they couldn't help fearing the worst. The leviathan could kill them all with a single swoop of its claws.

Vorlak was as far as he could be from Shadowmaker, while still staying connected to the group. He was holding Lord Coyzle's hand at arm's length, shielding his eyes and whining. Lord Coyzle couldn't help the bizarre pleasure he found in being Vorlak's shield from the man they both feared.

Traveler was the only one watching what Shadowmaker was doing. He wanted to understand how the legend was going to make an impossible light jump through heavy clouds and blackness. Shadowmaker's hand was open. He wasn't holding anything—light or unknown device. Was he waiting for a light source? Traveler couldn't think of any that were coming. He racked his mind, trying to guess. He had to admit, the mystery was fun. The only light he saw were random flashes of lightning.

"Impossible…" He looked back and forth between Shadowmaker's open hand and the storming sky.

Dumakleiza groaned, "Maker of Shadows, where is my Coobs?"

"He waits for you on Whewliss. He is safe, as I promised."

Dumakleiza nodded, coughs still cracking her lips. "I wish to hold him."

"You shall soon," Shadowmaker said. "Now—" He turned to Lord Coyzle. "—what is the fourth phase?"

Lord Coyzle was taken aback. "*That* is your one question." He'd prepared for a few possible queries, but this was unexpected.

"Yes," Shadowmaker said. "I tire of asking the same question multiple times. Answer it now."

"It's—" Lord Coyzle twitched as he contemplated lying. "It's a—there is an edge to the universe. The Wall. Have you not discovered it yourself?"

"I have," Shadowmaker said. "It is impermeable. There is nothing there."

Lord Coyzle couldn't help cracking a smile. "You haven't discovered the hole?"

A genuine expression of curiosity appeared on Shadowmaker's face. "There is a hole?" He smiled at the existence of something he knew nothing of.

"Yes." Lord Coyzle beamed, thrilled to know something Shadowmaker didn't. "It's where they—" He motioned at the others. "—are going to explore and study if we can successfully stop Abdabriel."

"Interesting." Shadowmaker went silent as his eyes moved around.

Gideon gave a curious expression. "Why don't you just kill him from here like you did with the coins? Wouldn't that be easier?"

"Three reasons," Shadowmaker said. "His reflection suit prevents me from using that method." The answer triggered a look between Lord Coyzle and Traveler.

"That's not good. He recreated it," Lord Coyzle said with a despairing slump. "That was designed to protect me from you," he said to Shadow-maker. "Do you know how to bypass its defenses?"

"No. Do you?"

"No."

"I will figure it out. Secondly, I have not mapped his pattern, so I could not accurately aim."

"And the thirßd reason?" Gideon asked.

Shadowmaker grinned. "One of the only Daemoanik traits I still possess. When there is someone deserving of death, I want to feel it in my hands." With that, he closed and opened his hand, and everything went white.

35

As the light faded from Gideon's eyes, a sharp pain flared. The jump still had him too cataleptic to make sense of it. He gasped at the sobering sting. It forced his mind to focus. After two heaving breaths, his vision cleared. The first thing he noticed was it was daytime. Without even processing that he was back on Whewliss, he looked over to see that his left shoulder was sliced open. He stared at it for a moment, still trying to rouse his mind. The cut was exact, absolute in its surgical precision— unlike his claw mark from Vorlak. It stung differently than he was used to. He'd had more than his fair share of injuries throughout his life, and he was no stranger to pain, but this felt different. Stranger still was that the wound was fresh, and yet it wasn't bleeding. Before trying to make sense of it, he looked over to see Shadowmaker sheathing a blade beneath his cloak.

"You will not lose your mother again," Shadowmaker said.

"W—what?" Gideon's eyes fluttered as the rest of his body regained feeling. "How? What do you mean?"

"The blade's edge has the same acidic chemicals used by the Daemoaniks to harden their skin. It's an aggressive strain secreted by resurrectors, a deep-sea jellyfish on Damoana and two other worlds I've visited. Before I destroyed Daemoana, resurrectors had gone extinct due to poaching for the sake of collecting their venom. Light will not remove it. Not even I can reverse its effect."

At first, Gideon didn't fully comprehend what he was being told. He grimaced and looked at the bubbling cut as the acid burned into his skin.

It hurt. It hurt a lot, but he appreciated what it meant. Never again would he lose the closure his scar provided. The only way he would ever see it missing is if his entire arm was cut from his body. Additionally, he could feel his returned energy replenishing his positivity. He smiled and looked around. Everyone else had made the jump safely. They were still in a recovering stupor since they hadn't had acid for a jolting alarm clock. As the bubbling cut burned, Gideon turned back to Shadowmaker.

"Thank you." Gideon smiled as more articulate gratitude eluded him. "Thank you."

Traveler was the most experienced light jumper aside from Shadowmaker, so he managed to move first. "Where are we?" He looked around, blinking until he recognized their surroundings. "Is this the City of Light?"

"Yes," Shadowmaker said. "Your cells' light compatibility has been restored, along with your implants. Abdabriel is preparing for his planetary address this evening. His soldiers are herding the Whewlights of this city to bear witness."

"We need to be careful," Lord Coyzle realized. "Abdabriel likely has drones patrolling the city. If they see us, they'll shoot on sight."

"I've destroyed all of the drones and bypassed your fractal gas," Shadowmaker calmly informed. "But there are still some soldiers. If you move quickly, you will not be found."

"If *we* move quickly? Where are you going to—?" Traveler looked over to see that Shadowmaker was already gone. He had no idea what Shadowmaker's plan was or how he intended to stop Abdabriel, but his sudden absence made Traveler feel vulnerable.

"That man is more difficult to figure out than a woman saying she's fine," Gideon said with a wincing smile. He turned and looked at Traveler, who was staring at him with an uncharacteristic softness. "You okay, Spaceman?"

Traveler walked over and placed both hands on Gideon's shoulders, pulling him in close. He hugged him and then stepped back.

"Thank you for everything, Gideon."

Gideon scoffed a vulnerable grin. "For what? We haven't stopped Abdabriel yet. Don't count your eggs before they——"

"That's not what I'm talking about. You just—I don't know. One of the only 'what-if' questions I don't like entertaining is 'What if I never met Gideon?'" Gideon smiled as Traveler looked at the slice on his shoulder. "I wish I could have met your mother. Maybe if we live long enough, you can take me to her grave one day. I would like to pay my respects and thank her."

Gideon took a satisfying breath and looked around. "One of the many things that made her beautiful was her belief when it came to that sort of thing. She never wanted anyone to visit her grave because her soul wouldn't be there. She said she wanted to be remembered in the smiles of strangers because we are, after all, not strangers but friends just waiting to meet."

Traveler nodded and smiled at how brightly Gideon's mother reflected in her son. "Sounds like the apple didn't fall far from the tree." As soon as he said it, he grimaced. "I'm afraid to know how I messed up that Earth quote."

"Actually," Gideon said, "that one was perfect. Verbatim." He patted Traveler on the back.

Traveler lifted a fist. "Yes."

Gideon chuckled. "Well done, Spaceman." He finally looked around and took in their surroundings. He froze. "What. The. Hell." He saw the city of skydrops spanning in all directions. He'd been so preoccupied with Shadowmaker, his scar, and then Traveler, that he hadn't noticed the enormous globular buildings floating around them. "What are those?"

Traveler looked at the two nearest skydrops. He recognized the names projected above them. The first read "Jella Cousel." It was an advanced gelatin-fashion store filled with innovative name-brand apparel and gelatinous accessories. It was typically exclusive to the wealthier Whewlights. Traveler cracked a smile, understanding why Shadowmaker had landed them where he had. It was more than just a subtle hint. He looked down at their dilapidated gelatin suits. His stomach growled as he looked at the second skydrop. Its sign read "Teal Platypus," a prestigious restaurant, normally too expensive for him to dine at. He smirked. Shadowmaker wanted them to eat and dress with luxuries normally unavailable. Maybe it was the Daemoanik legend's way of mocking the financial hierarchy. Maybe it was just sheer luck that he'd placed them in the richer part of the city. One way or another, Traveler was going to take advantage of it. Lord Coyzle would just have to accept that they were treating themselves before finding Abdabriel.

"I'll explain over some of the best Whewlight food there is," said Traveler. "And then we need to get new suits before anything else."

As Dumakleiza came to, she felt a familiar sensation of a tongue on her fingers. The cooing and paws against her legs expedited her recovery and immediately put a smile on her face.

"Coobs? Coobs!" She snatched the whining tanion up and held him in her arms, rocking him back and forth. "The Maker of Shadows didn't hurt you, did he?" She nuzzled his face, squeezing him tighter than she knew she probably should. "No. No, he would not have hurt my Coobs." She smiled, kissing his nose and forehead. "I would have killed him."

"Don't even say that," Izzy ushered with a sharp whisper as he looked around. "What if he heard you?"

Before Dumakleiza could respond, she found Gideon's arms wrapped around her and Cooby. He didn't say anything as he just held them. They embraced in silence, appreciating the simple miracle of survival. Gideon had been filled with doubts about allowing himself to open up to her before their jump to Fayde, but no longer. His protective instincts burned for her and only her. It had been years since he'd felt that way about anyone. It felt good.

Lord Coyzle squatted down, running his fingers through the soft grass. He didn't need to say anything for the others to understand. The Whewlight lord was back on his world. He'd survived Horror Planet, and he was appreciating the home he'd taken for granted. The grass appeared greener, the sky brighter, the air sweeter, and his smile more genuine.

Traveler ushered them to follow him to the restaurant's entrance pad. Dumakleiza, Izzy, and Vorlak stared in wonder at the massive spheres floating throughout the city. The looming giants made them feel dizzy. Vorlak wanted to climb one.

Lord Coyzle sped to the front of the line to join Traveler. Since they were back in civilization, his authoritative instincts felt comfortable taking lead. The familiarity was a welcomed relief after facing death on Fayde, and Traveler was happy to see his Lord resume leadership.

"I hope the others are alive," Lord Coyzle sighed. While he was concerned about Timrekka and Jasss, he was primarily worried about Master Brawd and Lady Melodeen. His friends had been taken by who he thought was one of his closest allies. He stepped onto the light pad and disappeared. One by one, everyone else followed.

The much-needed meal was bizarre and unique in the most delicious ways for the aliens. The recruits weren't sure if they felt more or less comfortable with the fact that there were no human servers or cooks. Everything in the restaurant was automated. Robots with uncanny human appearances took their orders and delivered their dishes. Throughout the meal, everyone lost themselves in the experience, temporarily forgetting about the danger they were heading toward. Traveler and Lord Coyzle proudly explained every dish: the foreign vegetables used to create the colorful salads, the antlered boar prepared to look like a flower in bloom, and the plastic tube containing the dessert. It was a flavored gas meant to be inhaled. Traveler explained that it wasn't necessarily a drug, but rather an aromatic experience so intense and decadent that physical consumption would indeedcreate addiction. Dumakleiza, in particular, enjoyed the dessert and immediately wanted more, as she'd had little experience with any form of narcotics. Lord Coyzle paid for everyone's meals, including the six helpings of antlered boar that Vorlak devoured alone.

Afterward, they replaced their ramshackle suits. They went through individual changing rooms, which provided ample privacy in the dazzling skydrop. Each included a chamber for stripping old gelatin before new could be applied. The old gelatin was drained through the floor and recycled. Once stripped, they stepped into changing rooms containing automated hoses with programmable designs. They were prompted using step-by-step screens that made up the walls, where they would select what style of outfit they desired. Once selected, the hoses went to work, spraying intricately designed patterns and layers of gelatin over their bodies. Finally, a wave of light zapped down through, solidifying the gelatin. Only Cooby was left out. He waited in the entryway.

Traveler exited first with a fresh grey suit accented by white and black edges. It was his favorite style whenever he got to enjoy extended stays on his home-world. Lord Coyzle followed close behind with a similar outfit. He wanted to avoid standing out with the elegance he was accustomed to donning. Izzy exited with earthy browns and greens covering him in a classy pattern of squares. Gideon made Traveler shake his head when he emerged with a purple suit, accented with white swirls decoratively painted around his body. Dumakleiza stepped out not long after. Her gelatin suit was pure brown. She'd contemplated playing with the array of colors, but she wanted to stay tactical in her approach, and brown was ubiquitously camouflaging. They all gathered and looked over each other's selections. It only took a moment to realize they were still waiting on Vorlak.

They waited, nervously staring out of the skydrop into the vacant city. They'd expected to see soldiers everywhere, but it appeared that Shadowmaker was right. Everyone had been called away.

Loud grunts and exasperated breaths caught their attention as Vorlak burst out of his changing room. He had an extra crazed look in his bloodshot eyes. They were surprised to see his taste in suit selection. The Daemoanik warrior was wearing blood red gelatin. It had gold accents and black cuffs around his wrists and a matching collar. Nobody wanted to admit that, for a monster, he looked good.

Vorlak grunted a fang-filled smile. "That was cold."

Gideon laughed as Lord Coyzle directed everyone to follow him. They exited the skydrop, quietly following his returned leadership. He'd been fed and dressed. Now he was finally able to focus on what mattered: taking back his world.

"What is our plan now?" Traveler asked as they left the skydrop's shadow.

Lord Coyzle stopped in the daylight and looked around. "I don't know. I was about to ask you that."

"Uh." Traveler shrugged. "My plan was getting Shadowmaker. We got him. I guess I kind of thought he was going to involve us in *his* plan if we got this far."

"How confident are you that he didn't trick us? That he's still going to help us?" Lord Coyzle asked.

Traveler looked at the cut on Gideon's shoulder. "I'm confident he will follow through on his promise."

Gideon was trying to be polite and let the high-ranking Whewlights decide on a course of action, but he was itching for involvement. There was a lot riding on their decision, and his gut was screaming with advice. He rolled his eyes with impatience and smirked.

"Well, as long as we're at a loss, we may as well show off our new outfits," he said while admiring his purple sleeves. "Why don't we go listen to Abdabriel's planetary address? May as well stay updated on his shenanigans."

Dumakleiza nodded. "And kill him, should the Maker of Shadows fail to do so himself."

"Hold on, Dumakleiza," Traveler firmly said. "Before we take action, we just need to—"

"Hey!" a commanding voice snarled as a handful of soldiers approached from behind. "Why aren't you Whewlights at Pinnacle Peak for the Holy One's planetary address? Get a move on."

They turned and looked at the soldiers, trying not to give anything away. Dumakleiza and Vorlak growled under their breath as they stared them down, itching for permission to engage.

Gideon grabbed Dumakleiza's arm and whispered through smiling teeth, "Duma, Vorlak, down. Play nice." He stepped forward. "Sorry, guys!" He laughed with a smack to his forehead. "We lost track of time and got ourselves all turned around. Where is it again?"

The soldiers approached them with flagrant irritation. Their impatience with rounding up straggling Whewlights was taking a toll on their friendliness, but Abdabriel had given them strict instructions. They looked the group of stragglers up and down, studying the odd ensemble. They paused when they saw Vorlak. Concerned expressions were accompanied by rigid fingers held by their sides.

Gideon and Traveler weren't sure what to do. The soldiers would likely execute the Daemoanik and then the rest of them for fraternizing with one. Vorlak wasn't helping. He was doing a good job staying his hand, but the hungry scowl on his face undermined any excuse Gideon could conjure up.

Gideon exaggerated an eye roll and a laugh. "Again, I'm so sorr—"

"Quiet!" One of the soldiers shook his head in disgust. He stared at Vorlak a moment longer. "Some Whewlights are so ugly." He scrunched his nose and motioned to the rest of them. "We'll escort you." He groaned. "Come on."

"Yes, sir," Gideon said, appreciating how lucky they were to be caught by aliens with no knowledge of Daemoaniks. "After you fine gentlemen."

36

On the outskirts of the City of Light, the landscape was comprised of flat, stretching terrain leading to other cities and towns, but on one end was Pinnacle Peak. It was the highest point of the only local mountain range. Its elevation towered above the rest of the city and was a landmark excursion for anyone interested in a grueling hike. Additionally, the City of Light often used it as a venue for large events. Public addresses, concerts, dances, sermons, and private events were frequently held at the universally renowned Pinnacle Peak.

The architect had spared no expense or detail. A massive amphitheater had been carved into the base of the mountain, leaving a perfectly smooth wall surrounding a stage just above ground level. Thousands of seats were built into the walls of the manmade cliff face, and tens of thousands more spanned out in front of the mountain. It was famous for the evening view of Whewliss's setting sun over the mountain range. The stage itself was an enormous, flat piece of marble with mirrors spliced into the stone. Layered on top of it was an unbreakable floor of clear plastic, infused with digital technology for projections and decorative lights. Spotlights, projectors, ornate flame throwers, and ultramodern theatrics of varying function were built into the mountain to enhance any production on the stage below. Pinnacle Peak was a state-of-the-art attraction, a historical location where many famed speeches and happenings had taken place. On any normal day, there was a packed schedule of events that appealed to the vast and differing tastes of Whewlights everywhere. It was an iconic landmark that Whewlights and world leaders of LOLA-abiding planets traveled incredible distances to attend, and Abdabriel was going to use the venue to instigate a paradigm-shift of cosmic proportions.

As the evening approached at Pinnacle Peak, the seats weren't just packed; they were forcefully beyond capacity. Over twelve-thousand of Abdabriel's soldiers were in attendance, and they had brought every single compliant Whewlight in the city to join. Countless Whewlights created a sea of faces spanning out from the stage for miles. Soldiers had been escorting locals and stragglers all day, and they weren't slowing.

With the majority of the Whewlight army executed or incarcerated, resistance was minimal. Abdabriel's Army of Light had only had to kill a few resistors throughout the day. For the most part, people were too scared to fight back, so they did as they were told. All the high-status seats carved into Pinnacle Peak's cliff walls had been reserved for the Whewlights who'd happily joined Abdabriel's vision. They were the esteemed, the privileged, the righteous who had seen the light. Abdabriel had handpicked them to ensure that the live recordings of his address would show only support and exuberance when broadcasted around the planet. Normally, any event at Pinnacle Peak would be an optional broadcast for any LOLA-abiding world's government to view on secure channels, but Abdabriel wanted each world's address to be restricted to only its own people, so he cut off interplanetary propagation. He couldn't allow other worlds the advantage of seeing a preview of what was to come.

Throughout the day, Abdabriel had instructed one of his favorite artists, a solo singer and musician named Gish-L, to entertain the masses. She was arguably Whewliss's most recognizable celebrity. After being given a passive-aggressive threat with a wink and a smile, she'd agreed to perform. She played through every one of her songs over the course of hours, repeating them whenever she ran out. Her fame exceeded the confines of Whewliss, to every world abiding by LOLA. Abdabriel's plan was working. Gish-L's songs brought comforting familiarity to the masses, thousands of them singing along as the last slivers of hope slipped through their fingers. In the shadow of Abdabriel's imminent rule, many hugged and wept, trying to console each other as they grieved executed family members, soldiers, and way of life. They were helpless and overpowered. There was nothing they could do except to accept their fate in the hands of a man they'd all once trusted and loved.

In addition to Gish-L, Abdabriel had instructed every catering service in the City of Light to gather throughout the crowd as venders to keep people sated. He had paid all of them handsomely for their services. Abdabriel had intricately planned the event, intending for it to be a joyous occasion. He'd worked tirelessly to blanket the pain of lost loved ones with celebration and entertainment. Surely, they could understand the painstaking lengths he'd gone to in order to assure a promising future bathed in light and harmony. Advanced fireworks of every color and design decorated the twilight sky as Whewliss's setting sun kissed the summit of Pinnacle Peak. Dancers joined Gish-L on stage, performing choreographed numbers and routines. Light shows shot out from the mountain, blanketing the masses in vibrant arrays. The people were fed, the entertainment was illustrious, and the stage was set for Abdabriel.

It was going to be a historic night that Whewliss would never forget. The history books would look back on this evening's presentation as the genesis of universe's unification. And most importantly, future generations would remember this night as the very instant that Abdabriel N'kowsky, the Holy One, had led humanity to the light. All his hard work was finally going to pay off, and he couldn't be happier with the turnout. The only issue lingering in his mind—the only whisper challenging his constitution—was the brief encounter with the cloaked stranger. Abdabriel tried to put it out of his mind. It really didn't matter. There were always crazies out there, and he would have to get used to their attempts on his life. In the end, he was okay. Everything was going according to his grand plan.

As instructed, once Gish-L concluded her most popular song illustrating hope and picking herself up from the ashes of painful life experiences, the music stopped, and all the lights simultaneously turned off. Two more fireworks exploded and filled the darkening sky with vibrant showers of orange and pink, and then they, too, went dark. Conversations died down to nothing more than occasional whispers of dread and anticipation.

Gish-L's voice broke the silence as it broadcast across the planet, "My fellow Whewlights, welcome!" Her professional eagerness sounded overdone, likely due to laser implants aimed at her from fingers the crowd couldn't see. "Look around," she echoed out. "Look around yourselves. What do you see?" Nobody could see her or whatever it was she was telling them to look at. "My beautiful Whewlight brothers and sisters, all I see is darkness. I cannot see your faces. I cannot see who you are. We are shrouded in literal darkness that perfectly exemplifies the darkness that has long been this world's government." The crowd murmured amongst itself as the setting sun further aided her speech. "Long have you been told minimal truths about the worlds beyond our own. Lord Coyzle and EBOO have kept secrets. They have ventured into the stars and seen planets and people beyond our wildest imagination, but has he shared the truths about what exists beyond our world with us—with the public who voted for him? Has he shared the knowledge about what other worlds our government meets with? Has he given us any information about our safety? Has he asked for our permission to speak on our behalf with planets we don't even know exist? Has he done anything other than keep secrets from us, the people he's sworn to protect?"

Her speech trailed off, allowing the amassed Whewlights to whisper among themselves in the darkness.

"No!" Gish-L yelled, her voice trembling. "But my beloved Whewlights, I am honored to have been selected. I am privileged to have been chosen. I am humbled by the opportunity to present to you the man who wants to tear down the walls that keep us in the dark. The man who longs to teach you about the secrets beyond our world. The man responsible for removing the blinds from our eyes. The man who will reassure our confidence in our world's safety and remove our fears of the unknown beyond it. The man who wants to teach us about everything we don't know. The man who guarantees peace across Whewliss and will expand that same peaceful empire of light across the stars. I present to all of you: The man who stares fearlessly into the light the rest of our government was blinded by. The man who happily shares that light with every single one of us, regardless of our status, age, planet, gender, race, or anything that up until now has divided us. Whewlights, stand to your feet and help me welcome the Holy One, Abdabriel N'kowsky!"

As soon as she finished, light exploded from every source available, illuminating Pinnacle Peak with radiant splendor, top to bottom. Celebratory music roared out over the crowd, accompanied by the largest spectacle of fireworks yet. The darkening sky became brighter than it had been at midday. Dazzling patterns of lights and colors danced across the stage, reflecting out over the people. All the waving lights focused together, spotlighting Abdabriel standing in the middle of the stage next to Gish-L. His charisma had lost none of its brilliance. The crowd thunderously applauded. They were afraid not to with the thousands of soldiers scattered throughout them. A projection of what was happening on stage was broadcast against the sky.

Abdabriel threw his hands in the air and smiled out over the ocean of faces. "Hello, Whewlights!" More forced cheering greeted him. "I am grateful for your attendance. Words cannot describe my excitement for what I am here to share with you all. There is nowhere I would rather plant the seeds that will one day grow into the most beautiful future than right here, in the hearts of my family, in the place that we all call home."

He looked around as uproarious shouts, whistles, and light shows responded to his introduction. After absorbing their adoration, Abdabriel smiled and motioned to Gish-L, who stood next to him with her hands clasped.

"Help me thank Gish-L for her incredible performance on this historic day." Genuine cheering erupted as the Whewlights screamed for her. Abdabriel nodded. "She was so blown away by what tonight holds that she did this concert free of charge!" A twinge of fear and shame washed over Gish-L's face as Abdabriel went on. "If that doesn't tell you how incredible tonight is going to be, I don't know whatwill." He graciously nodded toward her and smiled. "Thank you so much, Gish-L. You inspire us all."

"Holy One." She bowed and then took her leave, walking down off the stage, where she was met and escorted away.

Abdabriel took a deep breath and closed his eyes, relishing the spotlight as he paused. "I have spent my entire life representing Whewliss." He opened his eyes and looked over the crowd. "In my youth, I fought in the ULW. Many of you were there, as well, and I know I speak for all of you when I say that it was the most difficult time our planet has faced. We were invaded by Daemoaniks: Monsters we did not know existed until it was too late. We discovered that we were not alone—that the universe is home to countless more worlds like our own. We learned that, though it is a beautiful place, it can also be dangerous."

As he spoke, Abdabriel walked the stage, finding more comfort in his performance than anywhere else.

"Once we defeated the Daemoaniks, we anointed Albei Coyzle as our lord." Some cheering erupted at the mentioning of Lord Coyzle, and Abdabriel responded by ushering for silence. "The vote was nearly unanimous because of what he stood for. He promised to lead us into a brighter future—one where we would have observers on other worlds that would report back to us. He promised to keep us informed so that we would never again be surprised by an alien invasion." Abdabriel went quiet, walking a few steps while staring out. Once his voice had echoed away, he asked, "But what happened next?" His hands dropped to his sides as he gave a helpless shrug. "My friends, we were lied to. Lord Coyzle did not share anything he learned with the public. He did not tell all of you, the very people who were scared, the very people that needed to know that they didn't have to be scared anymore—he did not tell you anything about any other world. Instead, he met in secret with the alien governments of other planets. Personally, I believe that would have been permissible if afterward he had shared what was discussed with every one of you. After all, did you not fight alongside him during the ULW? Did your parents and grandparents not die in the dirt next to me while we bled for liberation? We have all paid the price to stay informed about other worlds that could repeat the atrocities of history." He paused as his pulse sped up. "After promising you a bright future, he kept you in the dark."

Abdabriel's confidence and stage presence were undeniable. Though the majority of the Whewlights despised him and what he'd done, they couldn't refute the validity of the truths behind his speech. He stopped at the front of the stage and glared out at them.

"When we united as a planet, we elected one world leader in the hopes that he would do better than past politicians. How disappointed were we when we were betrayed? And I promise you that we were indeed *betrayed*. Let me tell you why. Let me tell you what I have seen. Let me tell you what Lord Coyzle has kept from you." Abdabriel shook his head as his words grew sharper. "Esteemed Whewlights, I have represented you as your ambassador for decades. I have visited each world as they've discovered the properties of light. I have greeted them and informed them of the existence of the other worlds around them. I have kindly invited them into universal peace treaties, ensuring that their evolution would not endanger our lives or the lives of any other planet."

As his passion grew, Abdabriel started pacing again, growing more animated.

"Now, I could lie to you, as most politicians would prefer to do. I could tell you that it worked. I could inform you that every world I visited eagerly jumped on board and joined our peaceful ways. After all, Whewliss is the most peaceful world in existence. Why wouldn't others want to adopt our ways of life?" He shook his head. "But, my fellow Whewlights, I cannot lie to you. Not anymore. It has been eating away at me like a disease, and the only cure is truth." He cleared his throat. "While every world eventually agreed to our terms of universal interaction declared in LOLA, it did not guarantee that they stopped fighting among themselves. That's where I've foreseen the beginnings of an inevitable Armageddon." He paused to let his words sink in. "I have visited more planets than any other human in history. I have seen more governments, cultures, beliefs, and types of humanity than anyone else, and my eyes have been opened so wide that I will never be able to close them to the truth." He stopped, his expression burning with urgency. "Since the ULW, there has been no great war on Whewliss. We have effectively made war obsolete. That—*that* is a feat!" He all but laughed with how impressive it was. "We made the need to slaughter each other a memory by uniting. We don't kill each other in drones like we used to. We have established peace. And to Lord Coyzle's credit, he wanted nothing but peace with other worlds, as well. We never hungered for the bloodshed of other planets because we washed the taste of our own blood out of our mouths. Life has never tasted sweeter."

Abdabriel paced a couple times, running his hands through his hair as he sighed.

"But that's just it. That's where we differ from other worlds. *Every* other planet still wages war against itself. There are two abiding by LOLA that are nearly exceptions, but aside from those two, even the rest of the

LOLA-abiding worlds still slaughter themselves over petty differences, land, greed, or the desire for more power. They still have the taste of their own blood in their mouths, and as they continue to technologically advance, what is to stop them from hungering for ours?" He paused, allowing the full gravity of his point to take root in every Whewlight mind. "Should another world hunger for universal power, what is to stop them from turning their eyes toward us or any other planet? What is to stop the horrors of Daemoana from repeating?" Again, he stopped and walked the stage.

Susurrating murmurs slithered through the crowd. There was no way for Abdabriel to hear what they were saying, but he was confident that he knew.

"These are questions I have laid at Lord Coyzle's feet for years. For yearsI have given him worlds of evidence supporting my uncertainties and concerns. I believed he would share them. After all, he was my lord. I voted for him. He was my close friend, and I thought I knew the man of character he was. But I was wrong. Do you know what he would tell me? Do you know what the man appointed to look out for your well-being would say in response to my compounding evidence?" Abdabriel scoffed in disgust. "Lord Coyzlewould tell me it was none of our business." An angry chuckle exploded from his lips. "He told me that it was none of our concern if other worlds are fighting amongst themselves— that it was each people's right to conduct themselves however they wanted on their own home world." Abdabriel shook his head. "Lord Coyzle refused to get the Whewlight army involved because preparing for the imminent invasion of other worlds was 'none of our business.'" Abdabriel squinted as he stared out over the masses. "As the leaders of peace, we were too respectful of other planets' right to free will and privacy to put an end to their fighting. Lord Coyzle wasn't willing to make the difficult call in order to guarantee beyond shadows that Whewliss would be safe. He was more concerned with surface politics than protecting his own people."

A hush fell over the crowd. Nobody wanted to admit that what Abdabriel was saying was resonating within them, but it was. He was voicing many fears that most of them didn't even know they had. He informed them about worries they hadn't thought of.

"That is why I am here. All the violence over the last week has been appalling, but it was unavoidable. The blood of the dead is on my hands. I admit that. I will be honest with you about absolutely everything." Abdabriel nodded at the expected cold whispers spat at him from the thousands of angry faces. "But I would rather have the blood of millions of Whewlights on my hands than the blood of billions." His words made most go quiet. "I would rather bear the weight of your hatred and their deaths than to one day witness an invasion that leads to our extinction." His eyes welled up with heated passion. "Not when I know I could have prevented it. I promise you that the sacrifices of the dead will be eternally shared by the sacrifices I will continue to make on your behalf."

After prolonged silence, Abdabriel collected himself and continued, "My fellow Whewlights, I know you are struggling to accept my explanation. Your forgiveness, understanding, and compliance cannot simply be asked; they must be earned. Please hear me as I explain how I will earn them." He looked around, a sudden air of confidence filling his lungs. "I will lead my Army of Light to every single world. I will welcome those who wish for peace into our shared future of harmony. All threats will be eliminated humanely and immediately. I will lead a wave across every planet, uniting them. They will share our way of life. We will educate them, equip them, and govern them with our laws. And here is a revolutionary concept that I'm excited for: I won't keep you in the dark about any of it!" He smiled. "Every single momentous step will be public knowledge on Whewliss to keep you informed. Our way of life — our peaceful way of life — will become the universe's way of life. No longer will other worlds wage war amongst themselves because they will be united in our future. You will not only be educated about every known world, but you will be invited to visit them. Your travel options will be exponentially expanded, and your destinations will be safe." Abdabriel's smile grew with his enthusiasm. "Every planet will be an extension of Whewliss, every person will be governed by our peaceful laws, every world will interact in harmony, and my Army of Light will maintain strict protection against any individual, people, or planet that threatens that way of life. Punishment for the threat of hostility will be swift and absolute. No longer will any of us fear invasion. No longer will you be in the dark. No longer will we turn a blind eye to the violence festering on neighboring worlds. You will be safe. We will be safe. No longer will you be treated as lesser beings by your leader. My fellow Whewlights, we have experienced pain together, and the price paid will buy us a future brighter than anything we've ever envisaged."

He took a deep breath and smiled. "Welcome to my vision. Welcome to the future. Welcome to the beginning of universal peace. Welcome to the light!"

Cheering roared out, echoing through the air, ricocheting off Pinnacle Peak. Screams, yelling, and whistling grew and grew until it was deafening. Abdabriel soaked it up, holding out his hands. He nodded and pointed out at the people. He couldn't tell if their cheering and jubilation was forced or genuine, but it didn't matter. He knew that, over time, they would embrace everything that was to come.

As Abdabriel rejoiced, he brought his hand to his ear. He blinked a few times as he tried to listen to a frantic soldier's voice. He couldn't understand the onslaught of word vomit screaming through his earpiece. He turned away from the crowd and spoke under his breath, trying not to distract the cheering.

"What? You found who?" He waited as the voice repeated itself. Throughout his speech, one of his soldiers had recognized some of the faces in the crowd. Abdabriel's smile grew. "Really? They came back? All of them? Even—" He kept listening. "Even the Daemoanik?" He grinned. "No. No. No. Don't. Don't do that. I want them alive and well. Bring them here. Bring them on stage with me."

37

Abdabriel watched as the crowd parted to allow some soldiers to walk through. If what he'd been told was true, the next move was going to play into his hand even better than he'd scripted. It would effortlessly validate the corruptions he'd exposed. It might even win over some of the people clinging to their hatred for him. Loud whispers and comments susurrated as the Whewlights recognized who was being escorted to the stage. One soldier forcefully subdued a woman who rejoiced after screaming Lord Coyzle's name. Other soldiers postured themselves with fingers at the ready, prepared to pacify any sparks of resistance. It was all too possible for Lord Coyzle's appearance to incite a riot. The distant crowd grew restless as they watched the projection in the sky. Lord Coyzle reaching the stage electrified the masses with nervous curiosity.

Abdabriel smiled and nodded, waving his soldiers to come up. "Welcome. Welcome. What a surprise we have here. I was not expecting you to be in attendance tonight." He looked from the crowd to Lord Coyzle. "Come on! Don't be shy," he said. "Get up here. The people are waiting."

Soldiers led Lord Coyzle and the others past Abdabriel's four bodyguards and up onto the stage. The fugitives were forced to step into the spotlight at finger point. There were too many soldiers for them to attempt any kind of surprise attack. They would be put down instantly and easily, so they stayed their hands. The group averted their eyes as bright lights hit their faces. The spotlights were more illuminating and intense on stage.

They were forced to the front of the stage nearest the crowd, displayed for all to see. Their faces showed fear, nervousness, and disdain. Only

Gideon smiled and waved at everyone. They lowered their heads and winked, adjusting their optical implants to the brightness.

Abdabriel chuckled. "I am honestly surprised to see Lord Coyzle here. Let's, everyone, applaud his courage! Come on!"

The crowd nervously obeyed. Loud cheering erupted and then quickly died as Abdabriel marshaled them to quiet.

"My dear old friend," he said to Lord Coyzle. "Did you return to try and stop me?" He delivered the last part of his question with a click of the tongue. "With thisbunch?" He pointed at the recruits. All throughout the crowd, his soldiers laughed.

"No," Lord Coyzle said with an off-putting sense of confidence. A few armed fingers rose at him as he took a bold step toward Abdabriel. "*I* can't stop you. You've ensured that. So I hired someone who could."

Abdabriel brought his head back with a feigned expression of fear. His eyelids fluttered, and he couldn't help cracking a grin. "Oh! Yes. Yes. Yes. Right. Of course." He laughed in relief, realizing he knew who Lord Coyzle was talking about. "You mean that strange man in the cloak?" He smiled at the crowd and rolled his eyes. "Albei Coyzle here sent a man to kill me, and clearly—" He motioned to his unharmed body. "—you have poor selection in assassins." More soldiers laughed. "The future can't be stopped. My vision for mankind will not be hindered. Look around you." Abdabriel said with spread arms. "Whewliss is with me."

As the crowd mumbled amongst themselves, Izzy leaned over and whispered to Gideon, "While we were being chased by an owl, Shadowmaker was here doing reconnaissance?"

Gideon puffed out his bottom lip and whispered back, "The owl was a scary bird, but Shadowmaker is an odd bird."

Dumakleiza, Traveler, and Vorlak studied the stage and the soldiers around it, each conspiring in their own way. There weren't any promising options, but that didn't stop them from plotting.

Abdabriel clicked his tongue and shook his head. "Dear Whewlights, please observe what has happened. I had to remove our Lord from power to take the first steps toward the light, and as soon as I do, what does LordCoyzle do?" Abdabriel scoffed. "He broke the Daemoaniks free from EBOO's Winkloh Star. Now they're in cahoots." He motioned to

Vorlak. "At the first threat to his way of life, Albei Coyzle joined forces with the greatest enemy Whewliss has ever had." The crowd began booing. An uneasy wave of tension rose. Their beloved leader was, in fact, standing on stage next to a Daemoanik. The creature's hideous face redirected their hatred. They didn't want to believe what they were seeing. Abdabriel sighed and paced the stage around them. "And what's worse? He's poisoned the minds of some of Whewliss' greatest heroes: three of the fourth phase recruits." Abdabriel paused and stared out at the crowd, who he knew were confused, wondering what he was talking about. "Oh? What's that? None of you know about the fourth phase? Well, I guess that's just another one of Lord Coyzle's many secrets that I'm going to have to share with the public. Don't worry, though," Abdabriel said as he turned back to Lord Coyzle. "While they have been lost to your blind excuse for leadership, I have at least salvaged the bright minds of two." He grinned. "Timrekka!"

At his command, Timrekka shyly walked into the light from the shadows behind the stage. His slow steps had every gathered Whewlight in awe as they stared at the short, stout man from a world they didn't know. None of them had ever heard of Thamiosh. At most, some knew a couple of the names of LOLA-abiding worlds. Anything less advanced than those were not even glimmers in the public eye. Once Timrekka made his way across the stage, he stopped at Abdabriel's side. He glanced up at his friends through his thick goggles and then turned his eyes down.

"Yes, Holy One," he mumbled in shame.

"Timrekka of Thamiosh?" Dumakleiza gasped at his treachery. "Certainly, you are not in leagues with the pretty god?"

Timrekka held his head lower, refusing to look up at her or any of the other disappointed faces. He didn't want to say anything. He didn't want to discuss the last few days. He just wanted to disappear back into the skydrop laboratory.

Abdabriel smiled. "Timrekka is one of the brightest minds I have ever had the pleasure of knowing. He has seen the light and has been richly rewarded beyond anything his world or Lord Coyzle ever offered. For the last few days, he has been bathed in my mercy and grace. He's been provided resources from every reach of the cosmos, and he has learned that the future is brighter than the past you all still cling to. His cooperation and inventions will help pioneer us into a new technological age of abundance. It's a shame you refuse to partake." Abdabriel looked out at the confused crowd before turning his full attention back to Lord Coyzle. He paused when he saw the smug confidence still on Lord Coyzle's face. The defeated man was staring at him like he knew something Abdabriel didn't. Abdabriel was intrigued, but it made him uncomfortable. "Old friend, it's over," he said simply. "I have only one question before we resume this evening's celebration. Where was your inept assassin from? I didn't recognize him, and you certainly didn't find him while you were hiding from me at the Wall." He stared deep into Lord Coyzle's eyes, challenging this strange confidence.

Lord Coyzle started chuckling, making Abdabriel cock his head. Lord Coyzle's mysterious amusement only made Abdabriel laugh a little himself as he considered that maybe Lord Coyzle had lost his mind in the wake of defeat. Lord Coyzle composed himself enough to wipe his eyes and look up at Abdabriel.

"Oh, old friend, who told you we went to the Wall?"

Abdabriel squinted. "Master Brawd told me—"

"Ah," Lord Coyzle interrupted with his signature rosy cheeked smile. "For a self-proclaimed god, you are tragically gullible." Abdabriel was not amused, but he wanted to see what had Albei Coyzle so self-assured. Lord Coyzle turned out toward the crowd and gave an acknowledging bow. "People of Whewliss, Abdabriel N'kowsky is right about one thing." He stared at the wondering faces as his voice echoed away. "I have not told you as much as I should have throughout the years. It was out of my desire to protect you. Recent events have convinced me of the necessity of sharing many planetary secrets. But first—" He turned to Abdabriel. "Allow me to be honest with *you*. We did not go to the Wall. You deserve to know the truth."

"Where did you go?" Abdabriel tried to ask calmly to maintain his public rapport.

"We went to find help," Lord Coyzle said. "On H.P." His smile transformed into a confident glare. He raised an eyebrow, daring Abdabriel to doubt him.

All expression disappeared from Abdabriel's face. There was no returned glare, no fear, no confidence, no sneer, no smile—just a stunned shock as his mind rejected what Lord Coyzle said.

"I don't believe you," he chuckled as his body went cold. "I don't believe that for a moment." It was easy to convince himself that Lord Coyzle was lying. Even if they'd been reckless enough to go to Horror Planet, they wouldn't have been able to make it back. The clouds would have made sure of that. Even more absurd was the implication that they had found and persuaded Shadowmaker. He was a legend, a dead myth, a relic of war lost to history. All aspects of the outrageous claim made Abdabriel laugh. The man who had visited him in his office was certainly not Shadowmaker. Abdabriel had never seen Shadowmaker, but he knew the man had been too young and looked too normal. Besides, Shadowmaker was dead. Many years dead.

Abdabriel smiled, though sweat beaded on his forehead. Relief set in as simple logic explained away Lord Coyzle's preposterous fantasy. But even as he reassured himself, he couldn't help the voice in his head. He even glanced over at Timrekka, hoping to see the same guffawing expression, but Timrekka stared down at his own feet.

Lord Coyzle's eyes oscillated across the crowd. He couldn't see too far since night had come. The stage was so bright that it made the distant tens of thousands even more difficult to make out, but he smiled, nonetheless.

"I'm sure he's watching us right now."

"He's dead," Abdabriel snapped. His charisma was slipping, and everyone watching around the world was picking up on it. He cleared his throat and postured himself before turning to some of his soldiers "Execute them." The attempted cool in his voice shook with vulnerable trepidation. "Everyone must bear witness. They must understand the punishment for resisting the light. There are no exceptions. Not even for you, LordCoyzle. I was going to offer you the chance to bow before me, but you have lost that opportunity with your blatant disrespect and threats against my life."

At his instruction, a group of soldiers stormed the stage. The audience gasped as armed guards surrounded Lord Coyzle and the recruits. They couldn't bear to witness the leader they'd adored for so long be brashly shot down before them. Cries and pleas for mercy began spreading from all directions.

From safe distances, the soldiers onstage lifted their fingers and aimed. They wielded arachniblast implants. The executions would be overly effective and the display of power, absolute. They awaited Abdabriel's final command.

"Please don't kill them," Timrekka begged. "I will do whatever you want, just don't kill them, because they're my friends, please don't kill my friends."

"Enough." Abdabriel held up a hand. "Unless you want to join them."

Timrekka went quiet, tears pouring down his face as his hands shook.

Fingers were aimed, sights were set, and the soldiers' obedience to the Holy One was outright. They were ready to kill. Strangely, the recruits weren't trembling. They weren't begging for their lives or praying to their gods as expected. Gideon even waved while the others patiently waited. It seemed like he was saying goodbye, but to them. The juxtaposing attitude was haunting. His uncomfortable insanity was infecting the soldiers with doubt. Nerves polluted their steadiness as they yearned for Abdabriel to just finish it already.

Abdabriel sighed as he felt his supremacy return like a breath of fresh air. There was no real threat to his reign. There was only a hollow attempt by a slipping power's desperate last stand. He had Lord Coyzle at his mercy. All was well. Everything was still on track for his rule over Whewliss. But even with the reassurance, he hoped no one noticed him doing a quick sweep of their surroundings, searching for the implausible ghost. He saw nothing. Of course he saw nothing. There was nothing to see. He cleared his throat and glared at the seven criminals.

"Fraternizing with Daemoaniks is inexcusable," he growled. "Resisting the light is intolerable. You cling to the darkness of the past, and that is where I will leave you." He shook his head as his eyes narrowed, staring into the depths of Lord Coyzle's. He wanted to see the life leave them. "Goodbye, old friend." With that, he motioned for his men to fire.

The crowd was silent. No one moved. Even the little breeze had stopped as Pinnacle Peak itself waited for the executions.

Abdabriel blinked and looked impatiently at his men. "What are you waiting for?"

One of the soldiers turned to him, perplexed. "Apologies, Holy One, but—" He looked at the others to make sure they were experiencing the same troubles. "Our implants, um, aren't firing."

"What do you mean they aren't firing? Of course, they fire. Try again. Now!" Abdabriel commanded, frustrated with the anticlimactic moment. He watched as the soldiers continued trying to shoot but nothing was happening. The more they tried, the sillier they looked.

"Uh-oh," Gideon said loudly enough for Abdabriel to hear as he winked at him. "Performance issues." He shrugged. "Happened to Traveler on Horror Planet."

Traveler scoffed at him. "You're making jokes *now*?"

"What?" Gideon asked. "Every guy's been there."

Abdabriel fumed as he resorted to lifting his own hand. If his soldiers were going to fail him in this iconic moment, he would lead by example and demonstrate his power. He aimed his finger and squeezed his thumb. Nothing. His heart raced as he looked at his hand. There wasn't anything wrong with it. He aimed again and tried to fire. Still nothing.

"See?" Gideon said to Traveler. "He went from omnipotent to impotent."

"What is this?" Abdabriel bellowed. The entire planet was watching him nosedive in comical ineptitude. Firing a weapon was a simple task. He'd fantasized about this moment for years. "What is—"

"You have lost your temper," a familiar voice said from somewhere. "Meaning you have lost the stage."

Abdabriel jerked his head up and looked around. "Who's talking? Show yourself!"

The crowd and soldiers looked around. They could hear the voice, and Abdabriel's reaction to it had them curious. It didn't sound menacing. It sounded composed and unruffled amid everything unfolding on stage. Murmurs spread throughout the Whewlights and soldiers alike as Abdabriel searched. No one else stood on the stage, and no one else—he stopped. The hairs on the back of his neck stood as he sensed a presence behind him. He slowly turned around to see who had managed to sneak up on him. Standing in the same shadowed portion of the stage Timrekka had walked out from was the hooded stranger.

"You," Abdabriel's trembling voice barely managed. He hadn't seen him arrive, and none of his soldiers had indicated an intruder. The Holy One had had enough with the man's secrecy. "Who *are* you?"

The cloaked man stepped into the light. "For the sake of expedient understanding, I will make my introduction quick and simple. I am who you Whewlights refer to as Shadowmaker," he said with acceptance and ownership of the title. "I have deactivated you and your soldiers' implants. I, too, shall operate only with my flesh upon this stage. Should death prove a necessary dance this evening, I will lead with an intimate embrace."

Abdabriel gulped as his eyes went dry. He tried to say something, but nothing came out. It felt like his knees were ready to buckle. He managed to force himself to take a step back.

"You're not—you can't be." He blinked, desperate for his eyes to lubricate. "K—k—kill—kill him. Kill him."

His soldiers looked at each other, waiting to see which of them was going to engage the man claiming to be the creature from their nightmares. Most had heard of Shadowmaker, and they weren't going to test the legitimacy of his claim. Those who hadn't heard of him recognized terror. None of them were armed anymore. Without their implants, they were powerless. They didn't have any melee weaponry. They could attack him with their hands, but that felt foolish. Even with their vast numbers versus him alone, something in their guts held them back.

Izzy leaned toward Gideon again. "Do you think Abdabriel has anything real to offer?"

Gideon grinned and then cupped his hands around his mouth. "Show him something real! Like, um, oh! I know! Piss your pants! That'll probably do it."

Shadowmaker stopped a couple feet shy of Abdabriel and stared at him with disturbing focus. Everyone was silent. With how quiet the air had become, the crowd had seemingly vanished. There wasn't a single sneeze, cough, gasp, or whisper to break the tension. Only Abdabriel's sniveling was audible, and it was broadcasting across the planet.

Without adjusting his hood or removing his hands from his cloak, Shadowmaker calmly spoke. "While I'm not in any particular hurry, there is no need to prolong this." His fiery eyes burned through the tears in Abdabriel's. "Bow down on your hands and knees before Albei Coyzle on this stage, renounce your plot to conquer the stars, disband your army, and apologize to every citizen of Whewliss for your inane attempt at authority. Do this now and suffer only the wrath of the Whewlights. Do it not, and you will suffer mine. I will not say this again."

Gideon all but shook his fists up and down, dizzied by what was happening. He'd managed to convince the most dangerous man in the universe to deal with an extragalactic bully. It felt like he had a front row ticket to the greatest show on Earth. He chuckled at himself for the mental wording.

Lord Coyzle waited with his hands on his hips. "My friend, Abdabriel N'kowsky. There's no need for bloodshed. Give up on this dark path. It's not who you are. You're better than this. You are a good man. You've just gotten lost. I will help you remember who you are." His authoritative voice was saturated in pity.

Abdabriel's eyes darted around, his brain burning as it fought for a way out. His distorted expression worsened as he saw his soldiers uselessly standing around. They weren't even trying to step in. They weren't even trying to protect him.

Of course!

His eyes shot to his four bodyguards, who were blankly staring at him from in front of the stage. They were the solution. They were his retribution, his salvation, and hope. Their combined might dwarfed even that of the legendary Shadowmaker. Abdabriel reminisced over how the mightiest Whewlight soldiers had fallen without much of a fight against his four juggernauts.

"Mosh Elle! Get up here! This is what I pay you for!" He hurried backward until there was at least twenty feet between him and Shadowmaker.

At his instruction, the heavily muscled Mosh Elle leapt up onto the stage with her powerful legs. She grunted with a wild snarl, stepping between the two men. Her neck tightened in anticipation for the kill to come.

She beat her chest with a tightly curled fist, glaring at Shadowmaker. She snorted a few heaving breaths and then smiled.

Abdabriel glared at Shadowmaker. "Shadowmaker or not, you should run. Though I don't believe it would do you much good."

Shadowmaker delicately pulled his hood back over his head and stared at the vulgar female. He patiently observed her aggression before looking around at the skittish soldiers.

"Unlike the Dyfrulian troglodyte before me, the rest of you have chosen wisely."

"Your bones are mine!" Mosh Elle roared, every vein in her body on the verge of bursting.

Gideon smirked at what sounded to him like a tacky line from a cartoon villain. He recognized a flare of Daemoanik eagerness in Shadowmaker's eyes. The legendary warrior grinned ever-so-slightly, but he didn't say anything else to provoke. He didn't growl anything to antagonize or make any threat. There was no need. He simply walked toward his opponent.

Mosh Elle screamed and charged. She ran with thundering footsteps and swung. Faster than she could process, Shadowmaker used one hand to brush her fist to the side and crush her trachea. Her eyes shot open in surprise as she found herself facing Abdabriel with her lower spine snapped inward. She flew limp against Abdabriel's reflection suit, her mangled body bouncing off and skidding back across the stage. It all happened so fast that Abdabriel hadn't seen Shadowmaker kick her toward him. By the time he yelped, she'd already stopped moving on the ground.

Shadowmaker looked at Abdabriel. "You have opted for my wrath. There is no turning back from that decision." He rolled Mosh Elle onto her back, positioning her lifeless, horror-stricken face toward the sky.

Abdabriel's soldiers looked at each other and slowly backed away. There was no payment Abdabriel could offer that would convince them to attack the hooded man. Most hadn't seen exactly how he'd killed Mosh Elle. Some weren't sure if he'd even hit her at all. They just stared at her twisted body twitching on the stage.

Even Dumakleiza's eyes were wide. In her lifetime of violence and combat, she had never witnessed such absolute efficiency. In that moment, she had no difficulty admitting the terror she felt, along with her jealousy of Shadowmaker's abilities. She wanted to be feared like that.

Abdabriel stuttered a cracking yell, "Brothers Diabelicoff!"

Before he finished his command, the tattooed brothers jumped on the stage. They had no fear of the cloaked man. They were even grateful for him killing Moshe Elle, which set the stage for them to prove their superiority.

"Hello, wee one," one of them chuckled as he stared down at Shadowmaker. "We've eaten children larger than you."

The other nodded, his deep voice sharing his brother's amusement. "Don't run away, little man. Chasing you would only make us hungrier."

Gideon shook his head, almost bursting into laughter. "Really? The dude took out a *planet*, and you mongoloids don't think he can handle a couple gorillas?"

One of the monstrous brothers pulled out a knife. It was large enough to be a sword in anyone else's hands. He tossed it back and forth between his thick mitts, grinning down at Shadowmaker.

Shadowmaker didn't acknowledge the weapon as he spoke. "When you are finished with your toy, I will sheath it in your rectum."

Vorlak cringed. He knew when it came to promises, Shadowmaker didn't use metaphors, and he always followed through.

One of the brothers laughed louder as the other slugged his shoulder. They couldn't help their amusement with the small man. Especially since the thousands around them were so terrified of him.

Once again, Shadowmaker wasted no time on additional threats or banter. He walked toward the behemoths with a barely noticeable grin. He appeared to the crowd like nothing more than a holy man taking a stroll with how he moved in the modest robe.

The knifeless brother roared as he kicked a boot forward, large enough to cover Shadowmaker's entire torso. Shadowmaker's breathing didn't change as he reacted with a quicker kick of his own. His heel shot up into the descending brother's, the impact instantly splitting the giant's shin and dislodging his kneecap. The ogre roared as he fell back, clutching his knee protruding through his pantleg.

His brother lurched forward, plunging the tip of the enormous knife straight at Shadowmaker's chest. Shadowmaker gracefully slapped the flat end of the blade away from himself, redirecting its momentum into the falling brother's face. Before the other could process that he'd killed his sibling, three of his fingers were snapped backward from the knife's handle. The blade was instantly retracted from the skull, and with one fluid motion, spun up between his legs.

As soon as Shadowmaker fulfilled his promise, the sword lodged parallel to the giant's spine, he turned to face Abdabriel. A howling yell exploded and then deflated, curdling to silence. The deadweight thud behind him didn't even make Shadowmaker blink. He only glanced back to ensure both brothers were facing upward. Abdabriel, however, trembled as if he, himself, was constipated with razor blades.

Without waiting to be prompted, Greaper stepped between them with haunting grace. He was unimpeded by the three dead bodies on the stage around him. Their defeat didn't matter. He didn't care for them. He didn't care for anyone. Allegiance to Abdabriel didn't even motivate him. Rather, he'd joined the crusade for the promised opportunity to kill on new shores.

His hollow eye sockets stared directly at Shadowmaker as if he could see him—as if he could already taste his blood in his mouth, and he savored the anticipation. Aside from the reflection suit, he was Abdabriel's last line of defense, but it wasn't Abdabriel he cared about. All he hungered for was dethroning Shadowmaker and proving himself the devil.

The crowd was petrified. Their night had gone from an abyss of lamentation to the return of their greatest nightmare. They were bearing witness to history just as they had been promised but not in the way that Abdabriel intended. Shadowmaker was alive and on Whewliss. Even if he removed Abdabriel from the equation, he was the true monster they feared most.

Shadowmaker studied Greaper for a moment. "A hellrat from the World of Whispers." He smiled. "All gathered would be deprived of honesty if I denied the pleasure I will take from this. You, I will not offer any escape." Then, Shadowmaker whispered something shrill and cold, a whisper that no one else could understand but rendered a twitch from Greaper's hollow eye-sockets.

"I swear to you, Greaper," Abdabriel urged. "Kill him, and I will reward you with whateveryou want. Anything. *Anything*."

The world could hear him begging, pleading like a cowering sheep, and he didn't care anymore. Not staring at Shadowmaker, and especially not after what he'd just witnessed. The legend was alive, and the demon's eyes were solely fixed on Abdabriel. Nothing else mattered anymore.

As he did with Rauphel Dycitz, Greaper walked toward Shadowmaker with a sinister grin and an outstretched arm. His open hand was ready to envelope Shadowmaker's face. Shadowmaker was right. It was a dance of death, but it was Greaper who was going to take the lead. Greaper was ready to feel the mighty warrior squirm and twitch in his grip as air escaped his lungs. He wanted to feel Shadowmaker's lips desperately struggle for breath against his palm. With serpentine looseness, he prepared to move with the variability of water and instantly respond to whatever defensive tactics Shadowmaker presented.

Before he could reach Shadowmaker's face, he felt the expected swat to the back of his hand, but he was surprised by his fingers and metacarpals breaking. As the grievous whack flooded his brain, Greaper tried to yell out but found himself bereft of breath as eight, twelve, twenty fists pounded into his abdomen. Almost simultaneously, each of his internal organs burst with rapid and precise punches. Ribs cracked, chipped, and broke off internally as Shadowmaker's onslaught paraded him backward until he was bouncing back and forth between the Daemoanik's fists and Abdabriel's reflection suit.

"Holy—no," Gideon muttered in gruesome amazement. "Ah!" He averted his eyes, unable to stomach it.

Blood poured out of Greaper's mouth as it flooded his digestive tract. Everything in his torso was being beaten to mush so quick that he only managed to scream after dying. Shadowmaker stopped and retracted his soaked fist from where it had broken through Greaper's skin. He stood still and coolly fixated on Abdabriel as Greaper slid down between them. Before the hellrat's body reached the floor, Shadowmaker caught him by the throat and laid him faceup. He then stood, exhaled, and adjusted the folds of his cloak.

All of Whewliss could see what was happening. Nobody moved. Nobody cheered. No one screamed. They watched with wrecked expectations for the evening. Even the recruits were petrified witnessing the disturbing fruits of their labor. Shadowmaker had exceeded their expectations without even addressing Abdabriel, and in doing so, hadn't broken a sweat. His performance was effortless. All that was left to do was address Abdabriel.

Abdabriel couldn't look away from Shadowmaker's patient eyes. He couldn't feel his arms or legs. Crippling inferiority lay waste to his ability to think as he stared at the cosmic predator. Shadowmaker's supremacy was undeniable, his ruthlessness, deepened.

"Just…let me go." He started crying, his posture bowing. "Don't kill me. You can't. M—my, my suit won't let you." Saying what he hoped was true made him cringe at the possibility that it wasn't. "Just let me go."

"Yes. The next issue: your suit." Shadowmaker stepped closer, his fierce eyes searching for a weakness or fault in the seemingly impermeable reflection suit. "I will solve that puzzle." He reached forward, wanting to test its power. He was ready to be pushed back by it, and he saw no harm in feeling its effects for himself. It was something he'd never learned about. Abdabriel stared at his extending hand. He knew the suit would keep him safe, but he was terrified of the simple fact that Shadowmaker was dedicated to his apprehension. It was a nightmare that had never crossed his mind. He'd considered every way his plan could fail. But never this.

Then, in a surprising moment, Shadowmaker's hand reached Abdabriel's throat as if there was no deflective force between them. He wrapped his composed fingers around it and squinted, unimpressed. Abdabriel stared down in shock and disbelief. Shadowmaker's hand should have been thrown back. The force of his movement should have been equally reflected away. Even physics had betrayed him. Abdabriel froze. Instinctively, he wanted to reach up and pull Shadowmaker's hand away, but he feared that resisting would result in something worse.

"H—h—how?" He barely managed a whimper as his legs threatened to give out.

Shadowmaker studied the simplicity of his hand around Abdabriel's throat. "I do not know."

There was puzzling silence before, "I'm sorry, Master N'kowsky."

Timrekka's nervous voice called to Abdabriel like a foggy dream.

The shy scientist shuffled his big feet forward while looking at Abdabriel. "I lied, and I feel awful for misleading you because I do not like lying, but I did not request a reflection suit of my own for the sake of physical protection. It was for my peace of mind because I wanted to see if I could study it, break it down, and dissect its ability so I could shut yours down if I needed to, and it took me a couple days to find a way, and I'm kind of embarrassed about that, as usually I can deconstruct something's inner workings much faster, but with its reflecting function, that was obviously a little harder. It's really impressive technology, but I couldn't idly stand by and allow you to keep hurting people. I'm sorry, I just couldn't, and I understand if you're angry with me." He dipped his head as Abdabriel stared at him from within Shadowmaker's grasp. It was mortifying to hear his timid voice echoing out over tens of thousands of onlookers.

Abdabriel couldn't stop shaking his head at the damning betrayal. "How?" His whispering voice broke Timrekka's heart.

"Uh." Timrekka cleared his throat. "Well, I know the reflection suits can deflect anything physical, even fluids and gases, so any kind of sneaky and obvious answer was moot, but then I tried being more innovative and considered sound waves, and you're not going to believe what the actual answer was." Timrekka almost giggled at the dumbfounding solution. "I remembered this one time Gideon told me about how on Earth, there's a rumored tone called the brown note. The Earthlings theorized that it was capable of making people defecate themselves involuntarily when they hear it, and I don't know why I thought of that of all things, but it was never actually confirmed—only theorized. However, I found what I think to be it because it made me defecate unintentionally, so I took that, added a few tweaks of my own, and now it's capable of dissolving the reflective material, so I made this little emitter." He held out

a remote with a button. "And I just used it a few seconds ago when I realized your bodyguards weren't going to avenge you and kill me after
using it, but you didn't hear it, though, because it's too low for human
ears. Crazy, right?"

He laughed and then stopped as he realized how insensitive he was
being.

"Oh, I guess that means you'll need to work on that exposed vulnerability," he said to Lord Coyzle. "I'll see if I can help you protect against
anyone else using my hack against your reflection suit in the future. Sorry
about kind of just blurting that out for everyone to hear, my mistake." He
stepped back as he realized he was rambling beyond the necessary facts.

"Interesting," Shadowmaker said, genuinely intrigued.

Abdabriel was in hysteric disbelief. His losses in a mere matter of minutes were astronomical. Everything he'd worked so hard toward for so
long had been snuffed away. He slowly turned his fragmented eyes to
Shadowmaker.

"Are you going to k—kill me?"

38

"No," Shadowmaker said, still holding Abdabriel's throat. Abdabriel slumped, hesitant in his relief as he stared into Shadowmaker's eyes.

Lord Coyzle hoped Shadowmaker wasn't planning to do to Abdabriel what he'd done to King Slaughtvike for over a century. Though he knew there was nothing he could do to stop him, he wanted to prevent that extreme of a punishment, no matter how heinous Abdabriel's crimes.

Everyone watched in tense anticipation as Shadowmaker took a slow breath. "I am not going to kill you. I prefer condemning you to betrayal by the very light you've falsely claimed to lead others to."

"W—what?" Abdabriel asked.

"Stick out your tongue."

Abdabriel's eyes widened as he shook his head. "No. No. Please don't cut off my tongue."

"I'm not going to cut off your tongue. I'm not going to hurt you."

"I'll bow before Lord Coyzle now," Abdabriel sputtered. "I should have done it sooner. I'm sorry. I'll bow. I promise. I'll bow."

"It's too late for that. You made your decision. It's either this or I dokill you. Now, stick it out. I will not say it again."

Timrekka studied Shadowmaker with the utmost fascination. He hadn't been on Horror Planet, and he was surprised to see how disarming Shadowmaker appeared. Although, after witnessing him dismantle an entire army single-handedly, Timrekka gulped.

Abdabriel blinked thick tears as he slowly stuck out his tongue. Shadowmaker maintained eye contact as he placed a dissolvable tablet in the center of it.

"Swallow."

Abdabriel was apprehensive, but the only thing he wanted to do less than swallow the mysterious tablet was provoke Shadowmaker.

Gideon squinted, whispering to Traveler as quietly as he could, "What do you think it is?"

Traveler shrugged, an eerie sinking feeling in the pit of his stomach. "We'll find out soon enough."

Abdabriel pleaded with a desperate expression but to no avail. Shadowmaker waited with unsettling quiet. Finally, Abdabriel closed his eyes and swallowed. He winced, expecting to feel some kind of pain, but nothing happened. He waited a little longer, expecting something to burn, an internal organ to liquefy, his lungs to tighten, or some kind of unforeseen torture. Nothing happened. It was as if he'd just swallowed a bite of food. He opened his eyes and looked helplessly at Shadowmaker, who'd let go of his throat.

Shadowmaker gave a single nod. "As I promised, you will not feel immediate pain at the pill's expense. And if you follow my next instructions, you will remain free of any side effects from its consumption. You are now a host of Fayded Light, an aggressively advanced form of photodermatitis, compliments of the indigenous on Fayde."

Abdabriel's eyes darted around. "I don't——I don't know what any of that means."

"Of course." Shadowmaker nodded. "I am referencing Horror Planet, the cryptic title your world has given Fayde due to your fears of what you do not understand. The indigenous, named the Fayded, have provided the strain you are now infected with."

Abdabriel gulped. "What is, uh, what am I infectedwith?" He felt a hopeless knot in his gut.

"Never again can you expose your skin to the ultraviolet rays of light without accruing flesh-eating rashes and boils. Nor can you heal with light. Depending on the duration of a single light jump, you will either die in transit or land with injuries that will require weeks to heal. From now on, you will age and heal at a natural rate, and you will sleep as most of humanity does on other worlds."

Abdabriel's heart thudded in his ears as his eyes widened. His entire way of life was going to shift in a sobering direction. Every convenience and luxury he'd experienced due to light was no more.

Shadowmaker went on. "You will live a life of darkness. You will only venture out in the cover of night. You will hunt for your food as a nocturnal beast, and hide in caves during the day. If you break that rule, you will suffer the natural effects of the disease. No longer will you lead others to the light, for you are condemned to the dark."

Abdabriel was silent. His jaw slowly moved up and down as he tore his mind apart searching for anything he could do to beseech Shadowmaker. After all, he had nearly limitless access to anything, anywhere in the universe. There had to be an offering worthy of mercy.

"Is there anything I can do to convince you to give me the cure? *Anything*?" He dropped to his knees. "Please! I'll do anything! I can get you whatever you want!"

Shadowmaker looked down at him without pity or judgment. "I've never found a cure. As I said, there is no going back."

The answer hit Abdabriel with sobering cold. Tears welled in his eyes. He grabbed Shadowmaker's robe and buried his face in it.

"Please," he sobbed. "I'll do anything!"

The entire world watched, vicariously digesting the existence of Abdabriel's disease. If Shadowmaker said it to be true, it was true. Their way of life wholly depended on light and the abilities therein.

Abdabriel suddenly stopped crying and looked up at Shadowmaker through red eyes. "W—w—what did you mean I will hunt for my food?" That's the only part that didn't fit. Based on everything Shadowmaker had described, his life would turn into that of a hermit. He'd live in a home or cell without windows, sure, but he wouldn't have to resort to primitive hunting.

"I will provide you with one kindness," Shadowmaker said. "A choice. Where would you prefer to live out the remainder of your life: Fayde, where you will be safely bathed in darkness at all times, or a young planet with Neanderthal-aged humanity? The second option is more pleasant,

I assure you, but you will actively have to seek shelter from the planet's two suns."

Abdabriel's jaw wavered as he tried to think of a way out. "I—I—please,Shadowmaker, I will do anything! Just let me stay here. I will live alone in darkness. I won't bother anyone. No one will even know I exist! Please!"

"Choose soon before your body fully digests the tablet. Regardless of which you select, you will land with some minor boils and rashes from the jump alone. I suggest you pick now, or I will choose for you."

Tears streamed down Abdabriel's face as all expression vanished. There was no way out. He was at Shadowmaker's mercy. He took a deep breath and exhaled, his chest completely deflating.

"I don't want to go to...Horror Planet."

Shadowmaker nodded while grabbing Abdabriel's arm and lifting him to his feet. "Wise choice." He stared into Abdabriel's eyes while reaching toward the sky and closing his fist. "I suggest fishing for your food. The planet is home to a trout, recognizable by its green and silver tailfin that is delicious when cooked over fire—depending on your preference of course. A true delicacy when smoked. By the way, firelight will not harm you. This should be common knowledge due to the lack of ultraviolet light emitted, but I feel obligated to ensure you're aware. Most of the greens and berries there are nontoxic. Eat with caution and you will learn quickly which are not for consumption. I advise choosing your shelter from the daylight carefully. There are arachnids approximately half the size of you that live in many of them." He leaned into Abdabriel's terrified face. "What is that customary Whewlight farewell? Oh, right. May the light gui—actually, that will not fit your life anymore, now will it? Allow me to amend it for you." He paused as Abdabriel sniveled. "Abdabriel N'kowsky, may the darkness guide and protect you." With that, Shadowmaker opened his hand and Abdabriel vanished.

Gideon blinked a few times as Abdabriel's punishment sunk in. "Holy hell." He looked at Traveler. "The brown note may not have done it, but I'll bet he's shitting himself now."

As they had been for quite a while, the crowd was silent. Whewlights and soldiers alike couldn't speak. Everyone was scared and vulnerable.

For a moment, they were one people, yet they each felt alone in Shadowmaker's crosshairs. No one on stage said anything either. They were all waiting to see what Shadowmaker was going to do next. Abdabriel was gone, but they were more scared in that moment than they'd been before.

Shadowmaker casually stepped to the edge of the stage and looked out over the tens of thousands of faces. He looked up at the live broadcast of himself in the sky, and then back down at the people.

"People of Whewliss, do not fear me. As of now, and barring future disagreements, we are not enemies. However, every soldier under Abdabriel's command, I present to you two options. Release the remaining soldiers of the Whewlight army and surrender yourselves to them. Do that and you will face only their wrath. Do it not, and you will face mine. You will receive no additional warning."

In an unexpected turn of events, the majority of the soldiers in the Army of Light instantly turned to the nearest Whewlights and professed their surrender. The crowd of Whewlights was completely comprised of civilians, and they had no idea what they were supposed to do with all the self-admitting prisoners. Most remained still, baffled by the shift of power. Some grabbed hold of the surrendered soldiers' arms and waited for Lord Coyzle to resume command and tell them what to do. Some took pride in the turned tides, eagerly taking hold of the soldiers who had executed their friends and family. Many of the yielding soldiers cried out of panic, while others simply repeated their surrender over and over, hoping to ensure that it was understood by everyone close enough to hear.

Shadowmaker turned to Lord Coyzle. "Our deal has concluded. Whewliss is under your protection."

"Thank you" was all that Lord Coyzle could muster as Shadowmaker walked off into the shadows behind the stage. Every pair of eyes watched until he disappeared. They couldn't see him in the dark corner at the base of Pinnacle Peak, and yet somehow they knew he had gone. Wherever he had disappeared to, no one knew, and that made him all the more daunting.

In the silence that followed, Whewliss's population had no idea what to do. What came next? A few hundred soldiers from the Army of Light proceeded to free the jailed Whewlight soldiers. They had no interest in suffering Shadowmaker's wrath. People watching from home worldwide were stunned.

Gideon's desire for adventure was beyond satisfied with what he'd just witnessed. It was something he'd never imagined would unfold when Traveler first invited him along for the fourth phase. The adventure he'd joined was beyond anything he could have found on Earth. And what baffled him more than anything else was that it had led to him sharing his personal testimony about his scar—with the greatest assassin in the cosmos, nonetheless. His smile dwindled as something replaced it. A sense of peace washed over him like warm water. He'd achieved a level of closure he didn't even realize he'd needed for a long time.

Traveler was glowing. An immovable smile complemented recovering breath. He'd recruited a fourth phase team. He'd brought them to his people. He'd led a resistance against a powerful traitor when even his Lord had failed. He'd displayed more direction and courage than nearly every Whewlight in history. He'd survived Horror Planet. That fact alone blew his mind. He smiled to himself. No matter what the future had in store for him, he felt a sense of pride he'd longed for since first volunteering.

Dumakleiza scratched Cooby's chin as she stared at the dead bodies onstage. She reminisced over how incredibly satisfying their demises had been. She'd found righteous pleasure in the justice of it all. Even arousal. Cooby purred and cooed as Dumakleiza thought about the advanced abilities of the Maker of Shadows. She wasn't sure why, but she felt more emotional about everything than she normally did. Perhaps it was due to the magnitude of it all. Maybe it was because it had all come to an end. Tears welled. She choked them back and smiled at her pet. After a few composing seconds, she whispered to Grimleck. It was time to recalibrate her soul with some much-needed prayer.

Timrekka felt left out. He jealously looked at his companions. Even with all he'd done on Whewliss, he longed for the bonding they had survived without him. One thing that made him feel vital to the team was the success of his brown note. He felt a sense of involvement at having helped overthrow Abdabriel in their time of need.

Vorlak was unsure of the future. The Daemoanik warrior had assisted the very people he'd dedicated his life to conquering, enslaving, or eating. He'd helped them hunt down the one man he feared more than death itself. And what's more, he'd played a pivotal role in saving an entire world from a maniacal dictator. Everything was backward. What kind of monster had he become? Now that Abdabriel was defeated, he hoped Shadowmaker wouldn't change his mind about sparing him. Would he be executed or maybe returned to a Winkloh star? The idea depressed him.

Finally, Lord Coyzle cleared his throat and walked past the dead bodies to the edge of the stage. He looked out at his people, knowing it wouldn't be easy to salvage the moment. What was he going to tell them? Everything he'd kept secret for the sake of their safety had been exposed. Where should he begin? He cleared his throat again as he tried to think of the most appropriate approach to a planetary address after everything that happened.

"My beloved Whewlights. There—there is much we need to talk about."

39

It took a few days before Lord Coyzle was finally able to meet with the recruits. He'd been overwhelmed with the work needed just to begin reparations around Whewliss. The physical damage alone caused by Abdabriel and his Army of Light was going to take months to restore. The emotional damage, on the other hand, would take years. There were some scars that no amount of light could heal.

Lord Coyzle freed Master Brawd and Lady Melodeen from the City of Light's Winkloh Star. The other criminals and Daemoaniks within the same light prison were immediately returned to it once the two council members were successfully retrieved. Though, Lord Coyzle looked at them in a different light for a moment.

Master Brawd was reinstated as Whewliss' military leader. With his freed soldiers also returned from their imprisonment, he'd spearheaded the arrests and handling of the soldiers of Army of Light. Since he hadn't personally witnessed the events at Pinnacle Peak, he didn't understand why the soldiers were so compliant in their surrender. Not one of them put up a fight. In fact, most expressed that they felt safer in his hands than they did at the thought of going free. Many even offered to further surrender themselves and pledge their allegiances to Lord Coyzle and to Whewliss.

Furthermore, due to the exposure of what lay beyond their safe little world, thousands of Whewlight men and women had enlisted in the military. Many more started the steps for joining the police force. More poured in every day. They wanted to replenish the ranks and do their part in protecting their home from anyone like Abdabriel in the future. Never again would they be so easily duped. Civic pride had been ignited in hearts across the world, and there was no snuffing it out. With Lord Coyzle's leadership, Whewliss was pulling together with even more unity than before.

On the fourth day after the events at Pinnacle Peak, Lord Coyzle called for a private meeting in his office. The recruits and what remained of the council met in the capital skydrop.

Lord Coyzle stood from his chair and walked around his desk, taking time to hug each of them. He even hugged Vorlak, who was unfamiliar with the custom and even more uncomfortable with it. Master Brawd and Lady Melodeen squinted and turned away. They couldn't watch. The Daemoanik was still a monster.

Lord Coyzle stepped back and smiled. "Well." He sighed from mental exhaustion and sat back down in his chair. "Have a seat. Please. We've been through too much. There's no need for formality."

Before Lord Coyzle could say anything else, Master Brawd spoke. "I apologize, my lord, but I do not believe it wise or safe to have a Daemoanik in attendance during a private meeting." He glared at Vorlak. "I'm grateful for whatever assistance he provided you, but he should be returned to the Winkloh Star now that Abdabriel is defeated. He's not being put to death, and that is reward enough for one of them."

Vorlak glared back. He wanted to argue, attack, or at least growl, but he chose to sit in silence. The self-control made him gag, but somewhere deep down, he knew it was pertinent to his survival.

"No," Lord Coyzle firmly said. "I appreciate your concerns, Master Brawd. They are well-founded in the people as a whole, but this Daemoanik has earned my trust and respect. Therefore, he is permanently freed from the Winkloh Star, barring any future crimes. You and all of Whewliss will treat him with the respect he's earned. You don't have to like him, but you will not show him any incivility. Also, he shall not be addressed by his people, but by his name, which is Vorlak. And finally, while we're on the subject, Vorlak—" He turned to face the Daemoanik. "You are here at this meeting so I can inform you of what you will be doing. Rather than the Winkloh Star, I would prefer to provide you the chance to contribute on Whewliss. You will enlist in the Whewlight military."

Everyone's eyes shot open.

"My lord," Master Brawd urgently interrupted, but Lord Coyzle held up a silencing hand.

"Now, you will not get your own home and be treated as a planetary citizen, mind you," Lord Coyzle said. "You will be subjected to the same training as any Whewlight soldier and held to the same standard of professional conduct. You will obey every one of our laws. You still have much to prove in order to be treated as an equal in civilian population, and it will likely take years to earn the public's trust, but I believe military purpose would be a healthy beginning."

"Yes," Vorlak roared with excitement, practically wagging his non-existent tail. He lacked the words to adequately express how eager he was to take Lord Coyzle's offer. He would be permitted continued freedom from the Winkloh Star. He'd have a purpose again, and that purpose might include violence. He was an ecstatic monster.

"And," Lord Coyzle added with his signature rosy grin, "if I can make a personal request of you?" He smiled bigger as Vorlak nodded. "If you manage to earn the trust and approval of Master Brawd, I request you eventually join my personal detail as one of my bodyguards here in the City of Light."

Vorlak anxiously looked at Master Brawd's judgmental scowl like a dog ready to please its master. He blinked his red eyes a few times before turning back to Lord Coyzle and nodding.

"May the light guide and protect you during your training, Vorlak," Lord Coyzle said. "Master Brawd is a tough one to please, but you have at least earned the opportunity to try."

Master Brawd sighed, refraining from the insubordinate comments he wanted to scream into Lord Coyzle's face.

Vorlak shot an excited look to Gideon, who smiled and gave him two proud thumbs-up. Vorlak's hands trembled with delight as he pointed his jagged thumbs in the air, as well. Whatever the gesture meant, it seemed like a good omen.

While Master Brawd stewed in disapproval, Lord Coyzle turned to the recruits. "I just realized, when you released me before jumping to Fayde, Tsuna wasn't with you. Is he all right? Where is he?"

"I dropped him down the fourth phase after he executed Candelle to earn Abdabriel's trust," Master Brawd stated with flared nostrils.

Lord Coyzle's eyes widened as he stared at the hardened general. "Oh. Well. Good riddance then." He solemnly paused. "I'm so sorry, old friend."

Master Brawd gave an appreciative nod as Lady Melodeen squeezed his hand.

Silence settled in the room before Lord Coyzle turned to Timrekka. "Timrekka, I haven't had the opportunity to speak with you as much as the other recruits, and it saddens me that you were left behind when we went to Fayde. I know you were involved in the plan's conception. However, I am unable to express the magnitude of my gratitude for your assistance with Abdabriel. From within his grasp, your work made it possible to end his reign. Thank you. On behalf of Whewliss and every world that would have been invaded, thank you."

Timrekka gave a humble nod and grinned. "You're welcome."

"Did Abdabriel—" Lord Coyzle didn't want to ask. "Did he kill Jasss?"

Timrekka perked up and shook his head. "No, your lord, er, *my* lord, the Holy One, er, Abdabriel, ugh." He shook his head at his inability to speak. "Abdabriel gave her a group of his soldiers and sent them with her to her world to kill the slavers to prove his sincerity to her, so last I knew, she was alive, but she's on Ojīptian now, killing, uh, slavers with the Army of Light." Timrekka wasn't sure how they would take the news, and he felt nervous about possible repercussions.

"Ah," Lord Coyzle said as he squinted, turning his eyes to the floor. "Huh. Hmm." He tightened his lips. "I'm not sure what the appropriate response to that is."

Timrekka lowered his eyes and twiddled his thumbs.

Lady Melodeen looked inquisitively at Lord Coyzle. "Are you considering sending some of our troops there to stop them from interfering with Ojīptian's way of life?"

Lord Coyzle slowly looked up at her as he weighed his options, "I'm not sure. That's a...difficult situation. I'm not sure what the *right* thing to do is. That was over a week ago."

"If I may?" Gideon raised his hand. "Technically that'd be interfering with another planet's war and getting involved in a what's none of your business. I, personally, wouldn't try to police another world. That's an arrogance reminiscent of—dun, dun, dun—Abdabriel." Gideon gave a blatant head shake. "When it comes to your stance against interplanetary interference, there's more continuity in you staying out of it than you getting involved. Neither side is your people and neither cause is your cause. Personally, and this is just me, I believe you should just let this ride out. Besides, if another world's war results in freed slaves? Kind of sounds like this may be the one good thing to come of Abdabriel's crusade." Gideon shrugged. "Besides, once they've completed their mission, any surviving soldiers will return here, and you can then process them through the gelatin. Bam. Bam. Bam. All I see are wins, but I'm interested in any argument anyone else has."

Lord Coyzle stared at him for a moment and then looked around for opposing opinions.

Master Brawd nodded. "I agree. One of two results is most likely. One: The contingent of Abdabriel's soldiers is defeated by Ojīptian's forces, and we won't have to concern ourselves with them any further. Two: The Army of Light successfully kills all the slavers and then, as Gideon stated, they play into our hands by returning to Whewliss. I'm supportive of either outcome."

"But," Izzy chimed in with a disheartened tone, "what about Jasss? She could die."

Gideon nodded sympathetically. "Yes, that's possible. And if I were to venture a guess, she's probably happier risking death while freeing her people than she would be here, knowing her friends and family were still slaves. I'm sure she's obsessed over this idea, fantasized over it for years. And now it's finally coming true."

"Agreed," Dumakleiza said with an outburst that stood her to her feet. "It would be an unforgivable cruelty to rob her of this rare chance to avenge her people and break their chains. Whether she lives beyond their retribution or dies in the fires of combat, she is exactly where she needs to be. Don't let her live for nothing when she could have died for something."

Izzy slumped with a heavy exhale. "I know. I'm just worried about her."

"Do not drown in fear." Dumakleiza placed a comforting hand on his shoulder. "Pray for her aim to stay true, her ferocity to burn bright, and for her safe return. Pray, Izzy of Jurael."

Izzy gave an uncomfortable nod, afraid to argue with the medieval princess as her words did nothing to comfort him.

Lord Coyzle puffed out his bottom lip. "Well, I suppose we do have our hands full here on Whewliss. I, too, shall say a prayer for Jasss's successful and safe return." He nodded as the decision made more sense. "I never liked the Ojīptian slavers, anyway."

Lady Melodeen nodded with wide eyes. "Me neither. Awful people. So cruel."

"So," Traveler spoke up, "I don't mean to interrupt, but while you are busy with Whewliss, what is to become of our mission? Have we given up on the fourth phase?"

"Well." Lord Coyzle turned to him. "That's actually why I wanted to speak with you. I know you're hoping to pick up where you left off with the fourth phase expedition." He paused as he tried to think of how to delicately word his thoughts. "I was hoping I would be able to convince you all to stay here, and at the risk of sounding like Abdabriel, help me oversee Whewliss." He held up a hand, urging them to listen before responding. "Now, I understand that's not as appealing, but you've all shown such courage, leadership, wisdom, and creativity with how you — well, how you saved us, really. And the council has three empty seats."

He paused with reverent silence for the dead.

"I was hoping I could talk you all into forming Whewliss's new council, while still keeping Master Brawd and Lady Melodeen, of course. And before you answer, just know that I hold you all in the highest regard, and that this offer has never been made to aliens. But Whewliss needs people like you, no matter where you're from."

Traveler's eyes and jaw were as open as they could be. The honor and prestige of what was offered had him momentarily drunk on the idea. It was an impossible fantasy, a fool's dream, second only to the aspiration of becoming Whewliss's lord. He stumbled over an attempt at words before shutting his mouth and taking a moment to compose himself. After all his hard work, his status could be that of the most esteemed echelon. The council was so highly respected that they nearly came off as alien themselves, and now he had the opportunity to be one.

Timrekka looked up at Lord Coyzle. "I—" He twitched and adjusted his goggles. "I am grateful for the invitation, but I couldn't handle that kind of responsibility, and it's making my palms sweat just thinking about it because I don't have the wisdom, or knowhow, or experience, or ability to guide others, so I would lose my mind." He chuckled as he averted his eyes. "Being around too many people and being in charge of decisions that affect an entire world—" He shivered. "It's not for me. I couldn't handle it, even if everyone else accepts your offer, because I just hope you still let me go back to the Wall to study the fourth phase, even if it's just me. Sorry if it's not the answer you were hoping for, but I would just prefer to study and experiment with the unknown." He brought his eyes back down to the floor, hoping he wouldn't be in trouble for saying no.

Lord Coyzle nodded. "I understand, Timrekka. And I respect your position. But one thing you said that I will not tolerate is that you don't have the wisdom. Never undermine yourself like that. Not after who you've proven yourself to be. Anywhere your journey leads you—any place you visit—they will be lucky to have you *because* of the wisdom and kindness you possess."

Timrekka stared at the ground and nodded with a bashful grin. "Okay."

"I am in agreement with Timrekka of Thamiosh," Dumakleiza stated proudly. "I know not how to lead a giant world, and I still am not convinced that some parts of your 'science' aren't veiled magic." She nodded to Timrekka with stern support. "I, too, would prefer to test my courage and venture into the darkness on the Wall. And Sir Gideon is coming, too. He is allowed no choice, for he is mine."

Gideon chuckled. "Well, I guess that's that." He smiled and looked to Lord Coyzle with respect and admiration. "I know how much what you're offering means. It's something I don't think I deserve. But even more than the position of council member itself, the fact that you believe I should sit in that circle—well, that is a recognition I am incredibly humbled by. I've been given many special and sentimental things in my life, but this just—

it means the world to me, and I'm honored to even hear you say the words." Gideon scoffed. "And who knows? Maybe if we return alive and that mission is over, our curiosity is satisfied, and you have the answers you've sought—well, at that point, if that invitation is still open, then we'll talk." He smiled. "But I can't *not* go down that hole. I dipped my toe in, or head, rather, and there is something down there. Something or someone spoke to me, and I have to know who was in my head."

Lord Coyzle nodded at them as he sighed. "I would be remiss if I didn't tell you all how disappointed that leaves me." Another heavy sigh. "But I understand. The fourth phase is, after all, why you were recruited in the first place. It would be unkind not to allow you to explore it. And I admit that I am still quite curious about what's beneath the ripples I've heard so much about."

Gideon slowly shook his head with a smile. "You've never seen it? Like, ever? No, I guess you wouldn't have, huh?" He clicked his tongue. "You really need to visit the Wall." He smiled. "It's—it's beautiful. It's really difficult to explain what it's like to stare out at endless flatness."

"Oh, I've seen images and video relay," Lord Coyzle said with a nod. "And yes, it's unlike anywhere else I know of. I can only imagine what it's like actually being there."

"Dude." Gideon craned his neck. "No arguing. Your next vacation is the Wall. It just has to be. Have a sazeal cocktail, dig your toes into the black bead, and drop a fishing line down the hole. See what kind of creepy voices you can reel in. What else could a guy ask for?" He shrugged. "At least you've had onevacation from Whewliss, even if it was to Horror Planet."

Izzy spoke up, turning his eyes to Lord Coyzle. "I hope this doesn't disappoint the rest of you." He motioned to the other recruits. "But I would be interested in accepting your invitation, Lord Coyzle. That is if I'm included on your list of candidates."

Lord Coyzle smiled and nodded, bolstered with liveliness. "Of course, Izzy. I would be so happy to have you join us. Without your guidance in the swamps on Fayde, we would all be digesting in the stomachs of those reptiles. We would have never found Shadowmaker and would have subsequently failed Whewliss. Of course I want you on my council."

"Gratitude." Izzy beamed.

Dumakleiza cocked her head to the side. "Izzy of Jurael, you do not wish to venture down the hole with us? Is that not why you are here?"

Izzy sighed. "I've had enough danger and risk for a while. You already have one scientific mind filling that position, so you really don't need me. I believe my skillset would be put to better use here. Of course, I won't compare to Lady Skorric or Master Keevind, but I want to help as best I can. And I want to be here in case Jasss comes back." He blushed.

"One thing is certain," Lady Melodeen chimed in. "You will absolutely be an improvement over Master N'kowsky." She smiled through unhealed wounds.

Lord Coyzle nodded. "I think you will do exquisitely, Izzy."

Timrekka leaned toward Gideon. "Reptiles?"

Gideon nodded with a dopey grin. "Mhm! Big ones. Tried to eat Vorlak. There was also an owl half the size of this skydrop. Tried to eat Duma."

"And humans of night," Dumakleiza added.

"Tried to eat allof us." Gideon smiled.

Timrekka sighed, unable to conceal his jealousy. "I know I would have been terrified, and I probably would have cried, and likely urinated in my suit over and over but——"

"I urinated everywhere," Vorlak proudly added. "We could do it together."

Timrekka paused and then resumed. "I wish I would have been there. I wish I could have been there when you first found Shadowmaker. I can't begin to fathom how scary that must've been. How did you convince him to help us?"

Gideon just gave a small smile. "A story for another time. But don't be envious, big guy. We're going down the hole together. I can only imagine what we'll experience down there." His words trailed off as he remembered the whispering that pierced through him. He shook his head.

Once Lord Coyzle finished congratulating Izzy, he turned to Traveler. "Four Zero? Where does your heart lead you? The council or the fourth phase?" His energy calmed as he looked at Traveler. "Truly, after what we've been through together, there's no one else whose wisdom I would rather have guide me than yours. In fact, if I am ever to choose a successor, you would be my first choice."

Traveler was so lost in thought that the commendation failed to process. Once it did, he looked up at Lord Coyzle with yearning eyes. He looked over at Master Brawd and Lady Melodeen, their visible approval encouraging him to accept the offer. Traveler gave a subtle smile before looking at the recruits. He stopped when he saw Gideon. Gideon's face didn't beg him to go or show disapproval if he stayed. There was just understanding, support, and pride. Traveler's eyes narrowed, and his smile grew. He turned to Lord Coyzle.

"That's more than I've everwished for my life." His smile diminished. "You honor me, my lord." He gave a slow exhale that seemed to lift the weight of the world from his shoulders. "However, this was given to me." He pulled Gideon's backpack from behind his chair. "She goes by Sonder. And I, for one, can't imagine her collecting dust." He hoisted it onto his lap, the bag rattling and clinking with unknown items and trinkets. He stared at it, fascinated by its rugged character. "She belongs to adventure, and since she's mine to carry now, it'd be irresponsible of me not to go down the fourth phase with my team."

Lord Coyzle almost laughed as he nodded. "Well, Four Zero, should you return, there will always be a seat for you on the council."

"Thank you, my lord," Traveler said with an inexpressible amount of gratitude. "It has been an honor to have you actually join us on the perilous quest to save our people. Whewliss couldn't ask for a greater, more courageous leader. I believe there is truly nothing you wouldn't do for us."

"Thank you, Four Zero," Lord Coyzle said with rosy cheeks. He sighed heavily before looking to the recruits. "So, where wereyou with the fourth phase preparations before Abdabriel interrupted?"

Master Brawd thought back, realizing he didn't remember much before Abdabriel had taken the red spotlight of anger in his mind. "Uh, we had just—"

"Well," Timrekka enthusiastically took over, "we were discussing a solution to the darkness issue, and for the last few days, doctors Moybo,

Minkel, and myself have been creating prototypes of miniature Winkloh Stars, really promising, I think we're close. We just need to find something biological to shoot into it, and otherwise, we need to work out food rations, the language barriers beneath the ripples, and that's all I can think of right now."

"Miniature Winkloh Star?" Lord Coyzle asked with interest. "I'm curious to see what you come up with." His obsession with the fourth phase's mysteries was instantly refueled. "Well, Master Brawd, the mission is yours to direct from here."

"Actually," Master Brawd said and shook his head, "I was barely able to spare the afternoon for this meeting. Repairing our military is consuming all my time. I believe Four Zero is more than qualified to take lead on the expedition. Either way, I cannot."

Lord Coyzle turned. "Four Zero, the fourth phase is *yours* if you want it."

Traveler nodded. "That I will proudly take lead on. Thank you, Master Brawd." He nodded graciously as Master Brawd did the same. He turned to the recruits with an intense focus in his eyes. "First things first, Duma, would you do me the honor of leading us in prayer for our mission's safety?"

Dumakleiza stood to her feet. "Yes, Diviner, it would be my pleasure." She steadied her nerves and bowed. "Mighty Grimleck, it is I, Dumakleiza Yagūl. I humbly beseech you on behalf of the Diviner of Whewliss, Lord Coyzle of Whewliss, Master Brawd of Whewliss, Lady Melodeen of Whewliss, Gideon of Earth, Timre—"

"Duma," Traveler snapped with a little smile. He rolled his fingers in the air, ushering her to get a move on.

Dumakleiza nodded. "Oh, powerful Grim, send your winged warriors to watch over us. Though, if I may, I request they not be giant owls this time. In my previous prayer, I chose my words poorly." Gideon smiled at how honest and adorable he found her prayers to be.

She went on. "Keep us vigilant and alert beyond the white ripples. I pray that if any of us are to perish, we do it in the throes of combat against your enemies." Traveler loudly cleared his throat and chuckled at her insisting on celebrating violence in her prayer. She got the message. "Grim, if I can retract that last portion. It would be preferable if we were to live. All of us. To live." She glanced at Traveler, who nodded in approval of the revision. "I am grateful for all you have already done for us. Thank you." She nodded again. "So let it be made true."

Gideon smiled. "In Jesus's name, amen."

"Amen," everyone said.

Tears welled in Dumakleiza's eyes as she looked around at those she'd led in prayer. "Ugh." She wiped the wetness from her cheeks and shook her head. "I do not know why my happiness betrays me with tears."

"What do you mean?" Gideon asked.

"I have been crying with no reason," she said. "I am not one who cries without purpose. The curse of a woman's heart maddens me."

"Do you not know?" A voice turned everyone's attention around to see Shadowmaker standing at the top of the office's stairway.

"Holy spirit!" Gideon laughed, startled. "You're like freaking Space Batman, man. Do you ever use smoke bombs?"

"Why are you here?" Lord Coyzle asked, his happy tone transformed to firmness.

Master Brawd and Lady Melodeen recognized Shadowmaker from the footage they'd seen from Pinnacle Peak. They froze. While everyone else was merely tentative about his sudden appearance, their fear levels skyrocketed. Master Brawd's fists clenched. Even with the guarantee of his failure and death, he was ready to leap into action to defend Lord Coyzle. Lady Melodeen felt dizzy. She was less than ten feet from the one and only Shadowmaker. Terror consumed her. If she hadn't been sitting, she would have fainted.

Shadowmaker took two steps closer. Rather than his usual cloak, he was wearing what looked to Gideon like an astronaut's suit made of slick medieval armor. It was black and sheened, appearing to be made of steel or a similar metal. Minus Shadowmaker's head, he was fully covered in tactical gear. The sleek design was menacingly stylish, and they could only imagine what the armor was capable of. Shadowmaker showing up unannounced in body armor made the others wary.

Lord Coyzle repeated himself, "Why are you here, Shadowmaker?"

Shadowmaker looked past him to Dumakleiza. "You are with child. His, if my guess is correct." He turned his hazel eyes to Gideon.

Dumakleiza looked down at her flat stomach. Then, as if her shift in energy was contagious, Cooby reached down and touched her belly, curiously dragging his monkey fingers around it. He cooed and looked at her for guidance, but she was too taken aback by the suggestion to pay him any attention.

Gideon jumped to his feet and stepped over to Dumakleiza. "How do you know? Are you sure?"

"I'm certain," Shadowmaker said. "Pregnancy hormones aren't difficult to detect. I'm surprised the Whewlight suits haven't informed you of the child's existence."

Lady Melodeen flashed her eyes back and forth between Shadowmaker and Dumakleiza. "We've—we've been, uh, too preoccupied to check the suit reports."

Shadowmaker nodded. "In case it is a concern, do not worry about interplanetary breeding. There are only dangers in rare circumstances, but I believe you both possess compatible genetics. Your child will likely be healthy." He turned to Timrekka. "You, on the other hand, should not mate with a Whewlight. The child would not survive. Their wombs are not strong enough for a Thamioshling infant."

Timrekka nodded, unsure of what else he should do. "Okay." It was something he was suddenly curious about studying. His mind started racing with ideas.

Gideon placed his hand next to Cooby's on Dumakleiza's stomach. He was speechless. He didn't know if he was supposed to say anything, or if he even could. The possibility of her getting pregnant hadn't crossed his mind. They'd only been intimate once.

"Why are you here?" Lord Coyzle asked Shadowmaker more loudly. "*I* have asked three times now." He couldn't help smirking at stealing the Daemoanik's line.

Shadowmaker gave him a genuine smile. "Fair, Lord Coyzle. Congratulations on reclaiming your title, by the way. As for why I am here, I wish to ask for your blessing." He was speaking with a liveliness that didn't match his demeanor.

"What could *you* possibly want *my* blessing for?"

"I am here to lend my assistance to your venture into the fourth phase, as you call it. It is an efficient classification system you have invented."

Everyone stared at Shadowmaker while they considered the ramifications of his request. While they were all grateful for his assistance with Abdabriel, the idea of him tagging along into the fourth phase was a risk they hadn't considered. But if they were to refuse him, there was no foretelling how he would react. There was no stopping him from going if he wanted to.

Lord Coyzle took several deep breaths and composed himself. "Shadowmaker, I can't tell you how indebted we are to you. You have proven yourself to be more than your legend, and I dare even say that I consider you an unprecedented ally now. I am equally grateful to Gideon for paying your requested price." He waited, hoping Shadowmaker would get the hint.

Shadowmaker gave a subtle nod. "You fear the gamble of involving me. You are concerned that I would be a danger to your people. I understand. However, I assure you that I would not be any threat. None of you pose any threat to me, and I have no qualms with any of you. I have proven that I am true to my word."

"Why do you want to join us though?" Lord Coyzle asked. "In one light, it's flattering, but if we're being honest, you could find the hole and explore it yourself. You work alone, don't you? Why do you want to go with us?"

Shadowmaker nodded. "Yes, I typically operate in solitude, but it is not out of preference. It's how I have learned that I must live. Never before have I been sought out by those who know who I am for nonviolent reasons. If I am being honest, it was a refreshing. Usually when I come across someone who knows who I am, they either run or try to kill me." He looked at Gideon, who was still tuned out of the conversation and focused on Dumakleiza. Neither one of them were paying attention to the discussion around them. Shadowmaker looked to Master Brawd. The palpable eye contact lingered as Master Brawd glared. His stomach was twisted with hate.

Shadowmaker turned back to Lord Coyzle. "There is a unique courage in your group that suggests the rare opportunity for comradery. I would like to nurture that seed and prove my intention by helping with a mystery unknown to both parties. My hunt on Fayde has successfully concluded, and now this is where I have chosen to contribute my efforts, knowledge, and resources."

Lord Coyzle nodded. "And I appreciate that. But your hunts are exactly why I am unable to give you my blessing. No offense, Shadowmaker. Your business is your business, and I have no interest in lecturing you on matters that are none of mine." He stood up to meet Shadowmaker with sincerity. Just staring into Shadowmaker's face made Lord Coyzle's knees dare to buckle, but he forced his body to stand its ground. "I cannot support the idea of a man with sociopathic judgment. You have kept prisoners of war for an entire century, all for the sole purpose of torturing and hunting them. While I can, uh, empathize with your desire to ensure they suffer, I don't want someone like you along for the mission. We are striving for the future, Shadowmaker, and whether or not you see it, you are refusing to let go of the past. I'm sorry." He visibly trembled as he prepared for however Shadowmaker was going to respond. He had his new and improved reflection suit on, but it didn't make him feel any safer.

The others in the room felt a cold chill scratch down their backs. They felt vulnerable to attack with how blunt and honest Lord Coyzle's response was. They respected him all the more for standing up to Shadowmaker, but they were worried his moral rigidity would result in the entire skydrop inexplicably exploding with them still inside.

Shadowmaker gave a slow nod with a brief expression that was blurred between anger and disappointment. He didn't say anything as he digested the answer.

"Maker of Shadows," Dumakleiza said as she turned her attention back to the conversation, "*I* would feel safer knowing you are with us." She slowly walked toward him with an unusual softness in her voice. She swallowed as her eyes twitched with lingering surprise at the news of the baby inside her. After a deep breath, she continued. "I am still going to the phase of four, even if I am with child, and that is incontestable. I show no bump, so the stage is early enough to permit this one last voyage." She stepped up directly in front of Shadowmaker, whose dissatisfaction was still evident. "I would feel safer with you by our side. Not just for myself and my Coobs and my Sir Gideon, but also for the life you claim is growing within my womb." She blinked a few times, staring in disbelief at her stomach before looking back to Shadowmaker. "But," she said, bravely reaching out and placing a hand on Shadowmaker's cheek, "you must trust a higher power than yourself to judge the Daemoaniks you hold captive." Shadowmaker's expression didn't change as he stared into Dumakleiza's dragon eye. She lowered her brows. "If you truly wish to be free of your tether to Daemoana, you must free yourself of the war you still wage. Until you do this, you show us that you are still Cassiak Stagvayne of Daemoana." With that, she gave a stern nod from one warrior to another and gently slapped his cheek a couple times. Shadowmaker gave a subtle look of impressed shock at her audacity before she turned and walked back to Gideon.

Gideon met her with an agape mouth. "You're worse than I am." He smiled and then held her while looking at Shadowmaker. He was worried Dumakleiza would be killed for laying a hand on him.

After a painfully tense moment, Shadowmaker looked to Gideon. "How is your shoulder scar?"

Gideon smiled. "It's good, man. Thank you."

Shadowmaker gave a subtle nod. "Good." With that, he turned and walked down the stairs.

Lady Melodeen waited until she was sure he was gone. She gulped and looked at Lord Coyzle. "Should we be expecting him to just come and go as he pleases now?"

Lord Coyzle stared at the stairway. "He claims you've unknowingly welcomed him through the gelatin many times."

Traveler grinned at how nervous his superiors were. He didn't want to admit to them—and more importantly, himself—how much he was beginning to admire Shadowmaker.

40

Everyone went their separate ways for a few hours, knowing they'd be departing soon for the Wall.

Timrekka watched Cooby while Dumakleiza went to an appointment. She'd told him that he must treat Cooby as his own, "Or else." He'd apprehensively welcomed the tanion onto his back while taking Izzy to the skydrop lab. He introduced him to Moybo and Minkel, who were eager to get back to work. With so much unknown ahead, Timrekka wanted to be sure that Izzy was in good hands. Moybo and Minkel had been warm and welcoming, and the chemistry between the three made Timrekka wish he was staying to play.

Master Brawd begrudgingly took Vorlak to the City of Light's military headquarters. Even with his reservations, he knew there was nothing he could do to make Vorlak's life any more of a living hell than he'd done to himself. Rather, he decided to take advantage of Vorlak's lethality and make the best soldier he could out of him. As much as Master Brawd wasn't looking forward to it, he was more eager to work with Vorlak than he was to deal with the surrendered Army of Light. They shared a couple comments about their mutual distaste for the soldiers, and that was the closest to bonding they managed.

Lady Melodeen returned to her post at the gelatin. She was responsible for overseeing new scanning procedures and safety protocols. After her ordeal with Abdabriel, scrutinizing more efficient security measures had become an obsession. Never again would she let herself be caught off guard. Once her designs and concepts were laid out, she was going to bring them to Izzy and his team to see what they could do to improve Whewliss's peace of mind.

Lord Coyzle reluctantly returned to his duties, delegating planetary repairs, and dealing with public awareness. He enjoyed his lordship but selfishly wanted to spend more time with the recruits before their departure. Everything was peaceful, and Whewliss was saved, and if he was being honest, he found the tranquility boring. In hindsight, he realized just how much he'd enjoyed the action, the danger, the adventure, and the fear. It was all something he never thought he'd experience, let alone miss.

Traveler personally escorted Gideon and Dumakleiza to the City of Light's glowdrop: specialized skydrops designed for extreme medical measures. While Whewliss no longer had hospitals or career doctors, glowdrops were the technological amalgamation of both. The City of Light's was the bleeding edge zenith, a fully comprehensive artificial intelligence capable of scanning the human body for any abnormality or health risk. In response, it was a corrective tool capable of performing the most intricate and delicate procedures and surgeries using focalized light. Its use cost more than most of the population could afford, but Lord Coyzle had granted them access to check on Dumakleiza's condition free of charge.

Once inside, they looked around to see that it was designed like a reverse Winkloh Star. A two-way mirror coated the entire sphere, but the reflective side faced outward for privacy. Inside of the glowdrop, the hollow room was primarily empty. The darkening City of Light was visible all around, with nothing but clear glass for walls. There was no fancy equipment or hefty tools. There was only one floor in the middle of the skydrop, and it consisted of nothing more than a walkway around the perimeter. It had a handrail for safety and another railing lining an arched bridge across the center of the hollow glowdrop. In the middle of the bridge was a platform indicated for patients.

Dumakleiza looked nervously at Gideon, who smiled with her hand in his. They were beginning a journey that neither of them had planned for while also preparing for the fourth phase. Once Traveler joined them inside, a female voice, professional, calm, and disarming, spoke all around them.

"Welcome to the City of Light's glowdrop. I am PIM, your personal assistant in charge of ensuring that you receive the best possible care." The voice made Dumakleiza look around for the source that she assumed wasn't there. She swallowed the assumption of dark magic and listened. PIM spoke again. "Will the patient please walk to the master scanner?"

Dumakleiza looked to Traveler, who pointed to the platform. She gulped and nodded. After a lingering moment, she let go of Gideon's hand and walked over the bridge, cautiously stopping once both feet were on the platform.

PIM spoke again, "Alien genetics detected. Will the patient please state their name and planet of origin?"

Dumakleiza blinked a couple times as she struggled to accept the formless voice. "I am Dumakleiza Yagūl, last of the Yagūlamites. I hail from the world of Cul," she yelled, unsure of what direction she should be addressing.

"Cul calibrations set. Welcome, Dumakleiza Yagūl."

Dumakleiza looked around, frustrated. "Show yourself, PIM of Whewliss."

Gideon chuckled, "Duma, it's a—"

"I am incapable," PIM responded.

Dumakleiza narrowed her eyes, trying to understand the distressing voice. "Are you science speaking to me?"

After some silence, PIM answered, "Based on Cul's understanding of science, it is an understandable question. Yes, I am science speaking to you. For better comprehension, my name is an acronym for Personal Instrument of Medicine."

Dumakleiza gave an affirming nod and stared confidently around the inner walls. "I do not fear you, PIM of science. Proceed with your apothecary judgment."

"Yes, Dumakleiza," PIM stated without the amusement shared by Gideon and Traveler. "At this time, it is recommended that all people inside of the glowdrop please lower their optical aperture to their darkest setting."

Traveler grinned at Gideon while darkening his eyes. "Did you ever think you'd be a dad?"

Gideon shook his head with bubbling anxiety. "No. I mean I've always hoped and dreamed that maybe one day. But I don't know. I guess I'm nervous. Like, reallynervous." He chuckled out some energy before earnestly looking toward Dumakleiza. He stared at her, appreciating her exotic beauty. He took a moment to reminisce over the first moment she'd taken his breath away while coasting down from castle Yagūl, firing arrows at him. Since then, he'd witnessed her strength, resolve, sensitivity, and absolute courage. Gideon could feel his pulse quickening while whispering to Traveler, "Do you think I'll be an okay father? And please keep your lips away from my sweet ass." He slumped. "I never knew who my dad was. I mean, I probably met him, but you know what I mean, and I—I don't know. I don't know where to start."

Traveler smiled and grabbed the back of Gideon's neck, shaking him a little. "I think you have a lot to learn about what it takes. I know that I don't know how to father anyone. I can barely keep an eye on *you*. But something tells me that there's nothing you wouldn't do for your child, and that is something that I've found countless families across all worlds are missing. An existential issue with our species." He looked at Gideon more sincerely. "I think you'll be an incredible father, Gideon."

Gideon sputtered an exhale. "I'm going to try. I'm really afraid that I'll mess it up. I don't want to mess the little guy or girl up. Oh, god, what kind of role model am I going to be?"

Traveler chuckled, "Listen, just keep that mind of yours open, love your child, and for the love of all gods, *do not* mess up, or she'll kill you." He nodded toward Dumakleiza.

Gideon's stressed smile melted into a laugh. "Yeah. Yeah, that's true."

PIM spoke again, "If you are experiencing any difficulty with your optical implants, please leave the glowdrop immediately." She allowed some time for compliance before continuing. "Dumakleiza, please stand with your feet shoulder-width apart and arms extended straight out to your sides."

Dumakleiza mumbled a prayer to Grimleck as she assumed the instructed stance. The walls of the skydrop turned a foggy white as the glass began to glow. It only took a few seconds for the entire glowdrop's interior to be filled with bright white light.

"Please hold as still as possible," PIM instructed. "Master scan commencing now." The entire sphere glowed brighter as blinding light was shone at Dumakleiza from all directions, illuminating her body through her suit. Even with their limited vision, Gideon and Traveler could see the reddish glow of her figure as light blasted through her. Gideon stared in awe. He understood what was taking place, but he couldn't help marveling as he saw into his pirate princess. All he could see of her was the red glow, like a flashlight pressed against a fingertip, and though he couldn't make out her anatomical details in the extraordinary light, he could see the glow of her stomach. Just knowing that life existed within it brought tears to his eyes. After a few more seconds, the light died down and returned to normal.

"Scan complete. Patient's health: optimal. No abnormalities or risks detected. Child's health: optimal. Child's age: affected by multiple jumps throughout pregnancy. Estimated age is between twelve and sixteen weeks. Dumakleiza, would you like to know your child's sex?"

Dumakleiza scoffed and brought her head back. "This is possible?"

"Yes," PIM answered.

Dumakleiza refrained from laughing while looking over to Gideon and Traveler. "Surely, this is humor at my expense. How could one tell the sex of a child still in the womb without magic? My intelligence will not be so easily mocked."

Gideon smiled and nodded. "No, Duma, it's not magic. Even on my world, we can tell the genders of babies before they're born."

Dumakleiza stared down at her stomach in amazement. She placed both hands on it, slowly swirling her fingers around where her body held the small life. The entire concept blew her mind. Back on Cul, she would not have made any female or male preparations for a child until it was born, and the genitalia were identified. She blinked rapidly and then looked to Gideon for guidance. The vulnerability in her eyes caught him off guard. He froze. He'd been so preoccupied with convincing her that PIM and the baby's sex were the results of science that he hadn't actually considered what PIM was offering. He stared through her as he realized he could find out if he was having a son or a daughter. Both options triggered different reactions: both excited, breathless, and terrified.

PIM repeated herself, "Dumakleiza, would you like to know your child's sex?"

Dumakleiza looked around at the smoky glass sphere. She gulped and blew out her nerves. Recently the two things that scared her were Shadow-maker and abnormally large owls. But in an instant, the list grew. What if she couldn't protect her child? What if it was a boy? How would she handle a boy? Or worse, in her mind, what if it was a girl? It would be just like her. How would she handle such passionately bullheaded offspring? She was already in love with whatever was growing within her, but a dam had broken, and she was being flooded by every fear her imagination could conjure. Sweat beaded on her forehead as she considered the ways she could fail as a mother. More tears slipped down her cheeks. She looked to Gideon.

"Sir Gideon, will I still take away your breath, regardless of the answer given by PIM of science?" She knew her insecurity had no logic in it, but she feared losing him.

Gideon smiled at her with tears of his own. "Yes." He nodded. "You take my breath away every time I see you." He paused as he considered saying one of the few sentences that scared him. Every fiber of his being wanted to belt it out, but there was something holding him back. It burst.

"I love you, Duma."

He went numb as he realized he'd actually said it. A weightlessness liberated him from his doubts.

More tears spilled down Dumakleiza's face as she returned his smile. "Damn you, Sir Gideon, now *you* are the cause of my tears." She laughed as she wiped them away. "I love you as well."

Traveler smiled at them. "You two are as unlikely as they come, and you fit together perfectly." He patted Gideon on the back. "What was that thing you said the first time we met? Something about true love."

Gideon smiled, knowing exactly what Traveler was referencing. "That true love isn't a season that changes with time—"

"—it's the sun through which all seasons change," Traveler finished Gideon's words for him.

Gideon nodded. "Well, now that you've dragged me through the universe, I think I have finally found that sun." He beamed at Duma. PIM repeated herself again, "Dumakleiza, would you like to know your child's se—"

"Yes, PIM," Dumakleiza yelled out, clasping her hands over her mouth. "Use your science and tell me the gender of my child." She looked down and held her stomach as her heart pounded in her throat.

Before PIM had a chance to say anything, Gideon bolted to the bridge. "Wait! Wait! Wait! Wait!" he yelled as he turned the corner and dashed across to Duma. He wrapped his arms around her from behind and kissed her cheek three times. She tasted like sweat, electricity, and everything he never knew he'd always wanted. He took a deep breath and then looked around. "Okay, PIM, go ahead."

"By my observation of your interaction, I conclude that you are the father. What is your name and planet of origin?"

Gideon smiled. "Gideon Green from Earth."

"Congratulations, Gideon and Dumakleiza," PIM politely stated. "You will give birth to a girl."

The answer felt unreal. Dumakleiza's eyes lingered on her stomach as her smile grew. She wasn't showing yet, but all of a sudden she felt like she was. There was life within her, an actual life. She was going to have a daughter. She exhaled as peace overcame her. All her concerns and fears evaporated as if they never were. All her energy focused on what PIM had unveiled.

"My little princess," she whispered as she felt Gideon's hands clasp over hers, gently holding her stomach.

Gideon smiled with new tears in his eyes, "*Our* little princess."

"We will see," Duma said with a protective tone. "On Cul, a man must do more than impregnate a woman to prove himself a father."

Gideon nodded as fire flared in Duma's eyes. "I will happily work on being the best father I can be, oh, gorgeousqueen of mine."

"Yes," she said with a soft kiss to his chin, "I amyour queen. Thatmuch is true, Sir Gideon." She kissed his chin again.

Traveler chuckled, "I wish you luck, Gideon. Don't upset her, or chances are *you'll* need a new gubernaculum after she cuts your, uh, you know whatoff."

"Uh, yeah, pray for me, Spaceman," Gideon smirked at him before planting another kiss on Duma's lips.

✻

After leaving the glowdrop, they met with Timrekka and the other scientists. In the evening, the City of Light was beautiful and tranquil. The ocean of skydrops around them and the stars above them glowed. After sharing the news, Dumakleiza took Cooby on a walk so she could tell him about her daughter in private. She didn't want him getting jealous or worried that he would be discarded once the child was born.

Timrekka, Gideon, and Traveler stood together outside of the lab. They marinated in silence, taking a moment to appreciate the peacefulness after all that had happened, and the quiet before what was about to.

Timrekka's eyes darted around the ground before awkwardly looking up. "Uh, Gideon, I know you're excited about your baby, but I have questions, and I don't want to upset you with any of them, but I can't not ask, so bear with me, but if your baby was conceived during the night back on Borroke, there's a possibility that the Vulgair woman you shared a bed with is also pregnant. Does that worry you, and also, and this is the question I'm most worried about upsetting you with: Shouldn't you two stay behind while we venture into the fourth phase to ensure that your baby is taken care of, you know? What if something happens down in the hole and either of you are injured, or what if Dumakleiza suffers any kind of trauma and loses the baby? I just don't want that to happen because I'm too excited about you two being parents, and I know it would devastate her, and I'm sorry if I've upset you. I want you to come with us, I want that more than just about anything, and I'd be happier if you did — but I'm just trying to look out for what's best for the three of you, er, well, four of you because I can't leave Cooby out or miss Dumakleiza will hurt me."

As Gideon took a moment to process Timrekka's questions, Traveler considered the same ones. He didn't want to discourage Gideon in any way, but he couldn't deny that Timrekka's worries were well-founded.

Gideon smiled and sighed. "First of all, back on Borroke, the Vulgair woman joined us in bed, but Duma insisted that she was her plaything, not mine." He chuckled. "She'd already marked me as her property and wasn't going to share, but she enjoyed the Vulgair woman. It was pretty fun to watch. So violent." He wagged his eyebrow.

Traveler scoffed a smile. "She is one of the most unique and remarkable religious figures I've ever met."

"Duma told me she was so embarrassed by her jealousy that she wanted you two to think that both women were mine, when in reality both of us were Duma's." Gideon chuckled. "It was funny, actually. Once Duma'd had her fun with the Vulgair, she made the poor chick go stand watch by the door while we spent the rest of the night together. The poor woman was too scared to contest Duma, but she did watch for a while and Duma seemed pretty turned on by the voyeurism." Gideon's cheeks grew hot at the memory.

Traveler laughed. "I mean you're a rather embarrassing person to have feelings for."

Timrekka giggled along and then stopped. "She doesn't seem the type to be embarrassed."

"Well." Gideon puffed out his bottom lip. "I was her first crush. That's pretty typical behavior. Except she felt it later in life than most women. You know, killing every man she met through her teen years and whatnot." He raised an eyebrow toward Traveler. "Besides, did you see the Vulgair women? Hairy."

Traveler shook his head and feigned an annoyed groan. "Hey, you talked me into sex with those hairy women, remember?"

Gideon laughed. "That's true. You a freak." He nudged Traveler. "You slut."

"Shut up," Traveler scoffed a laugh. "Rude. But hey, at least the baby's out of the bag now."

Gideon furrowed his brows and then laughed. "Cat. The *cat's* out of the bag. How do you keep confusing babies and cats? Skinning them. Coming out of bags. You should probably let me do the talking if we ever go back to Earth."

Timrekka sighed. "I don't understand polygamy, not that it's a bad thing. It just doesn't make sense to me, but either way, knowing that you two have genuine feelings for each other makes me feel a lot better, so what are you two going to do about the fourth phase, and have you picked out a name yet?"

Gideon smirked. "No names yet. We've barely had time to accept that we're having a girl." His eyes widened as the realization hit him again. "Uh, and your other question: the fourth phase. I don't know." He sighed. "We probably shouldn't go. It would probably be wisest to stay behind and take care of Duma throughout her pregnancy." He nodded with disappointment. He was trying to conceal it but was failing miserably. His desperation for the fourth phase was killing him, but he knew Timrekka was right. After a painfully fake smile, he nodded again. "I'm going to tell her that we should stay."

41

The back of Gideon's head hit the wall of a private room he'd taken Duma to. With her hand pinning his throat in place, Duma glared with such lividity that her upper lip turned white.

"You wish to lie to yourself—that is your sin to reconcile—but do *not* tell me you wish to stay behind for the sake of a child," Duma seethed. Before Gideon could gurgle out a response, she flexed her jaw and barked, "You are a coward, Sir Gideon. Of what you fear, I am not certain. Perhaps you fear the Wall, the phase of four, or you are afraid the responsibility would fall upon you to provide my safety down the hole." She shook her head. "I am Dumakleiza Yagūl, last of the Yagūlamites, and while I do love you, Sir Gideon, I have never needed your protection." She let go of Gideon's neck, leaving him gasping as she paced around the room. "In fact, I have more often been the one saving your life and the lives of those around us. Why do you choose to treat me differently now? Because another life grows within my womb?"

"No, Duma," Gideon pleaded through glassy eyes. "I want to——"

"Use me as a shield," Duma finished for him. "You use my condition as an excuse to hide from the first adventure that proves too much for you. You fear the voice down the void to such extent that you leverage your feelings for me to disguise your cowardice."

"Duma, listen to me," Gideon begged, reaching for her hands to hold. Dumakleiza jerked them away, disgusted by Gideon's attempt to sooth her rage. "Duma, I love you. You are the first wom——"

"That word does not solve *everything*, SirGideon." Duma's eyes burned with such ire that tears didn't threaten to well, lest they be turned to steam.

"Love is one of the few magics I still believe to be true, and you taint its beauty with every manipulative use of its name."

Gideon disregarded Duma's violent posture and took a step toward her. "I love you, Dumakleiza Yagūl. I *love* you." He ached to scream it, to carve the words into her heart, mind, and flesh until she couldn't deny the truth of it. "It's not just a word to me. I don't say that lightly." Gideon's eyes darted around, searching for anything that could help him. "Duma, we've both been exposed to such a large universe. Bigger than I ever guessed it to be. I can only imagine how many men have taken advantage of it——how many have had 'conquests' on other worlds and vanished into actual thin air after impregnating strangers that they'll never see again——literally worlds apart."

"So, I should find gratitude in you crippling me?" Duma scoffed. "Perhaps in your culture women become weaker and dependent upon their impregnation, but it appears to me that *you* are the one who has lost their nerve due to the princess I carry."

"No." Gideon's fingers tensed. "I'm not bragging. I'm not expecting gratitude. I'm saying that I'm here. I'm choosing to be. I want to be. I'm here with you, and I'm not going anywhere. I'm not leaving you——either of you." He motioned to her belly. "The *three* of you. I love you, our child, and even Cooby has become a big part of my life. I have had every opportunity to walk away from a one-night stand and leave it as that. That would be easy. That's how I've handled my entire adult life. I run. I run away from everything and everyone that I begin forming connections with. Life is so much simpler that way, devoid of commitment and the work it takes to maintain love or a family." Gideon felt like Timrekka with how much he was pouring out without breathing.

"I understand that, Sir Gideon," Duma said as she instinctively grabbed at her hips where she normally kept knives. "I'm here with you, as well. However, I wish to go forward, regardless of what you would surrender to. A child is no cause for our dreams to wither away. I wish for us to venture into the phase of four *together*. Why do you deprive not only me, but yourself of that adventure?"

"Because you're——"

"Pregnant?" Duma hissed. "Oh, Sir Gideon," she angrily laughed to avoid hitting him. "On Cul, pregnancy is not viewed as the ending of a mother's life, but the beginning of an opportunity to build a family together. I will travel to the phase of four. I will kill any threat that exists within the Wall. Grim will protect me when——"

"Duma," Gideon yelled. "Cul's mortality rate is astronomical!" He grabbed his hair to avoid shaking her. "Do you know what that means? I'm not insulting your intelligence, but I am telling you that there are still many things you don't know."

"No, Sir Gideon, I don't understand your larger words of science." Duma stepped up to him, placing her face inches from his. "Tell me, oh, wise *man*, what do you believe my primitive brain needs learn?"

Gideon flexed his jaw, resisting the urge to yell something he knew he'd regret. "It means that they die, Duma! Babies. Mothers. Oftentimes both. Cul doesn't understand how to take care of women during pregnancy. It's not your world's fault. They're just not developed enough. Of course you still want to charge into the fourth phase. You're blissfully ignorant of the dangers you and the baby are susceptible to." Gideon smacked his own chest. "I admit that I'm not a warrior. I'm not qualified to protect you the way that you've protected me. I am a man, and I'm proud to admit that I need you, a woman, to save my ass every time we—— *I* get in over my head. But I *am* qualified to protect you from yourself based off what I've learned that you haven't yet."

"Grim will protect us down the hole," Duma confidently stated.

"It doesn't work like that, Duma." Gideon closed his eyes, trying to keep hold of his slipping composure. "I believe in prayer. I believe in God. But I also believe that if God teaches us something——say, knowledge through education——that we are meant to learn how to better and more wisely conduct ourselves based off those lessons. He didn't leave them available to us so we could ignore them."

Duma cocked her head to the side, preparing for an insult against Grim. "And what lesson am I not learning, Sir Gideon?"

Gideon took a deep breath as he saw Duma's hands clench into fists. "Well." He slowly shook his head. "What if the baby's breach, Duma? Not to sound insulting, but on Cul, are you aware of what breach is? What if there's internal bleeding that could lead to both of your deaths?

What if the baby gets wrapped up in its umbilical cord and is in danger of strangling itself?"

Duma's expression momentarily snapped from anger to fear. "That can happen?"

"Commonly," Gideon said. "That's only a short list of the few things I'm aware of, and I'm not very knowledgeable on the topic. There are *so* many possible complications. But they're not viewed as incurable nightmares here because you're monitored throughout your pregnancy. They take care of you every step of the way. They're fixable if you're around the people who can fix them."

Duma's face slipped back to defensive. "Timrekka, the scientist of Thamiosh, will protect me down the hole." She nodded. "The diviner himself proclaims Timrekka more brilliant than most."

"Ugh, it's not that simple." Gideon's eyes softened as he realized how scared he was to lose Duma. "Timrekka is incredible, genius even. I've never met anyone like him. I've never met anyone like you. But that's not the point. He won't have access to the medical equipment that's here. On Earth, I'd feel safe with the doctors taking care of you. On Whewliss, even more so. Plus, we don't know what's down the hole. There is so much that could go wrong and I'm not willing to put you in that position."

"You don't get to *put* me in any position," Duma snapped back. "I'm not a weak woman, subservient to your command—yours to tell what to do, where to do it, and how. I am——"

"Oh my god, Duma," Gideon yelled. "This isn't about feminism. I'm not trying to control you. I'm not throwing away politically correct etiquette to get my own way." He glared at her, bringing his face in close enough for her to hit. "You want to know what my selfishness wants?" Before Duma could respond, Gideon answered. "I want to go down the hole. I want to explore the fourth phase. I want to be the first human. Me. Gideon Green. I want to find out what was speaking to me. I've never wanted to go on an adventure so badly in my entire life."

"Then go!" Duma shoved Gideon backward. "Go with me. Be with me. I do not want any part in keeping you from the adventure you so desire."

"No!" Gideon ran his hands down his face. "I'm not going to. You know why? Because I *am* a man. You are a woman, and I am a man." He saw Duma about to snap something back, so he beat her to it. "Don't. Just don't. I'm not shitting on your lady bits. I am not belittling you. I'm not insulting you. I'm not telling you that you are less than me because of your sex. I'm saying that you're *better* than me! I'm trying to hold you above myself. I want to protect you. It's in my DNA, my bones, my soul. I want to take care of you, so you don't have to feel alone taking care of yourself anymore. Stop hiding from me." He clenched his fists, every iota of his posture pleading with her.

Duma hesitated. She felt herself softening, and it only angered her more. She held her stomach and glowered back at Gideon. "Why? Why, Sir Gideon? Why do you wish to stay with me? I am going to give birth to this child, but that does not make you and me family. Even in my developmental ignorance, I know that creating a child is that of science. Creating a family is that of faith. What do you wish to commit to?"

"I want us to be a family." Gideon couldn't help cracking a smile through the redness. "You, me, our baby, Cooby—we're a family—a family of misfits, and I'm going to fight for us. To keep us." He sighed, his back bowing. "I will do anything, sacrifice anything."

"It will take more than a keepsake from your beloved bag to convince me of that." Duma turned away. She couldn't look at Gideon and maintain her desired level of anger. "And what of the rest of our misfit family? What of the Diviner and Timrekka? Who will protect them down the hole if not me? Who will pray for them if not me?"

"Prayer isn't determined by proximity, Duma," Gideon said. "You believe that more than any of us. God, Jesus, Grim, whatever the right name is, they aren't limited by distance like we are." He was answered with silence as Dumakleiza stewed. Gideon's eyes began to well. "Duma, I'm not a coward, and I don't care if I come off as one. I'm not wanting to hold you back because you're a woman or because you're pregnant. I'm not trying to get in the way of your dreams. God knows I want to explore the fourth phase, too. And once Traveler and Timrekka have returned, as long as they do, they can let us know if it's safe for us." More silence. "Isn't our daughter's safety more important than the fourth phase?

Isn't it a priority for you like it's become for me? I'm willing to let all of my selfishness go to ensure that our princess lives to meet this world. Every world. With us."

Duma shook her head with her back turned to Gideon. "Of course I care for her above all else—even—even Cooby. I certainly care for her more than I care for you in this moment." She sighed, still refusing to look at Gideon. "The only benefit I see our absence providing Timrekka of Thamiosh and the Diviner is the opportunity for Timrekka to own his strength and be the shield." She sighed again. "Without a woman on that venture, there will be detriment, though. No amount of prayer can defend men against their own brutish stupidity."

It took a few breaths for Gideon to summon the courage to grab Duma's shoulders and gently turn her around. No fist or yell stopped him. He melted when he saw thick streams pouring down Dumakleiza's face and onto her shirt. Her bloodshot eyes bore holes through the floor as her quivering chin gave way. Her shoulders slumped and she crumpled into Gideon, burying her face in his chest.

"I'm scared," she confessed, digging her fingers into his back. "My father would feel such shame to see me consumed by fear."

"Oh, Duma." Gideon pulled her in and wrapped both arms around her. His own tears streamed into Duma's cornucopia of spiraling hair. "I may've never met your dad, but I would guess that he was filled with the same fear when he first held you. I'm terrified." He chuckled through stuttered breaths. "I wouldn't label either of us fearful people, but we're embarking on the adventure of parenthood, and that is scarier than any hole in the edge of space." Gideon lifted Duma's chin to plant a soft kiss on each of her puffy eyes. "Daughters are reflections of their fathers love. You are the most amazing woman on Earth." He paused. "Sorry. Habit. The most amazing woman I've ever met on any world. Honestly. And that tells me that your dad loved you more than anything. He would be so proud to see the woman you've become." Gideon's lip quivered. "I hope I can be enough of a man to raise my daughter half as well as your dad raised you."

Duma was past words. She whimpered something indiscernible and wiped her eyes.

Gideon took her right hand and placed it over the scar on his left shoulder. "More important to me than anything is that she knows who her father is." Gideon saw the instant heartbreak in Duma's eyes. He ran his other hand through her hair, tracing her eyebrow with his thumb. "There's a word back on Earth: hiraeth." He gulped, composing himself before explaining. "I can't remember what language it is—but it basically means homesickness for a home to which you can never return, or that you never actually had."

Gideon kissed Dumakleiza's forehead and then dropped to his knees. He kept his arms wrapped around her legs and pressed the side of his face against her stomach, wishing he could hear the baby's heartbeat.

"My hiraeth is not for an actual home made of walls and a roof, but for the arms of a father that I never knew." Gideon kissed Duma's belly. "I've always been afraid of having kids because I fear leaving them with that same impossible hole to fill."

Dumakleiza ran her fingers through Gideon's hair and sniffled. "You will be a good father, Sir Gideon." She exhaled until it felt like her lungs had collapsed. "And I, too, wish to aspire to be half the saint that your mother was." She gulped and tugged at Gideon's arms, ushering him to his feet. As soon as he was up, she buried herself in his arms again, closing her eyes and slowly rocking with her head on his chest.

"Perhaps Lord Coyzle will let you help train the new Whewlight soldiers," Gideon said. "As long as you don't overexert yourself, of course."

Dumakleiza cracked a grin. "What will you do?"

Gideon chuckled. "I have no idea. I've never been good at day jobs, but I'm sure there's something I'm qualified for."

Duma nodded, ready to vanish from existence and lose herself to sleep on Gideon's chest. "I love you, Sir Gideon. I do not know if I feel more excitement or fear for what is to come."

"I love you, too," Gideon said before squeezing her tighter. "I love sharing my excitement and happiness." He kissed the top of her head. "But I've never met someone I'm interested in sharing my fears with until you."

42

The next day's sendoff party for the recruits was unrecognizable in comparison. The first time they'd left for the Wall, there had only been a handful gathered to see them off, due to the fourth phase's secrecy. But since Lord Coyzle had opened up to Whewliss about its details, the mysteries surrounding the fourth phase had become public curiosity and excitement. Instead of a small group from EBOO, all the City of Light had gathered to revel in their journey. More Whewlights than had been forced to attend Abdabriel's planetary address had come to Pinnacle Peak. Thousands more had made the trip from other parts of Whewliss just to see the momentous occasion. Countless signs were raised with written praise and encouragement for the heroic aliens. Others had brought gifts and donations. The iconic event was broadcast live around Whewliss, and nearly every person not in attendance was tuned in.

The recruits and Cooby were gathered onstage before the amassing crowd. The cliff face seats had been reserved for the EBOO employees, and by Timrekka's request, Moybo and Minkel. Joining the recruits on stage were Lord Coyzle, Master Brawd, Izzy, and Vorlak, with a line of Whewlight soldiers forming a perimeter.

After Abdabriel and Shadowmaker, most of the public weren't concerned about the one Daemoanik anymore. They weren't ready to welcome him, but they had become unfazed by his presence. Besides, he seemed too preoccupied with excitement to be of any real threat. Vorlak flashed a fang-filled smile at the recruits and then gave a sloppy wave to Gideon.

Timrekka had the final product of his miniature Winkloh Star. The nearly indestructible plastic rendition dangled in his grip, connected to the end of a chain. It was already beaming bright light from a few small rodents that the scientists had launched inside. He'd fondly come to call the mini-Winkloh a "Wink," a name that he was actuallyproud of.

The ocean of people bubbled with eager conversation, their susurrating voices echoing against the mountain and into the sky. All of Pinnacle Peak was electrified. After being clued into what the recruits were doing, the public was impatient to discover what was inside the hole. They were curious enough about the Wall itself. After all, they'd just learned about its existence, let alone, the concept of the fourth phase. What could possibly lie in the darkness beyond the edge of space? Lord Coyzle had decided it best to not tell them about the voice beneath the ripples. He didn't want to scare them without having any answers to the obvious questions that would follow. For now, all he was willing to share were the basics.

The time had officially come. Lord Coyzle stepped to the front of the stage with open arms. He was met with uproarious applause, and he basked in the crowd's contagious energy. It was refreshing to feel happiness in the air again. They were all there to celebrate the progress of mankind instead of mourning the lost, and he did not take the moment for granted. After basking a moment longer, he ushered for silence.

"Whewlights, it is a beautiful day to make history." His opening line was met with more cheering, and his rosy cheeks soaked it up. He nodded. "We have endured a lot together over the last few weeks. Our people have been hurt, and we have grown. We have been lost, and we have learned from the depths of this journey. We have been defeated, but we did not give up. We strived for the impossible, and we have survived." He held his hands out and smiled at his people as they cheered for their victory over the Army of Light.

Lord Coyzle's expression grew solemn as he turned and looked at the recruits. "And these brave Whewlights and aliens alike are the ones responsible for where we are today." He stared at the recruits with indebted gratitude as the crowd screamed for them. "They risked their lives for our world, a world that is not their own. When the light betrayed us, it was they who braved the darkness that we, as a planet, have been too afraid to even acknowledge. With the most ill-advised plan I've ever heard of, they found our salvation. I've seen firsthand the bravery they possess, and I

cannot begin to tell you the horrors they've overcome together. I mean—
" He shook his head in disbelief. "—they went after Shadowmaker and
asked him to help us. I don't need to tell you how insane that idea is, and
they jumped at it willingly simply because it was the right thing to do."
Some of the crowd cheered, while most just stared in residual admiration.
Lord Coyzle scoffed. "In fact, calling them aliens feels too cold and unfamiliar. We have bled together. I would prefer to just call them friends.
Heroes. Because that's what they are." He turned and looked at Gideon
specifically. "Perhaps even saints." No one in the crowd understood the
gravity, but he saw the vulnerability in Gideon's eyes. They shared a smile
before Lord Coyzle looked at the other recruits. "Whewliss will never forget
what you have done for us. Our people will tell your story for as long as
we have voices to speak."

The recruits smiled back at him. Even with the Whewlights' limited
understanding of the recruits and the sacrifices they'd made, they were
beyond grateful for anything and everything that had got them to where
they were.

Lord Coyzle sighed, sad to be saying goodbye, even if just for a while.
"Well, I could talk about them all day. I could tell you story after story
just about the last couple weeks, but I don't want to waste theirtime."
He chuckled. "Maybe someday I'll publish a book on the courage of the
fourth phase recruits, and then all of Whewliss can know the details of
what has been done on their behalf. Until then, it's time we saw you off."
He motioned to the recruits. "Is there anything any of you would like to
say before you go to the Wall?" He shook his fists with anticipation.

"May I address Whewliss?" The familiarity of Shadowmaker's voice
was etched into every Whewlight's memory, and they recognized it immediately. The entire world turned their attention to the front of the
crowd, where the armored Daemoanik myth was standing. The Whewlight soldiers directly in front of him lurched backward. He'd appeared
out of nowhere, and all their military training disintegrated as childlike
fear devoured their postures.

Lord Coyzle's breathing stuttered. He gulped and stared at Shadowmaker. There were many reasons he had to carefully consider his
response. Dealing with Shadowmaker presented a dangerous risk, and

he also had to consider that everyone was watching. There had to be a balance between firm control and tactful diplomacy. He took a deep breath and then forced a smile, followed by a nod.

"Get up here, Shadowmaker!" Lord Coyzle extended his hands toward him, as if to honor a distinguished guest. "I was just recognizing the heroes responsible for our liberation. You have perfect timing." Shadowmaker stopped right next to him, staring unwaveringly into his eyes. Lord Coyzle's blood ran cold as he placed a wary hand on Shadowmaker's shoulder and looked out at the crowd. "Whewlights, please help me thank Shadowmaker for his assistance with Abdabriel."

With Lord Coyzle's fearless embrace of the legend, most of the crowd felt comfortable with a cheerful response. Thousands chanted, "Shadowmaker" and glued their eyes to the warrior on stage.

Lord Coyzle smiled at him and nervously asked, "You wish to say something?"

Shadowmaker gave a subtle nod as he turned to face the crowd. He paused and looked around at the faces staring back at him.

"It has been many lifetimes since someone last lectured me. Yesterday, your lord, Albei Coyzle adjudicated me with outright moral expectation and unrelenting leadership." He paused. "I chose to digest his council, though it was difficult to swallow. As someone who has seen the atrocious shortcomings from most world leaders, allow me to congratulate you on having a leader who possesses the courage to stand up for what he believes in, even at the risk of violent consequences."

The crowd cheered through tense confusion as Shadowmaker continued. "I make one last offer, Lord Coyzle." He spoke quietly, so only they could hear one another. "It will be my final attempt at your approval." It was clear by the eye twitch that he wasn't happy about whatever he was about to say.

The crowd's noise died down. They were trying to hear the private conversation on stage, but Shadowmaker didn't allow it. Not even the recruits could hear what was being said.

"I do not possess the constitution to free or kill Slaughtvike. It goes against what I believe to be necessary. However, your judgment—I regret having to admit—is what I've needed. I will provide you Slaughtvike's location on Fayde. If you wish to free him or end his life, I trust your judgment to be sound. Do that and allow it to appease your conscience enough to give me your blessing." He stepped back and raised his voice for all to hear. "In return, what I offer is the technological knowhow in jumping from worlds such as Fayde, along with limited other technologies I have selected to share with you. Additionally, I will provide your recruits with these supernova suits. They are of my own design and will keep them safe from nearly anything or anyone." He motioned to his black armor. "And I can also solve the communications issue I've heard you discussing. I speak each of their languages with enough efficiency to translate for them." He wasn't sure why their translators wouldn't be enough on the Wall. He'd been there before and never experienced any difficulty with his equipment. "Lastly, I will provide my assistance throughout the duration of your fourth phase expedition. The wealth of knowledge I've accumulated extends far beyond combative and will prove helpful in whatever circumstances your recruits encounter. This is what I offer."

Lord Coyzle waited a moment as he weighed the potential ramifications of everything Shadowmaker offered. He couldn't deny that whatever advanced knowledge he offered would be useful, but there was nothing Shadowmaker could do to make Lord Coyzle trust him. Without breaking eye contact, he squinted.

"You really aren't afraid of the hole, are you?"

Shadowmaker's expression flared curiosity at Lord Coyzle's haunting tone. "I have not felt fear in a long time, Albei. There is no one and no thing I've found in this universe that provides me with the excitement of fear. In truth, I miss it, the intensity it provides a single moment." He had no idea what the hole was, but he doubted it would trigger anything other than new questions for him to study and new mysteries to solve. "I long for fear to consume me as it did in my youth. Perhaps then I would feel the flames of passion reignite."

Lord Coyzle stared at him for a moment, studying the empty longing in his eyes. He believed there was truly nothing that scared Shadowmaker, and that it was torturing him. He sighed and turned to the recruits.

"You have my blessing—to ask *their* permission. After all, it's their lives that would be risked alongside yours. Not mine."

Shadowmaker gave an understanding nod as he turned to face the recruits. He didn't repeat himself. They weren't stupid. They didn't need a reminder.

As Traveler and Timrekka struggled to think of a good response, Gideon gave a hesitant smile. He walked up to Lord Coyzle and Shadowmaker.

"Actually," he said and patted them both on the back like old friends. He left his hands on their necks as he spoke. "Dumakleiza and I have an announcement." He glanced back at her and then turned to the crowd. "We've got a crib midget in the oven." He smiled at the confused Whewlight faces. The crowd looked at each other as the words caught them off guard. Gideon chuckled and reworded himself. "We're pregnant!"

A few people chuckled at the misunderstanding as the crowd erupted in celebratory cheering. Shouts of congratulations decorated the air as tens upon tens of thousands of Whewlights joined in their happiness.

Gideon danced around and motioned for Dumakleiza and Cooby to join him at the front of the stage. With Cooby on her back, Duma awkwardly stepped forward, unsure of standing before so many people. The overwhelming amount of attention made her uncomfortable. Cooby was quiet while he maintained a death grip around her neck.

Gideon put his arm around them both and then spoke as the crowd quieted. "So, uh, I don't know how else to say it. But due to our little bun in the oven, we have agreed that it is in our child's best interest that we stay behind."

His juxtaposed delight for the pregnancy and disappointment in staying behind was palpably evident. The crowd responded with understanding nods and some dying shouts of congratulations. Gideon gave half of a smile and nodded again.

"We're excited to hear what those two—" He pointed at Traveler and Timrekka. "—discover." He reached up and scratched under Cooby's chin with his free hand. The anxious tanion cooed and relaxed a little at the affection.

"Wait," Dumakleiza blurted as she stared at the crowd through softening eyes. She turned and glanced at Shadowmaker before looking back out at the faces. Hearing her voice echoing out for miles was an unfamiliar sensation. She recognized her own sound, and it felt like she was shouting from all around herself. She blinked a few times to recalibrate her mind and then turned to Gideon. "Sir Gideon, I wish for you to go with them."

Gideon shook his head with a confused grin. "No." He chuckled, unsure of what was happening. "We're staying behind for the baby, baby. We've talked about this."

She nodded. "I know this. It is wise that I stay behind for the sake of my princess's life. I agreed it best for you to stay with me for more than just my selfish desire for your company. It would be a tragedy for my princess to grow without you, and that would not be possible if you were to perish down the hole. However, now that you would be provided additional protection, I believe you would be kept safe."

Gideon scoffed until he saw Duma's eyes fill with tears. "I'm not leaving you here. I'm staying. We're staying together."

"No." Dumakleiza shook her head. "My princess will have a complete father or no father at all. You will never be whole if part of you is lost in the adventure upon which you never embarked." She caressed his cheek while staring into his eyes. Cooby looked back and forth between them, confused and agitated by whatever was happening. "Much of your soul resides within the unknown. I am too selfish to survive with only half." Gideon's eyes sank as Dumakleiza spoke. "I have seen your full soul, and it is beautiful."

"Duma."

Without acknowledging Gideon's confliction, Dumakleiza turned to Shadowmaker. "Maker of Shadows, if you venture into the phase of four and protect my Sir Gideon until he returns to me, my eyes will see you as a friend." She glared at him as his intense stare fixated on her.

Gideon stepped between them, putting himself into her line of sight. "Duma, I'm not leaving you."

She reached out and held his cheek. "There is no further argument, Sir Gideon. All of who I am is yours. I require the same of you, or I will not have you. That is the end of this debate. You will go find the rest of your soul and only then return to me. Should you not return, or should you perish down the hole, it would be better than the decay of regret here." Tears streamed down her face as she held the bottom of her stomach.

Gideon blew full cheeks through his lips as his own tears welled. He couldn't imagine how selfless Dumakleiza was being, but he was torn right down his center. It felt like he was leaving his heart behind to find his soul, and he wasn't sure if he would survive. For the first time since he'd met Duma, he felt like she was literally taking his breath away—literally killing him. After another trembling exhale, he gave a nod with his head hung. He cleared his throat and forced a small smile for the crowd.

"Okay, Duma," he sighed as he studied the details of her face. "It doesn't matter where adventure takes me, I have finally found my home—the sun to my universe." Duma smiled at him with warm understanding. After marinating in the pressure of everyone's silence, Gideon looked over to Traveler while holding Duma's hand. "I guess you're stuck with me, Spaceman."

Traveler slowly nodded toward Dumakleiza with empathetic eyes. "I will do everything in my power to keep him safe." He adjusted Sonder on his back.

"That is not your duty," Dumakleiza clarified. "You must assist my Sir Gideon in finding himself. Shadowmaker's duty is ensuring his safety." She nodded, feeling more confident in her decision after correcting their respective roles.

Lord Coyzle cleared his throat to redirect the conversation. "Four Zero, the final call is yours." He awkwardly nodded toward Shadowmaker.

Shadowmaker turned his eyes to Traveler, who reactively flinched.

After rushed deliberation, Traveler chuckled and shrugged. "Uh, well, if it guarantees us Gideon and, well, I mean, the armor will probably be helpful." He shook his head and took a deep breath while his thoughts collected. All of Whewliss was watching, and he was choking on a simple yes or no. "To quote Gideon: Why not?" He exhaled the words, slapping his hands against his sides with another shrug. "Welcome to the expedition, Shadowmaker."

Shadowmaker gave an appreciative nod. "Your supernova suits await you at your settlement on the Wall."

Timrekka ducked his head, flashing his eyes up at Shadowmaker. "You scare me a lot, and I don't know if that'll ever change, but as someone who's never had any real friends until meeting these people, I can tell you that you're gambling with the right group." He sunk his head as it flooded with unrealistic fears of Shadowmaker killing him for speaking.

Traveler looked around at the thousands of faces staring at them. Once again, Shadowmaker had managed to surprise them with an unexpected turn of events. Traveler chuckled to himself before turning to the others.

"Well, shall we?"

Gideon looked to Dumakleiza with a pained expression. "I don't think I should—"

A soft kiss silenced him. "Return to us." Dumakleiza placed Gideon's hand on her stomach. After looking at each other for a moment longer, she stepped away with Lord Coyzle.

Everyone backed up as the recruits gathered at the stage's center. It was time. Gideon's heart beat in his neck as he backed toward the others. The crowd's eyes bounced between the recruits and the sky, but Gideon's lingering gaze was stuck on Duma.

Traveler took a moment to give an acknowledging nod to those he was leaving behind. He was sad to be saying goodbye, but his heart was racing knowing it was finally time to go. Hopefully they would return one day. He looked up with an outstretched hand. Gideon placed his hand on Traveler's collar and held on. Timrekka held Gideon's other hand, and Shadowmaker gripped Gideon's neck. Timrekka stared at Shadowmaker, afraid that he might crush Gideon's throat on accident. Traveler closed his fingers and then turned his gaze back toward everyone staying behind.

"May the light guide and protect you all."

Almost in perfect unison, all tens of thousands of Whewlights replied with the same farewell, "May the light guide and protect you."

Lord Coyzle put a supportive hand on Dumakleiza's shoulder while they looked to the recruits. "May death not find any of you sleeping," he said, singling Gideon out with a smile.

Tears slid down Gideon's cheeks as he smiled back. "Nor you, my friend."

They all stared at each other in a moment of silence as they waited for Traveler to open his hand.

"I love you, Sir Gideon," Dumakleiza said with a shaky voice. Cooby licked her face and held her tighter as he cooed. He didn't understand why they weren't with Gideon. Even with his limited intelligence, he knew they were saying goodbye, and he didn't like it. He reached his paw toward Gideon and whimpered, torn between squalling for him and tending to Dumakleiza's sadness.

"I love you, too." Gideon's breathing quickened as he struggled to contain the maelstrom of emotions threatening to burst within him. "Take care of her, Coobs." He smiled through his tears at the tanion.

Shadowmaker looked at the Earthling who inexplicably intrigued him. "I know that on Earth, they call gravity a law. Do you feel fear before light jumps?"

Gideon took a deep breath and composed himself before turning to respond. "Well, I suppose if gravity is the law, only criminals will fly." He raised an eyebrow.

Shadowmaker grinned with approval.

Traveler opened his hand, and everything went white.

43

As the light faded from their eyes, they found themselves in the open center of the eight Wall Post buildings. The flooding brightness dwindled away, leaving only the clarity from the Wall's low atmospheric line. Millions of stars shone so crisp and vibrant, it felt like they could just reach out and touch them. Cosmic clouds of every color painted nebulas and galaxies forever away. Just seeing the glassy, blue haze in the distance all around them brought smiles to their faces. Everything was ready. And they were, too.

Shadowmaker had recovered first, heading straight into the Wall Post to ensure everything was ready. He could sense the others' reverent fear for wherever they were going. He didn't understand, but he longed to feel the same raw emotions. While the Whewlights were less advanced, he knew they had experienced their share of exploration. It was still odd to him that they invested belief in any kind of mysticism, such as imagined fears down the simplicity of a hole. It didn't matter. It was their prerogative. What did matter in his mind was the fact that there was something he knew nothing about. He was eager to see what had all Whewliss so rattled.

Gideon's heart ached knowing that he was impossibly far away from Duma. It wasn't a normal scenario that he'd heard a thousand times before, where families were divided across the Earth, states apart, seeing each other occasionally. No, this was something vastly different. Dumakleiza was so many trillions of miles away that it was difficult to wrap his mind around. He knew a single light jump could bring him back to her quicker than he'd ever imagined possible, but that wasn't the point. It felt strange not having his pirate queen by his side for the journey. Even not having Cooby crawling around made him feel empty, like something vital was missing from his body. He took a few deep breaths and closed his eyes, whispering a prayer for his bizarre little family. He prayed that he would find what he needed to and then be returned to them in one piece. He opened his eyes and felt a sense of relief wash over him. He had to surrender their lives and their fates. In his eyes, mind, and heart, their future was in God's hands. Whether that god was Jesus or Grimleck, he felt the reassurance of some higher power looking out for them. *Parachute your mind, Gideon,* he reminded himself.

The instant Timrekka was alert, he took his Wink and darted into the Wall Post to gather supplies. The hefty scientist was beside himself with giddiness. He had no emotional tether to anyone left behind. There was nothing he had to overcome, no anchor made of guilt or remorse holding him back. He was free. He was off to explore the greatest scientific anomaly ever discovered, and he giggled with every breath. He was not only being allowed but *instructed* to unleash his mind's full capacity. Along with the Wink, he'd brought a handful of new inventions that he was looking forward to sharing with the other recruits. Additionally, he was eager to see what the supernova suits were like——if Shadowmaker had even managed to make one his size.

Traveler stood still for a while, gazing up at the dreamlike sky. He'd seen it many times before, but this time was different. The oceans of stars and distant thousands upon millions of planets were all familiarities he was leaving behind. He didn't know if he'd ever see them again or if he'd ever return to Whewliss for that matter. It was surreal to say farewell to the universe he was so conversant in, and yet, still knew so little about. The swell of emotion within him wasn't what he'd expected it to be. He had expected jubilation and fear, and while they were present, he was primarily filled with a burning sense of purpose. He was responsible for leading the journey, and it felt right. He was finally where he belonged. After everything, he wasn't an observer anymore. Nor was he even a recruiter. He had become an adventurer, a force of nature itself.

Gideon walked over to him, following his gaze into the effervescent sky. "You're not getting cold feet, are you, Spaceman?"

Traveler smiled with his eyes still up. "Just the opposite. I'm saying goodbye to everything I know."

"Oh, don't be so dramatic." Gideon smiled. "Go with 'see ya later.' Just blow it a little kiss. Not a sloppy one. Gotta leave it wanting more."

Traveler smiled. "What if—"

Gideon eagerly waited to hear what scenario Traveler was going to pitch, but after a quiet cliffhanger, he leaned in and whispered, "What if what?"

Traveler scoffed, "I don't know. I had too many. That entire hole is a what if. It's *the* what if, and we're finally going to find out."

"Yup," Gideon blurted out with a mischievous giggle. "Well, shall we go inside and make sure Shadowmaker and Timmy are getting along?"

"Indeed." Traveler sighed and brought his gaze down to the black bead beneath his feet. He stared at it for a moment and then smiled at Gideon. "Is that really the saying? Cold *feet*? I could have sworn it was knees. Like someone's fallen to them."

Gideon chuckled as they walked to the Wall Post. "Maybe your translator was broken the entire time you were on Earth."

"Maybe. Oh." Traveler stopped and unslung Sonder from his back. "I know this was a gift but—" He held the backpack out toward Gideon. "—now that we're not going to die in a cave, I think it belongs with you."

Gideon grinned as he accepted his backpack back. "You don't want to carry a big ol' bag of junk around the fourth phase?"

Traveler smiled and patted Gideon's left shoulder. "All of the junk in there is worth more to me than anything, but only when it's brought to life through your stories. Besides, I want to be a part of the adventures that result in new additions."

Gideon nodded and slung Sonder around his back. He sighed at the familiar weight. It felt right to be reunited with his souvenirs as they resumed their walk to the Wall Post.

"There are many stories yet to tell but—and I'm sure you already know this—most of these items are results of mistakes I make along the way. Hope you're ready to get stuck in a lot of pickles."

Traveler smiled and rolled his eyes. "Yeah, I get that those are part of what I sign up for with you as a friend."

"Yup." Gideon nodded. "I'm glad I get to go with you, after all."

"It wouldn't have been the same without you."

"So." Gideon smirked. "With Duma staying behind, does that make Shadowmaker our spiritual leader?"

Traveler laughed. "Oh, I would be very interested in hearing what kind of prayer hewould lead us in."

As they entered the warm light of the Wall Post, they saw Shadowmaker assisting Timrekka with his supernova suit. It appeared that Timrekka had momentarily forgotten his crippling fear of the Daemoanik and was instead bouncing up and down like a child as Shadowmaker dressed him. His eyes darted around in his goggles, gobbling up the sight of his new protective outfit. It looked like Timrekka's suit was custom made. It fit him perfectly, as if Shadowmaker had only put their suits together since meeting them. When had he measured them? Gideon didn't know. How had he measured them? Gideon chuckled in his head at some guesses and smiled at the subtle effort at friendship.

With a few finishing touches, Shadowmaker clasped some pieces together and then stepped back. They looked Timrekka over. The black armor complimented the stout Thamioshling's form surprisingly well. He stretched his arms and legs around, bending and bowing to test the movement. He was pleasantly surprised by how flexible the material was. Even with his already superior strength, he felt even lighter. Gideon loved the look's ferocity. Protective plates covered each individual muscle group, while some sort of alien material connected it all underneath. Timrekka smiled up at Shadowmaker.

"It's really comfortable, and I'm interested in what kinds of materials you used, and what all purposes it's served you, and with my initial observations, I assume it could be an effective windbreaker, possibly even a functional underwater suit, perhaps warming in subzero locations. It feels like it could deflect all kinds of weaponry and artillery, but are there health factors, like with the Whewlight gelatin suits, or is it primarily for protection?"

"It assists with all of your expressed concerns, guesses, and more," Shadowmaker answered. "Along with exploring habited worlds, I enjoy studying uninhabitable planets, moons, and any celestial body I can land on, as well. The supernovas are the eclectic pinnacle of my protective knowledge. I mine dead stars for most of the materials. I call the finished plating 'galactic graphene.' My manipulation of that raw material is the fundamental element that makes these suits virtually indestructible. I do not understand why Whewlights limit themselves to the habitable universe. They would glean much through the exploration of the uninhabitable. There is just as much, if not more, to learn there than there is on worlds distracted by human life." He motioned to the table in the room, where five matching helmets waited for them.

Gideon gasped at the menacing headgear. Each helmet appeared to be slightly different in shape, presumably tailored to their individual heads. Gideon paused as he realized that one of them had been intended for Dumakleiza. It made his heart heavy.

He studied the black helmets. They looked similar to motorcycle helmets in aerodynamic design, but rather than a visor, two red lenses provided visibility on the otherwise smooth surfaces. The headgear was simple but foreboding, and Gideon couldn't wait to wear his villainous supernova suit in its entirety.

"Red on black? Aw, Shadowmaker, you flirt like a son-of-a-bitch." He could only imagine how elated Duma would have been to don the armor.

Shadowmaker gave a proud nod. "The optical specs offer infrared, night vision, heat detection, predictive motion sensing, electric—"

"Sorry to interrupt," Traveler said, "but just so you're aware of what you're dealing with, everything operating on electricity or a battery source of any kind won't function down the hole."

Shadowmaker turned. "Why is that?"

Traveler smiled, reveling in knowing something that Shadowmaker didn't. "Let's get everything together and then you can just see for yourself."

Shadowmaker gave another grin at the unknown. "Suit up."

Without wasting time on further questions, he grabbed the left side of his breastplate and clicked a small latch to demonstrate how the suits fastened. When he did, the protective sheet of black armor over his torso loosened with an airy hiss, exposing the tattoo on his chest again.

Gideon immediately nodded toward it. "What's the story behind your tat? It looks kind of like a teddy bear. Not gonna lie, you with teddy bear ink is *a*dorable."

Shadowmaker glanced down, staring through his tattoo before turning his eyes back up to Gideon. "This supernova is yours." He motioned to one of the three remaining suits armor magnetically suspended above the floor.

Gideon nodded with sarcastic suspicion. He assumed it would probably take some prying to get the tattoo's backstory. It was an answer he was willing to work for, though he hoped it wouldn't take too long. After all, it would only be fair after Shadowmaker badgered out the story of his shoulder.

He and Traveler began climbing into their suits. While they figured out how they fit and sealed, Timrekka grabbed three of the backpacks Moybo and Minkel had delivered. They were made of a white material that, though soft to the touch, was durable in extreme weather. Sturdiness was a prerequisite for exploring down the unknown chasm in the edge of space. Each backpack contained weeks' worth of MREs, basic medical equipment that operated without electricity, and some powerless tools. Timrekka brought them over to his teammates and placed them on the ground. He went back and grabbed an armful of more MREs and added them to the pile. He looked at Gideon.

"We—" He motioned to the others. "—will be carrying these back-packs, and I'm assuming you'll be carrying Sonder, so I have a plenty of extra food packs for you to stuff into it, and I have the Wink, so I think we're ready to go." He looked around while bouncing with anticipation.

As Traveler finished suiting up, he and Shadowmaker grabbed a back-pack while Gideon filled the rest of Sonder to the brim.

Gideon, Traveler, and Timrekka took a moment to assess themselves. They were impressed with how comfortable the supernova suits were. They could feel tactical compression supporting their bodies. Their lower backs were principally supported, making them feel almost invincible. Every inch from their necks down had unique and individualized protection. Even their hands were protected by robotically enhanced gloves. Shadowmaker had spared no expense or detail when creating them. It helped that his resources were only limited by where he was willing to go to get the materials.

As they walked around the room to test their movement, they felt some kind of hydraulic system built into the legs and boots. They could tell by each motion that it was mechanical, not electricity or battery powered, and they could only imagine how many surprises the outfits contained.

"There is much I will teach you about the supernovas," Shadowmaker said as he watched the three of them bound around. "Ensure that your helmets fit your heads."

They stopped and turned toward the table in the middle of the room. Their hesitation was forgotten after feeling how protected the suits alone made them feel. They wasted no time. As soon as they squeezed their heads through the fitted head slots, another hissing sound sealed the helmets in place. Through the blood red eye slits, everything looked normal. Surprisingly, there wasn't a red tint. Breathing felt clear and unstifled. In fact, the suit's filtration system was immediately noticeable. The concentration of oxygen was energizing. Timrekka was relieved to find that he didn't feel claustrophobic.

"Mine's cozy," Gideon said as he moved around, testing his neck's range of motion. "I feel like a space knight." He chuckled. "Sir Gideon, the space knight."

Shadowmaker assessed their mobility. "If it's true that electricity and batteries will be useless down this hole, the majority of the suits' functions won't work. However, enough of them have manual options to still be helpful." He put on his helmet and sealed it shut. "If nothing else, they will provide protective cushion and support if we fall."

Timrekka paused at the thought, sweating before the suit whisked it away. "That would be a dreadful fall."

"Well," Traveler said with suppressed excitement, "is there anything else we need?"

Timrekka turned and started out the door. "No, Moybo and Minkel had the Whewlights that brought our supplies set up our climbing gear, and it should already be there, so let's go." With that, the Thamioshling left the Wall Post.

Gideon smiled at his enthusiasm and then chuckled to Traveler and Shadowmaker, though neither of them could see his expression through his helmet.

The short walk to the hole was more thrilling than usual. Normally it consisted of trekking through the sazeal trees and looking at the stars, but this time, the recruits bounded effortlessly across the Wall, as the supernovas amplified each movement. Gideon couldn't stop laughing and howling as he jumped, somersaulted, flipped, and ran around like a child on a sugar high.

"These are awesome! They make the entire Wall a trampoline," he said.

Timrekka, on the other hand, had to limit himself and minimize each step. He was already at risk of leaping out of the atmosphere on accident. With the suit, he had no idea just how far he could possibly throw himself if he got greedy. Each step was potential suicide. He stuck with cautious shuffling, even though he wanted to join Gideon.

They emerged from the sazeal forest and walked into the clearing around the hole. While the others made their way over to its edge, Timrekka shuffled to a group of trees with long ropes fastened around them. He held the ropes up close to ensure they were the plasma-braids, interwoven with rubber and steel strands as he'd instructed. One by one, he examined them all with his Wink to make sure they were secured and that they could each support many times their bodyweight. It didn't matter how much he trusted the Whewlights, he didn't want to fall to his death down the hole. He tugged a few times but resisted the urge to pull as hard as he could and possibly uproot the trees themselves. The trees didn't budge or even groan, and he hoped that'd remain true during their descent.

Once he was satisfied, he followed the trail of ropes away from the sazeal trees to the edge of the hole, where the lengths were rolled up into collective piles. Each was abundantly long to ensure that they would at least reach the bottom. Beyond that, they were going to have to find their own way with only the tools in their backpacks. Timrekka stopped next to the others and joined them staring into the abyss. He'd forgotten just how vast and black it was, spanning a few hundred feet across.

Gideon smiled back and forth between the hole and Shadowmaker. "Shadowmaker, this is the fourth phase. Fourth phase, Shadowmaker."

Shadowmaker stared into the darkness without acknowledging Gideon. Even with his helmet concealing his face, the others could visualize his expressionless fixation. Silence played the catalyst for his introduction to the ominous beast as he quietly spoke.

"There is greater depth to this hole than just physical."

"That's what she said," Gideon chuckled.

Shadowmaker looked at him from within his helmet. "What?"

"Oh, nothing. Nothing." Gideon smiled, refraining from annoying him further. "Check this out, though." He squatted and grabbed a handful of black bead. After a dramatic pause, he tossed it out over the openness. Everyone watched in silence as the trickle of beads broke the unseen surface. The white ripples of light instantly spread out from each individual breach and then slowly faded away into nothingness.

"What is that?" Shadowmaker asked with curbed intrigue.

"Don't know," Gideon said with a quick shoulder raise. "But that's where all of our science-y rules change." He reached beneath the surface and waved his hand around, causing light ripples to swirl like magic water. He smiled at the anomaly and then looked up at Shadowmaker. "There's something down there."

"The fourth phase?" Shadowmaker clarified.

"A voice," Gideon whispered. His playfulness melted away as he relived hearing it for the first time. Shadowmaker recognized Gideon's sudden shift in energy.

Traveler, who had been standing back observing their interaction, motioned toward Shadowmaker. "Stick your head down it. I'm curious what *you* will hear."

"Oh!" Timrekka nodded. "Maybe you'll hear something different than Gideon did. I wonder if it's like a prerecorded message or if it's individualized, or perhaps it's a machine, or I guess it could be a person, but how would it surround you the way you've described?"

Shadowmaker studied their sincerity. The reverence with which they approached the hole aroused a cautiousness he hadn't felt in a long time. It made him uneasy, which only intrigued him further. While keeping his eyes on the others, he squatted down to his hands and knees a few feet from Gideon. Before doing anything else, he reached out and slowly inserted his hand. White ripples of light spread around his fingers, but he felt nothing. He retracted and stared until the light completely disappeared. Nothing had physically happened to him, so he lowered his head. The others watched in tense anticipation as his helmet breached the surface. There was no breeze, no crickets, and no speaking. Shadowmaker didn't move as he held his head beneath the ripples in silence. Gideon was all grins. The most terrifying man in the universe was experiencing the most mysterious discovery of mankind for the very first time. The moment was unprecedented, and Gideon was dying to know Shadowmaker's every thought.

Shadowmaker ripped his head out of the ripples and lurched backward, leaping to his feet. Within his commotion, he reached up and removed his helmet so he could breathe in the open. The others jumped back, startled by his abrupt and uncharacteristic reaction. Shadowmaker was audibly hyperventilating, and what was more unsettling, he was shaking.

"W—what did you hear?" Gideon whispered, afraid to speak too loudly.

Shadowmaker tried to calm his breathing as he looked around, spooked, almost defensive. It took a few breaths before he took some steps back toward the hole. He stood over it and peered down into the blackness.

"I *felt* a child's voice." Shadowmaker's breathing quickened. "It warned me not to 'blend to grey.'" Nobody said anything. They didn't know what was more unsettling: the cryptic message or Shadowmaker's fear of it. They weren't sure how to react to him afraid. Before, they had been excited to show him something new, but now that he'd reacted so adversely, they suddenly wished he had answers to reassure them with.

Gideon leaned forward, captivated by Shadowmaker's uneasiness. "Don't blend to grey? What does that mean? Do you know what that means?"

"No." Shadowmaker shook his head. "I don't understand but—" He unlatched his breastplate again and looked at Gideon. "—it scares me." He stared back down into the abyss as he placed his hand over his tattoo, gripping the flesh it was inked into. He wanted to claw into his own heart and manually pump it.

Gideon grinned, captivated by the answer. "Really?"

Traveler squinted, looking from Shadowmaker to the hole. "Don't blend to grey." He puzzled over it.

"Hold up," Gideon said. "How are we communicating right now? Didn't that just scramble your translator or whatever you use?"

"Yes," Shadowmaker said, still trying to catch his breath. "But I speak all three of your languages, and your translators are still intact, so you understand me."

"Oh, I like that," Timrekka said, distracted by the convenience.

Sweat beaded on Shadowmaker's face as he continued trembling. "On Daemoana, we had a species of bear called honey bears." His wide eyes didn't leave the hole as he spoke. "They were a medium-sized bear, only weighing up to seven-hundred-pounds."

The others listened with their own hearts racing.

"Honey bears were violently territorial and were known for being one of the most protective mammalian mothers. With that reputation and the name honey bear, they became one of the most popular stuffed toys for children." He sighed as the story contended with the emotions brought forth by the voice in the hole. His eyes struggled to hold still as he looked around the pit. He was looking for something, as if a creature from within the blackness was going to emerge. "Helethro, my son, called his honey bear Oorrabak, a Daemoanik name meaning guardian or protector." He heavily exhaled at his son's memory after the voice tore his regular composure apart. "Helethro imagined Oorrabak as a real friend of his. It was normal behavior for a child of his age. Whenever I would leave for another world, Helethro would tell me, 'Father, I send Oorrabak to protect you until you return to me.'" Shadowmaker's eyes welled, which only confused him as more composure slipped away. "Helethro would keep his toy, but the spirit of Oorrabak would accompany me to keep me safe. Daylucia used to tell me Helethro would not play with his toy until I returned its soul home." Shadowmaker paused. "When my family was taken, Oorrabak was protecting me." Shadowmaker hung his head. "Helethro didn't have either of his guardians when he was killed." Shadowmaker stifled tears as he looked up at the others. He removed his hand from his chest, allowing them to see his tattoo as he, too, stared down at it. "Oorrabak's protection was the last gift that my family gave me." His voice trailed off. "This marking is my conduit, the few remaining ashes of my faith. It's all I can offer to any higher power still willing to look at me."

Everyone was silent as Shadowmaker's eyes drifted into the blackness of the hole. His breathing slowed and his trembling calmed, but his energy remained disturbed.

Gideon looked from Shadowmaker to the hole. "New life from ashes is always more bountiful."

Traveler stepped up next to them. "Perhaps the answer is down there." He turned toward the hole. "It's time." Goose bumps compressed his body after saying the two words he'd dreamt of for so long.

With Cooby wrapped around her back, Dumakleiza held her stomach and stared up at Whewliss's night sky. "Grim, watch over my Sir Gideon," she prayed under her breath as she searched the stars. Even her dragon eye, with all its Whewlight enhancements, couldn't find Gideon among the heavens. Tears flowed freely.

"I beg of you, with everything that I am, return him to me. I do not know if I possess the strength should he perish."

Timrekka walked to the piles of ropes and tossed them down into the chasm. As light ripples spread and the ends of the ropes fell, the four of them watched in silence. The lengths of rope slapped against the cavern walls, echoing out until they came to a stop and only silence remained.

Gideon turned to Shadowmaker. "Now that you've heard the voice, what do *you* think is down there?"

"I don't know," Shadowmaker said as he put his helmet back on. He paused and repeated the cautionary voice under his breath. "Do not blend to grey."

Gideon grinned and squatted by the edge. He grabbed one of the ropes and clipped it to his hip. After a few quick breaths to amp himself up, he pulled it taut against the tree it was fastened around and backed up to the edge. He slowly leaned back, preparing to descend, carefully feeding the rope through. As he took the first step down through the ripples, he paused and looked at Traveler.

"What if?" he asked.

Traveler smiled as he clipped a rope to his hip, as well. "Why not?"

Gideon laughed, bursting with readiness. His energy echoed down into the hole and out through the sazeal trees. His heart raced so fast that it almost went down the hole without him. He looked from Traveler to Timrekka to Shadowmaker and ultimately down into the next adventure. With that, he began the descent into darkness.